Left Field Love

Left Field Love

Copyright © 2023 by C.W. Farnsworth

Cover design by Mary Scarlett LaBerge

CONTENTS

LEFT FIELD LOVE

C.W. FARNSWORTH

CHAPTER ONE

LENNON

Freshman Year

A ny hope of today being better than I expected dies a slow death as soon as I step inside the open doors of Landry High School. The soles of my ratty sneakers squeak against the scrubbed linoleum as the smell of grass and sunshine is replaced by the scent of ammonia and new notebooks.

I only catch glimpses of the gray lockers that line the walls between the hordes of teenagers crowding the hall. My heart travels up to my throat, lodging in an uncomfortable lump that expands with each side glance and every whisper.

My gaze remains straight ahead as familiar faces flash by. Eyes dart away. Heads tilt together.

I keep my expression impassive.

I woke up prepared to face stares.

This is the first time I've been inside Landry High, but I know where I'm going...I think. It takes a special kind of idiot to get lost in what is essentially a cinderblock rectangle. Walk long enough, and you'll end up back in the same exact spot.

My steps don't slow until I arrive at the glass door that leads into the main office. Once I do, I suck in a deep breath. The wrinkled paper I'm clutching makes a crinkling sound as I attempt to smooth it against my thigh before pulling the heavy door open.

The hinges groan, announcing my arrival to the school secretary. The middle-aged woman glances up with a prepared smile that falters slightly when she registers my face. The curse of living in a tiny, pretentious, *nosy* town.

No secrets exist in Landry.

I feel the weight of her sympathy settle over my shoulders like a lead-lined blanket as I shuffle up to the front desk.

The worst part of grief is the expectations. How everyone thinks they know exactly what grieving should look like. How they're uncomfortable when it's displayed yet judge its absence.

I keep my face blank, although I'm tempted to wrinkle my nose in response to the lemon scent saturating the air. The aroma is overpowering.

I cast a nervous glance over my shoulder, chewing the inside of my cheek as the two girls across the hallway don't bother to hide the way they're staring at me through the glass.

"Hi. I just need to drop this off." I rush the words out, anxious to have them expelled. Eager to be rid of this form and be one step closer to getting through this day.

According to the state of Kentucky, the school year is one hundred and seventy days. High school is four years. After today, I'll only have six hundred and seventy-nine days to get through.

Six hundred and seventy-nine days.

Rather than comforting, the countdown sounds…long.

I set the paper on the counter, watching the secretary's brown eyes dart between me and the wrinkled sheet. "Of course. I'll add this to your file."

"Thank you." I whirl around, eager to leave.

"Lennon?"

"Yes?" I take my time spinning back toward the desk, uneasy. I'm so sick of sympathies, especially forced ones.

"We have a new student starting today. I just pulled up your class schedule, and you two have the same homeroom. Would you be willing to show—" The wooden door behind her opens, interrupting her question, and revealing a face I've never seen before. A rare statement in Landry, Kentucky; home to just over five thousand people.

The guy walking toward me might be a stranger, but I know *exactly* who he is. I knew the moment I heard the words "new student."

No one with the name Winters needs an introduction in the state of Kentucky.

It didn't take long for the residents of Landry to move past the news of my father's death last month, although the whispers in the hallway confirm people haven't forgotten about it. Not only because he was an outsider. Not only because of the circumstances surrounding it. But because it was overshadowed by the speculation about why Austin Winters was moving back to Landry with his wife and only child. Overshadowed by excitement that Landry's most respected family was expanding their presence in town.

Caleb Winters *looks* wealthy. Important. He also appears annoyed.

A scowl mars otherwise attractive features, suggesting he's about as thrilled to be here as I am. His black hair is ruffled, like he's just run his hand through it; his blue eyes blaze, like the flame at the base of a candle absent of soot.

3

He strolls through the main office like he's walking along a red carpet rolled out exclusively for his arrival. Condescending, purposeful steps shorten the distance between us. I can practically feel the entitlement wafting off of him, cloying the citrus-scented air.

"Perfect," the secretary says, conveniently ignoring the fact she never actually *asked* me anything and that I never answered— much less accepted. "Caleb, Lennon has the same homeroom as you. She can show you the way since you missed orientation."

My black mood darkens. I could make this awkward for everyone and remind her I *also* missed orientation last month—to attend a funeral. Or I can suck it up and get this over with.

Blending into the background is where I'm comfortable. Caleb Winters comes with his own spotlight.

"Okay," I manage. I basically flee from the office, flinging my full weight against the metal bar so the glass door swings open and striding out into the rapidly emptying hallway. Attempting to act as if I don't have a care in the world. As if this is just an inconvenience on an unremarkable day.

In reality, I'm listening for the sound of footsteps behind me. There's nothing, more nothing, and then…

"You're a terrible tour guide." The words are a dry, judgmental drawl.

I scoff in response as Caleb Winters falls into step beside me, but I feel more like smirking. Weirdly, I welcome his rudeness. More of the stony silence he displayed in the office would have been easier to ignore, but I'm already in a foul mood. I'm angry. Embarrassed. Sad. I wanted to snap at the secretary simply for doing her job.

Caleb is testing me.

And I'm happy to push back.

"Don't expect any special treatment from me, Winters."

4

"You know who I am."

It's not really a question, so I don't bother answering.

"Doesn't seem fair," Caleb adds, when he realizes I'm not going to respond. "I don't know who you are."

I laugh, because the town golden boy saying something is unfair is amusing. If the gossip is to be trusted, Caleb has been living in Landry for a week. As soon as he arrived, he automatically received the acceptance I pined after for all of middle school.

"Life isn't fair," I reply. "But I guess I could see how that's a difficult concept for someone like you to understand."

There's a sudden, warm pressure on the crook of elbow. My body reacts before my brain can catch up, electric shocks of awareness skittering across my skin while a red flush crawls up my neck. It's an unfamiliar, unexpected, *unpleasant* reaction that's also the most thrilling sensation I've ever experienced.

"Have we met before?" Caleb asks seriously, ignoring how I'm gaping at him.

"*No.*" I jerk my arm away so we're no longer touching. It makes it much easier to think. To *breathe*, even, which is especially annoying. That's supposed to be a simple reflex.

"So you approve of judging strangers?"

I open my mouth. Close it. Stare at him. I hate the whispers when people hear my last name, and it bothers me that Caleb has a valid point. There's a difference. The Winters name is associated with power and money and prestige. My family is the subject of scandal and pity. But both are pre-determined associations. Stereotypes.

Caleb doesn't break my gaze the way I'm expecting him to. He stares back, his expression more searching than superior.

Shocking me further, he asks, "Do you know what number our homeroom is?"

One dark eyebrow rises, emphasizing the question. Caleb has a couple of inches on me, which adds an unfamiliar dynamic I don't appreciate. At the end of eighth grade I was taller than all of the boys in my class.

"204," he says, when I don't respond.

I scowl at Caleb before tugging my crumpled class schedule out of my backpack. His expression is serene. A warm flush creeps across my skin, accompanied by the sinking suspicion he would only look that confident if he knew the correct answer. Sure enough, my homeroom is listed as 204. The closest classroom has a placard reading 225.

I spin in place and start stalking in the opposite direction, down the hallway that is now empty. Evidently no one else had any issues navigating what I thought was a foolproof system.

Instead of rubbing it in, Caleb remains silent as we walk down the hall past decreasing numbers. 221...214...209...

I hate the quiet. It feels like a physical presence lingering between us.

Over the past few weeks I've spent more time thinking about Caleb Winters's arrival than I'd care to admit. Mostly calculating how much attention it might pull away from me.

Unfortunately, that's not what I'm considering right now. I'm wondering how he can simultaneously be exactly what I expected and nothing like it.

I thought I came prepared today. Arrived with an impenetrable wall built up. But in a matter of a few minutes, Caleb has managed to throw me off completely.

And he stays silent until we reach the door placard reading 204. I yank at the door handle and another squeaky set of hinges announce our arrival.

I've spent many sleepless nights recently imagining how

uncomfortable encountering my classmates this August morning
might be.

Being entirely ignored was best-case scenario.

Arriving late with Caleb Winters in tow is the total opposite of
the incognito entrance I was hoping to make.

"Lennon Matthews, I presume?" My attention is drawn from
the sea of familiar faces gawking at me to the middle-aged
woman standing at the front of the room. Her lips are pursed. A
tight bun and crossed arms exacerbate her stern expression.

My manners kick in automatically. "Yes, ma'am," I confirm.

There's a sharp intake of breath behind me. I battle the urge to
look over my shoulder and witness the moment Caleb Winters
realizes I'm a member of Landry's most disgraced family.

What little is left of it, anyway.

"And this must be Caleb Winters with you?"

"Yes, ma'am." Caleb steps forward, stopping about five feet
to my left. Distancing himself from me. "I'm Caleb Winters."

Confidence saturates his voice. Attention shifts from me to
him. Judgmental murmurs morph into excited whispers. Pitying
stares become admiring glances.

It doesn't surprise me. It doesn't sting, because pain is easier
to ignore when you expect it. But it does piss me off.

"I'm sorry we're tardy. Caleb thought the room was the other
way."

I regret the hasty, *false* words as soon as they leave my mouth.
I'm not a liar. Or I didn't use to be. But it's easy—disarmingly
easy—to act poorly if that's what people expect from you.

Everyone in the room is staring at me. But the gaze of the guy
standing next to me feels different. Feels heavier, like a weight I
can't avoid. His attention crawls over my skin as an inescapable itch.

I want to ignore Caleb.

To be unaffected by his attention and presence. But I'm ...*not*.

"I'll let it slide since it's the first day," our teacher announces. "Just make sure it doesn't become a pattern. Take your seats, please."

There are exactly two open seats left. One in the second row and one in the very back. I head toward the rear of the room, disparaging stares following my journey from front to rear. A wave of snickers travels through the room when I stumble a foot from the chair.

I drop into the seat, willing the heat in my cheeks to disappear as the classmates around me shift at their desks, like unpopularity is a contagious disease.

I focus on my notebook, ignoring everyone in the room except the teacher.

Especially the guy sitting in the second row.

I stop off at my locker before lunch to dump the three heavy textbooks I've already accumulated this morning.

Landry takes its academics *very* seriously.

My plan is to avoid the cafeteria and eat lunch in the library instead. I'm about to head in that direction when I hear a voice that belongs to someone I'd really rather avoid.

Ryan James is a stereotypical jock. He's been Landry's quarterback since whatever age boys start playing football, and the status of that position combined with a seemingly endless supply of self-confidence has granted him some form of popularity.

He spent the first half of the summer directing more concentrated attention my way than I thought him capable of. My best friend—now *ex*-best friend—Madison was convinced he had a thing for me.

Nothing my dad's death didn't take care of.

As I hide behind my locker door, I wonder how Ryan is handling Caleb's arrival. It's the first challenge to his alpha male status since kindergarten.

As if I summoned him, I hear another voice I recognize immediately. I shouldn't know Caleb's voice well enough to identify it instantly. But I do, it turns out. "Hey. It's Ryan, right?"

"Right," Ryan confirms. I smile a bit at the annoyance I can hear in his voice.

"Colt said I should meet him here," Caleb explains.

"Oh. Cool," Ryan responds. There's a little less hostility in his tone. "So, what do you think of Landry so far?"

My initial reason for stalling at my locker was to wait for Ryan to leave and avoid an awkward encounter. But now I'm waiting for another reason. I'm curious what Caleb will say. I want to know if he'll mention the rude girl who led him the wrong way this morning. If he'll share anything I don't already know.

"It's all right. I already know Landry pretty well from visiting in the summers. Not that much of a change."

He's lying. I'm not sure how I know, but I do.

Ryan's oblivious. "The whole school wants to show you around, man. Just go with it."

"Won't be necessary," Caleb responds. There's a pause, and then, "You play?"

There must be some football paraphernalia in Ryan's locker. Probably a framed photo of himself in uniform. "Yeah," Ryan replies. "Quarterback. You?"

"No. Baseball."

"Oh, good. You're here. Was worried you might get turned around." Colt Adams's voice joins the conversation. "Must have been Lennon's fault you got lost earlier."

Colt laughs. I cringe.

"You know Lennon Matthews?" Ryan asks; to Caleb, I presume. Colt and I have gone to school together since we were five. New students are rare here, which makes Caleb a novelty even if you ignore his last name.

"Not really," Caleb replies.

"But you heard about her dad, right?" Ryan questions. "Not that much of a surprise, really. I would have overdosed too, if I had to live on an old farm that's falling apart. Poor dude. And you know her mom was looser than—"

I slam my locker door shut, a brief thrill of satisfaction racing through me as I watch Caleb, Colt, and Ryan jump along with everyone else in the immediate vicinity. The three boys remain silent as I walk toward them, giving up eavesdropping and heading in the direction of the library.

"Don't stop your conversation on my account, *dudes*," I comment as I pass them by, barely registering their expressions. Colt looks concerned; Ryan uncomfortable. I can't get any read on Caleb. His face is blank.

But as I continue down the hall, he ends up being the first one to say anything.

"The cafeteria's the other way, Matthews!"

And that's the moment I decide I hate Caleb Winters.

CHAPTER TWO

LENNON

Senior Year

The coil of dread tightens in my stomach as soon as I hear his name called. When mine immediately follows, I miss a loop in the elaborate pattern I'm drawing.

I knew it was coming for the last four and a half minutes. Mr. Tanner isn't known for his innovation. He prides himself on his predictability. One doesn't have to look any further than the course syllabus I'm currently doodling on. It's lined with title after title of revered, classic literature, no doubt copied directly from the state curriculum.

As soon as Mr. Tanner announced Ellie Nash would be working with Jillian Baker, I had a sinking suspicion who my partner would be. I didn't need to spend the past few minutes running through a list of the last names of everyone in this English class to come to the inevitable conclusion Mr. Tanner just announced. But I did so anyway, hoping bad luck and I were finally parting ways.

"Lucky," Cassie Belmont whispers from her desk next to me.

Since Cassie is the one person I consider to be an actual friend at this school, I don't correct her assumption.

Good luck, for me, would be never having to see Caleb Winters again.

Being paired with him on an assignment that will determine a quarter of my English grade and require spending more time with him than the past three and a half years combined? The worst start to a new year I can imagine, and we're only four days in.

It's a sad testament to my lone friendship that Cassie isn't aware of how much I hate Caleb, even considering she only started at Landry High last August. This is the only class I share with Landry's golden boy this year. I've barely had to see Caleb, much less talk to him.

That made everything easier.

"I'm reserving the rest of class to begin discussing the project with your partners," Mr. Tanner announces. "Remember, this is worth twenty-five percent of your final grade in this course. This is a chance to finish strong, not to slack off because it's your last semester of high school. Please rearrange to sit with your assigned partners."

Cassie stands and heads to the front of the room. I don't so much as shift in my chair. Partly because I'm hoping I somehow misheard Mr. Tanner, but mostly because I know I didn't and I want to force Caleb to come to me. Petty as it is, he has enough handed to him.

The chair next to me scrapes against the floor. I resume my doodling in a hasty attempt to appear nonchalant.

"Happy New Year, Matthews."

I grunt, focusing on my lopsided loops like they're a puzzle that needs solving.

The chair squeaks. I stay focused on the paper, refusing to look at him. Mature, I am not.

"I hope you didn't apply to any art schools."

Caleb's voice is closer than I'm expecting. *Too* close. I drop my pen and glance over at him. He's leaned across the narrow aisle to study my doodles. And he's actually looking, scrutinizing the drawing like there's some hidden logic in the loops.

I flip the paper over and cross my arms, expecting him to move away.

He doesn't.

Caleb shifts his attention from the paper to me, his blue eyes amused and bright. He's proud of the dig at my artistic ability, I guess. Maybe it wouldn't bother me, if I'd applied to *any* school.

When I say nothing in response, he doesn't either. We hold a silent stare-off, during which I unfortunately notice he got tan during the baseball team's trip to Florida. The only school sports team to go anywhere over winter break, and also the only school sports team Caleb Winters plays on. Not much of a mystery how that trip was funded.

"Why don't you request a change of partners?" I suggest.

"I'm good. At least I know you'll do your part of the project."

I scoff. "You mean *both* parts?"

Something shifts in Caleb's expression, amusement and aloofness shifting into annoyance. "I mean *your* part. I do my own work, Matthews."

"Just like the baseball team funded its own trip to Gainesville?"

Caleb finally leans back, picking up his pen and spinning it around his finger as he studies me with a mixture of irritation and incredulity. "I'm first in our class, Lennon."

13

"No, you're not."

"Yes, I am."

There's a slow, sinking sensation in my stomach. "Fall grades haven't even come out yet."

"They were released last night."

Absurdly, my eyes start to sting. I bite the inside of my cheek and reach down to pull my water bottle out of my backpack. I haven't cried since my father's funeral. I won't cry *now. Here*. In front of *him*.

Unlike most of Landry High's senior class, I won't be attending an elite college this fall. I haven't worked twice as hard as everyone else so I could get into a university with a single digit acceptance rate. The truth is, I probably could. But I already have a full-time job waiting for me after graduation, taking care of Matthews Farm. Looking after my grandfather.

I thought I'd have the satisfaction of everyone knowing I chose that path. Knowing that I had other options. When all of my classmates leave for their shiny futures, I figured I would know I'd beaten them all in one way.

Of course, Caleb Winters would be the one to ruin that, too.

And he realizes it.

"You were first, weren't you?"

I take a long drink of water, ignoring him.

"That's the only reason you'd care what *my* ranking is."

"Drop it, Winters," I grit out, growing increasingly incensed.

He grins, showing off the star pitcher smile that I've seen rob many girls of speech. And their senses. "Well, between the two of us, we should manage to get a decent grade on this."

"I'll do the whole project and you can take half the credit. How does that sound?"

"We took the same classes, with the same teachers, and I did better than you did last semester. You're seriously going to act

14

like I'm going to mess this up for you?" He raises one eyebrow, still spinning the damn pen. I'm tempted to snatch it from him.

Caleb handicapping this project is not what I'm worried about, not that I'd ever admit it to him. Whoever came up with the *dumb jock* stereotype never met Caleb Winters. I didn't need to know his class ranking to think he's smart.

Honestly, he's the only classmate who's challenged me in every class we've shared. Landry's wealthy inhabitants ensure it's consistently considered the best school district in the state. But it churns out perfect test scores and elite college acceptances by ensuring its students are prepared, not by handing out easy A's.

Not wanting to partner on this project with Caleb has nothing to do his academic ability and everything to do with the way he throws me off-kilter. I find him interesting, and it irritates me.

"Have you two decided on your book and topics?" Mr. Tanner appears, glancing between me and Caleb.

I don't think it's a coincidence we're the pairing he chose to check in with first.

"We're still discussing," Caleb answers.

Mr. Tanner looks between us again, then nods. "All right."

I blow out a long breath as soon as he moves on, tempted to start doodling again. Anything to help ignore Caleb's presence. He's too much. Too close and too attentive. I can smell him, but it's not the overpowering cologne too many guys wear. It's something more subtle that makes me want to lean closer.

I resist the urge.

"I fully intend to do half the project, so we're going to need to agree on a book," Caleb says.

"Fine."

"Any ideas?"

"*Moby Dick*?" I challenge.

Caleb rolls his eyes. "Pass."

"*Great Expectations*?"

"You're joking."

"*Crime and Punishment*?"

"Your suggestions are punishment enough," Caleb drawls.

"I don't hear you coming up with anything."

"What about *Frankenstein*?"

"I don't like horror."

"It's not horror; it's a classic," Caleb argues.

"Just because it's on the reading list?"

The bell rings, shrill and loud.

"Outlines detailing the book you chose and the three literary devices you'll be analyzing are due next class," Mr. Tanner calls out. "One outline per group. See you tomorrow."

The classroom erupts in commotion. Students scramble to return to their belongings.

Only four minutes separate each period, making it impossible to linger without receiving a tardy slip. Not that I need any incentive to get as far away from Caleb Winters as possible. And thanks to the fact I'm one of the few who stayed in their original seat, all I have to do is shove my binder back into my backpack and rush out the door.

My hasty departure is tracked by a few questioning glances, but the only one I acknowledge is Cassie's.

"See you at lunch," I tell Cassie as I pass her by on my way out. My next class is Calculus, and the math wing is on the opposite side of the building.

By the time Calculus ends, I've almost managed to forget my conversation with Caleb. The first of the new year. And thanks to Mr. Tanner, definitely not the last. For attending a high school as small as Landry High, I've managed to do a surprisingly good job of avoiding Caleb for the past three and a half years. Up until now, apparently.

Rather than head straight to the cafeteria when the lunch bell rings, I turn in the direction of the library. I spent every lunch period as a freshman, sophomore, and junior among the stacks of books. It allowed me time to perfect assignments my chores rushed me through, with the added bonus of avoiding sitting alone in the cafeteria.

Cassie asked if she could sit with me at lunch the first day of senior year, her first day at Landry High, and I couldn't bring myself to tell her no. Or admit I'd spent the past three years eating alone in the library.

Starting at a new school is never ideal, but in Landry? Almost everyone can trace their family back for generations.

Newcomers are rare, and they receive a frosty reception. Cassie was the only new student to start here since Caleb arrived freshman year. And she didn't coast in on the winning combination of ancestry and affluence, the way he did. Cassie's family is wealthy but doesn't have any roots in Landry. Money buys some favor—literally—but even after living here for six months she's mostly treated like an outsider.

Unlike me, Cassie tries to see the best in people. That is the solitary, or at least the main, reason we're friends. Her unassuming, warm personality has also defrosted a few of our less pretentious peers, expanding our lunch table of two slowly over the first half of senior year.

I'm not retreating back into old habits of eating solo today.

I'm checking Caleb's claim that he's the top student in our year.

The library is empty when I enter it, same as every other time I've been in here during lunchtime. Mr. Gibbs, the elderly librarian, looks up and gives me a warm smile as I enter, before promptly turning back to his crossword puzzle.

I walk across the beige carpet toward the computer terminals, inhaling the comforting smell of paper and ink.

Unlike the ancient contraption I use at home, the brand-new computer whirs to life as soon as I move the mouse. It only takes a few seconds for the school's homepage to load. Once I sign into my account my grades appear instantaneously.

Next to class ranking is the number two.

My fingers form a fist as I scroll down through my past semester's grades. All A's and one A- in Biology. He must have gotten all A's.

I exhale deeply, attempting to let out my anger with the air. I turn off the computer and head back into the hallway. This time, I walk in the direction of the cafeteria.

The noise is startling after the quiet library and empty hallway. A long line of students is still waiting to buy lunch. I have to weave through it to get to my usual table. In a twist on the typical stereotype, Landry High's cafeteria food is universally considered to be quite good. Not that I would know. Bringing a sandwich from home is cheaper.

I finally reach my usual lunch table and take a seat next to Cassie.

"Hey, what happened to you?" she asks.

"Had to stop at the library," I explain as I pull my lunch out of my backpack.

"You're not already working on that English project, are you?"

I'm pretty sure Cassie thinks I'm an insane overachiever, which isn't entirely inaccurate. But my work ethic at school has a lot more to do with the fact that by the time I finish the chores, homework is the last thing I feel like doing.

"Definitely not," I respond, before biting into my peanut butter and banana sandwich.

"So, what's the deal with you and Caleb Winters? Did you guys date?"

A glob of peanut butter gets caught in my throat. That's about the last question I expected Cassie to ever ask me. "*Date?*"

"Yeah. People were...talking. Earlier." Cassie's expression turns apologetic, like listening to gossip is a betrayal.

Nothing involving me ordinarily interests anyone besides Cassie, but the entire table's attention is suddenly focused my way. I scoff loudly, eager to dispel any confusion on this topic. "We've never dated. *Would never* date."

"Everyone knows Caleb and Lennon don't get along," Shannon Jones says.

I'm grateful Shannon is agreeing with me, but I also have to suppress a sigh. That's all I'm known for in Landry: my last name and my contentious interactions with the star pitcher.

Eliza Gray laughs from her spot across from me. "Remember the spelling bee freshman year?"

Tina Smith leans forward to speak past Cassie. "Oh my God, I forgot about the spelling bee. I had culinary with them sophomore year. Caleb swapped out your sugar for salt, right Lennon?"

"Right." I take another bite of my sandwich, growing increasingly annoyed with the topic of conversation. More of the girls mention encounters between me and Caleb, most of them moments I hadn't even realized others noticed.

"Don't forget that debate they had in History last year!" Shannon adds.

"I still say Johnson shouldn't have been impeached." A new voice joins our conversation from directly behind me.

A familiar one.

A male one.

The only thing worse than being caught in a conversation

about Caleb Winters? Having Caleb Winters overhear it. *Knowing* he overheard it.

An immediate, total silence falls over the table.

"Eavesdropping, Winters?" I keep my voice as nonchalant as I can manage, glad Caleb can't see my face.

I have no idea what he's doing over here. The baseball team rarely strays from its coveted corner table, lording over the rest of the school from its spot at the top of the high school social hierarchy.

"Doubt I missed hearing anything good if you were involved in the discussion, Matthews."

I glance over one shoulder at Caleb, ignoring the wide eyes of my tablemates. "Did you need something, or did you just come over here to annoy me?"

"What makes you think I came over here to talk to you?" Caleb grins. It's dimpled. Devilish. I pretend it doesn't affect me, but there's an annoying flutter in my stomach. "Maybe I came over here to talk to someone else."

"Don't get my hopes up."

Caleb smiles again, but this time it's more genuine. It's wry, not polished or practiced. "We never decided on our project details. Hell, I'm not even sure we settled on a book. And then you ran as soon as the bell rang."

"I did not *run*. The bell signals the end of class. And I had to get to the math wing. I'll do the outline, okay?"

"Without me?"

"I'll put your name on it, Winters."

"Do you really want to have this conversation? Again?"

I heave out a long sigh that I fill with as much exasperation as I can muster. Which is a sizable amount. "Why do you have to be so freaking difficult?" I ask Caleb as I stand up and grab the rest of my sandwich.

"*I'm* the difficult one?"

I scoff before striding over toward a mostly empty table about twenty feet away. Only a few other students, who look to be freshman, are huddled at the opposite end. I drop down on one side, and Caleb takes the seat across from me.

"So…how often do you spend lunch gossiping about me?"

I should have known he wouldn't let that drop so easily. "First and last time," I inform him.

He smirks. "Yeah, right."

I sigh. "It can't be news people gossip about you."

"No. It's not."

There's a dissatisfied edge lurking beneath the words. One I'm surprised to hear and too uncomfortable to acknowledge.

"We can do *Frankenstein*," I blurt.

Ending this conversation as soon as possible suddenly feels like a top priority. Something about sitting here, with him, all alone is creeping under my skin and taking hold.

Caleb studies me with a strange, speculative look for a minute. "What?" I ask.

"Nothing." Caleb gives his head a small shake. "Okay, so we've settled on a book."

"Miraculous," I mutter dryly.

"So, you have any favorite literary devices?" Caleb asks.

"Please tell me that's not one of your pickup lines," I can't help but quip.

Caleb gives me another one of his rare, genuine grins. I take a bite of sandwich. "I've got better game than that, Matthews."

"I don't see why you'd need to. Perk of being the hottest guy in school, and all that." The words slip out past the piece of banana I've just swallowed. Unthinkingly. And I regret them as soon as they leave my mouth.

"You think I'm the hottest guy in school?" Caleb asks, a wicked, speculative gleam appearing in his eyes.

Shit. "That wasn't a personal opinion," I hurry to say. "I just meant, that's what people say, is all." I'm flustered, and I'm pretty sure Caleb can tell. Mostly because I *do* think he's the hottest guy in school, and that's something I *never* wanted him to know.

Uncharacteristically, he doesn't press the topic. "Foreshadowing?"

I breathe a subtle sigh of relief. "I'd hope so, considering the subject."

"Two to go, then."

"Imagery?" I offer.

"Isn't that a given in every book?" Caleb contends.

"Did you notice how I didn't criticize your suggestion?" I retort.

"Fine. Personification?"

"Done," I state, eager to be finished with this discussion. "Do you trust me to write the outline now?"

"Yes," Caleb replies simply.

"Good." I ball up the plastic baggie I transported my sandwich in, expecting that to be the end of our conversation. But Caleb doesn't move, so I feel obligated to stay seated too.

We stare at each other in silence. It's a stark contrast to the din of voices surrounding us.

"How was your break?" Caleb finally asks.

I don't answer at first, too taken aback by his unexpected question. We don't exchange pleasantries. We bicker and argue.

I feel like it's a test, and so I don't bother with the glossy answer I offered to Cassie and the one other person who bothered to ask. "It...wasn't great," I admit. Maybe honesty will fracture this bizarre moment. "Yours?"

If Caleb's surprised by my answer, he doesn't show it. "Not great, either."

His answer isn't what I expect. I spent most of break arguing with Gramps, who is still insisting he could handle the farm if I went off to college in the fall, despite the fact he struggles to walk to the barn some days. I know that's not how Caleb spent his. Maybe he feels obligated to mirror my melancholy answer, but I don't see why he would. I'm well aware of how charmed his life is. Everyone is aware.

"Great," I finally say, because something needs to be said. I can't sit in more silence.

A smile tugs at the corners of Caleb's mouth in response to my obvious sarcasm.

"Well...I'm going to go."

I stand. Caleb says nothing, eventually giving me a small nod. His sudden muteness is unnerving. I hesitate for a second, then turn to walk back toward my table. I should have just told him what I narrated to Cassie in homeroom earlier. The last thing I want from Caleb is pity.

"Matthews!" I spin back around.

Caleb is standing now. "You've got some peanut butter on your nose," he informs me.

Heat flushes my body. I swipe at the center of my face repeatedly while glaring at him. "This whole time? And you're just telling me now?"

Caleb shrugs, giving me a lazy smirk. "You called me hot, so I decided to be nice and let you know."

"I did *not* call you hot." I snarl the words before stalking the remaining distance to my table.

"How did it go?" Cassie asks me tentatively as I plop back down beside her.

"Great," I growl.

23

"That's...good," she replies, her voice suggesting she doesn't believe me.

I sigh and fish around my lunchbox for a granola bar. "Do I have any food on my face?" I ask.

Cassie studies my face. "Uh...yeah. There's some peanut butter right *there*." She points to my nose.

I grab a napkin and scrub it over my whole face. "Gone?"

Cassie nods.

I toss the napkin. "Could this day get any worse?" I mutter.

After seventeen years, I really should know better than to tempt the universe.

CHAPTER THREE

LENNON

Dusty could go out with Stormy, but then I'd need to put Commie out solo. Maybe all the mares should…

"Lennon? Lennon!"

"What?" I ask, tapping the pencil against my notepad and trying to act as though my attention only just drifted from the newsroom, when in reality I've tuned out most of the school paper's hour-long meeting.

Our editor, Andrew, is a senior like me. Meaning he views the next five months as his final chance to leave an everlasting mark on *Landry High Times*.

His "vision" for the next few issues took up the first forty minutes of the meeting.

I zoned out after five to plan the turnout schedule for the next week.

"You'll be covering the baseball interview, Lennon."

I sit up straighter. "Baseball interview? What baseball interview?"

"It's Caleb Winters's final season. He finally agreed to do an interview with the paper."

I've never seen Andrew look so enthused. He's practically beaming as he delivers the news that makes every other member of the staff perk up as well.

"How thrilling," I drone. "I'm not writing it, though."

"You have to!" Andrew pushes his tortoiseshell-framed glasses back up the bridge of his nose. I recognize it as one of his nervous tells. The two of us have had several creative differences since both joining the school paper freshman year.

"No, I definitely do *not*," I inform Andrew. "Me writing an article about Caleb Winters is a terrible idea. You know that we don't get along. And I don't know anything about baseball. Simon is the sportswriter!"

Simon startles when I say his name, looking nervous rather than eager.

Despite my personal misgivings, I know Andrew is right to be excited. An interview with Landry's star pitcher will be huge for the paper.

But Simon still isn't jumping in and offering to do the interview for me, which is strange. I've personally been subjected to hearing him drool over Caleb multiple times.

"Actually, you do," Andrew states. "Caleb said he'd only do the article if you were the one who interviewed him."

"He said *what*?" I blink at Andrew, stunned. "I'm sure he only said that because he knows I won't agree to it. Or he won't show up. Or he'll make up all his answers. This is his way of getting out of it. Using me."

Andrew doesn't disagree. "Not a chance we can take," he replies, then shrugs. "Winters never talks to the press. No one knows where he wants to play next year. What he thinks about his final season. This is our chance to get a serious scoop. There's not a single person in this town who wouldn't read an interview with Caleb Winters."

"I wouldn't." My voice is petulant.

"Not sure you'll have much choice, considering you'll be the one writing it."

The school paper has always been a refuge for me. None of the other members of the staff are people I'd consider to be friends, but none of them have ever treated with me with any form of derision. I've carved out a grudging respect here. And writing for the town paper, the *Landry Gazette*, is my sole and best opportunity for employment following graduation.

Not only do I not want to quit the school paper, I can't.

Despite the many hours we collectively pour into each issue, I've never even seen any of my classmates read the school paper. There's no way I'll be able to convince Andrew to do anything to endanger this story.

Which means I'll have to take this up with the instigator of this infuriating predicament.

"Fine," I state, slumping back in my chair. Andrew eyes me suspiciously, skeptical about my sudden lack of objection. "I'll give him one chance. But don't say I didn't warn you."

"I can send you some questions to ask, Lennon." Simon finally chimes into the conversation.

I sigh. "Thanks."

Andrew shoots me another wary glance, but moves on. "Julie, you'll be covering Mr. Barnett's retirement. Steve, the plans for the new running track. Good work, everyone! Drafts for the new issue by the end of next week, please."

The huddle in the middle of the room breaks apart, all of us heading back to our assigned desks.

"I guess the rumors are true," Julie Larson muses as she takes a seat at her desk, which is adjacent to mine.

"What rumors?" I ask, shoving my notebook inside my backpack.

"That you hate Caleb Winters."

"We hate each other," I correct.

"Then why would he have you do his interview?"

"To torture me. He's a jerk." I zip my bag up, annoyance reigniting.

"I've never talked to him," Julie states. I glance at her, surprised. That's something I haven't managed to do in a small school while actively attempting to avoid him. "But if he is a jerk, he's a hot one." Her tone has turned wistful. Admiring. And I can't summon the amusement that used to appear when I saw girls fawn over him. Instead, I'm picturing blue eyes.

"The most dangerous kind," I warn as I grab the last of my belongings and head toward the door. "See you tomorrow, Julie."

"Bye, Lennon," she calls after me. "When you do the interview, ask if he's single!"

I grimace as I head out the door of the newsroom. Good to know she took my warning seriously.

I told Cassie I'd stop by the boys' basketball game after the paper meeting, so I head out the front doors and make my way over to the sports complex.

It's not the route I usually take. And it brings me directly past the baseball field. Despite the chilly temperature and the fact the baseball season doesn't start until—actually I have no idea when the baseball season starts, but I know it hasn't—I recognize enough of the navy-clad figures to realize the team is out on the field practicing.

Which means *he* must be out practicing.

I alter my course slightly, veering to the left of the parking lot and alongside the stretch of metal bleachers.

"Winters!" I disregard the half dozen guys gathered around Caleb and march right up to him. He's leaning against the chain-link fence, tossing a baseball back and forth between his hands like he doesn't have a care in the world.

Must be nice.

Caleb says nothing in response when I call his name, just cocks a brow maddeningly.

"I need to talk to you."

"Feel free."

"Somewhere else?" I ignore the mutters the words prompt among the other baseball players.

Lunch earlier illuminated an alarming level of interest in my interactions with Caleb, and I'd like to avoid feeding further speculation. Caleb either doesn't know about the gossip, or more likely doesn't care, because he remains in place.

"I'm in the middle of practice."

"You're leaning against a fence."

He doesn't move. "You want to talk, *talk*."

"Fine. What the hell is your problem?" I hiss.

Caleb doesn't look nearly as apprehensive as I think he ought to. "You're mad at me? That's a nice change."

I scowl. "If you stopped trying to purposefully *piss me off*, you wouldn't have to deal with me being mad at you."

Caleb merely arches an arrogant brow.

"You told Andrew you wouldn't do an interview with the paper unless it was with me? Why the *hell* would you do that? It's not bad enough we're partners on that English project? You want to spend *more* time together?"

There's a low, husky laugh behind me. I glance over one shoulder at Colt Adams. He turns the sound into a cough as soon as our eyes connect, but I'm not fooled. I narrow my eyes at him, then turn back to Caleb.

"Well?"

He sighs. "After three plus years of being *begged* to do so, I agreed to do an interview with the school paper that will probably mean more than four people read it. I didn't realize that was a problem. More like it merited a *thank you*."

"Four people? God, you're *such* a jerk." The fact he's probably not wildly off on his readership count is irrelevant.

"Are you done? We're still in the middle of practice." Caleb gestures to the loose grouping of his baseball teammates, none of whom are making any attempt to act like they're not hanging on to every word. I don't know why girls are the gender associated with loving gossip.

"I'm not doing the interview with you." I leave no room for argument in the statement.

But Caleb finds some. "Then why are you here, yelling at me about it?"

I grind my teeth, probably doing some damage to my molars. "Do the interview with someone else, Caleb." I speak each word as if it's a sentence, the final threads of my patience fraying like worn rope.

"You're the best writer on the paper. It's you or no one else, Lennon."

Caleb emphasizes my first name slightly, and I know it's to let me know he caught that I used his. But I'm more distracted by the fact he just *complimented* me.

At least, I think he did.

I'm waiting for the punchline.

But it doesn't come. "I have a busy schedule. You'd have to work around it."

Caleb doesn't hide his grin, and I know it's because he thinks I'm just continuing to be difficult. I keep to myself. Aside from the paper, I'm not involved in any school activities. Honestly, I'm shocked Caleb even knew I'm on the paper.

"You've got a busy schedule?" He scoffs. "Okay, fine. When

do you want to meet?

"Tomorrow at five thirty," I reply promptly. Meaning I'll have to get up at…yeah, not thinking about that.

"In the morning?" Caleb lets out a laugh of disbelief.

"Yes. That's my final offer. Take it or leave it." I smirk, certain he'll leave it.

But I underestimated Caleb's stubbornness. Or his dedication to torturing me. Or maybe both.

"Fine."

I study him for a moment, testing his resolve. He doesn't waver.

"Fine," I finally retort. "I'll meet you here."

"Here?" Caleb glances at the baseball field.

"Don't be late." I spin around and walk away, silently seething. I thought Caleb would back down after teasing me a little. There's no way he *actually* wants me to interview him. It will be torture for the both of us.

My annoyance lasts for the short walk from the baseball field to the gymnasium. The bleachers along the far wall are only half-full when I enter the gym. My ears begin ringing from the sound of rubber soles squeaking against the varnished floor. The pungent, unpleasant scent of sweat burns my nostrils.

Cassie is easy to spot among the couple dozen spectators. She's the only person not paying any attention to the game. At least until I take a seat on the wooden bleachers beside her. Cassie finally glances up; first at the game, and then over at me.

"Hey," she greets. "What took you so long? The game's practically over."

"I got held up at the paper," I explain, which is partially true. I don't elaborate any further than that, although I know Cassie, along with the rest of the school, will eventually hear about my latest assignment. I'm still holding out hope the interview will get

31

derailed. Caleb showing up on time tomorrow morning seems unlikely. "Surprised you noticed I wasn't here," I tease. "You looked invested in the game."

Cassie makes a face. "Basketball was big at my old school," she tells me. "Not so much here, I guess?" She nods toward the small, unenthusiastic crowd.

"I don't really follow the sports scene," I remind her. "But if I had to guess, I'd say your best bet for a big crowd is a baseball game."

"Yeah, I probably should have figured that out." Cassie looks at me thoughtfully. "Because of your English partner, right?"

I grimace at the curiosity in her voice. There were times I would go days—weeks, even—without having to think or hear about Caleb Winters. How I've suddenly gone from that to frequent reminders he exists is irritating.

"Right," I confirm. Baseball has always been big in Landry, but Caleb certainly hasn't impeded its popularity. Far from it. Despite the rock I've tried to shove myself under when it comes to him, I know he's racked up an impressive number of athletic accolades in the sport.

The basketball game ends ten minutes later, with Landry winning handily. Cassie and I filter into the lobby with the few other attendees.

We're heading toward the front doors of the sports complex when Cassie pauses and nods to our right. "I'm going to run to the restroom. Do you mind waiting?"

"No problem," I respond, stopping and leaning against the cinderblock wall. "I'll be here."

Cassie flashes me a grateful glance before disappearing into the lobby's bathroom. I'm studying some of the shiny trophies on display when I hear a male voice say my name.

I turn to see Will Masterson, my freshman year lab partner,

looking at me with surprise. He's still wearing his basketball uniform from the game.

"Hi, Will," I greet. I could count on one hand the number of conversations we've had since sharing a blacktop table freshman year. Not for lack of trying on Will's part. He always says hi to me in the halls or waves from a distance. He's one of those rare people who is genuinely nice.

Every conversation we have, I feel like I have to carefully consider each word I say, worried some snark or sarcasm will slip through and reveal my cynicism.

As he approaches me with a wide smile, I'm reminded of the other reason I keep our interactions short: I've gotten the sense Will's friendliness might not be entirely platonic. The few other guys who have flirted with me have been easy to dissuade with a few sharp retorts. I feel badly doing that to Will, but I don't want to give him the wrong idea either.

I return his smile. "Nice game."

"Thanks, Lennon." He beams in response to my compliment. "It's really nice to run into you. I feel like I never see you around."

"Senior year, you know." I keep my reply evasive, hoping he'll fill in the blanks with what I've been busy with himself. With normal activities, like college visits and applications, rather than what actually takes up the bulk of my time: running a horse farm.

"I sure do." Will lets out a low laugh. "Hard to believe it, huh? Seems like not that long ago we were lab partners."

"It doesn't feel like that long ago," I agree. Probably because my life doesn't look all that different. Gramps is more forgetful and has a harder time getting around. But my mornings still start early and I usually collapse into bed as soon as I finish my homework.

Aside from Cassie's presence, high school never improved much from the disastrous first day Caleb Winters became my nemesis, and the hours spent in Will's friendly, upbeat presence were an unexpected bright spot in an otherwise dismal year. Impulsively, I tell him so. "That class was the best part of freshman year for me."

"Really?" Will asks. He looks shocked by my comment, which is probably warranted. It's not exactly common for me to be nostalgic.

"Really," I confirm, smiling slightly. "You were always nice to me, and most people…weren't."

"Most people are idiots," Will states, his tone emphatic.

My laugh is wry. "Won't argue with you there."

Will leans a little closer and opens his mouth to say something else. I hope it's unrelated to my pariah status. I hate talking about my parents and I don't discuss Gramps with anyone.

I'm distracted by a sudden gush of cool wind and the slap of cleats hitting the lobby's linoleum, but I force my eyes to remain on Will and resist the urge to watch as the baseball team walks by.

Unfortunately, Will doesn't do the same, turning to face the commotion and taking my excuse to appear oblivious with him.

"Masterson! How'd it go?" Luke Evans pauses next to us.

"I'm insulted you have to ask." Will grins. "Decimated them."

"Nice work," Luke congratulates, and then tucks his baseball glove under one arm so he and Will can do one of those half-hand slap, half-fist bump greetings guys seem to apply to every possible interaction.

"You guys are already practicing?" Will nods to Luke's dirt-streaked baseball attire.

"Already? We never really stop," Luke replies. "Fall ball has started running right into the spring season."

Will whistles. "Wow. That's a lot of baseball."

Luke nods. "Sorry I didn't catch any of the game. Our practice ran long. It got interrupted, so Winters had us stay later than usual."

I wasn't sure if Luke was among the guys huddled around Caleb earlier, but now I know for certain. I look at him for the first time since he stopped next to Will and me, and he's sporting a cheeky grin.

It dims when I glare at him.

"Really? What happened?" Will asks curiously, missing our brief exchange.

"Just some equipment issues," Luke responds.

I tense.

I haven't been keeping track of the players walking past us. In fact, I've been doing everything I can *not* to look at them, but somehow I know Caleb has just entered the lobby. Most of the basketball team and other spectators are gone, and Luke was the only baseball player who stopped during the team's trek to the locker room.

Meaning I can hear every footfall as the spikes of Caleb's cleats hit the tiled floor.

"Congrats on the win, Will. I've gotta get changed." Luke is suddenly in a rush to depart, and despite the fact I still haven't looked over, I know that means I'm right. Caleb is in the lobby, and Luke doesn't want to be seen with me.

It's too late, though. I can feel the weight of Caleb's gaze as Luke hurries off. Which is why I turn my undivided attention back to Will. If I have to suffer through a fourth encounter with Caleb today, I'll likely end up resorting to physical violence.

"Sorry about that," Will apologizes. "Hadn't seen Luke since winter break."

"It's fine," I reply, injecting a little extra cheerfulness into my voice as I hear footsteps grow closer.

35

"We were talking about how much some people suck, right?"

I let out a loud laugh as the footsteps reach their crescendo and then start to fade away, ignoring the puzzled look my unexpected mirth earns me from Will. He misses the irony of the timing. "Yes, we were."

"Hey…" I let out a sigh of relief when I see Cassie has finally reappeared. She looks surprised to find me standing with Will rather than waiting alone.

"You know Will, right, Cassie?"

"I think we had gym together last semester," Will supplies helpfully.

"Yeah, we did." Cassie smiles. "Nice to see you, Will. Did you have a nice break?"

"Yeah, I did. You?"

"It was good," Cassie replies simply, and then silence falls over our trio.

"Well, we'd better get going," I say when it becomes clear neither of them are going to say anything else. "Have a good night, Will."

"Yeah, you too," he replies. "And thanks for coming, Lennon. It was really nice to see you."

I smile at him before I head toward the main doors. Cassie follows me.

"He likes you," she informs me as soon as we emerge outside. Dusk is just beginning to fall. I watch our shadowy shapes stretch alongside us as we head toward the parking lot.

"Yeah, I know," I admit.

"Did he ask you out?"

"What? No!"

Cassie deflates. "Bummer." Seconds later, she perks back up. "He's definitely interested, though. I bet he will next time you talk."

I blanch. "I hope not."

"Why? He's cute! And he seemed really nice."

"Maybe you should date him."

"I wasn't the one he couldn't stop staring at."

"He's too nice."

"You won't go out with him because he's too nice?" A mixture of confusion and amusement fills Cassie's voice.

"Yes," I reply simply, unwilling to delve into the other reasons.

None of my classmates—the few who might care or the many who wouldn't—are aware of the fact I'll be staying in Landry after graduation. Watching everyone else embark on their exciting futures will be difficult enough without getting romantically attached to someone.

I owe it to Cassie to tell her about my lack of college plans. But I definitely won't ever tell her—or anyone else—the second reason I avoid dating.

My mother had a certain reputation when it came to men, one that is still associated with my last name. Part of the scandal my father heaped onto. People already find plenty to gossip about. There's no need to give them more fuel.

"You guys could be perfect together," Cassie says, oblivious to my inner thoughts. "He could make you a little friendlier, and you could make him a little more…intimidating?"

I shoot her a mock-glare, and she laughs. "I like that he's nice. I just don't want to date someone I feel like I can't be myself with."

Cassie nods. "That makes sense. But I still think you should give Will a chance. You can just go on one date with him. Maybe he's not as *nice* as he seems."

"I'll think about it," I reply as we reach the end of the sidewalk. More to get Cassie off my back than actually meaning the words. "I'll see you tomorrow, okay?"

"I can drive you home. It's almost dark out."

"I'll be fine," I respond. "It's not far."

"Okay," she agrees. I'm sure she's noticed I've never invited her, but she's never said anything about it. "See you tomorrow!"

Cassie continues into the parking lot and I keep walking. The sun is continuing its rapid descent, showcasing a brilliant spray of color across the darkening sky.

Only a whisper of orange remains by the time I finish my hike across the east pasture.

Gramps is on the phone when I enter the farmhouse. I wave at him before dropping my backpack in the kitchen and heading upstairs to change into my barn clothes and boots. The ancient hinges let out a familiar groan of greeting as I push the door open, revealing the light-yellow walls and white lace curtains of my childhood bedroom. The decor is better suited for a ten-year-old girl than a seventeen-year-old one, but I haven't had the heart to change any of it.

Redecorating my room so it was suited for a "big girl" was part of my mother's final attempt to break free of her many vices, before an aneurysm ensured she'd never have the chance to conquer them permanently.

Gramps is still on the phone when I emerge downstairs, so I head straight out to the barn. It's completely dark out now, much later in the day than I usually start my chores.

Rather than bring the horses in right away I flick on all the lights and start preparing the evening grain and hay allotments, delivering them to each horse's stall. I mucked out this morning before school, so the stalls are all clean.

The horses are eager to get inside and eat. Dusty was ridden this morning, but Geiger won't be getting his scheduled exercise tonight. The practice track doesn't have any lights, and galloping an ornery stallion in the dark is a surefire way for something to go terribly wrong.

It takes me an hour to finish the evening chores. Gramps has already made dinner when I enter the kitchen. It's tacos, which are a bit adventurous for him. I'm too hungry to care he over-salted the meat and some of the tortillas are still cold.

Dinner is spent discussing one of Gramps's old trainer buddies, who was on the phone earlier. He was calling from Florida, where he's training two-year-olds for the upcoming racing season. I nod along as Gramps narrates their conversation about breaking from the gate, but I'm not really listening.

I'm surprised and relieved he remembers as many training techniques as he apparently does. It eases some of the worry that appears every time he can't find his keys or leaves the oven on.

After we finish dinner, I help Gramps clean up the kitchen and then say good night. I shower off the barn grime and put on my favorite pair of striped flannel pajamas before settling in the rickety wooden chair to complete my assignments for tomorrow.

The English outline only takes me ten minutes, but the study guide for my Oceanography class takes a lot longer to complete. I quit when the words start swimming across the page in a black-and-white river.

I should have time to go over it again in the morning. Even if —and that's a big if—Caleb actually shows.

I pack up my bag for tomorrow, get ready for bed, and then slide between the soft sheets, letting out a deep sigh. I love this moment. Nothing that needs my attention. There's no looming task or assignment. Just silence and my warm, cozy bed. I try to savor it, relish the tranquility.

But I drift toward unconsciousness as soon as my head hits the pillow.

CHAPTER FOUR

LENNON

There's already a figure sitting on the bleachers when I hop over the gate onto the far edge of the baseball field.

My stomach sinks as I walk across the brown grass. I was confident—certain—he wouldn't show.

"You're early." I state the obvious as I take a seat one row below Caleb on the hard metal. I'm not sure what else to say to him.

The metal bleachers are the same temperature as the early morning air. I shiver as I sit, glad I bundled up in extra layers. The first streaks of sunrise are only just beginning to creep across the horizon; nowhere near powerful enough to warm the metal.

"So are you," Caleb observes. His words are casual, just like his stance. He's slouched between two of the risers, and the brim of his baseball cap is pulled low, masking most of his face. "Hoping to wrap this up early so you can leave for your Arctic expedition?"

I roll my eyes, and he gives me one of his rare, genuine grins.

Maybe it's the time. I'm not used to interacting with other

people this early, and I haven't had time to raise the protective shield that's fully in place by the time I arrive at school. I'm uncharacteristically honest with him. "I was going to leave at 5:31," I admit.

Caleb chuckles. "Why do you think I showed up early, Matthews?"

"I'm offended you think so little of me." I'm not; I'm surprised he predicted I'd try to get out of this again, and that he made certain I wouldn't be able to.

"You already admitted to it, Lennon. No need for the fake indignation."

Ordinarily, it's a comment I'd bristle in response to, but Caleb's voice isn't mocking. It's matter-of-fact.

"Let's get started," I say, biting back the sarcastic comment I have ready.

Despite the chilly temperature and early hour, Caleb actually seems to be in a decent mood. Pissing him off is probably not the best way to get this over with quickly and painlessly.

Caleb doesn't say anything, which I take as an agreement. "Where do you want to play next year?"

"Pass."

"You can't pass on an interview question."

"I just did," Caleb retorts.

I grit my teeth. So much for a decent mood. "I can't write an article about 'pass,' Caleb."

"Then ask a different question."

I exhale, loudly enough for him to hear. "Fine. What's your favorite thing about playing baseball?"

Caleb's blue eyes swim with humor. "That's your second question?"

"I'm not the freaking sportswriter. I don't know *anything* about baseball. What do you want me to ask you?"

41

Caleb scoffs, but the exasperated sound doesn't reach his eyes. He's still amused. "I'm good," he states.

"What?"

"You asked me what my favorite thing about playing is. I'm good."

"You've got to be kidding me." Between that answer and "pass," I'm picturing this article stretching about two lines.

"It's the one thing I never have to think about," Caleb continues. "When I'm out on the mound, everything is simple and straightforward. Throw the ball as fast as I can to the spot where it needs to go. Yeah, we practice a ton, and I've had great coaches, but I've always been good at it. Technically, baseball is a team sport. But when I'm pitching, it's all on me. It's the one thing that clicks, you know?"

A snarky response is waiting on the tip of my tongue, but I don't voice it. Maybe I have some sense of what he's talking about. There are moments, when I see an A on a paper or am galloping around the practice track, that I feel like I'm where I'm supposed to be, doing what I'm supposed to be doing. But more often than not, I feel like I'm too busy doing exactly what's expected to explore anything else. To find that sense of belonging Caleb's describing.

Maybe because I've grown up in this town that's intent on driving my family out.

I clear my throat and move on to the next question on the list. I've read all of Simon's past sports articles. Almost every one of the athlete interviews he's done have been verbatim retellings of the conversation, printed in question-and-answer format.

That's not going to work for my conversation with Caleb, for obvious reasons. My best bet is to keep Caleb talking and hope he gives me enough information I can cobble together for a decent story. Commenting about how, of course, throwing a baseball seems simple and straightforward probably won't help.

I ask Caleb about his first baseball game (he won), his pregame rituals (according to him, he has none), and his favorite game he's played in (quarterfinal junior year).

I sigh. "I'm out of questions," I admit.

Rather than look irritated, Caleb appears entertained. "I'm flattered you over-prepared."

My eyes narrow. "This was kind of short notice. I've never covered sports, and Simon and Julie didn't exactly have helpful suggestions."

Caleb leans back against the bleachers again, looking intrigued. "What were their suggestions?"

"Simon sent me some bullet points with a lot of abbreviations in them. Julie wants to know if you're single."

"Did you look up the abbreviations?" Caleb asks, disregarding my second sentence.

"Of course. His questions still didn't make any sense." I sniff. Although I did research them while trying to both tie my sneakers and eat breakfast.

"To you," Caleb surmises with a smirk.

"To me," I concede. "Plus, I figured anyone who truly cares about an RBI or a WHIP would know where to look that up."

Caleb laughs, and the husky warmth of it somehow infiltrates the three layers I'm wearing. "Probably true." He stands and pulls on his backpack. "You coming?"

"What? Where?"

"To the library. I can't sit on these bleachers anymore. It's a miracle anyone watches our entire games."

I stand and stretch. "Uh, yeah, I guess." That's exactly where I was planning to go, but I'm wary of spending any more time with

Caleb alone. I doubt anyone but Mr. Gibbs will be there this early. I don't have a better option, though, so I climb down after him.

We walk side by side along the deserted sidewalk, and it's incredibly bizarre. I'm hyperaware of everything: the thump of my heavy backpack, the slap of my sneakers against the pavement, the rapid pounding of my heart. The back of my hand brushes Caleb's once, accidentally. I snatch it back, cheeks burning as I keep my eyes aimed straight ahead.

We're almost to the front doors when Caleb speaks. "I am, by the way."

"What?" I glance at him. He's focused on the brick building we're approaching. It's an imposing facade better suited for a university than a public high school, complete with columns and framed windows. Landry doesn't do anything in half-measures.

"Single." Caleb glances over at me, his indifferent expression becoming a smirk, probably in response to the confused expression I can feel wrinkling my brow. "You said someone asked."

"Someone?" For whatever reason, that's the word I focus on. Maybe because I'm weirdly…relieved that's his answer. "I *just* told you her name is Julie."

Caleb looks amused by my response. "Fine, *Julie* asked."

"You only bother to learn girls' names if they're popular?" I snap.

Suddenly, I feel like I'm witnessing this conversation from a distance, watching what will come next but unable to stop it. Around most people I think, then react. Around Caleb I react, then double down.

Caleb reaches out and pulls open one of the four front doors, gesturing for me to walk in first. I stalk through the opening, annoyed at him for being nice to me when I'm not being nice to him for essentially no reason. This is the worst possible time for him to try being a gentleman.

He catches up to me easily. "I know *your* name. And popular isn't exactly the first adjective that comes to mind."

I should probably be affronted, but I know he's right. I doubt a single person in Landry would consider me popular. I'm being ridiculous but am too stubborn to admit it. And wondering what adjective *does* come to mind.

"What an honor," I mutter before marching into the front office to sign the early arrival sheet.

The school secretary blinks sleepily as she looks up from her steaming mug of coffee.

"Good morning," she greets us.

"Good morning."

I wonder if I'd be standing here with Caleb if I'd showed up to this office the first day of freshman year after he'd already left. I quickly block the thought. Too many tiny moments have determined major parts of my life. It's easier to think we were destined to spend high school arguing no matter what.

I lean over the desk to sign my name, then step back so Caleb can do the same. The secretary's eyes bounce back and forth between the two of us. I've never shown up this early to school. I'm usually running late after rushing through the morning chores. Maybe she doesn't even recognize me, since I'm no longer a gangly freshman. Maybe she's staring because she's as enamored with Caleb as the rest of the town.

The only sound in the small office is the pen scratching against paper as Caleb signs his name. As soon as I hear the sound stop, I head toward the door that leads into the school hallway, pushing the metal bar to fling the glass door open. Unlike the last time I left this room with Caleb Winters behind me, I don't drop the door on him. But as soon as I feel him start to hold the weight, I lower my hand.

"You think she remembers us?"

I glance at Caleb, surprised and somewhat alarmed to realize we were both thinking the same thing. It suggests a familiarity I didn't think we shared. "Remembers what?"

He grins, likes he knows I'm only feigning forgetfulness. "The day we met."

Not the first day of freshman year.

Not the day I got him lost.

The day we met.

"You're hard to forget." As soon as the words are out, I wish I could shove them back into my mouth.

"I didn't think you knew what a compliment was, Matthews."

"I didn't say it was a good thing, Winters."

We reach the library with an uneasy truce hanging between us. As expected, Mr. Gibbs is the only person in sight. He gives me the same nod of greeting as every other time I've entered this library before turning back to whatever book he's reading.

I head straight toward my usual table. Caleb follows, taking the seat across from me as I pull out the study guide I made for my Oceanography test.

I'm shocked he's sitting with me. It's not like there aren't other seats available. But I try not to show it. I focus on my notes instead.

Motion across the table draws my attention back to Caleb. I watch him pull a binder out of his backpack and begin flipping through the pages.

My gaze drops back down to my own papers, but I glance up again just a few minutes later.

Caleb is attractive. I've always known that. I've heard the admiring whispers when he walks down the hall. But I don't typically allow myself to focus on the way his dark hair falls across his forehead or to think about how straight the line of his jaw is when we're arguing. Unfortunately, there's nothing to distract me from either of those things in the silent, empty library.

Except for the blaze of embarrassment when he glances up and catches me staring at him. "What?" he whispers, looking at me curiously.

"Nothing," I reply hastily, dropping my eyes back down to the study guide in front of me.

I don't let my eyes wander again until the first bell rings, signaling the start of homeroom in five minutes. I continue to avoid looking at Caleb as I pack up my belongings and stand.

Based on the shuffling sounds coming from the opposite side of the table, he's doing the same.

"I'll do the interview with Simon, if you want."

"What?" I freeze, then glance at Caleb. It's not what I expected him to say. And, I'm surprised to realize, not something I'm thrilled to hear.

"I'll do the interview with Simon. If you want me to," he repeats.

"Is that what you want?" I ask.

"After everything it took to get you to agree to do it in the first place?" Caleb raises a brow as he looks at me expectantly.

And I have a stroke. Or a brain freeze. Or some other impediment that stops me from telling Caleb there's nothing else I'd love more than *not* having to write an article about him.

"I'll talk to Simon…and get some better questions for a follow-up interview," I tell Caleb as we walk out the doors from the library.

I'm not a quitter.

The hallways aren't crowded, but other students are trickling in, and we attract more than a few double takes as people pass us by.

"I'll, uh, I'll see you in English," I say as we linger just outside the library doors.

Something between me and Caleb suddenly feels tenuous. Off-kilter. The easy annoyance that's always hovered between us has vanished.

Caleb opens his mouth to reply.

"Lennon!" I turn to see Will walking down the hallway in our direction. "Morning," he greets cheerfully, grinning at me.

"Hey, Will." I smile back.

Will seems to notice who I'm standing with for the first time. "Hey, Winters," he greets, a hint of surprise in his voice.

"Masterson," Caleb replies, sounding bored. "I'll see you later, Lennon."

I give him a quick, jerky nod. "Bye, Caleb."

It seems like something shifts in his expression, but he turns and heads in the opposite direction before I have enough time to study it.

"I didn't think you and Caleb got along," Will remarks, studying Caleb's retreating back with a look of confusion.

"We don't. I have to write an article on him for the paper."

"Oh," Will says. After a moment he adds, "I didn't know you covered sports."

"I don't," I state, with a fair bit of irritation in my voice.

"Okay…" Will replies, obviously looking for more of an explanation.

"It's a long story," I tell him. That I could have just ended and didn't for a reason that eludes me.

"Your article isn't due tomorrow, is it?"

"No. Why?" I ask.

"Marcus is having a party tonight to celebrate our win yesterday. I was hoping you might want to go, since you were one of the few people who bothered to actually come to the game."

"Oh." I start to form a refusal automatically, but then stop to reconsider. Maybe Cassie's right. What could the harm be? "Yeah, sure," I say instead. "Is it okay if I bring Cassie?"

"Of course. Do you want me to pick you up or meet you there?"

"We'll meet you there. I know where Marcus lives."

"Cool. See you then," Will says, before continuing down the hallway.

I start in the opposite direction, quickening my pace when the warning bell echoes around me. Thankfully, my homeroom is a quick trip down the hall and to the right. I drop into my usual seat next to Cassie just as the final bell rings.

The morning announcements boom overhead, but I don't listen to what is being said. I lean over as far as the small desk will allow.

"I need you to go to a party with me tonight," I whisper to Cassie.

She turns to me, her brown eyes full of surprise. "What?"

"I saw Will on my way here. He invited me to a party tonight, and I need you to go with me. Please."

"Of course I'll go with you. We can—" The announcements end and attendance starts. "We'll talk at lunch," Cassie says, then leans back in her chair.

The rest of the day passes quickly. Mr. Tanner's class is a lecture on literary devices for our upcoming papers, but we don't separate into partners. I caught Caleb's eye when I dropped our outline on Mr. Tanner's desk, and he gave me a nod. That was it.

I head home straight after school ends, glad the paper doesn't have a meeting today. I shirked on chores this morning since it was so outrageously early, and I rushed to ensure I'd beat Caleb to the field.

A wasted effort, in retrospect.

At lunch, Cassie made me promise I would come over after dinner to "prepare for the party." I have no idea what that means. The last party I attended was a birthday party in middle school that definitely didn't require two hours of preparation. Cassie insisted a couple of hours were necessary, though, and she was so enthused I couldn't bring myself to tell her no.

I also have a feeling this will be my first and final high school party.

Might as well make the most of it.

Despite the chill in the January air, Gramps is sitting out on the front porch in one of the ancient rocking chairs when I get home. He looks up from the magazine he's reading when the creaky steps announce my arrival.

"How was school, Lennie?" he asks, taking a sip from the mug set beside him.

"It was fine," I reply. It's my standard answer.

"You left awfully early this morning," Gramps remarks.

"I had to work on something for the paper," I tell him. "I'm heading back out to the barn to finish things up now."

"Don't worry about the feed bags. They were already moved."

I shoot Gramps a hard look. "You didn't." Disapproval is heavy in my tone.

"No," he responds, sounding disgruntled. "Tom stopped by earlier for a visit. He moved them."

"Good." I let out a sigh of relief. "Did he happen to say anything about those articles I sent him?"

Tom Stradwell owns the *Landry Gazette*, along with a host of other local papers, and is one of my grandfather's oldest friends.

He's also my best chance at having something to do besides muck out stalls and clean tack in the fall.

"He liked them," Gramps tells me, still sounding disgruntled. And disapproving. "Said to come see him in May if you're still interested in some work."

"Of course I'll still be interested," I stress. "I hope you made that clear."

"Schools are still taking applications, Lennie."

"Gramps, we're not going through this again. You can't take care of the farm yourself."

"Then we need to sel—"

"We're not selling the farm," I state firmly. "This is your home. My home."

"I just wish…" He lets his voice trail off.

"I know," I mumble. Sometimes, I really hate my parents for the respective messes they left behind. "Look, lots of people take gap years. I'll have more time to do things around the farm when I'm not in school. I can make some repairs, market the stallions better. We'll have Stormy's foal to sell. Maybe that'll be enough for me to take some online classes, at least."

Gramps opens his mouth with what I can already tell will be an argument, so I take evasive action. "I really need to get started on the chores. I'm headed to a party after dinner," I inform him.

Sure enough, that tidbit derails him completely. "What?" Gramps looks stunned. Saying I don't get out much is akin to suggesting Landry's residents have a mild interest in horse racing.

"I'm going to a party tonight," I repeat. "I mean, as long as that's okay?"

"I—yeah, of course," Gramps fumbles. In addition to the surprising flicker of activity in my sad social life, he's also thrown by me asking permission. Our relationship is usually defined by me taking care of him.

"All right, then." I take advantage of his lingering shock to slip inside the empty house.

Rather than dump my backpack in the kitchen like usual, I carry it upstairs with me so I can change out of my jeans and sweatshirt into rattier jeans and a dirty sweatshirt. I typically don't bother changing on Fridays, since Saturday is the designated laundry day, but I don't really want to show up to the party smelling like manure and covered with horsehair.

By the time I finish all the barn chores and exercise Gallie, it's pitch black out and I'm starving. I finish brushing down the massive black stallion and head inside, happy to see dinner is already waiting on the table.

Whispers of steam rise from the freshly cooked burgers. I eagerly lather plenty of ketchup and mustard onto the warm bun before delving into my food. Some of Gramps's culinary creations are questionable, but his burgers are always good.

Gramps surveys me curiously as I eat. "You're hungry tonight."

"It was Gallie's day," I explain. The youngest of our remaining seven horses, Sir Galahad is feisty on a good day. Like all of them, he should really be ridden more than twice a week, but my schedule is already stretched trying to accommodate two rides a day. Exercising Gallie is like trying to stay aboard a rocket ship. He was born when I was in fifth grade, and won every race he entered, just before my dad died and everything really fell apart. Gallie's stud fees are our main source of income these days.

Gramps shoos me away from doing the dishes after supper, so I head upstairs to change back into what I wore to school. I stare at my reflection in the full-length mirror attached to the back of my door, trying to see myself the way a stranger would.

My hair is my best feature. It's thick and straight, and thanks to a lack of any recent haircut, hangs almost to my mid-back.

52

Ordinarily it's a mundane shade of light brown, but in the sun I have coppery highlights that emphasize the green in my hazel eyes.

Right now, in the artificial light cast by the lamp on my dresser, it's difficult to find anything remotely special about my appearance. My brown color is boring and my eye color is over-shadowed by the dark circles beneath my eyes. The sweatshirt I'm wearing hangs loosely around my thin frame, jumbling what few curves I have.

I walk over to my closet, swinging the slightly ajar door fully open so I can peer at the contents. There are only a few hanging items to flip through. A jean jacket, which is out because I'm already wearing denim, a sweater that shrunk last winter, my rain jacket, and a navy blouse. I actually like the blouse a lot, but it's entirely unsuitable for January.

Sighing, I close the door and resign myself to my current outfit. I'll be wearing a coat over it, anyway.

I head back downstairs. Gramps is still in the kitchen, finishing up the dinner dishes. He looks up when I enter the room.

"Okay, I'm going to head out," I tell him. "I've got my cell. Call if you need anything, all right?" I hesitate. I'm gone all day to school, but hardly ever at night. What if he needs something? What if…

Gramps reads the uncertainty on my face. "I'll be fine, Lennie. Won't ride one of the stallions or move any hay bales. Just a Jays game and bed for this old man." He grins, and it creases the skin around his eyes, the exact same shade as mine. Even when his face relaxes, the lines remain, the folds firmly etched in his face after decades of squinting in the sun at horses galloping by. His expression sobers, and his voice gains a bit more authority. "Go have some fun, all right?"

I nod reluctantly and head out into the chilly evening.

CHAPTER FIVE

LENNON

The Belmonts live on the outer fringes of town, part of a newer subdivision on land that used to be a horse farm. A development exactly like what would happen to Matthews Farm if we ever sold it.

Land in Landry is too valuable to graze horses on when the coveted zip code ensures people pay outrageous sums to live on the same patch of earth.

The truck wheezes ominously as I reach the final hill that Cassie's family's house is perched on, so I press harder on the gas pedal. Despite constantly sounding like it's on its dying breath, I've never actually had the truck break down on me before. Hopefully that will remain true.

I park behind Cassie's car and hop down from the truck, glancing around her neighborhood. I've visited her house before, but this is the first time I've come over at night. Lights blaze, not only in her house's windows, but in the neighbors' as well. It's a foreign sight to me. Matthews Farm is about fifteen acres. There's no one who lives close enough for any lights to be visible.

The winding, stone path leading up to the front door is also well-lit. Trimmed hedges that line it have been wrapped with hundreds of small, twinkling lights. They weren't up the last time I was here, so I assume it was part of the Belmonts' holiday decorations.

I ring the doorbell. Only a few seconds pass before I hear the pounding of footsteps.

The black door swings open to reveal a guy I've never seen before. He looks older than me, but probably not by more than a couple of years. Cassie has mentioned her two older brothers, so I figure he must be one of them. It's pretty obvious they're related. He has the same dirty blond hair and brown eyes as Cassie. And the same friendly grin, although his is tinged with a bit of mischief I don't ordinarily associate with my sweet friend.

"Hi... Is Cassie home?"

"Yup," he replies, still smiling broadly. But he doesn't move to open the door any further.

"Can I come inside?" I ask. "She's expecting me."

I feel him look me up and down. A roguish smirk forms. "I'd rather you hang out with me instead."

I roll my eyes. Where does this endless supply of cocky, over-confident guys come from? "I don't thin—"

"Josh! What the hell?" Cassie suddenly appears, shoving her brother to the side with one elbow and giving me a wide smile. "Ignore him. Come on." She opens the door so I can enter the expansive front foyer of the house.

"I was just getting to know your friend," Josh says, completely unabashed.

Cassie grimaces and waves a hand between me and her brother. "Josh, Lennon. Lennon, my annoying brother Josh, with awful manners. Introductions done!" She grabs my hand and starts pulling me toward the stairs.

"Are both your brothers home?" I ask curiously as we climb the wooden staircase.

Cassie sighs. "No, just Josh. He's still on break from college. He was supposed to be off skiing, but his flight got delayed or something. He's been driving me crazy. He doesn't know anyone here, so he's got nothing to do. But I don't know what he's complaining about. He's not the one who had to start over at a new school senior year. He just has to live here for a few weeks." She glances at me, her expression apologetic. "Not that I don't like it here, I just—"

"I get it. I can't imagine moving senior year. And Landry's not exactly an easy place to live."

Understatement.

Cassie leads me inside her bedroom, which is massive, especially compared to mine. It's decorated entirely in shades of white, which sounds boring, but is actually kind of cool. I take a seat on the cream-colored loveseat while Cassie perches on an ivory stool in front of a matching vanity with a vast array of makeup spread across it.

"I'm almost finished with my eyeliner, then we can do yours," she informs me.

"Do my what?"

"Your makeup." She gives me a *duh* look.

"You don't need to do that," I assure her. "I'll just watch you get ready."

"Why? Do you not think people will be dressed up?" Cassie asks me, her expression nervous. She sees me as some sort of guide for all this, and I have no idea how to break it to her that I'm far more clueless than she is.

"No, I'm sure they will be. It's just—well, I don't want people to think I care," I admit. "It will just give them more to talk about."

Cassie's face softens. "I'm not going to pretend like I understand the social dynamics of this town, because I don't. At all." I laugh. "And I know some people are shitty. But I also think some of them might surprise you if you give them more of a chance. I know Shannon really likes you. So do the rest of the girls. They all think *you* don't like *them*."

I open my mouth to reply, but she keeps talking, so I snap it shut again.

"Just think about it, okay? If you don't want to wear makeup because you don't want to, that's fine. Just don't decide based on what others might do or say."

I know she's right. "Okay," I sigh. "Just a little, though."

Cassie beams. "That's all you need, anyway."

"Why wouldn't Shannon or any of the others say anything to me?" I ask. "I mean, no offense, but I've known them all a lot longer than you have."

"Are you serious?" Cassie asks. She answers her own question. "I guess you are. You're intimidating, Lennon. You're smart and gorgeous, and you might care what other people think, but you don't act like you do. And you always know just what to say. People are *envious* of you."

I scoff, and it's thick with disbelief.

"I mean it," Cassie insists. "You should have heard the girls at lunch yesterday after you went to sit with Caleb. I mean, he's *Caleb Winters*." Her voice holds the same blatant admiration I've heard so many times before.

I shrug. "He's just a guy." My voice is indifferent, but I'm not. Not entirely. I keep picturing him sitting across the table from me in the library this morning.

Cassie shrugs, evidently not sensing my mixed emotions. Maybe she's right; I am better at hiding my true feelings than I

57

thought. "True. But he's a very hot, very popular guy this entire town seems to have some sort of unhealthy obsession with."

"Yeah, I guess so," I acknowledge.

Cassie keeps talking as if I hadn't spoken. "None of us could come up with anything to say to him, but you acted completely normal. Not that it mattered. He didn't pay attention to anyone but you."

She's right, I realize, with a jolt of surprise.

Cassie doesn't bother waiting for a response, too excited about me agreeing to a mini makeover. She beckons me over to the stool and sets to work. It's a surprisingly relaxing process. A swipe of lip balm and some moisturizer is usually the extent of my morning routine. I have a new appreciation for the girls who show up at school with a full face of makeup when I realize how long it's taking Cassie to do what she assures me is a minimal amount.

Finally, she finishes, and I have to blink at my reflection a couple of times. The liquid she spread across my whole face has given me a glowing, dewy complexion. My lips look soft and shiny. And my eyes look green again, thanks to the flattering lighting that surrounds the vanity and the black Cassie has rimmed my eyes with.

"Wow, thank you," I tell her, hesitantly raising a hand to touch underneath my left eye. The patch of skin that normally appears almost bruised has been seamlessly altered, making me look well rested rather than sorely sleep deprived.

After makeup, Cassie moves right along to clothes. I lounge on the loveseat as she tries on outfit after outfit, before finally settling on a pair of black skinny jeans and a sparkly sweater.

Then, her attention shifts to me. I end up changing out of my oversized sweatshirt and into a clingy, maroon sweater Cassie insists looks amazing. As we head out the door to go back downstairs, Cassie hands me a gray woolen jacket to wear over it. The material and sleek design look fancy enough to be an outfit all on their own. I feel completely transformed as we head back downstairs. Only my jeans remain unchanged, but I know that's mainly because I'm several inches taller than Cassie.

"Nice Guy is not going to know what hit him," she tells me on the stairs.

I laugh, but it morphs into a yawn.

"Lennon! It's not even ten yet!"

"I know," I reply. "Early morning, that's all." Not to mention I usually go to bed *at* ten, never mind when I've been up since four thirty.

The faint sound of raised voices is just audible as we prepare to depart. Cassie seems to rush to put on her shoes, but she doesn't say anything, so I don't either. Avoiding uncomfortable family drama is certainly something I can understand.

We've just reached Cassie's SUV when a shadow emerges from the side of the garage. I study it curiously, but Cassie jumps a few feet in the air.

"Josh!" she exclaims when the twinkling lights reveal her brother's features. "What are you doing out here?"

He jerks his chin in the direction of the house. "Avoiding them. Can I come with you? Just for a bit?"

"To a *high school* party?" Cassie scoffs. But her gaze wanders to me, and I can see the conflict reflected there.

"I'm nineteen, not thirty," Josh retorts.

Cassie holds my gaze, and I can see the silent question hovering.

"Marcus is the youngest of five," I inform her. "There will probably be some older kids there."

After another moment of hesitation, Cassie nods. "Okay, you can come," she tells Josh. He grins. "But if you embarrass me, I'll tell Mom and Dad some things that will make their current argument look tame, got it?"

Whatever she's threatening Josh with must be pretty bad, because he nods furiously. The three of us pile into Cassie's car, and she immediately turns the stereo up, assaulting our ears with some pop ballad about a broken heart. I don't know if she's trying to prevent Josh from speaking or keep me awake, but she accomplishes both as we whizz along the empty roads.

More than awake, I feel...normal. Listening to a song about making an ex pay while headed to a party with a friend might be commonplace for most high school girls, but for me it's a rare event. Exceedingly rare. I savor the feeling as best I can while simultaneously feeling like I might keel over from exhaustion, despite the fact I'm already sitting.

I give Cassie directions for a while, but stop bothering once we turn on to Marcus's street. It's obvious where we're headed toward. The actual house is quiet, with only a couple of lights on, but the path to the right of it is lined with cars, and the sound and sight of activity is evident through the trees as we all climb out of the car.

There are a few other groups arriving at the same time as us, and I attract a lot of stares as we walk along the mowed path. I'm not sure if it's simply because I'm here, or if it's because I'm here with the "new girl" and a strange guy, but it's annoying either way.

Josh notices. "You a local celebrity or something, Lennon?"

"Or something," I mutter back as we emerge into the clearing. And that's all it is. A large patch of browning grass ringed with trees and filled with people.

This is it? I can't help but think.

For years of Monday mornings, I've heard about the wild Friday nights that take place here. The stories I'm accustomed to hearing don't seem to fit with the scene in front of me. I don't know what I expected, but it wasn't this. I feel strangely let down; like an illusion has been shattered.

Cassie takes in my lackluster expression and laughs. "Come on. Let's get a drink and try to find Will."

"I'll catch up with you guys," Josh says, before heading toward a group of girls.

Cassie tracks his movements closely as we head in the direction of the two kegs perched on the periphery of the clearing, next to the few cars fortunate enough to avoid being parked on the sloping path.

"He better not embarrass me," Cassie mutters as we walk along. I don't answer, busy taking in my surroundings.

I study each group closely as we pass them by, feeling like an anthropologist sent to observe a foreign culture, rather than a high school senior in the midst of people I've known since kindergarten.

Although, the peer I'm most concerned about encountering has only attended the same school as me since ninth grade.

I scuff my sneakers along the tufts of grass, interspersed with dirt patches worn by decades of teenagers partying at this very spot.

"Come on, Lennon," Cassie urges, finally losing patience with my pace and grabbing my hand to tow me along faster. "Try not to look like you're being tortured just by being here, please."

I paste the widest, fakest smile I can muster on my face as she drags me past a couple making out against the truck parked closest to the keg.

Cassie laughs at my expression as she fills two plastic cups with beer. "Much better."

I drop the fake smile and try to muster a real one as I take a long sip of the cold, frothy liquid filling the cup she hands me.

The malty smell is strangely comforting, reminiscent of lazy Sunday evenings spent sprawled out on the living room rug studying while Gramps nursed a bottle of beer until it was luke-warm at best.

"Let's go over to the bonfire to wait for Will," Cassie suggests.

"Okay," I agree, feeling a little less like an outsider with a red cup in hand and hops coating my tongue.

The power of peer pressure.

I spin around to follow Cassie toward the roaring flames, and then the next few seconds seem to happen in slow motion. My left foot catches on something—an errant stick, or maybe an empty beer can—and I'm suddenly off-balance, falling forward when I want to be upright. I take a quick half-step to right myself, and watch in horror as beer sloshes out of my full cup and drenches one half of the couple kissing against the truck.

The person I soak turns out to be Madison Herbert. The girl who, as she'd be the first to tell you, is considered Landry High's most popular is now dripping with beer, courtesy of my clumsiness.

Despite the fact she ranks quite high on the long list of people I don't like very much, horror hastens my apology. "I'm so sor—" The last word dies on my tongue when I realize who she was kissing.

Blue eyes burn mine. All of a sudden, it feels like the oxygen has been sucked out of my lungs.

I tear my gaze away from Caleb. "It was an accident," I inform Madison.

My ex-best friend glances up from her dripping clothes with venom spewing from her eyes. "What the hell are you even doing here, Lennon?"

"I invited her." I glance over at Will, who's approaching with two other guys. Uneasily, I realize they aren't the only ones looking this way. Most of the clearing's attention is aimed over here.

"Of course you did," Madison drawls. "You two make *perfect* sense."

Maybe I'd walk away, if it was just me she was insulting. That's a storm I've successfully weathered many times before. But it bothers me she's dragging Will into it, that she's willing to slight him just to take a dig at me.

I toss my mostly-empty cup and cross my arms. "What does that mean?"

"It means you walk around with your nose in the air, like we don't all know your dad was a deadbeat druggie and your mom was a slut who—"

"That's enough."

It takes me a moment, to work past the ball of pain and rage and realize who spoke.

Madison—everyone—is gaping at Caleb.

"I'm just stating facts." Madison recovers first, pairing the statement with a fake laugh.

No one joins her. It's eerily silent, everyone frozen in place like scared animals. But they're not staring at Madison—or me. They're all focused on Caleb, like they're waiting for him to react.

"Whatever." Madison flips her hair. "Help me get cleaned up?"

"Not a fucking chance."

I thought I'd heard Caleb angry. But the ice in his voice is new. Its cold edge cuts through the night air like a sharp blade before he turns and walks away.

I flinch, and I'm not the only one. Madison glares at me before she spins and disappears into the crowd too.

"Whoa," Cassie breathes. "I, uh, I can't believe that happened."

I'm still frozen, staring at the spot where Caleb was standing.

"Hey, Lennon." Will approaches, hands in his pockets. "Hi, Cassie," he adds.

"Hey, Will," she responds, and I smile.

"Can I get you ladies anything to drink?" he offers.

I chew on the inside of my cheek and nod, appreciating his effort to act like that scene didn't just happen.

"Drinks would be great," I tell Will.

"You okay?" Cassie whispers, while Will's over by the coolers.

"Yeah, I'm fine."

Cassie excuses herself a couple minutes after Will returns with our drinks in an obvious attempt to leave the two of us alone. We chat easily, although Will does most of the talking. He's in the midst of explaining the joke gift holiday tradition in his family when one of his basketball teammates stumbles over to us, clearly drunk.

I tell Will I'm going to grab another drink, and he nods, preoccupied with keeping his teammate upright. Rather than head for the beverages, I hike up the edge of the small hill that slopes into the clearing and take a seat on a random truck's tailgate. I spot Cassie standing next to the bonfire and watch her chatting with a few of the girls we eat lunch with before turning my gaze upward at the stars. I've just started tracing the shape of the Little Dipper when I feel the tailgate dip from the added weight of another body.

"Heard you soaked Madison." When I glance over, Colt Adams is also looking upward.

"Unfortunately, it wasn't on purpose," I reply, glad my voice doesn't reveal how shocked I am Caleb's best friend is voluntarily speaking to me. That's happened...never.

Colt chuckles. "He's pissed."

Something twists in my stomach. Worse than the confusing state of things between me and Caleb is others noticing it. Whenever people talk about me, it's always in a negative context. "No idea what you're talking about, Colt."

"How much do you want to bet he's going to come over here? Twenty bucks?"

"I don't have twenty bucks."

My honest admission doesn't have the effect I hoped for, because he keeps going. "Fine. If he doesn't come over here, I'll give you twenty bucks. If he does, I'll have the satisfaction of knowing I was right."

"Whatever." I resume staring at the star-strewn sky.

"So...why did you come?"

I glance over at him. "You sound like Madison."

"Probably because she's worried about the same thing I am."

"Once again, I have no idea what you're talking about."

"I know." Colt sighs. "That's the whole damn problem." He shakes his head, then hops off the tailgate in one smooth motion.

"You're leaving before our bet is resolved?"

He nods to the right. "Better luck next time."

Colt pauses to say something to Caleb, then disappears into the clearing. Caleb continues toward me, taking the open spot next to me silently.

"You just lost me twenty bucks."

Caleb is silent for a few minutes. "Why'd you come, Lennon?" He sounds frustrated. Angry, even.

"If you're mad that I interrupted your makeout—"

He scoffs. "Has she always treated you like that?"

65

"*Everyone* has always treated me like that, Caleb. Including you."

That's enough to turn Caleb's attention from the stars to me. "Are you fucking kidding me, Lennon? I've never—"

This time, I interrupt him. "Never insulted my parents? Never called me a name? Which one qualifies you for sainthood?"

Caleb leans closer. Too close. I'm suddenly very aware we're not at school. As stupid as it sounds, that's where we always interact. There are schedules and witnesses and *light*. Sitting here in the darkness feels different. "I think you like it."

"What?"

"I think you like it," he repeats. "I think you like arguing with me, Lennon Matthews."

"You're wrong."

"Am I? If I ignore you on Monday, you wouldn't care?"

"I'd be thrilled. Best day of high school." I'm saying the words. But I'm thinking, *Would I?* Because I've always taken Caleb's presence—his attention—as a given. I've wished for its absence but never considered what the reality would feel like.

Caleb doesn't say anything, and I make the mistake of looking over at him. Those piercing blue eyes aren't looking at the party, or the sky. They're looking at me. My clothes. My face. I don't know how much he can see in the dim light, but something tells me Caleb has noticed the changes in my usual appearance. A warmth that has nothing to do with the borrowed wool I'm wearing works its way through my body. I lift my gaze back up to the stars, thoroughly unsettled.

"I didn't know you'd be here. You never come to these things."

"What difference does it make?"

"None, obviously. Have a good night, Matthews."

I open my mouth to respond but nothing comes out. Caleb

shakes his head, then jumps off the tailgate and walks away. Something sinks inside of me, like an anchor dropping into my stomach.

If I ignore you on Monday, you wouldn't care?

I have my answer.

And it isn't the one I wanted.

CHAPTER SIX

LENNON

He approaches me while I'm switching books out in my locker. Since Landry High assigns lockers alphabetically and we've kept the same ones since freshman year, seeing Ryan James isn't a rarity. Talking to him is. We remain in a comfortable state of not acknowledging the other exists.

Ryan leans against Ellie Nash's locker, shooting me a cocky grin. The same one that swindled me out of my first kiss, back in eighth grade.

"Wanna hang out tonight?"

I'm shocked. I figured he was coming over here to pile on about my disastrous Friday night. "You feel like slumming?"

Ryan's grin widens as he shakes his head. "Come on, Lennon. We both know you have more confidence than that. It's one of my favorite things about you."

"Oh, yeah?" I grab my Calculus textbook and then slam the door shut, satisfied when Ryan flinches at the loud noise. "What else is on the list?"

"What list?"

"Your list of favorite things about me."

"Oh. Well." He runs his fingers through his hair, obviously not expecting the question. Most of the girls at this school smile and blush in response to anything he says. Maddeningly, I used to be one of them. "I've always thought you were cool. And, well, before everything happened…"

"By everything, you mean my dad dying? That's when I could have used a *hang out*, Ryan. You're about four years too late."

"It's only too late if you say it's too late."

"That's literally *exactly* what I just said."

He laughs. "Yeah, I heard you. Just think about it, okay?"

Ryan is gone before I can respond, lost in the crowded hallway. The warning bell rings a few seconds later, and I basically have to sprint to get to Oceanography in time for the start of class.

The Oceanography teacher, Ms. Lyons, begins class with the announcement we'll be spending the class period performing an octopus dissection. She allows everyone to choose their partners, which pleases everyone but me.

Shannon is in my class, so I decide to test Cassie's claim the girls we sit with at lunch aren't only there because of her. I don't fully believe her. I'm guessing it's Cassie's way of "helping"— and by helping, I mean forcing—me to better integrate with her friends.

"Do you want to work together?" I ask Shannon, plopping down on the empty stool next to her.

"Sure," she replies, appearing genuinely enthusiastic, which I take as a promising sign. "I'm not sure I would have taken this class if I'd known we were doing dissections."

"Hopefully it won't be too—" I'm cut off when Ms. Lyons sets a metal tray in front of us that's mostly covered by a slimy, gray lump. It jiggles when the tray hits the table. "Gross," I finish.

Although it appears gelatinous, the slippery surface of the mollusk proves challenging to pierce. After we've pulled on surgical gloves, Shannon attempts to hold the sides of the dead octopus while I try to slit the skin with the scalpel. It's a difficult, disgusting process.

"I don't think I'll be able to eat seafood again," I comment once we're finally finished.

"I'm sorry," Shannon replies.

"I never really liked it all that much, anyway."

She lets out a little laugh. "No. I'm sorry about the way I—the way so many people—treated you freshman year. That some people still act that way." I know she's referring to Friday night. "I can't imagine what that must have been like."

"It sucked."

Shannon nods. "If it makes any difference, I've always been impressed by how you handled it. I know I never would have been able to keep my cool the way you did. I don't think many people could."

"They probably wouldn't have to," I state.

Shannon doesn't deny it. My father's fatal overdose the summer before I started high school wasn't the first scandal Landry ever experienced. The main difference was Gramps and I chose to remain rather than relocate. Gramps's roots are sunk too deep to ever leave Landry voluntarily. It's why I won't allow him to consider selling the farm. It's part of who he is.

"But thank you," I add, acknowledging her words. And the courage it took to say them.

Shannon smiles at me, and I feel like my social "line" might have just become a triangle. At the very least, I feel less isolated than usual.

On my way toward English, I run into Andrew. He's hurrying down the hallway, perpetually in a rush, but stops when he spots me.

"Lennon! Just the person I wanted to see," he tells me.

That worries me slightly, but I smile anyway. "About what?"

"About the article on Caleb Winters! How is it going?"

"Um…" I haven't seen Caleb since he walked away Friday night. Somehow I forgot, during that moment that felt like a closing chapter, that we have both a project and an article to get through together. "It's going."

"You'll get me the draft on time?"

"Have I ever turned in a draft late?" I ask.

Simon sent me some professional-sounding questions this weekend, so all I need is an opportunity to ask Caleb them before I have to turn in a draft to Andrew. Which will require…talking to Caleb.

The warning bell rings, indicating there are only two minutes left until the start of third period. Andrew startles. "I'll see you tomorrow," he tells me, and then sets off at a brisk walk. I'm not surprised. He's absolutely the type who arrives early to class to get a front-row seat.

The hallways are rapidly emptying. I only pass a couple of other students as I turn into the long hallway that comprises the south wing. There's another figure just rounding the corner ahead of me.

I recognize the dark hair and broad shoulders instantly.

Might as well get this over with. If I time it right, maybe he won't have a chance to bring up Friday night before we reach the classroom.

"Caleb!" No reaction. "Caleb!" I try again, a bit louder.

Does he have headphones in?

"Caleb!" Finally, he turns.

"What?" His voice echoes in the empty hallway, loud and annoyed.

I falter, then recover. "Are you deaf? I called your name three times!"

"Yes, Lennon," he drawls. "I'm deaf."

"Did I say deaf? I meant an asshole," I retort.

His expression hardens. "Ever think I just didn't want to talk to you?"

"Then maybe you shouldn't have made certain *I have to*! Andrew is breathing down my neck about the article *you* insisted I write. I could barely come up with more than a paragraph based on last week's conversation."

The final bell rings, signaling the start of English.

"Why didn't you pass it off to the sports guy?"

"What?"

"You heard me. I said I'd do it with him, and you chose to still write it yourself. Why?"

"I—"

"I thought I recognized the voices of two tardy students. Class isn't being held in the hallway today." Mr. Tanner appears in the doorway of our English classroom.

"Sorry, Mr. Tanner," Caleb says, his tone vastly different than the one he just used with me. Instead of angry, he sounds exhausted.

"It won't happen again," I add meekly.

He nods, and ducks back inside the classroom, clearly expecting Caleb and me to follow. We do.

"I can meet on Wednesday at the same time as before," Caleb mutters as we finish our trek to the classroom door.

"Fine."

CHAPTER SEVEN

LENNON

W hen the numbers on my phone display a four and a five, I realize Caleb isn't coming. I arrived at the field just before 5:30, again.

The smug satisfaction over having beaten Caleb here has long since faded; first I was annoyed, and now I'm smack dab in the midst of anger. Instead of being thrilled he stood me up, I'm pissed. Worse, I feel foolish. Caleb not showing didn't even occur to me when I woke up extra early this morning.

The school won't even be unlocked for another fifteen minutes. I literally have nothing to do except sit here and stew.

The parking lot fills slowly as the time ticks past. I should take advantage of the opportunity to accomplish something, but I'm too aggravated to focus right now. I just sit and stare out at the empty field, not really seeing anything in front of me.

Eventually, I leave the bleachers and head toward the entrance to the school. Andrew is walking along the sidewalk from the opposite direction. I march right up to him.

"I can't do the article on Caleb. I tried. I really did. But I can't do it."

Shockingly, Andrew nods. I figured he'd freak out. Instead, he looks…understanding? "I get it, Lennon. I know where you're coming from, but unless he tells you he can't—"

"I *told* you this would happen, Andrew! The whole news staff heard me say it was a bad idea, but you insisted I do it."

"Wait. What are you talking about?" Andrew asks.

"The interview with Caleb! I gave it a chance, and fine, he showed up the first time but this time—"

He cuts me off. "You haven't heard?"

"Heard what?" I reply. A trickle of unease interrupts the indignation when I see Andrew's expression has turned somber.

"Senator Winters was rushed to the hospital last night. He died a couple of hours ago."

"Oh." That one syllable is all I can manage for a minute. "I hadn't heard," I add unnecessarily. I'm pretty sure my shocked expression already conveyed that to Andrew.

He nods grimly. "Needless to say, we'll forget about the article for now. We'll revisit it…later." Andrew doesn't expand on when that will be before continuing along the sidewalk, leaving me standing here.

News of Senator Winters's death spreads like wildfire through the halls of Landry High. Everyone speaks in muted tones. Teachers offer amateur counseling services. A giant scroll of white paper is spread across three folding tables in the front lobby. A rainbow of scrawled condolences soon cover every inch.

I spend most of the day comparing the reaction to Senator Winters's passing to my parents' deaths, and I hate that I do. Loss isn't any sort of competition. But I can't help but compare the outpouring of support to the awkward condolences and subsequent shunning Gramps and I were subjected to.

Caleb isn't back in school on Thursday. Or Friday. According to the rumor mill, he's with his parents in the nation's capital, attending some sort of memorial service being held there in honor of the late senator.

It's announced a funeral will take place at the Winters's estate on Sunday, so I know he'll be back in Landry by then.

For years, I've wished Caleb Winters hadn't moved here. But instead of appreciating his absence in English, I spend the class staring at his empty seat.

Sunday morning dawns dreary and overcast, matching my dismal mood. Wet weather always makes Gramps's bad hip act up. After twenty minutes of hobbling around the farmhouse, he admits he won't be able to attend Senator Winters's funeral alongside what is sure to be most of Landry.

I was surprised to hear he was planning to go in the first place. As far as I know, my grandfather never so much as met the man. Caleb's grandfather was like a legend; often discussed and rarely seen. It's irrefutable he meant a lot to this town, so maybe that's why Gramps was wanting to go.

Unfortunately, Gramps's change of heart lands me in the uncomfortable predicament of deciding whether *I* should go. I thought the choice had already been made for me.

I deliberate for the entirety of the morning chores and my usual ride on whether I should go without him. A gathering of all of Landry's snobs is ordinarily the last place I would choose to be, but I feel some strange compulsion to attend. Not going feels wrong, somehow.

Cassie replies to my text seconds after I send it, saying her family will pick me up on their way. Gramps seems surprised when I tell him I'm still going to the funeral. Over the years, he's heard me complain plenty about Caleb. But he doesn't ask why I'm attending, and I don't offer up an explanation.

I own one black dress: a long-sleeved, sheath style. Paired with pantyhose, black flats, and a black cardigan, I look appropriately mournful. I hope. My bulky winter coat ruins some of the effect, but the moist air has a chilly bite that makes it a necessity.

After making certain Gramps is comfortable on the couch, I walk down the long driveway to wait for Cassie. Matthews Farm is a bit out of their way, so it will save some time, but the main reason I walk is I don't want her family to see the rundown property. Once a majestic, maintained plot of land has become nothing more than a collection of buildings in desperate need of repair. If I had the time, money, or ability, there's no shortage of pressing projects.

A shiny car pulls up a few minutes after I reach the mailbox. Josh gives me a wide grin when I climb in beside him, and Cassie's parents greet me warmly as well. Every time I've interacted with them, they've both been perfectly polite, but I can't help recalling the echo of their angry voices when we left for Marcus's party as they say hello.

Cassie smiles across her brother at me.

It's a five-minute drive to the massive wrought-iron gates that mark the entrance to the Winters' estate. I've driven past the imposing ingress countless times on trips into downtown Landry. Like everything else in this town, location is a status symbol.

The properties closest to the center of town are some of the largest; claimed by those who settled here first and wanted to stable their horses close to the racetrack. All the properties surrounding the immediate downtown area, including the high school and racetrack, are owned by those who can actually trace their family lineage through our tiny town's history.

Ironically, it's the only way Caleb Winters and I are on equal footing when it comes to our families.

I thought the front gate of the Winters' farm was ostentatious, but all it does is mask the majesty of the rest of the property. The tree-lined driveway winds and weaves for at least a mile before depositing us in a cobblestone circle comprised of light gray slabs of stone scrubbed so clean they gleam. Cassie's dad parks half in the shadow cast by the main house.

Main house, because there's more than one residence.

It's obvious which one the Winters family lives in. Columns soar upward, framing the white front porch, the white front door, and the white shutters that frame every front-facing window.

Everything is white.

The house stands out like a drop of snow amongst the greenery that rolls out like an emerald carpet in every direction.

The second house is smaller, but not by much, and no less grand. The basic architecture is identical to that of the main house, only without some of the additional, more ornate details, like the front porch and scrolling columns. It looks like it could comfortably house at least a dozen people, and I'd be surprised if it doesn't. I can only imagine the number of employees it must take to not only run a farm of this size, but to maintain the impeccable condition it so clearly is in. I barely have time to care for seven horses while neglecting every square inch of our property.

Last I heard, the Winters housed close to a hundred horses, and I know from personal experience pasture grass doesn't look so green and plush naturally. Especially in winter.

There are a few groups of people milling around on the cobblestones, but everyone else seems to be heading behind the main house. Cassie's parents and brother follow them, and she and I trail behind.

"This place is insane," she whispers to me. "Can you imagine living here?"

"No, I can't," I reply honestly.

We round the side of the house. My eyes widen when I catch a glimpse of the crowd. The backyard is expansive, but it's not nearly large enough to accommodate everyone. Two sides of the yard are buttressed by split-rail fencing, and those who weren't able to claim one of the hundreds of folding chairs that have been set up have already taken spots along the wood to lean against.

Uniformed attendants are setting up more chairs on the paved patio connected to the back of the house, so Cassie and I follow her family over there. Her parents grab two of the few remaining seats. Cassie, Josh, and I all sit down on the stone wall that encloses the periphery of the patio.

Josh lets out a low whistle as he takes in the view. "This is crazy," he remarks. "I thought people hated politicians."

Silence suddenly falls, and everyone who was fortunate enough to claim a seat quickly takes it. A minister clad in a black robe walks toward the lectern that's been set up, closely followed by Caleb's parents. Then a woman who looks to be in her fifties, who I've never seen before.

Caleb appears last. He's wearing a black suit that's perfectly tailored. I can only see his profile, not his expression.

The minister thanks everyone for attending and then begins speaking. I tune most of what he says out, more interested in people-watching.

Until the minister's gravelly voice is replaced by a familiar one.

"My grandfather was an important man. A proud man. He cared about this community. Where he came from. What legacy he wanted to leave behind. If you asked him why he decided to go into politics, he would say it was because he wanted to contribute something back to a place that had given him so much. That when he left Landry for college is when he truly appreciated all that it had given him. I thought it was just a soundbite one of his aides came up with during his first campaign."

Polite laughter ripples through the crowd.

"But once we moved here, I understood what he meant."

I frown at that, but everyone else looks enchanted.

"My grandfather did a lot of incredible things," Caleb continues. "For this country. For this state. For this town. But no matter what happened with his career, what he loved most was the land we're standing on now. He was never happier than when he was sitting in his study or watching one of his horses win the Landry Cup. Those moment are always how I'll remember him. How he would have wanted to be remembered. Thank you all for coming. I know it would have meant a lot to my grandfather."

Caleb steps away from the lectern, and the minister's voice replaces his. "That concludes the service. The Winters family would like to invite you all to remain for some light refreshments. There will also be guest books circulated for any messages you'd like to convey or memories you'd like to share." The service ends, my view of the lectern obscured as attendees rise from their seats to mill about.

"Did you know Caleb was giving a speech?" Cassie whispers to me.

"No, I had no idea."

"Weird his parents didn't speak, no?"

"I guess." Truthfully, I know nothing substantial about Caleb's family. Whether he's close to either of his parents.

Cassie's no longer paying attention, busy scanning the crowd instead. "I see Shannon and Eliza." She waves. "Let's go say hi."

"I'll come find you guys in a few minutes. I'm just going to grab a drink," I tell her before weaving through the crowd over to where the refreshments are spread out.

I fill a glass with lemonade and head toward the periphery of the nearest field. There's a gray filly grazing only a few feet away from the fence. I lean against the closest post to study her. I hold my hand out, but the filly doesn't venture over. She trots to a fresh patch of grass, tossing her mane haughtily.

"Is the whole town obsessed with horses?" I turn to see Josh walking over toward me. "No one here seems to want to talk about anything else."

"Pretty much."

"They are nice to look at," Josh states. "Is this one old? He's all gray."

I laugh. "You don't know much about horses, huh?"

"Nothing." He grins.

"I'd guess *she's* about two," I inform him. "Wrong on both counts."

"Tell me something else," Josh says.

"What do you want to know?" I ask.

"You came." A new voice joins our conversation.

I look to the right, and Caleb is standing there, hands tucked into the pockets of his slacks.

"Yeah." My voice comes out too quiet, so I clear my throat. "I'm really sorry, Caleb. About your grandfather."

"Thanks." That's all he says in response.

A heavy pause stretches between us, exacerbated by the sound of dozens of conversations happening around us. Moist mist swirls, coating my skin and infusing some texture into my ordinarily straight hair in what I hope is a flattering way but probably is not.

Josh senses the awkward tension, taking a few steps away.

"I'm going to grab some food," he states, before disappearing into the crowd.

Neither Caleb nor I say anything once he's gone.

I can't think of anything to say besides bringing up how our last conversation was not exactly a cordial one.

He takes a couple steps closer. "I'm sorry—"

"It's fine," I interject, cutting off his apology.

"I would have called to say I wasn't coming, but I don't have your number."

I figured—understandably—that Caleb had totally forgotten he was supposed to meet me Wednesday morning. The knowledge he didn't isn't entirely welcome, causing an uncomfortable twinge in the center of my chest.

"Your speech was nice." Caleb scoffs. I think it's in response to my words, so I feel obligated to explain them. "I judged what people said to me after my parents died. But it wasn't because I knew what they should say instead. I still don't, obviously."

"He was a dick." The words are so quiet, I barely hear them.

"What?"

"My grandfather. He was a dick."

"Oh." I look away, back at the gray horse. I know I should follow that solitary syllable with more, but I'm too busy processing the curveball Caleb just threw at me. Why didn't he just say thanks?

His honesty draws a little of my own out. "At least you tried," I offer. "I didn't—couldn't—say anything about my dad. I just tossed some dirt. And that was that. I didn't say anything. True or made up."

I feel Caleb's eyes on my face, so I keep mine fixed on the gray horse moving steadily away from us. "What about your mom?" he asks.

A long exhale of air rushes out of my mouth as I run a finger along the top of the rail. The white paint is flawless. There's not even a small chip. "I read a poem. I was too young to come up with anything else, and it—losing her was different. She didn't choose to go, you know?"

"Yeah," Caleb says softly. "I know."

And then he reaches out and rests his hand on top of mine. An electric jolt travels up my arm and shocks my entire system. It's the accidental brush of our fingers amplified times a thousand. Because this *isn't* accidental. It's purposeful.

Heat spreads throughout my entire body, making my lungs tighten and my heart pound erratically.

"I should, uh, I told Cassie I'd be right back." I pull my hand away, gnawing on my bottom lip.

Caleb nods, his face impassive. "Okay."

"I'll see you?"

"Yeah," he replies. "You'll see me."

"Okay." I feel off-kilter and confused. Unsure. It shouldn't be this difficult to have a conversation with Caleb Winters.

I turn and head back into the throng of people in search of Cassie.

Leaving him standing there.

CHAPTER EIGHT

LENNON

The damp paper towel helps, but my face still feels sweaty and gross even after I've wiped it repeatedly. Glancing at the clock above the sink, I ball up the paper towel and toss it into the trash.

Landry High requires students to take one semester of gym each year, and that we do fitness tests as part of the curriculum. I didn't need to wheeze around the track four times to know I'm not in the best of shape. I prefer to let the horse do the running, and I don't exactly build up much cardio endurance hauling hay bales.

To make matters worse, I had to watch all the other seniors with the unfortunate fate of having gym second semester— including Madison and Caleb—jog around the football field effortlessly.

With one last anxious glance at the clock, I leave the locker room and hurry in the direction of the newsroom. Andrew hates when we're late.

Instead of the usual hustle and bustle, I'm met with complete and utter silence when I walk inside. No one has moved from their desk to the center of the room where we usually hold our meetings.

It doesn't take me long to figure out why.

"What are you doing here?"

Both Caleb and Andrew turn at the sound of my voice. Andrew looks relieved; Caleb amused.

"Did you get lost, Lennon?" he asks me, smirking. "Been waiting a while."

"Gym ended ten minutes ago," I reply. "You couldn't have been waiting that long. And I'm guessing you spent most of that time trying to *find* the newsroom."

Caleb makes a show of glancing around the small, sparsely furnished room. "At least there was a sign on the door. Otherwise, I might have confused this with a janitor's closet."

"Feel free to tell the school committee they should reallocate some of the athletic department's funds, and we'll redecorate."

Caleb grins. "Nah, on second thought, I like it. Very minimalistic."

"You shouldn't have any trouble finding your way out. The door is two feet from you and marked *Exit*."

I can tell from the way Andrew opens and closes his mouth twice he would love to rebuke me for directing that comment at the subject of our biggest story.

Caleb appears completely at ease as he strolls toward me. I'm painfully aware every member of the paper is tracking his movements.

There's a reason we were relegated to a room in the far corner of the school. People who are not on the paper do not just stop by the newsroom.

Especially not popular people.

Especially not Caleb Winters.

"What are you doing here?" I hiss as he leans against my desk and studies the clippings from past articles I have posted. "You can't just show up in the newsroom!"

"You showed up at my practice."

"That was different!" I protest.

"How?"

"It...just was!" It's far from a compelling reason, but it's all I can come up with.

The corner of Caleb's mouth curls up. I wait for him to pounce on the inadequacy of my response, but instead he changes the subject. "You're avoiding me."

"No, I'm not." It's my automatic reaction to disagree with anything he says, but in this case, he's right. I am avoiding him. The only time we've spoken since his grandfather's funeral was forty minutes ago when he asked me if it was my first time running.

Unfortunately, I think his own pace was fast enough he missed seeing the gesture I responded with.

Caleb is obviously expecting my denial, because he speaks before I've stopped. "Yes, you are." His voice is confident. "Because of what happened at my grandfather's funeral."

Julie's desk is closest to the door—closest to us—and she loses the battle pretending like she's not listening to our conversation. Her head jerks toward us involuntarily, before she catches herself and quickly looks back at the computer screen.

"I don't know what you're talking about." I hoped—thought, expected—the weird moment we shared on Sunday would be easily forgotten.

"Why haven't we met about the article?" Caleb crosses his arms over his chest. The move makes his biceps bulge, and I have to swallow twice before I can answer.

"I was giving you some...time," I reply, in what I hope is a tactful way.

"I don't need time." Caleb glances at Julie. "Hey, do you have a pen?" he inquires.

"Uh, yeah…sure…here," she stutters, handing a blue ballpoint to him.

Caleb smiles at her. "Thanks…"

"Julie," she supplies.

His grin widens. "Nice to meet you, Julie. Any guys give you trouble, be sure to sic Matthews here on them. I can tell you from personal experience she'll—"

"Caleb!" I snap.

Caleb smiles as he grabs a sticky note off the desk and jots something down on it using Julie's pen. "Call me when you're free tonight," he says, handing me the fluorescent square of paper. "I have practice until six. We can meet up after that."

I glance down at the series of numbers. Caleb hands Julie her pen and heads for the door. He turns back around right as he's about to reach it. "Bring your English stuff too," he calls. "We can work on the project."

"What was *that*?" Julie asks me as soon as the door swings shut behind Caleb.

"That was Caleb Winters," I say sourly, dropping into my swivel chair.

Julie rolls her eyes. "I know. What I don't know is why—"

"Lennon! Would it have killed you to be nicer to Caleb?" Andrew appears alongside my desk, looking annoyed.

"Yes. It actually might have."

Andrew shoots me a sharp look. "Please do not do anything to mess this up, Lennon. I already told the printer to double our order for next month's issue, before… If Caleb is still willing to do the article but *you* mess it up and we have to lead with Steve's story about the new running track—we're going to end up with a lot of wasted paper."

I sigh. "I'm not making any promises. But if it makes you feel any better, Caleb still seems set on doing the article. If nothing I've said to him so far has dissuaded him, I seriously doubt he's going to change his mind now."

"That does *not* make me feel any better," Andrew replies, which is probably fair.

"Look, I'm apparently meeting him tonight—" I grit my teeth in annoyance. "So I'll have a draft ready for you next week, all right?"

"Fine." Andrew lets out a long-suffering sigh, sounding more like a sixty-year-old than a high school senior.

I roll my eyes at his dramatics. "You insisted I do this, remember?"

"He said he'd do it with you, or no one else," Andrew replies. "What was I supposed to do, Lennon?"

Andrew may act like he runs a global news organization rather than just a small school paper, but he did what any reasonable editor would to ensure a good story. He didn't have a choice, but I did.

I could have gotten out of this, and I didn't.

There's nothing worse than realizing the person you should really be angry with is yourself. Because I didn't take the out when Caleb offered it. Because I have been avoiding him since his grandfather's funeral last weekend.

"The article will be fine, okay? Good. Great, even."

Andrew eyes me dubiously, but nods. "Okay."

He heads toward the center of the room, where the rest of the staff has already begun to assemble for the meeting. I grab a notebook and follow.

"Happy Hump Day!" Andrew calls out, falling comfortably into his favorite role: overseer of everything.

"I thought you said good reporters don't make sexual references," Joe Watkins replies with a cheeky grin. Out of everyone on the paper, he's probably my favorite peer. Mostly because he seems to enjoy teasing Andrew about how seriously he takes his role almost as much as I do.

"My mistake. I thought I was dealing with near adults, not with reporters who have the maturity level of middle schoolers," Andrew retorts.

"You should probably start calling me Mr. Watkins, then," Joe informs him. "Treat people the way you want them to act, and all." That comment draws a few guffaws from the rest of us.

Andrew exhales deeply. "Joe, you can go first."

Joe leans back in his chair and crosses his ankles. "I'm working on a piece detailing the two new courses they're adding in the fall. One is a medieval history class I would actually take if I was still going to be here. The other is some super advanced chemistry for the nerds who already made it through regular and advanced. Don't expect any details on it because I didn't understand a word of what Mr. Johnson said when he explained what the course would cover. Should make a splash on the fourth page."

Andrew lets out another long sigh, but the rest of us are all grinning. "Great. Just avoid using the word 'nerd' in your article, all right? We're trying to foster an inclusive atmosphere and demonstrate the academic rigor our curriculum offers."

I have to bite my lip to keep from laughing out loud, and I'm not the only one. I have no idea where Andrew comes up with this stuff. He must read the school handbook for material.

"Sure thing, boss," Joe replies, adding a mock salute for effect.

"Steve, what about the running track?" Andrew asks.

I tune out the next few article updates in favor of worrying about tonight. So, it's fitting when Andrew reaches me and I have no idea what we're talking about.

"We already know how Lennon's article is going," he states dryly.

I roll my eyes.

"I totally thought people were exaggerating about you and Winters," Joe comments.

"What do you mean, exaggerating?"

Joe shrugs. "People talk, is all."

I'm no longer finding Joe's commentary amusing.

"Julie, what's the running track update?" Andrew asks.

"On time and on budget," she reports. "It's going to be a struggle to write a thousand words on it, to be honest."

"Finish the draft," Andrew instructs. "And then let's see if we can add a new angle to it. There's talk of a new auditorium. Maybe we can get a quote from Principal Owens on that."

Julie nods.

Our meeting lasts another twenty minutes. I rush out of the newsroom as soon as it ends, eager to avoid any conversations about the entertainment Caleb and I provided prior to the meeting.

The truck is missing when I finish the trek around the barn, indicating Gramps is at one of his two local haunts: the racetrack or the post office.

Rather than start with my chores the way I ordinarily would, I decide to go for a ride first to burn off some of the nervous energy fizzing inside me.

After dropping my backpack in the kitchen and getting changed, I head into the barn. Eat My Dust, better known as Dusty, whinnies when I head to her stall first.

"Hey, sweet girl," I murmur, rubbing the soft hair directly beneath her forelock. She nudges against me, soaking up the attention. "You ready to run?"

Dusty's warm breath saturates the fabric of my fleece jacket as she continues to nuzzle me, looking for treats.

I grab her halter from its hook and slip it on, before leading her out into the shavings-strewn aisle. Dusty tosses her head impatiently after I clip on the crossties, eager to get outside. I tack her up quickly; my fingers so well-trained they move through the familiar motions without requiring any thought.

I lead Dusty outside, over to the empty water bucket propped upside down for this very purpose. I balance on it and swing my right leg over her broad back, then shove both feet into the stirrups. She dances beneath me as I settle in the saddle, my knees bent forward to compensate for the short stirrups. I keep a tight grip on the reins, but not to guide her. She knows the route to the training track as well as I do.

Dusty's literally champing at the bit. The leather reins dig into my palms as she makes her impatience with the slow pace clear.

"Easy, girl," I murmur as we cross the driveway.

The training track is nothing more than an oval stretch of dirt, but it serves its intended purpose. It used to be surrounded with fencing, but most of the rails have sagged, giving it a forlorn, tired appearance. Not that the energetic horse snorting excitedly beneath me minds. The starting marker is still standing. I guide Dusty over to it as I rise into a crouch over her black mane, making sure I'm balanced evenly over her withers.

I watch Dusty's muscles ripple and tense beneath me as I tug her to a stop. I ensure the reins are taut and weave my fingers into the fine strands of her mane.

Then, I let her fly.

I lost track of how many times I've ridden a horse a long time ago. My mother returned to Landry while she was pregnant with me. Living on Matthews Farm is all I've ever known. I remember the day Dusty was born ten years ago. I remember watching her place second in our last season as a working farm, back when we still had the money for trainers and jockeys and grooms and entrance fees. Horse racing's an expensive business.

No matter how many times I do this, the thrill is just as spectacular. There's nothing in the world quite like it.

My eyes tear with water.

My thighs burn from the effort of holding upright and still.

My skin prickles as chilly wind sneaks underneath my fleece and combs through my hair.

Any discomfort fades from my mind as I look down at Dusty's loping strides eating up the sandy dirt. The familiar scenery of Matthews Farm flashes by in a blur of color.

I may not have a lot of things, but I have this.

The rest of my chores drag. Partly because I don't have my usual ride to look forward to after they're finished. But mostly because I'm overflowing with apprehension about seeing Caleb tonight.

I finish feeding the stallions their dinner, and head inside. Gramps is back from his outing. I head to the kitchen sink first to wash the grime off my hands. Gramps leans over to kiss the top of my head as he pokes at what I think is soup on the stove.

"Good day?" he asks as I dry my hands on the threadbare towel hanging on the stove door.

"It was fine," I respond. "Newspaper meeting ran long. I've got a new article to finish for the next issue."

"Oh, really?" Gramps frowns at the bubbling liquid he's stirring.

"Uh-huh," I confirm, brushing past him to grab two bowls from the kitchen cabinet.

"What's the article about?"

I sigh. "Baseball. It's an interview with Caleb Winters."

"They assigned that to you?" Gramps raises his grizzled

eyebrows in surprise. He's well aware of my distaste for both the sport and the boy.

"Yes."

"Huh," is all Gramps says at first. "Might be good for you, Lennie. A chance to branch out."

It's exactly what I expect him to say. Gramps is a perennial optimist. Part of why I'm such a pessimist. Together, we represent some semblance of actual reality.

"I guess. I don't have a choice, really. I need to stay on the school paper if I want to work for the *Gazette*."

Gramps purses his lips, the same way he does every time the topic of my fall plans comes up. "Dinner is ready. You ready to eat now?"

"Yeah, I am." I hesitate. "I have to meet Caleb for the interview tonight."

Gramps does a remarkable job of hiding his surprise. Me meeting a boy at night? Even for a school assignment? Unheard of. "Well then, let's eat."

"What are we having?" I ask, a little apprehensively.

Gramps chuckles. "Potato soup."

Well, that explains the unappetizing color, I guess. I ladle some soup in one bowl and give it a tentative sniff. Not bad.

Before Gramps injured his hip last year, we used to share in the barn and household chores. Now that he's significantly less mobile, I've almost entirely taken over caring for the horses, leaving Gramps to handle the cooking and cleaning, for the most part. It's far from a perfect set-up but we've managed to make it work.

As soon as we finish dinner, I take a shower and change into clean clothes. Hair still dripping, I pull out my phone. Caleb said to call. So, in a small attempt at revolution, I text the number I memorized instead of paying attention during the paper meeting.

Lennon: *Free whenever.*

Immediately, I second-guess my choice of words. But before I have time to overanalyze for too long, he replies.

Caleb: *I'll pick you up in ten minutes.*

I didn't expect him to respond so quickly. Or at all.

I rush downstairs.

"I'm, uh, I'm going to head out," I tell Gramps, grabbing my backpack from the corner of the kitchen where I dropped it earlier. "I'll see you in the morning."

Gramps is in the middle of loading the dishwasher, but I'm sure he'll be retiring to the living room and a baseball game within minutes. I'd be surprised if he's not asleep in the next hour.

"Okay, Lennie," Gramps replies. "Have fun." There's a teasing lilt to his words, and I'm tempted to roll my eyes in response before heading out the front door.

The wind has died down. It's not as cold outside as I braced myself for, especially with wet hair. I hurry down the dirt driveway, skirting around potholes that make the truck's suspension groan every time it leaves the property. I make it to the end of the driveway before any headlights come into sight, breathing a sigh of relief when I reach our faded green mailbox before the ten minutes have passed.

I'm not ashamed of the ramshackle property, although most people probably would be. But Caleb setting so much as a foot on Matthews Farm feels too intimate. Too personal.

Caleb was right earlier. I *have* been avoiding him. I *am* freaked out about the moment that transpired between us at his grandfather's funeral.

Headlights appear.

Nerves knot in my stomach as the window of the shiny black truck rolls down. "Were you planning to walk, Matthews?" Caleb asks.

"Just trying to speed things along," I reply, opening the door and climbing into the passenger seat. His car smells brand-new, and the soft leather seat feels like sinking into a cloud. I expect there to be junk food wrappers and baseball equipment strewn about, but the interior is immaculate.

"You'd rather walk down your driveway in the dark than spend an extra two minutes with me?"

"You said it, not me," I say as I snap my seatbelt. "And… you're the one going out of your way. I figured it was the least I could do."

I say the words as a peace offering, but they're true. I'm not used to other people taking care of me. Helping me.

He seems to hear the honesty in my voice, because his turns serious. "It's not a problem."

The quiet crooning of a country song about a broken heart serves as our soundtrack for the five-minute trip from my house to his.

The Winters' estate is just as striking at night as it was during daylight when I was here on Sunday for the funeral, maybe even more so. The main house is entirely lit up, illuminating the sprawling yard and immaculate landscaping. It looks even larger empty, without crowds milling about.

Caleb parks right in front of the mansion, then climbs out and heads straight for the stairs that lead up to the porch. After about twenty feet, he glances back and realizes I'm not following him.

He says nothing, just arches an eyebrow.

I blow out a breath, well aware he'll probably make fun of me for this. As far as I know, Caleb is about as interested in horses as I am in baseball. But I'll never be back here. This will be my one chance to see Kentucky's most famous stable.

"Can we—can we look inside?" I ask, nodding toward the huge barn.

Both eyebrows rise now. "You want to go in the barn?"

"Yeah. Just for a minute?"

He shrugs. "Okay. Sure."

Caleb veers left, heading toward the looming structure that houses the horses that have won a majority of the Landry Cups over the last decade or so.

Soft lights glow all around the exterior of the barn, showing off the clean concrete that surrounds it. Caleb approaches a small side door tucked next to the massive sliding one and types a code into the keypad attached to white siding. A light flashes green and he pulls the door open, gesturing for me to walk inside first.

I mutter a "thanks" before stepping into the barn. Being cordial toward Caleb—Caleb being cordial toward me—still feels strange.

Automatic lights flicker on as I enter what turns out to be a kitchen filled with shiny appliances and granite countertops.

Not what I was expecting.

Almost everyone in Landry has obscene amounts of money. The Winters family has the most, so it shouldn't surprise me that this is the nicest kitchen I've ever been inside.

But it's in a *barn*, which is unexpected.

"Through here," Caleb says, not bothering to stop and admire the spotless kitchen the way I am.

The next door leads into the center aisle of the stable. More lights flicker overhead.

It's exactly what I expect, and nothing like it.

There are familiar elements. It smells like hay and horses and liniment and pine and leather, same as every other barn I've been inside. But there's no dust or manure or even a stray shaving.

The black rubber mats that run down the center of the aisle look like they've been freshly vacuumed. Unlike the worn, chewed walls that enclose our horses, every horse here has a stall

95

that's constructed from a mixture of black iron and mahogany wood.

The entrance to each stall reaches about four feet high, allowing the horse to stick its head out into the aisle. On either side of the door, wrought iron slopes up gradually, creating a "U" shape that frames the front of each stall. To the right of each door hangs a leather halter and a golden nameplate.

The only sound aside from our footfalls on the rubber is the quiet munching of hay. A few horses duck their heads out of their stalls, but most of them just continue eating their dinner, unbothered by our visit.

The stalls seem to stretch endlessly, even though I know they must end eventually. Occasionally, I think I feel Caleb's eyes on me, but every time I glance over he's focused on the barn.

Finally, the stalls stop, transitioning into a grooming and bathing area filled with fancy equipment and racks of brushes. I halt but Caleb keeps walking, heading toward a massive sliding door just past a shelf filled with shampoo and bug spray.

"There's *more*?" I ask. I haven't been counting, but we've already passed dozens of stalls.

"I thought you'd want to see the stallions." Caleb slides the wooden door open, exposing a cement hallway that veers abruptly to the left. As we walk down the hall, snorts and stamps sound.

The stalls down here are bigger, allowing the massive horses more space to pace. Eight heads pop out into the aisle, pricked ears and proud profiles appearing left and right.

A huge, coal black stallion whinnies, straightening the elegant slope of his neck as he shakes his thick mane. Caleb approaches the horse and begins stroking the skinny white blaze that runs down the center of its wide face.

I take a step toward the stall, trying to see the horse's name plate. The stallion snorts, eyeing me suspiciously. There's a wild savagery and a barely-restrained power that's captivating to witness.

"This is Grand Slam."

"Last year's Landry Cup winner."

"Yeah." Caleb's hand moves lower, stroking the rippling muscles of Grand Slam's neck. "He's mine now, technically."

"Your grandfather..."

"Yeah."

"You named him?"

"It was between Grand Slam or Babe Ruth," Caleb replies.

I smile. "Of course." I study the majestic animal. He must be close to seventeen hands. "It suits him. He's handsome."

"He's handsome, but I'm just hot? That's cold, Matthews," Caleb teases.

I roll my eyes. "I knew you were going to find some way to bring that up again," I mutter, moving on to the next stall.

This stallion's not as skittish as Grand Slam was, and he lets me stroke his neck for a couple of minutes before I turn back around and we head back into the main section of the barn.

"Thanks," I tell him, about halfway down the aisle.

"For what?"

"For showing me around."

"You're big into horses, huh?"

I glance over at him, eyebrows raised. "You *are* aware we live in Horsetown, USA, right?"

"Yeah. But you can live somewhere and not subscribe to everything it stands for," Caleb responds. My steps slow as his words register. I'm not sure we're still talking about horses.

"Well, you didn't grow up here," I remind him. "It's different when it's all you've ever known."

"Meaning you wouldn't like horses if you hadn't grown up here?"

"I don't know," I reply honestly.

"Your grandfather doesn't race them anymore, though."

I'm surprised he knows that. Based on Caleb's low level of involvement in his own family's horses, I wasn't expecting him to know anything about my family's. "Uh, yeah. He stopped racing after…" I clear my throat. "He just decided it was time."

"But he kept all the horses? That's a lot of work for…well, nothing back."

I scoff, well aware of exactly how much work it is. "It's not *nothing*," I reply, miffed. "We still breed them. They've all got championship bloodlines. And I ride them… sometimes."

We emerge outside. The night air feels especially chilly after being in the warm barn.

I pull my jacket tighter to keep any wind from sneaking underneath. "Simon gave me some questions. There's only ten, so it shouldn't take long to get through them. That should give me enough for the article. Andrew can't wait to get my draft, especially after your unexpected visit earlier." I emphasize the last three words. "Thanks for that, by the way. Andrew's convinced I'll scare you off and we'll have to lead with a story on the running track that no one will read."

There's a pause before Caleb replies. I play with the zipper on my coat, wondering when I started feeling nervous around him, instead of annoyed. Has this giddiness always been there, hidden beneath irritation? Or is it new?

"You should take that as a compliment," he finally says. "Not much scares me."

"You're saying *I* scare you?"

"You pack a hell of a punch, Matthews."

"What does *that* mean?" I ask. As tempted as I've been on multiple occasions, I've never actually hit Caleb.

"It means you tell it like it is. Not many people do, or want to have to confront it. Why do you think people act so nervous around you?"

"Because my mother gambled away all our money, made some questionable choices when it came to men, and then dropped dead out of nowhere. Then, my absentee father felt some misguided sense of obligation, so he returned, only to overdose at the racetrack when parenting became too much for him," I say, summarizing my messy past succinctly.

Caleb lets out a short, surprised laugh, and then quickly glances over at me, like he's worried his amusement at the expense of my parents' demons will offend me.

"I, uh, I didn't know the details," he says.

He's lying.

My mother died when I was in sixth grade; my father the summer before I started high school.

It feels like a long time ago—it was a long time ago—but the drama surrounding my parents is far too juicy not to be still gossiped about regularly. I'm certain Caleb has heard far worse about my family than what I just shared with him.

"That's not why people are intimidated by you, Lennon."

I shoot him a look of disbelief as we climb the front stairs to his house. "You're joking, right? That's all people care about."

"No, I mean it," Caleb insists. "I never see you talk to anyone at school besides that new girl…"

"Cassie," I supply.

"Right, Cassie," Caleb agrees quickly, probably worried I'm going to lecture him about remembering girls' names again. "I'm just saying, if you opened up a little… Some people might surprise you."

It's remarkably similar to what Cassie said before Marcus's party, but I'm more willing to believe Caleb on this. Given our history, I don't think he'll sugarcoat anything.

"*Some* people might." I stress the first word, because I'm pretty sure I know who we're talking about. "But most won't. You walked into homeroom with me, the first day of freshman year. You saw how they all looked at me. I'm still the same person I was then."

"Maybe other people aren't." Caleb holds open yet another door for me—this time the imposing black one that marks the entrance to the house.

I step inside the front foyer and open my mouth, ready to respond. I close it again when a stunning blonde woman appears in front of us.

"Caleb, where have you been?" she asks, patting the elaborate twist her hair is pulled back in. "I texted you three times. You were supposed to look over the color schemes for your graduation party."

"I was at Colt's. Then picked up Lennon," Caleb replies. "You can choose whatever colors you want, Mom."

Mrs. Winters fixes her gaze on me. I experience the uncomfortable sensation of being closely scrutinized and found lacking. "You're the Matthews girl, aren't you?"

"Yes, Mrs. Winters, I'm Lennon Matthews," I reply. "It's nice to meet you."

"You didn't mention you were having a visitor tonight, Caleb."

I mimic Mrs. Winters's cool indifference. "Caleb and I have a school project to work on."

Caleb's mother looks relieved to hear I'm here on a strictly academic basis. "I'll leave you to it, then." She sweeps out of the front entryway as dramatically as she appeared.

"I feel surprised," I tell Caleb.

He grins. "Yeah, my mom is probably not the best example.

100

She tried to acclimate to living here by becoming the snobbiest snob of them all."

Caleb walks toward the central staircase. I trail behind him, registering the inside of the house for the first time. It's similar to the minimalist exterior of the house but paired with polar contrasts. The ivory walls meld into ebony floorboards. The floors are dotted with woven rugs, and the white painted plaster is covered with black-and-white framed photographs.

Once we reach the top of the stairs, Caleb turns right, leading me down a long hallway. It has a similar color scheme, interrupted by the occasional flash of color. An oil painting of the Tuscan countryside here, a vase of blue hydrangeas there. Finally, Caleb pushes open a door at the end of the hall.

I let out a low whistle as I walk inside. "Ran out of money to pay the interior decorator?"

His chuckle vibrates in my chest, low and husky. "Decorating my own room was a bribe for moving here."

After the carefully matched, neutral tones in the rest of the house, Caleb's room is an assault to the eyes. The walls are painted an outrageous shade of red; one that reminds me of expensive sports cars or outlandish flowers. The bold color is mostly covered by posters depicting various logos, bands, and baseball players. Lots and lots of baseball players.

There's a massive four-poster bed in the center of the room, pushed up against the wall between two windows that are exposed to the exterior of the house. A desk sits to the right, and a dresser to the left. Just past the dresser, there's a door that I can see leads to an attached bathroom.

"You did a great job," I tell Caleb dryly, dropping my heavy backpack down next to his desk.

Caleb disregards the sarcasm in my voice. "Thanks." He

drops down on the bench at the end of the massive bed, so I take a seat at his desk.

It doesn't take long to run through the questions Simon gave me. Caleb answers them seriously, and in a manner that tells me these are the types of questions one is actually supposed to ask in a sports interview. Suggesting Simon should have been the one writing this article all along. But neither of us bring that up.

I take careful notes recording his answers, knowing I won't remember the baseball jargon otherwise.

After the interview questions are finished, we switch to English. It's shockingly easy. Past project partners were always content to let me do the bulk of the assignment, but working with Caleb feels like completing a project with a clone of myself.

I even find myself saying, "Yeah, that's a great idea."

Caleb looks at me with shock. "Did you just compliment me?"

I roll my eyes. "I can think you're smart *and* an annoying, entitled jock, okay? Plus, you were the one who made certain I knew you'd knocked me out of first in our class."

He shoots me a triumphant grin that reminds me I hadn't exactly conceded that fact to him. "You were first?"

"You knew that."

"You confirmed it."

"Well, don't get too comfortable," I retort. "We still have one semester left, and I fully intend to finish first."

"Game on, Matthews," Caleb says with a smirk.

By the time we finish outlining our paper, I know we're way ahead of everyone else in our class. The paper's not due for another month, and the accompanying presentation is a few weeks after that.

Caleb realizes the same. "We're basically done," he tells me. "We can meet again in a couple of weeks." I wait for the dread to accompany his words, but it doesn't appear in the pit of my stomach.

"Okay," I reply.

Silence falls between us. I shut my notebook, then fiddle with the metal spiral.

"Do you want to watch a movie?" Caleb asks. His voice is casual, but serious.

In my mind, I'm screaming *Absolutely not! Terrible, stupid, dangerous idea.* Whatever this strange shift between us is, it won't end well. For me. Despite living in the same town, Caleb and I are from two very different worlds.

But what comes out is, "Sure."

Caleb rises from his sprawled position on the bench and walks over to the built-in cabinet directly across from the bed. He opens it to reveal a large flatscreen television, then he walks over and flops down on the lime green comforter that clashes horribly with the red walls.

I hover awkwardly, already regretting agreeing to stay. Caleb appears the picture of ease, tucking one arm behind his head. His sweatshirt rides up, exposing a sliver of skin. A flock of butterflies appears in my stomach, fluttering uncomfortably. Being alone in a bedroom with him suddenly feels like a bad idea for a completely different reason.

"Come on, Matthews." Caleb pats the bedspread. "Don't make it weird."

I inch over to the bed, and finally take a seat on the edge, before lying down on the soft comforter. I make a point to keep as much distance as possible between us, which turns out to be a couple of feet, thanks to the oversized bed.

"Want to watch *Frankenstein*?" Caleb jokes as he flips through movie titles on the screen.

I scoff. "Pass."

"What about this?" Caleb asks. I glance at the screen to see he's pulled up some action thriller.

"Fine," I say, raising a hand to mask the yawn I can feel coming. Lying down was a bad idea. Every limb of my body suddenly weighs a hundred pounds, sinking down into the foam mattress that's way more comfortable than my own bed.

Caleb starts the movie. Gunshots and shouts sound from the television's speakers. It's not the silence I'm used to falling asleep to, but it doesn't matter. I'm losing the battle with my eyelids.

I'm too tired to talk.

I'm too tired to insist Caleb drives me home.

I'm too tired to care that falling asleep in Caleb Winters's bed is a really bad idea.

And then I'm too tired to think at all.

CHAPTER NINE

LENNON

There are a lot of places where I never expected to wake up. I've lived in Landry my whole life. Left the state of Kentucky exactly once and never been out of the country.

Waking up in Canada would have been less shocking than realizing I spent the night in Caleb Winters's bed.

I bolt upright into a sitting position. The room's mostly dark, despite the fact that the window shades on either side of the bed are wide open. The sun hasn't risen yet.

The only light comes from the television, which casts a dim blue glow over the bed.

The bed I'm currently in.

With Caleb Winters. Who's lying next to me, flat on his stomach, fast asleep.

"Caleb," I hiss. He groans, but doesn't otherwise react. "Caleb!" This time, I give his shoulder a light shove, and it's enough to open his blue eyes.

He looks straight at me first, then lets his gaze wander to our surroundings, checking to confirm we're still in his bedroom. His lazy perusal wanders back to me as he sits up slowly. "This is a surprise," he admits, running a hand through his hair.

The action ruffles the dark strands into what should be comical disarray, but instead they manage to look perfectly tousled on purpose.

I clear my throat, shifting away so we're not so close.

"A *surprise* is rain that wasn't on the forecast. Waking up in bed with *you* is more of a traumatic event," I snap.

Caleb has the audacity to laugh. "We fell asleep watching a movie. Not sure what's so shocking about that."

Maybe for him. I've heard the gossip at school. I saw him kissing Madison. I see a *little* of the appeal. But this is in no way, shape, or form a normal occurrence for me.

I slide off the soft comforter and stretch. Conversing with Caleb while on a bed next to him is not conducive to thinking clearly. His hair isn't the only part of him that looks attractive first thing in the morning.

"I need to get home," I say, crossing my arms.

Gramps always goes to bed before me, so I'm not worried he'll have missed me last night. But if he wakes up and I'm missing, that will be difficult to explain. Plus, there's a long list of chores waiting for me out in the barn.

Caleb rolls off the other side of his bed. "Just give me a minute to change, and then I'll drive you home."

He disappears into the adjoining bathroom, leaving me with the tantalizing opportunity to poke around his bedroom unsupervised. I resist the urge for about thirty seconds before wandering over to his desk. I run the pads of my fingers along the varnished wood surface as I study the bulletin board mounted above it. A few photos with his baseball teammates, a copy of his class schedule, a ticket to a baseball game. I open one of the desk drawers, only to discover it's filled with nothing but old school notebooks. I slide it shut and open the next one. It's filled with letters from colleges. Recruitment letters. A much-needed reminder of another way in which Caleb and I are completely different.

"Finished snooping?" Caleb's voice startles me. I knock two books off his desk in my haste to spin around.

Not incriminating at all.

"I was just…sightseeing."

Caleb's smirk makes it clear he doesn't believe me. "If you're done *sightseeing*, I'm ready to go."

He's changed, I realize, into a pair of jeans and a different sweatshirt than the one he woke up in. He's also combed his short, dark hair so it lies flat, making me miss the messy bedhead.

I grab my book bag from the spot where I abandoned it last night. To my surprise, Caleb grabs his own as well.

"What are you doing? Aren't you coming back here?"

Caleb shrugs. "I'm already up." He opens his bedroom door and starts walking down the hallway.

I hurry after him.

"What if your parents see us?" I whisper. As embarrassed as I am about waking up next to Caleb, it would be infinitely worse for anyone else to find out. And based on the sneer Mrs. Winters gave me last night, she would be equally displeased.

"My dad's out of town and my mom won't be up for hours. As long as I'm not out besmirching the Winters name, they could really care less what I do."

I don't have anything to say to that aside from informing Caleb hanging out with me is probably the worst form of name besmirching he could engage in. But I don't feel like pointing that out.

I'm just as struck by the opulence of the Winters' mansion on my second trip through it as I was last night. Morning light is creeping in through the windows, bathing the soft shades surrounding us in hints of color.

"I've always wondered what these houses look like inside," I muse as I follow Caleb through another hallway lined with antique side tables and expensive oil paintings.

Caleb studies what I'm guessing is an awestruck expression. "It's awful," he offers. "Like living in a museum."

"Grass is always greener, I guess," I reply, as I follow him through the soaring foyer and outside, pulling my fleece tighter around my torso to combat the early morning chill. It takes a few minutes for the water to turn hot in the farmhouse and the radiator pipes clang in the middle of the night. I bet the heating in this place works perfectly.

"Or bluer, based on our location." Caleb's grin is wide, obviously pleased with himself for coming up with that reference to Kentucky's nickname.

I roll my eyes. "That was lame."

"Then why are you smiling?"

"I'm not," I lie, quickly wiping any traces of amusement from my face as I climb into his truck.

"You're a terrible liar," Caleb informs me as he climbs into the driver's seat.

"I'll take that as a compliment," I respond as I snap the seatbelt into place from my spot on the passenger side.

"Well, normally you take everything I say as an insult, so I'd call that progress."

"I don't *take* it as an insult. Most of what you say to me *is* insulting."

"I think that's a matter of opinion."

"Exactly. *My* opinion." Caleb opens his mouth to voice what I'm certain will be an argument, so I speak again before he has a chance to. "Can we get going, please? I've got a lot to do before school."

"You have a lot to do at—" Caleb glances at the clock on the dashboard. "5:30 a.m.?"

"Yes." I sigh, exhausted by the thought of all the tasks waiting for me. "I didn't make you meet me this early for the last interview just to make you miserable, you know."

"It was just a bonus?"

I glance over at Caleb's grinning face as we start rolling down the gravel driveway. The soaring oaks lining each side of the road block some of the rising sun, but the golden glow still manages to spill inside the car between each branch, bathing the interior of the truck and Caleb's features in brilliance.

"Maybe," I admit, turning my gaze to the white fence line we're whizzing past.

I deliberate on asking Caleb to drop me off at the end of the driveway for the entirety of the short drive. But when he takes the turn, my mouth stays shut.

Matthews Farm looks especially ramshackle after just having come from the immaculate Winters estate.

I fling the truck's door open as soon as it comes to a stop outside the barn. Impatient whinnies pierce the cool air as I climb out of the warm car, the horses annoyed by my tardiness.

"I'll see you at school, Caleb," I say. "Thanks for the ride," I add before I close the door and then rush toward the house, not giving him a chance to respond.

The farmhouse is still and silent when I slip inside the front door. I let out a sigh of relief. Gramps is one to make his presence known, slamming frypans and clomping around in his heavy boots from the moment he wakes until he passes out on the couch at night.

I sneak up the stairs, carefully avoiding the spots I know will creak. Reaching my bedroom door, I twist the handle and step inside, letting out a long exhale of air when I close the door behind me and drop my backpack on the floor.

There's no time to savor my successful sneak in. My first, and likely last. I quickly change into a fresh pair of jeans and a clean shirt before pulling my fleece jacket back on. I yank a brush through my tangles and pull my hair back in a careless attempt at a bun before darting back down the hall to use the bathroom.

Gramps emerges from his bedroom at the same time I exit the restroom, face washed and teeth brushed.

"Morning, Gramps," I call out as I hurry toward the stairs.

"Where's the fire, Lennie?" he calls, stomping down the stairs after me.

"I overslept. I haven't been out to the barn yet," I yell back as I grab a banana from the kitchen and sprint out the front door. Only to come to a screeching stop on the porch.

Caleb's black truck is still parked in front of the barn.

I swear under my breath before I start walking again, pausing when I reach the driver's side of the car. He's not inside.

Loud stamping and snorts are coming from the barn. I leave Caleb's empty truck and head into the barn. As soon as the horses see me, the din increases substantially. Hooves clang against wood and excited nickers fill the air.

"Caleb?" I call out, feeling ridiculous. Whenever I'm in the barn, I'm alone.

"What?" his voice replies. I track the sound to the feed room.

"What the hell are you still doing here?" I ask, entering the small space to find Caleb slouched against the table where I normally mix feed and supplements, studying the board that has the turnout schedule written out.

"What did you call it earlier? Oh yeah, I'm *sightseeing.*" He looks over and smirks.

"Also known as trespassing," I correct, grabbing two feed pails from the floor. I'm too far behind schedule to waste time arguing with him.

"Interesting how one's perspective shifts," Caleb comments. Humor glints in his blue eyes.

I drop the buckets next to him on the table with a little more force than usual. "Fine, I was snooping earlier. Will you please leave now? I've got a ton to do, and I—"

"What do you mean? Don't you have..." Caleb's words trail off as realization replaces amusement. "You take care of all these horses yourself?" The astonished pity displayed on his face is more than I'm equipped to handle following what has already been a draining morning.

"Just leave, Caleb. I don't need—"

"Lennie?" My grandfather's booming voice interrupts me. He's close by. Meaning he already saw the strange truck outside.

"Shit," I whisper under my breath. "What is it, Gramps?" I shout back.

"I wanted to see whether you—" The door to the feed room opens.

Gramps stops speaking the second he sees Caleb. We don't have many visitors. Certainly none that are my age. And definitely none that are male.

"Who's this?" Something in his expression tells me he already knows.

"Nice to meet you, Mr. Matthews. I'm Caleb Winters." Caleb steps forward and holds out a hand, which Gramps shakes.

"Caleb Winters, eh? I thought that was the name of the fella you're always complaining about, Lennie." Gramps has never been one for subtlety. He knows exactly who Caleb Winters is and exactly how I feel about him. He's also a troublemaker.

"It is," I reply bluntly as I start scooping.

"Lennon has a tendency to take everything I say the wrong way," Caleb offers by way of explanation.

Although my back is to him, I can picture the charming grin I'm sure he's giving Gramps.

Sure enough, Gramps chuckles. "He seems nice enough to me, darling."

"Traitor," I mutter under my breath.

"And how did my granddaughter manage to get you on our property at this ungodly hour?" Gramps asks Caleb.

I interject before Caleb has a chance to answer. "I asked him to pick me up before school to finish the interview for the paper. We didn't get it all done last night."

"Well, get out of here, then," Gramps says. "I'll finish up the chores."

"I've barely started, Gramps. They all need to be turned out still."

"I'll manage."

I raise both eyebrows. We both know he can't. He hasn't done anything more than some light lifting since his hip injury. He certainly hasn't tried to lead any of the spirited stallions out to the west pasture. "No you won't, Gramps. If I rush, I can get it all done."

He heaves out a long sigh. "You worry too much, Lennie."

"And you don't worry enough," I retort.

Gramps turns to Caleb, who's been watching the two of us like a ping pong match. "Can I get you a coffee or anything, Caleb?"

"No, sir, I'm all set. Thank you."

"No need for the formality. Just call me Earl," my grandfather says before he hobbles out of the barn.

I sigh as he disappears. "There goes my last sympathetic audience."

Caleb turns his gaze on me. "What?"

"I can't complain to anyone at school about the shit you pull without them acting like I'm insane. Gramps was all I had. Now he'll take your side too." I let out another exasperated exhale, but it's not as genuine as it once would have been.

Caleb surprises me by laughing. And it's not brief or stiff or mocking, a sound I've heard many times before. It's genuine. Warm. "Sorry to disappoint. With the exception of you, most people seem to like me, Matthews."

I make a small sound of incredulity, although I know he's right.

"So, what can I do to help?" Caleb asks.

"What?" I reply, shocked.

"I'm stuck here until you're ready to leave. Might as well help out."

"You're not stuck here. We took *your* truck," I reply. "You can leave right now and I'll walk to school like usual as soon as I finish."

"We're due at the same place in—" He pulls out his phone to check the time. "Forty minutes. I'll wait. Help."

I mask my shock with irritation. "Do you even know anything about horses?"

Caleb snorts. "I think I can handle it, Matthews."

"Fine." I hold out the two buckets I've already filled. "Give these to the two mares on the right. First two stalls."

I have to bite my bottom lip to keep from grinning at the sight of Caleb balancing the two buckets as he tries to open the swinging door with his arms full. It slams shut behind him once he finally manages it.

"You said the left, right?" he calls from the aisle.

"The *right*!" I holler back, and hear him laugh.

After all the mares are happily munching on their breakfast,

Caleb follows me over to the stallion barn. Feeding Geiger and Gallie is a much quicker process. There's only two of them, and their diets are identical, speeding up the measuring significantly.

As soon as the stallions are fed, I head back to the main barn, grabbing four halters from the row of hooks to the right of the door. "Can you handle two?" I ask Caleb.

He nods. I slip halters on Ransom and Stormy. Ransom's our oldest mare, and Stormy is expecting a foal in four months. I'm certain Caleb notices I've given him the two most docile horses, because he lets out a quiet snort. He doesn't comment, though, just follows me along the path that leads to the east pasture where the mares spend most of the day.

We let the four horses loose, then head back toward the barn for the rest of them.

"So you do all of this, *every* day?" Caleb asks as we walk along.

"Gramps helps out how he can, but he injured his hip last year, and horses tend to move at the pace they want to, not how fast you want them to go."

"Couldn't you get someone else to help?"

"Yeah, I'm sure someone would help. If we could afford to pay them."

"Oh," Caleb says as he realizes.

He doesn't make any more comments about my long chore list as we put the rest of the horses out to pasture and then start the smelly process of mucking out the stalls.

I keep waiting for Caleb to bail, especially once manure is involved, but he scoops up the soiled shavings quickly and efficiently. He contributes enough I realize I probably wouldn't have had time to finish all the chores before having to leave for school.

"I've just got to grab my backpack, and then we can go," I say as soon as the last stall has been cleaned. "Do you, uh, want to come inside for a minute?"

"Sure." Caleb agrees easily, not realizing what a leap it is for me. Back when I thought Madison and I were still friends, I overheard her telling a group of our classmates how much she hated coming over to my house. And it was in a much better state back in middle school. Even if I'd had friends to invite over in the past few years, I doubt I would have. All Cassie has visited is the end of the driveway.

I can see Gramps bustling around in the kitchen through the front-facing window as we approach the house. "Ignore anything my grandfather says," I warn Caleb. "I don't have many"—more like *any*—"people over, so he'll probably try to embarrass me somehow."

Caleb's smile makes me think the prospect of Gramps embarrassing me in front of him is not an unwelcome one. It only falters when we reach the rickety front porch. Caleb glances down at the wooden boards nervously as they creak. Under our combined weight, they do sound like they're about to give out any minute.

"I've yet to fall through," I tell him.

"Comforting," Caleb remarks.

Gramps is standing at the stove frying an egg when we enter the kitchen.

"I'm just going to run upstairs to grab my stuff," I tell Caleb. "Feel free to help yourself to whatever." I gesture vaguely around the kitchen and then give Gramps a quick glance that I hope conveys he better behave himself.

I rush up the stairs and into my room. My backpack's sitting on the floor next to my desk. I pick it up and head back toward the door, only to hesitate. Letting the bag drop down to the floor once more, I unzip my fleece and fling it onto my desk chair. I pull my favorite sweatshirt out of my dresser. It's a soft crewneck style that's a vibrant shade of dark green. Then I pull the elastic out of my hair, releasing my long strands from the knot. I swipe the brush through it a couple more times before picking up my backpack again and heading downstairs.

Gramps is chuckling when I enter the kitchen. "You're definitely right about Roberts," he tells Caleb. "I know the Jays can find better."

They're discussing baseball. Of course.

"We'd better get going," I announce. "Or we'll be late."

Caleb looks over from his spot next to the kitchen sink. Nothing in his face indicates he notices the changes to my appearance, but he keeps his eyes fixed on me as he takes a long sip from the mug of coffee he's now holding.

Gramps hands me my lunchbox and a thermos of hot coffee, and I give him a grateful glance. "Thanks, Gramps." I snag a couple of cereal bars from the cabinet and head toward the front door. "See you later."

"Thanks, Mr. Matthews," Caleb adds. "Nice to meet you."

"It's Earl," Gramps corrects. "And you too, Caleb."

I hold out a cereal bar to Caleb in a silent offer as we walk down the rickety porch stairs and cross the overgrown yard. He takes it. "Thanks."

"I should be thanking you," I admit. "I never would have gotten everything done this morning without you."

Caleb doesn't say anything at first. Then, "I like your grandfather."

"Me too," I agree, taking a bite of my breakfast bar.

"He's your mom's dad, right?"

"Right." I'm surprised he's asking. Interested.

"What happened to your grandmother?"

I don't answer, and Caleb quickly backtracks. "Never mind. It's none of my business."

"No, it's fine. I just…" *don't know why you care.* "She died right after my mom was born. I never knew her."

We reach the truck and climb inside.

"I'm sorry," Caleb says quietly.

"Not your fault," I say, uncomfortable with his sympathy. "It was a long time ago. We're going to actually be late." I nod to the clock on the dashboard. We only have four minutes to get to school.

Caleb nods, then starts the truck.

I think we're running late enough to avoid seeing more than a couple of people. If I'd taken my usual rushed route across our field and through the rear entrance, I would've.

The rare times I've driven I always arrive early, so I incorrectly assumed most of the student body will already be inside school.

Instead, what looks like the vast majority of Landry High is milling around the blacktop. The parking lot is packed and swarming with familiar faces; most of whom turn in our direction when Caleb's truck appears. There are only a few spots left, all in the furthest row from the entrance.

But Caleb drives right past them.

"What are you doing?" I ask. "You just passed the only spots."

He just grins as we approach the front row, which is where the majority of people seem to be gathered. I spot some of Caleb's baseball teammates, Madison, and the rest of the popular crowd I'm not a part of.

There's one spot left open in the very center. Based on how full the rest of the lot is, I know this was left for Caleb on purpose.

"Front and center." The many stares I can feel on us are putting me on edge. I can feel my usual snark rising, erasing the fragile peace that settled between us last night and this morning. "A late slip would have been better than *this*."

Caleb appears overly amused by my obvious irritation with the attention. "Most girls aren't quite so horrified to be seen with me."

"You do this a lot, don't you?" Caleb opens his mouth. "Actually, don't answer that. And now everyone's going to think…" I bang my head back against the soft headrest once. "Don't say a single word to anyone about this if they ask. Aside from saying nothing happened, okay?"

"Nothing *did* happen, Matthews," he drawls. "I'm well aware if I'd so much as tried to touch you last night you would have slapped me."

I try not to think too hard about his words. Not to imagine him touching me. Because I'm not sure that I *would have* stopped it. And that's highly concerning.

"You're missing the point, Winters. No way am I ending high school being considered one of your groupies. Anyone asks, shut it down."

"I get the point, Lennon."

"Good." I grab my bag and swing the passenger door open, preparing to leap down onto the asphalt. "Uh—thanks again."

"For the sex?"

I slam the door on his grinning face. Hard. Forcefully enough that if we'd been in the farm's old jalopy, the spotless blacktop would be littered with flecks of rust.

I stride toward the front doors without looking back at the black truck. My irritated stride eats up the pavement quickly. I'm almost to the front doors when I hear Cassie's voice.

"Beautiful morning, huh?" she asks, appearing next to me.

I grunt, eyeing Cassie's bright smile suspiciously. It's warmer than it's been and the sun is out. But I think she's referring to something I'd rather not discuss.

"Anything interesting happen?" she continues, confirming my suspicions.

"Nope," I insist. Cassie lets out a maddening humming sound. I sigh. "I'm not a groupie."

"What?"

"We were working on…" Belatedly, I remember I haven't told her about the interview for the paper. "We were working on our English project before school."

"Hmmm," Cassie hums again, her eyes glinting mischievously. "Interesting."

"It wasn't, really."

"Okay." Cassie drops the subject, reminding me why she's my favorite person at this school. We talk about the trip her family is planning for spring break until we reach my locker. I'm barely focused on our conversation, paying closer attention to all the stares aimed my way.

Right as Cassie's about to continue on to her own locker, I crack. "How often does Caleb drive girls to school?"

She stares at me, eyebrows raised. "That I've seen? Never."

Never.

"Would you? Have…seen?"

"Yeah. I always get here pretty early. Only person I've seen him arrive with is Colt Adams."

I look away, fiddling with the lock. "I didn't think people would see. We were working on the project, and it made sense to drive together. How the hell was I supposed to know everyone loiters around the parking lot?"

"I guess you wouldn't," Cassie acquiesces. She knows I usually walk and come in through the back entrance. "But Caleb knows."

"Yeah, I guess so," I reply.

Caleb knew we'd been seen together, and didn't care. I'm not sure why that matters to me so much, but there's a strange warmth in my chest that remains even as I catch more than the usual amount of stares the rest of the day. These aren't contemptuous. They're intrigued, maybe a little awed.

Everyone seems to think something might have changed between Caleb and me. I hope they'll quickly realize that's not actually the case.

Me, most of all.

CHAPTER TEN

LENNON

I hate gym.

"Choke up on the bat, Lennon! We're not fishing here, straighten up!"

I would love to yell at whoever came up with Landry High's requirement that students have to score a run to pass the baseball unit of twelfth grade gym class.

"I'm holding the grippy part of the stick," I reply.

Our physical education teacher, Mr. Evans, gives me an encouraging look before tossing the baseball at me once more. I miss, again.

"Okay, give someone else a turn. We'll try again next week."

"Wait a minute."

I freeze when I hear his voice. Tense when I hear the whispers from everyone watching my humiliating attempts to hit a baseball.

"What the hell do you think you're doing?" I hiss at Caleb as he appears beside me.

"Helping you pass gym. I've gotten the sense grades are kind of important to you."

"I don't need your help." Or the scrutiny.

Caleb Winters is not the guy who offers his help freely. As evidenced by the undivided attention from our previously disinterested classmates that feels like a spotlight. He's the guy who's untouchable. Unbothered by the problems of mere mortals. Hot and rich and popular, with the whole world within his reach.

I've avoided him ever since the accidental sleepover, and was finally making some headway in fading back to normalcy.

With three words, Caleb eradicated that progress.

"I've got about thirty witnesses who would say differently," Caleb replies. "Stop being stubborn. I'm good at baseball, okay?"

I can't help the small smile that forms in response to his massive understatement. "Fine," I agree.

Aside from the unwelcome attention, it's not like I have anything to lose.

At least I didn't *think* I did, until Caleb steps behind me, close enough I can feel his body heat. Until he grasps my elbows and readjusts my stance.

I'm grateful my long sleeves hide the goosebumps appearing on my skin. I'm struggling to keep my breathing even, but Caleb doesn't seem the least bit affected by my proximity.

"You're holding the bat all wrong," he informs me. "Move your hand a little down here." His instructions are unnecessary, since he shifts my grip himself. Ripples of heat race through me, relentless and confusing. "Okay, angle it a bit more, lean forward, and...*yeah*, right there. Just swing at the ball, okay?"

"I know that much, Winters."

"I wasn't sure, after your eleven strikes," Caleb retorts.

I'd love to roll my eyes at him, but I can't turn to look at him without messing up what I hope is a gym-passing posture.

"Okay, one last try," Mr. Evans states.

He's not looking at me. He's looking at Caleb, just as

confused by him helping me as the rest of the class undoubtedly is.

Mr. Evans tosses the baseball again, a slow, easy toss that I would knock out of the park if this were a movie. But this is my actual life, so I only manage to graze the edge of the ball, sending it skittering harmlessly in the direction of the dugout. Not exactly the home run I was hoping for.

"Progress," Mr. Evans congratulates, since the bar was low. "We can try again Monday. We'll get you there by the end of the unit, Matthews."

I nod, distracted by the unfamiliar emotion overshadowing my annoyance with the stupid requirement. I didn't think there was anyone in Landry whose opinion I cared about, besides Gramps's.

Turns out there might be.

And he tried to help me, which makes me feel worse. I'm worried I let Caleb down somehow, which is a ridiculous, inconvenient thing to feel. I know it is. But that knowledge doesn't allow me to shake it.

Two more students take their turns at bat, and then class ends.

"Let's head in, folks!" Mr. Evans calls out after Lucy Howarth manages a single. "Only five minutes before the bell. Halloway, Josephs, grab the equipment, please."

I scrape my hair together, twist it, and snap an elastic around the bun in a lazy attempt to keep the strands from blowing around in my face as I trudge back toward the brick building to change.

"You swung too late."

I'm still grappling with the uncomfortable aftermath of shame, and in no mood to talk to the boy who incited the emotion. "Really? I thought it was my grip on the bat."

"At least you've learned it's called a bat, not a stick," Caleb replies.

"I always knew that," I grumble. "Gramps watches a lot of baseball."

"You're not going to magically improve by Monday, you know."

"Obviously I know that, or else I would have already passed the stupid requirement."

"You're right," Caleb agrees easily. "It is a stupid requirement."

I eye him suspiciously, curious why he's agreeing with me when ordinarily he's willing to argue about anything. "A stupid requirement? I thought having everyone else forced to play the sport you worship would be your first choice for a gym requirement."

"I thought so too. Until I had to watch you butcher a simple swing for twenty minutes."

And…there's the catch. "It was *not* twenty minutes."

"Ten, at least."

I scoff, but that's probably accurate.

"There's not much I could do for one swing, but regardless of how uncoordinated you are, anyone can hit the ball once," he tells me. "Especially if they've got a good teacher."

"I'll let Mr. Evans know," I state dryly.

Caleb sniggers. "*I'm* offering to help you hit a baseball, Lennon."

"You're what?" We've almost reached the gym entrance. I stop too soon, caught completely off guard.

"I'm offering to help you," Caleb repeats, pausing as well.

"But…*why*?" Disbelief drips from my voice.

"Because you need help."

I scowl. "You're messing with me."

"No, I'm not."

"Why would you help me?"

"Because you suck at baseball, and I'm good at baseball." Caleb enunciates each word, as though I'm unaware of the reality of our respective skills when it comes to the sport and need it explained to me.

"That didn't answer my question. Why would help me, and get nothing in exchange?"

"What did I get out of mucking out stalls with you?" I don't answer; he keeps talking. "Do you want my help, Lennon? Yes or no."

"Yes."

"Okay. I'll text you later." Caleb heads inside the gym, leaving me standing confused and alone.

Wondering what the hell I've just agreed to.

I finally follow him inside, taking my time changing out of my gym clothes. Having gym last period is the only upside to having gym at all.

I leave the locker room and head back toward the main building of the high school. I forgot to grab my history book earlier, and I need it to complete a worksheet due tomorrow.

The halls are bustling with activity, everyone buoyed by the sense of freedom that the final bell provides. Caleb is standing at the end of the hall, talking with a group that includes some of his baseball teammates. Madison and a couple of her friends are also included. I avert my gaze as I pass them and continue to my locker.

"You free tonight?"

I grab my History book and shut the locker door. Ryan is standing in front of me, one corner of his mouth turned up as he studies me. The genuine interest on his face unsettles me. He hasn't spoken to me since his last visit to my locker, and I was hoping it was a one-time thing. "No."

"Tomorrow night?"

I sigh. "Ryan, I told you it's not going to happen."

He tilts his head. "You know, you're the last girl I thought would go for Winters. I thought you hated all the elitist bullshit."

"I don't know what you're talking about."

"You're not into Winters?"

"Ryan. We never dated. We're not friends. I don't know why you'd—"

Ryan looks past me. "Hey, Winters."

"James."

I straighten, automatically, as soon as I hear Caleb's voice.

Ryan glances at me. "Guess that's my answer. See you later, Lennon."

"What was that about?" Caleb asks, as soon as Ryan is gone.

I shove the History textbook in my backpack before meeting his gaze. "He asked me out."

"What did you say?" The words are flat, like he's purposefully hiding any inflection.

"No." I fiddle with the strap of my backpack. "What do you want? Change your mind about helping me already?"

I make the mistake of looking past Caleb after asking that question. Everyone he was standing with earlier is staring at us.

"I didn't change my mind."

"So…what's up?"

"I wanted to give you this." Caleb hands me a few sheets of paper, stapled together neatly.

"What is it?" I ask as I take the packet from him.

"Our English outline. I included everything we discussed during our sleepover."

I cast him a *look* for that reminder, but my irritation fades after I flip through the first couple of pages. It's more than an outline. He's basically written our entire paper in bullet point format. "You didn't have to do all this, Caleb."

He shrugs. "It didn't take me long."

I'm pretty sure that's a lie, but I'm distracted by Madison walking past with a couple of friends. She sends me a spiteful look even more venomous than usual. I'm guessing it has a lot to do with the guy who's standing a foot away from me.

Caleb follows my gaze. "We used to be friends, you know," I tell him, for some unknown reason.

He looks at me with surprise. "You and Madison?"

I let out a short laugh. "Yeah. Best friends, actually. Her thirteenth birthday was just a couple days before my dad...died. It was a pool party. I got her a sparkly headband."

"What happened?" Caleb asks quietly.

"Life. High school." I shrug. "She cares what people think. I've never had that luxury."

"What do you mean?"

"People judge me for things I have no control over. Nothing I can do about it. Maybe it was just bad timing, but I think high school has a funny way of turning friends into foes no matter what."

"Yeah, maybe you're right," Caleb says softly.

"I've got to get home," I tell him. "I'll see you...later?"

Caleb nods. He said he would text me about batting lessons, but I don't know if he actually will. Don't know if I really want him to. It will only confuse everything more.

I start down the crowded hall, feeling his eyes on me the whole way.

I'm sorely tempted to turn around.

But I don't.

CHAPTER ELEVEN

LENNON

The incessant beeping is getting to me.

"I forgot to grab rice," I tell Gramps, which is actually true. "I'll be right back." I duck out of line to head back into the main section of the supermarket.

It doesn't take me long to find the correct aisle and grab the light blue bag. There's only one grocery store in town. Gramps and I have been coming here every Saturday for as long as I can remember to stock up on food for the week.

Gramps has moved up to second in line by the time I return to the check-out. I toss the rice in the cart and try not to wince as the scanner keeps beeping nonstop.

Finally, it's our turn. Gramps chats with the owner as she rings up our groceries.

"I'm going to put these in the truck," I tell Gramps, grabbing two of the paper grocery bags and heading toward the door. He nods as he continues making small talk.

I spin around to push open the door with my back. When I turn back around, I'm standing on the sidewalk just outside the store.

Face-to-face with Caleb Winters.

We stare at each other as we contemplate what to say.

At least, that's what I'm doing.

"Hi." Running into Caleb outside of school is strange, especially following his unexpected offer to help me pass gym. It added another layer to our already complicated…something. Not a friendship, *definitely* not a relationship, but something more than nothing.

"Hi," Caleb repeats. All I can see on his face is surprise. Unlike me, he's not alone. Jake Barnes, Colt Adams, and Luke Evans all hover behind him. Jake looks bored; Colt and Luke amused. "Good weekend?"

"Thrilling. Can't you tell?" I nod at the two paper bags I'm clutching to my chest.

"Yeah, it's pretty obvious."

I shift the weight of the bags I'm holding. "How about you?"

"It's been all right," he responds.

"Winters! We gotta go," Jake calls. He, Colt, and Luke have drifted down the street, and are now standing about twenty feet away from us. It's disconcerting to realize I was so focused on Caleb I didn't even notice their departure.

"I've got to put these in the truck, anyway," I say, giving him an easy out. "I'll see you on Monday."

Caleb doesn't acknowledge Jake. Doesn't look away from me. "Do you want to come?"

"Come?" I echo.

"To see a movie. We're headed there now." He jerks his head to the left, toward the town cinema located a couple blocks further downtown. His voice is casual, but the invitation is anything but. The most popular guy in school is asking me to hang out with him. It feels like a cliché that I'm stunned speechless by the offer.

But I don't find Caleb's popularity appealing. It's a reminder of everything I hate about this town.

"Why are you asking?"

A muscle pulses in Caleb's jaw as he glances down the street at his waiting friends. "I have to have a reason?"

"Caleb…"

The door behind me clangs open and shut. I turn to see my grandfather emerging from the store, carrying two more paper bags. "Gramps," I admonish. "I was coming back for those."

"I can manage a couple bags, Lennie," he informs me, before his gaze moves to the guy standing in front of me.

"Well, hello there, Caleb."

"Hello, Mr. Matthews," Caleb replies.

Gramps shakes his head. "I told you to call me Earl."

I don't miss the glances Caleb's friends exchange following the revelation he's met my grandfather previously. I wish I'd realized they were still in earshot sooner.

In a town as small as Landry, it's rarer not to know someone than to know them. But Gramps and I don't exactly frequent the events where most of the local socializing takes place. Not anymore.

Caleb smiles. "You did, sir. Earl," he tacks on hastily when my grandfather gives him a sharp look.

"Better," Gramps praises. "What are you boys up to?" Gramps asks, shifting his gaze from Caleb to his posse hovering nearby.

"We're headed to see a movie," Caleb replies. "I was just seeing if Lennon wanted to come."

I know what Gramps's response will be even before I catch a glimpse of his delighted expression. "You should go, Lennie."

I glare at him. "What about the groceries?"

Gramps waves off my question. "I can handle it. There are only a couple more bags to grab."

"I can help." Caleb doesn't hesitate to offer his assistance, and to my surprise, his friends help too. I end up watching all four of them load our groceries for the week into the back of the old farm truck. I expect Gramps to take advantage of the opportunity to strike up a conversation about baseball with four of Landry High's starters, but he drives off as soon as the truck is filled.

Probably eager to leave before I can come up with an excuse to depart with him.

"This better not be a horror movie," I tell Caleb as we walk back toward the sidewalk where his friends are waiting.

"I thought you'd come around on those," he replies. "Aren't we doing *Frankenstein* for our paper?"

"That's a book, not a movie," I inform him. "Plus, I wasn't about to spend all of lunch arguing with you about other options."

We reach Luke, Colt, and Jake.

"Hey, you look really familiar. Have we met before?" Jake asks as we continue in the direction of the movie theater down the street. He pairs the question with a cheeky grin.

"I assume you're referring to the fact that we've gone to school together since kindergarten, Barnes?"

Jake laughs. "Yeah, that's probably it."

I roll my eyes. I'm trying to act casual as we walk along the brick sidewalk, but it's a challenge to pretend like this is anything normal.

Hanging out with Caleb is bizarre enough, but the last few years of animosity have established some familiarity between us. I can't recall the last time I spoke to Jake Barnes. The only time I've talked to Colt Adams was when he approached me at Marcus's party. And Luke Evans barely bothered to acknowledge my existence when he stopped to talk to Will after the basketball game.

Even before my family drama made me the school pariah,

131

these were never people I was friendly with. Walking down the sidewalk now, it feels like I've stumbled into some bizarre alternate reality where I'm friends with four of the most revered guys in school. It's a jarring shift compared to the infamous solitude I settled into freshman year.

The movie theater is bustling with activity when we enter it. It's a dreary, overcast day, and there are few forms of entertainment in town during the winter months to begin with. The cinema is connected to an arcade and a diner, making it a popular spot for everyone to congregate.

After we buy tickets for a spy thriller, the guys all decide to buy snacks from the concession stand. I stay in the lobby, claiming I ate lunch just before Gramps and I went shopping. In reality, I don't have any money to spend on overpriced candy.

Leaning against a wall watching others buy their tickets gets old fast, so I wander into the arcade area. I haven't been in here since middle school. I'm surprised by how nostalgic I feel looking around at the flashing lights and listening to automated trills. The air hockey table was always my favorite, and it's empty right now. I send the puck flying into the opponent's goal for old time's sake.

"Lennon?" I turn to see Will standing a few feet away, with Marcus Freedman beside him.

"Hi, Will," I greet. "Marcus. How's it going?"

"Not bad," Will replies, giving me his usual friendly smile, then glancing at the table behind me. "You're playing some airless air hockey?"

I smile. "Yeah, I guess I am."

"Are you here with Cassie, or…"

"Oh. I, uh, I—" I stammer and stall, trying to figure out how to respond. Will may be nice enough to pretend otherwise, but I know he's aware I'm barely perched on the first rung of Landry High's social ladder. There's no easy explanation for why I'm here with those comfortably situated at the top. Mostly because I don't understand it myself.

"Thought you were staying in the lobby, Matthews." Caleb's voice joins the conversation.

"I got bored," I reply, internally cringing as I see Will's wide eyes bounce back and forth between the two of us. Marcus looks shocked, too. "I'll see you guys around." I shoot Will a small smile, then turn to head back to the lobby.

"Masterson's into you," Caleb comments, falling into step beside me.

"Maybe."

A warm hand encircles my wrist, tugging me to a stop. I face Caleb, raising an eyebrow. His throat bobs with a swallow. "Lennon…"

"We thought you left." Jake approaches, Colt and Luke right behind him. Caleb's hand drops, releasing mine.

I figured Jake was addressing Caleb, but his gaze is on me. "I just walked into the arcade."

"Thank God," Luke mutters.

I glance at him, confused. "If I wanted to leave, I would have," I reply. "It's not like Caleb would have bothered to stop me."

Colt looks highly amused by my response for some reason. "Good luck, Winters."

Caleb rolls his eyes. "I wouldn't have invited you if I didn't want you to come, Matthews. Hurry up." He starts down the carpeted hallway that's lined with movie posters and smells strongly of buttered popcorn.

"Winters is weird about missing the previews," Luke informs me as we all struggle to keep up with Caleb's brisk strides. "God forbid we just arrive on time for the movie we actually came to see. We have to be embarrassingly early, like we're here for the senior discount special."

"Yeah, he would watch movie trailers in History last year." The words are out before I've thought them through, and Colt gives me a weird look.

I'm just as confused. *Why do I know that? Why did I remember that?*

Despite Luke's complaints, the movie theater is already close to full when we enter the dark auditorium. I follow the guys to the top row of the stadium-style seating.

"Nice of you to finally join us." Caleb smirks. I flip him off. I reached the top of the stairs only a few seconds after he did.

"Ladies first," Jake says, holding his arm out like a game show host presenting the winning prize. Only instead of a brand-new car, I receive the gift of having to shuffle past all four of them down the row.

There's some whispering at the top of the stairs, and then Caleb is the one who walks down the row and takes the seat next to me.

"You draw the short stick?" I mutter.

"Yep. They're making me share my popcorn with you, too." He holds the container out to me.

"I don't like popcorn," I lie.

"Then why did you eat some at lunch last week?" Caleb counters.

I raise both eyebrows. "Why do you know what I ate for lunch last week?"

"So I could catch you in a lie when we went to the movies this weekend," Caleb says sarcastically. "Just take some, Matthews."

I cave and scoop up some of the salty, buttery snack. "Thanks," I murmur begrudgingly. I finish the handful before the movie has even started.

"Here." Caleb holds out the bin of popcorn again, and this time I don't argue with him.

He goes to take some at the same time I withdraw my hand. His palm grazes my knuckles, and the contact feels like touching an open flame. I react immediately, hastily yanking my hand back into the sanctuary of my seat as though I've just been burned.

The movie finally starts. I focus my attention on the massive screen, acting as though the film featuring a hunky actor I vaguely recognize, along with a lot of guns and gore, is all that matters in the world at this moment. In reality, the back of my hand still tingles. I'm excruciatingly aware the tall frame silhouetted in the seat next to me is Caleb Winters.

The darkness makes it seem like there's no one else here besides the two of us.

I keep my eyes trained on the screen in front of me, but the movie can't distract me from Caleb sitting only a few inches away.

I listen to him munch popcorn.

I watch him bounce his knee.

I feel his elbow bump my bicep when he shrugs out of the hoodie he was wearing.

And…I'm attracted to Caleb Winters. I don't just find him objectively good-looking. I like talking with him, knowing he'll have a response ready for anything I say. I like how he doesn't seem to care I'm a loner and an outsider. I even enjoy the fizziness when I'm around him, how my awareness of everything is heightened.

By the time the movie ends I'm just as clueless about the plot as I was before it started. Thankfully, no one asks for my opinion as we exit the auditorium. Jake and Caleb are engaged in a detailed discussion about one of the stunts.

"Hang on," Jake says as we approach the lobby. "That slushy ran right through me."

He ducks into the men's restroom. I take the opportunity to escape for a moment as well. "I'll be right back."

I walk through the doorway marked with a stick figure wearing a dress, then take a sharp right to head down the hallway lined with stalls. I lock myself in the first one that's available and tap my head against the plastic door three times, hoping it will knock some sense into me.

No such luck. The memory of sitting next to Caleb in the pitch black still causes goosebumps to rise on my skin.

This is bad. Really bad. I can't avoid him until graduation in June and wait for this silly crush to fade.

I wash my hands and then head back down the hallway toward the exit. I'm just about to round the corner to re-enter the hallway when I hear Colt's voice.

I pause in place. "—think it's adorable you had to use her grandfather to trick her into spending time with you."

"This is the sort of shit I'd expect from Jake, not you," Caleb responds. "We happened to run into each other. She's writing that article on me, and it'll be easier if we try to get along. It's not a big deal, okay?"

Colt snorts. "You're not fooling anyone with that crap, Winters. It's obvious—"

Footsteps sound behind me, and I have no choice but to round the tiled corner and leave the bathroom before they reach me. Both Colt and Caleb fall silent the second I appear, and that only increases my curiosity about what they were discussing.

Caleb scrutinizes my face closely as I approach. I'm pretty sure it means he has an idea I might have overheard some of his conversation with Colt. Jake and Luke are standing closer to the lobby, waiting for the rest of us.

"Are you heading home from here, Jake?" I ask, once we've reached the exit.

"Uh, yeah," he replies.

"Can I get a ride?" Instead of answering, Jake glances at Caleb. So do Colt and Luke.

I don't.

Jake lives in an upscale gated community located only a couple of blocks from the high school. There's no such thing as "out of the way" in a town as small as Landry, but there's no denying the fact Jake lives closest to me.

"Sure," Jake replies, although the words don't sound all that welcoming. Maybe he's worried someone from school will see us together.

Relieved about managing a ride home with someone other than Caleb, I turn to the other three boys with a bright smile. "See you guys Monday. That movie was great...exciting."

Exciting can apply to any action movie, right?

I'm avoiding looking at Caleb, but both Colt and Luke nod their heads before I head toward the exit doors.

A few seconds later, I hear Jake behind me. I hold the door for him as we emerge outside into the damp air.

Jake Barnes is known for being a jokester. I'm not sure I've ever seen him without an easygoing grin stretched across his face.

But he's silent and serious as we walk down the sidewalk. Aside from turning on the radio and instructing me to play whatever I want, Jake doesn't say a word as we make the short trip back to Matthews Farm from downtown Landry. There are a couple of times when he opens his mouth, as though he's about to speak, but he always closes it before any words actually escape.

"I'll, uh, walk from here," I say when he pulls into my driveway. I can't handle any more of the awkward silence.

"You sure?" Jake asks.

"Yes," I confirm, opening the door to climb out. "Thanks for the ride."

I jump out and start walking up the dirt driveway, trying to put as much distance between myself and this weird afternoon as I can.

CHAPTER TWELVE

LENNON

I t feels like I've only just climbed into bed when my phone vibrates from its spot on the three-legged stool I keep to the right of my pillow for the sole purpose of making sure I hear my alarm in the morning.

I fumble my fingers across the slab of oak for my phone, unwilling to open my eyes just yet. Once I convince my eyelids to open, I have to blink at the phone screen about a dozen times to make sure I'm not misreading the text I just received.

Caleb: *Baseball field. 1 p.m.*

It's 5:15 in the morning. My alarm hasn't even gone off yet. And Caleb is texting me? About playing baseball? What is he even doing up at this hour?

There's no way I'm falling back asleep now. With a long sigh, I abandon the warm covers to get dressed. I only had fifteen minutes of sleep left, anyway.

I've just pulled on my usual fleece when my phone buzzes. It's from Caleb again. A series of obnoxious question marks.

Lennon: *Fine.*

I send just the single word, biting back some of the snarkier ones I wouldn't mind adding. The main reason I hold back is because he's doing me a favor. Caleb's my best hope that I won't have to spend gym class on Monday listening to overdone sighs behind me as I repeatedly miss hitting the ball.

There's a whisper of warmth in the air when I step out onto the front porch; the first I've felt in months. The barest hint of color is edging across the brightening horizon, silhouetting the barn and the broad oaks that surround it in a pastel hue.

Landry doesn't look so bad right now. This image? Spread before me like one of the oil paintings that line the hallways of Caleb's family's estate? It kindles a warmth that sits in the center of my chest.

Thanks to Caleb's text, I'm running ahead of schedule, and I don't have the constraint of school since it's a Sunday. I head into the stallion barn first to tack up Geiger.

Fifteen minutes later, I'm appreciating the sunrise as a streak of color from my perch atop his broad back. The world flashes by in a series of slowly brightening hues as we circle the practice track again and again. My thighs are burning by the time Geiger is willing to slow his pace. I slide out of the saddle, letting out a quiet *oomph* when I hit the ground harder than I expected to.

Gramps has already started distributing the mares' grain by the time I've untacked Geiger and fed both him and Gallie.

"Morning, Gramps," I greet as I enter the tack room.

"Morning, darling," he responds, giving me a broad smile. "Good ride?"

"Yeah, it was," I reply.

"You were up early… Everything all right?" As much as Gramps would love for me to become more social, his apprehensive expression suggests he's realizing that actually happening could come with its own challenges. I wasn't exactly forthcoming with details about how my trip to the movies went.

"Everything is good." I rush to assure him. "I just happened to wake up extra early this morning. Yesterday was fine. A bit weird, but fine."

Gramps nods, looking relieved.

After we finish the chores and I shower, I head into town to meet Cassie. Spending Sunday mornings at Landry's sole coffee shop has become a weekly tradition ever since the first time she suggested we meet there. I do homework, while Cassie tends to people watch and draw.

She's already waiting outside when I cross the street. Downtown is livelier than it was yesterday, more people taking advantage of the nicer weather.

Cassie gives me a quick hug of greeting before we head inside the cafe. "Cute fleece," she teases.

I roll my eyes at her. Cassie is a fashionista. I've never seen her wear the same outfit twice. One of the many ways in which we're complete opposites. "It's new," I inform her.

Cassie scrunches her nose in distaste as she surveys the gray fabric I'm wearing. "It looks the exact same as all your other ones."

I shrug. "It's a different color."

Cassie shudders. "Let's get breakfast. I'm starving."

We join the long line of people waiting to order. Despite its length, the line moves fairly quickly, and soon we're ordering.

Cassie decides on a veggie omelet and a latte, while I opt for my usual muffin and a cappuccino. The barista hands Cassie a beeper to alert us when our food is ready. There aren't many open tables, but we finally find one close to the front door.

I'm pulling a notebook out of my backpack when the bell above the door clangs, announcing Madison's arrival. Close behind her are a few other members of the popular crowd, including Ryan James and Colt Adams. No Caleb, and I hate that I look for him first.

Madison makes a point of not looking in my direction. Ryan gives me a subtle nod but doesn't say anything. But Colt pauses, greeting me with a casual, "Hey, Lennon."

Madison whips her head around in shock.

"Hi, Colt." Thankfully, my voice doesn't betray any of my shock.

Colt nods in acknowledgment and keeps walking, shrugging when Madison whispers something to him that I'm certain is about me.

Cassie is staring at me with both eyebrows raised. "What was that about?"

I take my time pulling my Oceanography textbook out of my backpack. "No clue," I answer.

It's not really a lie. Based on Jake's behavior on the drive home, I was convinced Caleb's friends were merely tolerating my presence.

Cassie shrugs, pulling out her sketchpad. "I got accepted to Lincoln yesterday."

"You did? That's amazing! Congratulations!"

"Thanks." Her smile is bashful. "I wasn't sure I would get in."

"They're lucky to have you."

"You didn't apply early anywhere, right?"

I exhale. "I... I didn't apply *anywhere*, actually."

Her eyes widen. "What?"

"I'm not going to college. At least not in the fall."

"Oh. I—I just assumed..." Cassie clearly has no idea what to say, and I don't blame her.

"My grandfather has some health issues. He can't manage the farm by himself. And we can't afford to pay someone."

"That's really selfless of you."

I shrug. "It's what family does."

Cassie nods.

"I'm sorry I didn't tell you sooner. It's not something I love talking about."

I love Gramps. I love Matthews Farm. But the closer it approaches, staying in Landry feels an awful lot like being left behind.

"I get it, Lennon. Well, maybe not entirely," Cassie corrects. "But I understand it. We're good."

I give her a weak smile, relieved to see our buzzer light up on the table. We head to the counter to retrieve our food and coffee, effectively abandoning any heavy conversation.

I leave the coffee shop a couple hours later and drive straight to the high school.

There's no sign of Caleb yet.

I walk out onto the field and take a seat on the grass, tilting my face back and closing my eyes.

It rarely dips below freezing here, but it's been months since it's been warm enough I've purposefully prolonged my time outside. The rays of sunshine soaking my face feel heavenly. My breathing turns deep and even as my muscles relax.

A car door slams, effectively ending my daydream. I open my eyes and shade them with one hand, watching Caleb walk toward me, carrying a duffel bag I assume must contain baseball equipment. He didn't forget, and I'm surprised by how happy that makes me.

"Hey, Matthews," he greets.

"Hey," I reply, standing and dusting off my jeans.

Caleb drops the bag on the grass next to me and unzips it to reveal a bat and glove on top of a bunch of other sports equipment.

"Here." He holds out the bat to me, tucks the glove under one arm, then continues to rifle through the bag.

"Thanks," I reply, taken aback by how brusque he's being. I walk over to home plate, and Caleb takes his spot on the pitcher's mound.

"I'm just going to toss a few to start," he tells me. "So I can figure out what's messing you up. I wasn't paying close enough attention during gym."

"I thought the whole reason you're doing this is because you had to watch me mess up?" I ask, a bit testily.

It looks like Caleb clenches his jaw, but I'm too far away to tell for certain. He throws the baseball. It's faster than Mr. Evans's throws. I instinctually jump back, so it hits the chain link behind me with a loud clang.

"If you don't swing, I can't help," he calls.

"I wasn't ready," I shout back, feeling my face warm.

Caleb grabs another baseball. I step closer to the base and lift my arms, prepared to swing. But he doesn't throw it.

"What are you waiting for?" I finally ask.

"Oh, are you ready to hit it now? I couldn't tell." Caleb's voice is nasty. Mocking.

"Ass," I mutter. I know he couldn't have heard what I actually said, but his derisive smile deepens, like he has a pretty good idea.

He finally pitches the ball. I swing this time, but it's a few seconds too late. The next time I swing too early. After the tenth failed attempt, I start to lose patience.

"Lower your stance," Caleb coaches. "And straighten your arms a little more."

I try to follow his instructions, but I still don't come close to connecting with the ball. With each failed attempt, I grow more annoyed. More embarrassed.

Finally, I drop the bat. "This is a waste of time. I'm sorry."

Caleb starts walking toward me. "Lennon…"

"It was really nice of you to offer to do this, but I'm hopeless. And I'm sure there are a million other things you'd rather be doing right now, so…"

He's getting closer and closer. I compensate by stepping back. I retreat until my spine is pressed against the hard ridges of the chain link. Rather than give me space, Caleb follows.

He tosses his baseball glove down, creating a small cloud of dust as it hits the dirt. "I thought you *were* hopeless, Lennon, for a long time."

"Well, that's ru—"

Caleb keeps talking like I never said a word. "But everyone else seems to think you're just clueless. And so I don't know what the hell to think now, except that I'm running out of damn time."

My brow furrows. "What are you—"

Again, he interrupts. "You go on and on about how I have everything handed to me because of my last name. How I've never worked for anything and how I can do whatever I want. That my life is perfect."

I gnaw my bottom lip, because phrased like that, it sounds terrible. "That's not *exactly* what I—"

"*Stop talking*, Lennon. For once, just stop talking and let me say this."

He's so close I feel the mint essence from his gum prickle my face as he speaks. Caleb tilts my chin up and forces me to look straight at him. Storm clouds are gathered in his eyes, darkening what's usually the same shade as the light blue sky behind him. Even if I wanted to say something right now, I'm not sure I could.

"You think I do whatever I want, but you always make excuses when it involves you. If I bring you over to my house or talk to you at a party or invite you to the movies, you never seem to see it for what it is. So, fuck it. You think there are a million other things I'd rather be doing right now? Wrong. There's *nothing* I'd rather be doing right now, Lennon. You think this is a waste of time? It's going to be the highlight of my day. I'd watch you swing and miss at a baseball all day. I'm doing this to help you. So you can stay or you can go, but either way stop acting like I wound up here on accident, okay?"

I gape at him, stunned, as his hand drops from my face. Unexpected, shocking, life-altering moments have happened to me before. But none of them rendered me frozen and mute, the way this has. My body feels numb; my mind blank.

Caleb closes his eyes, hangs his head, then exhales. "Dammit," he mutters, before looking up at me again. "Sorry, I didn't mean to unload all that. We can just—"

I finally decide how to react, rising up on my tiptoes and pressing my lips to his. For a split second, we stand like that. Then I'm moving backward, once again leaning against the fence. This time, I don't even notice the hard metal.

Caleb kisses me hungrily. Eagerly. Like he's been wanting to do it for a long time. And I realize, following the confession I haven't fully processed, that he has.

I melt into him, responding in a way I never have with the few other guys I've kissed. There's no second-guessing, or really *any* thinking at all. Every time my brain starts to catch up to what's happening, Caleb does something different that overwhelms me all over again. His hands slide under my shirt or his tongue brushes mine.

He tastes like spearmint. His body is warm and solid, caging me against the backstop. Heat spreads through my body like a fever, a reaction that has nothing to do with the spring weather or the sunshine.

We kiss and kiss, until my lips are tingling and my legs feel like jelly.

I pull in deep breaths of air when we separate, glancing down at the dirt instead of meeting Caleb's gaze straight away. When I do look up, he's staring at me, lips wet and hair tousled. There's a tentativeness in his expression, an uncertainty that's oddly endearing.

"I thought you hated me," I whisper. "That first day, I was in a dark place. My dad had just died, and it was all people were talking about. Well that, and *you*. They'd make fun of my dad one minute, then be starstruck over you the next. And I got us lost and blamed it on you, so I figured you'd look down on me like everyone else. Worse, because I'd given you a reason to. Everything after... I never let myself consider that you paid attention to me for any good reason, I guess."

And before this semester, when we started spending time together outside of school, I'm not sure I'd have believed him. Part of me still thinks this moment isn't tethered to reality.

"I get it, Lennon. If I could go back, I'd do a lot of things differently."

My hand rises without me consciously telling it to, my fingers running along the sharp line of his jaw. Caleb looks surprised by the contact, but he doesn't pull away. His hands, still tucked beneath my shirt, press tighter against my lower back.

Foreign urges course through me. I want to kiss him again. I want to do *more* than kiss him.

"What now?" I whisper.

He smiles, and it hits me differently. It's like walking outside after being in a darkroom. Jarring in a welcome way.

"Now, I'm going to kiss you again. And then, I'm going to teach you how to hit a baseball. Okay?"

"Okay."

His lips meet mine again, warm and electrifying.

I'm surprised—and unsettled—to realize I would happily stand here all day.

And that's a massive problem. Because everyone knows Caleb Winters is destined for big, impressive things. In places bigger and far more worldly than Landry, Kentucky.

And I'm...not.

I'll be here, long after he leaves.

CHAPTER THIRTEEN

LENNON

It happens gradually: the shift in my life to accommodate the different way I view Caleb Winters.

I oversleep on Monday morning, since there was too much bouncing around my head Sunday night to fall right asleep.

Instead of avoiding Caleb, I look for him in the halls between periods. But I don't see Caleb until English. He's talking to Marcus Cooper when I walk into the classroom. Our eyes connect and we share a smile, but that's the extent of any interaction.

Throughout the rest of the day, my nerves about Gym multiply. I managed to hit the ball three times before Caleb and I left the field yesterday, but that was out of too many unsuccessful attempts for me to feel any confidence. And it feels like there's a lot more riding on this than a grade.

"You're up, Lennon," Mr. Evans calls, halfway through class. I'm the only person who has yet to successfully complete the requirement

By the time I reach home plate, my palms are so sweaty it's a struggle to hold the bat. I run the advice Caleb gave me yesterday on repeat, praying it'll be enough to get me through this.

Mr. Evans throws the first pitch. I swing too early, missing the ball by millimeters. My stomach clenches, dread and nerves swirling around. The second pitch glances off the top, skittering to the side as a foul ball.

I try to block out the whispers behind me, but it's a challenge. My grip tightens around the bat as I glance over my shoulder, finding Caleb's gaze immediately. He gives me a small nod.

I turn back around, choking up on the bat a little and waiting for the next pitch. When it comes, I swing at the perfect moment. Ball and bat connect with a satisfying crack. I watch with a mixture of shock and satisfaction as the baseball goes flying. Farther and farther, until it disappears from sight.

Mr. Evans is just as stunned as I am, his eyebrows flying up his forehead. "Congratulations, Lennon. You passed." He glances past me. "Nice work, Caleb."

I chew on the inside of my cheek, burying the urge to snap at a teacher. "Lennon is the one who hit the ball," Caleb replies.

Mr. Evans smiles. "Of course, if you want to be modest. No wonder the baseball team is so successful."

I drop the bat. The blatant favoritism is hard to stomach. Just one of hundreds of examples of Landry's snobbery.

Everyone stares as I walk back toward the dugout. I pause in front of Caleb. "Thanks for your help, Winters." The words come out snarkier than I mean them to, Mr. Evans's dismissal fresh in my mind.

A muscle jumps in Caleb's jaw. "That's it?"

"Is there something else I should be thanking you for?"

He shakes his head. Scoffs. "Nope."

I keep walking. We don't speak for the rest of class.

~

Three days later, I grab a racquet from the bin in the equipment room. We've moved on from baseball to tennis.

When I turn around, Caleb is standing there.

Impulsively, I grab another racquet and hold it out to him. "Hi."

"Hi." He studies me as he takes the racquet, like he's surveying a puzzle. Half-assessing, half-confused.

We haven't talked since gym on Monday. Haven't *really* spoken since Sunday at the field. I don't know what to say to him. How to act around him. Part of me is still processing the fact that we kissed.

"Dude! What's taking forever? Oh. Hey, Lennon."

"Hi, Luke." I glance back at Caleb. "I'll, uh, see you."

He nods. I give Luke a small smile as I pass him.

Once everyone has grabbed a racquet, Mr. Evans marks pairs off on his clipboard. I'm pretty certain he would be my least favorite teacher based on nothing but the subject he teaches, but that title is solidified when he calls out, "Matthews, you'll be with Herbert."

There aren't enough tennis courts for us all to play at once. Mr. Evans sends Madison and me, along with a few other pairs, to the grassy knoll to the right of the courts. I plop down on the grass, glad it's a sunny day and the blades aren't damp. Madison lowers herself down gingerly after scrutinizing the ground. I swallow a snort.

She's always been prissy. It drove me crazy when we were younger. I'd be racing around the playground, while she'd sit on a swing and refuse to play tag.

"Sure you don't want to get a chair?" I ask her.

She glares at me and tosses her long mane of blonde hair over one shoulder. "I just have standards. Unlike some people."

I adopt my most serious tone. "You're right. Sitting on grass is definitely evidence of a massive character flaw."

Madison scoffs, then turns to talk to Poppy Tisdale about the upcoming senior trip. It's still three weeks away, but I'm not surprised they're already discussing it.

High schoolers start planning for the trip to a nearby campground as freshmen. The senior-only trip is that legendary. Back in freshman year, I even had some vague fantasy I might be able to go. It feels far away now. There's no way Gramps could manage the horses all by himself for three nights. I've been bracing for an argument about it, because I know he'll try to convince me he can, but the topic hasn't come up yet.

"No, I'm bringing my straightener anyway," Madison is saying. "I know they said it draws too much power, or whatever, but Amanda Stephens said she used hers last year and it was totally fine."

I bite my bottom lip, trying to contain my amusement over the thought of Madison blowing a fuse at the campsite and depriving everyone of electricity, just so she can straighten her hair.

"Okay, I'll bring mine too, then," Poppy says.

Madison and Poppy move on to discussing their outfits. It's a struggle to keep a straight face as they describe the tank tops and dresses they're planning to pack.

For a trip to a campground. In the woods. In April.

I keep my mouth shut, though, as I mindlessly pick at blades of grass.

"Time to switch!" Mr. Evans calls out.

Everyone waiting, including me and my reluctant partner, stands to take the place of the losing pairs. Mr. Evans sends partners out onto the court in the order they arrive at the metal gate that leads onto the green asphalt.

Based on how Madison is literally dragging her feet, I figure out who we'll be playing even before Mr. Evans says, "You two will be paired with Winters and Kelly."

That definitely gets Madison's attention. She perks up as we head toward the nearest court. It's my turn to walk slowly.

Caleb hasn't noticed us yet. He's talking to his partner, Harper Kelly. She was on the paper with me freshman year, which was probably the last time we spoke.

Right now, she's entirely absorbed in whatever Caleb is saying, looking at him with the worshipful expression I've seen aimed at him many times before.

It bothers me in a different way than the reverence usually does. I'm...jealous.

Madison clears her throat loudly as we cross the baseline. "Ready to play?"

"Ready," Caleb replies. His gaze shifts to me. A grin forms, surprising me. "You any better at tennis than baseball, Matthews?"

"I'm batting 500 these days, Winters," I reply, relaxing into our usual banter.

His grin deepens, making his dimples pop. "Impressive."

"Can we start the game already?" Madison butts in.

"Serve away, partner," I reply, moving closer to the net.

I am better at tennis than I am at baseball, but not by much. Harper misses more tennis balls than she hits too, but Madison is actually pretty good. And Caleb seems genetically programmed to be good at any sport, so the teams are pretty even.

Mr. Evans blows his whistle halfway through our third set. "Time's up. Grab your gear and head back to the locker rooms."

"Good game, guys," I call out to Caleb and Harper.

Madison scoffs loudly beside me. "No longer playing hard to get, Lennon?"

"Well, I saw how well being easy was working out for you," I retort. "You've been dating Caleb for how many months now?"

She sends me a glare filled with loathing and then stalks off.

"You two best friends again?" Caleb appears beside me.

"What gave it away?"

We walk off the tennis court, following the rest of the class. Caleb lets out a quiet chuckle, and I know his next words are going to be teasing before they leave his mouth. "So are you just generally uncoordinated, or…"

I shove his arm without thinking. He looks just as surprised by the unexpected contact as I am.

"I ride horses."

"Isn't the horse the real athlete?"

"I guess," I reply. "But it's not exactly easy squatting on top of a horse running thirty or forty miles an hour."

"I guess not," Caleb acknowledges.

"You ever ridden?" I ask, as we follow the gravel path that winds back in the direction of the gym.

"No," Caleb responds. "When we'd come here in the summer, it felt like we'd spend half the visit at the racetrack. I got my fill of horses then. Became white noise after a while."

Only a Winters could get away with insulting Landry's pride and joy like that.

"Do you ride a lot?" he asks me.

"Twice a day. Once in the morning and once after school, so they all get exercised a couple of times a week."

"Wow. I'd like to see that," Caleb comments, which I'm not expecting.

"You can come watch whenever, if you're really wanting to."

"You're inviting me over?" Caleb asks. There's a teasing undertone to his voice, which almost sounds like flirting.

154

"I didn't think you needed an invitation," I respond. "Last time you just invited yourself to stay."

"Is that why you asked Jake for a ride home from the movies?"

His tone is no longer playful. I glance over at Caleb, surprised by the fact he's bringing it up. His expression doesn't give me any indication of what he's thinking.

It's completely blank, almost purposefully so.

"He lives closer to me," I answer. "And I was...clueless."

Neither of us have acknowledged what happened between us on Sunday since then. I wait anxiously to see what Caleb will say in response. It's underwhelming. He just nods, not providing me any insight into what he's thinking. And we've reached the entrances to the locker rooms, so I have no more time to analyze his expression.

"See you, Lennon," is all he says before disappearing into the boys' one.

After I've changed back into my usual jeans and sweatshirt, I head to the newsroom for our meeting. I'm anxious about it. This is the first paper meeting since I handed in the draft for my article about Caleb to Andrew. I didn't want to write it in the first place, but the stakes have risen exponentially since I received the assignment. In a way I definitely didn't expect.

"Hey," Julie greets when I take a seat at my desk next to her.

"Hey," I reply, glancing around the newsroom. "No Andrew yet?"

"Nope," she replies. "Joe said he was here earlier. Was muttering something about you and then left."

"Oh. *Great.*"

My anxiety increases.

I have almost every sentence of the article memorized. I run through the words I spent hours agonizing over, trying to figure out what might have caused Andrew to be late for a meeting for the first time ever.

The newsroom door flies open a couple minutes later, announcing our editor's presence.

"You're late," Joe calls out to Andrew.

"I know," Andrew replies. He looks almost…giddy. Julie and I exchange a quick glance, trying to figure out what's going on. She shrugs. Maybe this isn't about me?

"Well?" Joe prompts.

"I had to talk to the printer," Andrew says. "And up our order for the next issue to two thousand copies."

Julie's mouth literally drops open. That's a hundred times our normal order. A quarter of Landry's population. More copies than students who attend Landry High.

"What? Why?" I ask, unable to keep my mouth shut. No one else is saying anything.

Andrew grins. "Funny you should be the one to ask, Lennon. I read your article in study hall earlier. One of the best things I've ever read, and I'm not going to be the only one who thinks so. Everyone else, pay close attention to my notes on your articles. This will be the issue people read. Make sure it's your best work."

He pulls a packet of papers out from under his arm and starts distributing them around the room. He drops Julie's article draft down in front of her, dotted with red ink. Mine falls next. Without a single mark. That's never happened.

Andrew continues moving around the room, dropping off articles and sharing feedback. I remain seated, in a state of shock.

"Can I read your article?" Julie asks.

"Uh, yeah. Sure." I slide the papers over toward her.

My pen taps against the surface of the desk, trying to reconcile the last few minutes with the berating I was bracing for.

Two *thousand* copies? I should be flattered, and a part of me is. But I also know the more people who read the article, the more attention the student body will pay to me and Caleb. I've spent the last three and a half years being defined by my so-called hatred of Caleb Winters. Now I'll be known as the girl who wrote the article about him. It's an upgrade from being judged for my parents' mistakes, but it still has nothing to do with *me*.

"Wow. This is really good," Julie comments.

"You sound surprised."

"No, I'm not," Julie insists. "I just…based on how you reacted to getting it assigned, I thought…"

She trails off, but she doesn't need to finish her thought. I already know what she is trying to say.

"Yeah, well, if I decide to do something I don't see any point in half-assing it," I respond.

Julie laughs. "Clearly. But I hope you know this is going to seriously boost his reputation." I must look confused, because she laughs again. "I mean it. *I* like him more after reading this. The fact that you wrote it? People are going to give it way more credence."

I replay her words for the rest of the meeting and the walk home. Caleb can already do no wrong in the eyes of Landry. Why would one semi-complementary article change that? That implies people care about what I think or say, which is not an impression I've ever gotten.

The paper meeting ran longer than usual, and I have a pile of Calculus problems waiting for me, so I rush through the evening chores.

I hop off Dusty's back just after dark and lead her back to the barn. Its lights are shining like a beacon, visible for miles. Untacking her only takes a few minutes. After I finish brushing her, I release Dusty into her stall.

When I turn around, Caleb is leaning against the adjoining stall's door, just inside the barn's entrance.

My heart stutters, then picks up in double time.

"You said I could come over whenever," he reminds me.

"I know. I just didn't think you would."

"No?" Caleb straightens. Steps closer.

"Did you win?" He's still wearing his baseball uniform, and I really wish he weren't. Especially now that I have the memory of all those muscles pressed against me.

"Yeah," Caleb responds, then smiles.

I tilt my head. "What?"

"I threw a no-hitter."

There's a buoyant note to his voice, some barely restrained excitement. "That's good, right?" I surmise.

His smile grows. "Yeah. It's good." He takes a few steps toward me.

I suck in a deep breath. Caleb doesn't stop until he's only a few inches from me. I can see the darker flecks of blue in his eyes. The shadows beneath them.

"I'm really good at blocking distractions out," he tells me.

His warm, hard body is pressing against mine now, but I don't feel trapped. I feel protected. Shielded. Safe.

"But do you know what I keep thinking about, Lennon?"

Caleb's hand coasts down my side, landing on my waist.

"This."

He kisses me first. But I'm expecting it. There's no surprise or uncertainty. Shivers race up and down my spine as tentative touches turn hungry. Fierce. Ravenous.

I learn that when I suck on his lower lip, he groans.

We don't pull apart until "Lennie!" echoes across the front yard. Caleb and I survey each other for a minute, both out of breath.

"Be right there," I shout back.

"This mean anything to you, Matthews?"

"*I* don't go around kissing random people, Caleb."

He realizes what I'm referring to immediately. "I wouldn't have touched her, if I'd known you were coming that night. If I'd known you'd *care*, Lennon."

"I never said I cared."

"Right." He glances down, running a hand through his hair. "I'll see you later."

Caleb is halfway down the barn aisle before I speak. "Do you want to stay for dinner?"

He slows. Stops. Turns.

"Okay."

And that's how I end up entering the kitchen with Caleb right behind me. Gramps gets over his shock quickly and starts gushing over Caleb.

Apparently, the fact he pitched an entire game without allowing the other team to hit the ball is kind of a big deal. Which explains some of Caleb's amusement in the barn. My *grandfather* is more up-to-date on town news than I am.

Thankfully, dinner is one of Gramps's better creations. He and Caleb talk easily, while I mostly observe. It's not as strange as I expected it to be, having a third person sitting at the rickety kitchen table. Having *Caleb* sit at the rickety kitchen table.

And that's sort of terrifying.

He wasn't supposed to fit.

The next two weeks fly by. Caleb's schedule grows more hectic thanks to baseball, and mine was already packed.

But he continues coming over to the farm, mostly at night, but sometimes in the morning, and we talk. About everything and nothing. The only thing we never discuss is the future.

I'm guessing Caleb never brings it up because he knows the entire school is eagerly trying to figure out which elite Division I university he'll be pitching at next spring. And I have my own reasons for avoiding the subject.

"Caleb's been spending a lot of time over here lately," Gramps comments one evening at dinner, right after Caleb left.

"I guess," I reply, thrown by his cautious tone.

"Just be careful," Gramps warns. "The Winters, they…well, Elaine—"

A shockwave rolls through me at the sound of my mother's name. "What about Mom?"

"The Winters family has been worshipped here for a long time," Gramps says. "Caleb's father, Austin—well, people treated him the same way they treat Caleb now. I'm glad you're having some fun, but I don't want you to get hurt, Lennie."

Gramps reaches under the kitchen table and pulls a blue bundle of fabric out. He hands the roll to me.

"What's this?"

"A sleeping bag," Gramps replies. "Figured you could use it on the senior trip. It gets cold up in the mountains at night."

"I'm not going on the senior trip, Gramps. I—"

"Yes, you *are* going." There's an undercurrent of authority I rarely hear from him. "I let college drop—for now." He gives me a stern look. "Because you're partially right. I don't have any good options for taking care of things around here myself for that long. But three nights I can handle. And, before you ask, I have friends coming to help out. Go be a kid for a bit, darling. I know you had to grow up fast, and I'm sorry you did. But life is short. You already know that. You'll regret not going one day."

I want to argue, but studying his weathered, wrinkled face, I realize this is for him as much as for me. He wants to do this.

"Okay." I blow out a breath. "I'll go."

I stand to clear our empty plates, and then circle the table so I can wrap my arms around him, chair and all. It reminds me of the days I used to spend traveling around the farm on his shoulders.

"I love you, Gramps."

He pats my arm affectionately. "Love you too, Lennie. Just no shenanigans with the Winters boy on the trip, all right?"

"Gramps!" I exclaim. My cheeks are burning, making me glad he can't see my face right now.

He laughs and stands. "What sort of guardian would I be if I sent you off on an overnight trip without mentioning it? I was a young man once myself."

"Stop talking! I'm going out for the night check now," I inform him, still blushing.

Gramps's chuckles follow me out of the house. The mare barn is still and quiet when I enter it, but the horses hear the door creak open and start rustling around. I head inside the tack room to grab the hay bags I already prepared earlier.

I divvy them out among the five mares the same way I do every night, and then feed the stallions.

It's a clear, starry night. I stand in the doorway for a few minutes, looking out at the pasture and contemplating the end of another day. They all blur together, sometimes.

Senior year is speeding by, the end of high school drawing closer and closer. The only thing that's been different lately has been Caleb. And now I have Gramps's warning echoing right along with my own caution.

I thought this thing between us would fizzle out on its own. But it hasn't. Now it feels like the longer it lasts, the harder it will be to end.

With a sigh, I head back toward the farmhouse.

CHAPTER FOURTEEN

LENNON

I've spent years judging the girls who fall over themselves to talk to Caleb Winters. And yet here I am, anxiously scanning the halls for a head of dark hair.

I glance to the right again, but there's still no sign of him. Annoyed with myself, I focus on my locker, transferring the books for my first three periods into my backpack. When I turn around, I spot Caleb standing at his locker, talking to Colt.

Shouldering my backpack, I shut my locker and head his way.

"Hey, guys."

They break off mid-conversation.

"I'll see you later, man," Colt says. After a nod to me, he continues down the hall.

I take a step closer, fiddling with the strap of my backpack nervously. I'm already second-guessing this. Despite the many things that have changed between me and Caleb, our interactions at school really haven't. From the outside looking in, you wouldn't think he ate dinner at my house last night.

"What's up?" Caleb asks, grabbing a textbook and then shutting his locker door.

"I was, uh…" I take a deep breath. "Did you read the article?"

"What article?" Caleb asks, completely straight-faced.

"So, you hated it?"

"Lennon!" Ryan approaches, smiling widely.

"What is it, Ryan?" I ask impatiently. My irritation only grows when I realize what he's holding.

Ryan glances between me and the copy of the school paper. "Have you seen this, Winters?"

"Yeah."

Ryan's attention turns back to me. "If you're taking over the sports section, I know some other athletes who'd be interested in a feature."

The bell rings, saving me from answering.

"See you guys later," I say, then rush off.

Cassie is literally bouncing in her seat when I enter the classroom, a copy of the school paper sitting on the desk in front of her. Surprisingly, I realize most of my classmates already have copies as well. That's definitely a first.

I'd be able to enjoy the interest more, if I had any idea how Caleb feels about it. Considering he was the one who pressured me into writing the article, his lack of reaction feels especially unfair.

"Nice article, Lennon," Harper Kelly comments as I pass her.

"Uh, thanks," I respond.

I sink down in my usual seat next to Cassie just as the announcements start. Cassie doesn't pay Principal Owens's voice any attention.

"Oh. My. God," she tells me, leaning across the aisle so she's closer to me. "I can't believe you wrote this, Lennon!" She shakes the paper in my face.

"In a good way or a bad way?" I whisper.

"Good! I mean, 'there's a reason that every resident of Landry, Kentucky knows the name—'"

"I know what it says, Cassie."

She laughs. "Right. Yeah. I guess you would."

It turns out maybe Andrew wasn't insanely optimistic about the number of copies. All day, I keep passing peers clutching copies of the paper.

Caleb shows up at dusk, right as I'm finishing in the barn. I walk out as he's climbing out of his truck, running a hand through my hair to catch any stray hay.

"I'm mad at you," I tell him.

He shuts the door and walks to the front of the truck, leaning against the hood and crossing his arms. "That's a nice change."

I roll my eyes. I haven't been mad—genuinely mad—at him in weeks, and he knows it. With a grin, he shoves away from the truck and walks toward me, eating up the distance between us in a few quick strides.

"Why are you mad at me?"

"Because the article was your idea! You talked Andrew into it, and if I hadn't gone along then I wouldn't be able to…" My voice trails as I remember I haven't mentioned my fall plans to Caleb. "Do you have any idea how long I spent writing that? And then *nothing* from you."

"I loved it, Lennon." All of a sudden, Caleb's voice is very serious.

"You-you did?"

"Yeah. Wanna know what my favorite thing about the article was?"

He's closer now, near enough I can see his eyes beneath the brim of his ballcap. He smells like grass and sweat, and I realize he came here straight from his game.

"What?" I whisper.

164

"You wrote it."

"I'm going on the senior trip." I blurt the words as a distraction. For me, from Caleb. Because I need the reminder that high school is close to ending. That *we* are close to ending.

"Really? I thought you said…"

"Gramps is basically shoving me on the bus. He really wants me to go. Be normal, you know?"

"Maybe he's trying to get used to the idea of you being gone next year."

This is the closest we've come to discussing college. And this is when I should tell Caleb the truth: that I won't be leaving Landry this fall.

That those big, exciting things I wrote are waiting for him aren't ones I'll share in. That this uncertain, fragile feeling between us has a set expiration date. Something I once imagined him mocking me for somehow became something it seems like he should know.

But I don't *want* to tell him. He's become an escape, a way I can ignore all the messy parts of my life and feel like a normal seventeen-year-old with a crush on a cute boy.

Once I tell him, I know things will be different. Everything between us will change. And I'm not ready for it to.

We're surrounded by a bubble that's bound to pop. I can't forget that. Being left behind is bad enough without a broken heart.

So I fist the polyester material of his jersey and pull him toward me in a kiss instead of saying anything.

CHAPTER FIFTEEN

LENNON

Departure day for the senior trip dawns warm and sunny. Despite my initial reluctance to attend, I feel the first glimmers of excitement as I head toward the gym to drop off my duffle bag. Anticipation swirls around the hallways so thickly it feels like a tangible presence.

Mr. Tanner is the one who checks me in and hands me a paper tag to attach to my bag. He must be chaperoning, which I'm a little surprised by. I've never gotten the impression he got into teaching because he loves spending time with young adults.

"Add it to the stack," he tells me in an unenthused tone once I've written my name on the tag. I toss my duffle bag amongst the designer luggage, and then head toward my homeroom.

I sit down right as the final bell rings, then glance at the empty seat beside me. I work my phone out of my pocket and send Cassie a quick text under the table.

Lennon: *Where are you??*

She's never late, so something must be wrong. Cassie's response comes immediately.

Cassie: *I woke up with a fever.*

A leaden weight appears in my stomach, guessing what that means. She confirms it a second later.

Cassie: *I can't go on the senior trip.*

Any excitement I was experiencing disappears. Cassie is my life vest. Without her, I'll be adrift, bobbing on the periphery.

I text back saying I hope she feels better soon. Cassie's been talking about the senior trip for weeks. I'm sure she must be devastated to be missing it.

The school day passes quickly; probably because I'm dreading its ending. After the final bell rings, the senior class separates from the crowd of underclassmen to rush toward the coach buses already loaded with our luggage.

I'm one of the few who trails behind reluctantly.

The inside of the bus is plush. Far from a wheezing, yellow one. The air is being circulated, blowing the artificial scent of cleaner throughout the massive vehicle. The central carpet is a light gray. Oversized seats line it, upholstered with some sort of dark gray leather.

I walk halfway down the aisle until I spot a pair of seats that are empty. I sink down in the one closer to the window.

"This seat taken?" I look up. Will's hovering in the aisle, looking down at me with a friendly smile.

"Nope," I reply, smiling back. Since Cassie isn't coming, I assumed I'd be sitting solo.

Will sinks down beside me. "I figured this was exactly the sort of school-sponsored outing you'd try to avoid."

I laugh. "I tried. My grandfather thought it would be an important life experience."

"Survival training would qualify, I guess," Will replies seriously.

My smile widens. "Yeah, I guess so. Cassie's sick, though, so it could be a lonely weekend."

"What do you mean?" Will asks.

"Will. You don't have to pretend like I have friends aside from Cassie. I got comfortable with being an outcast a long time ago."

"You're not an outcast, Lennon," Will replies. I raise both eyebrows, and he correctly interprets my disbelieving expression. "I mean it. Marcus talked about you showing up at his party for like three days." Will pauses. "And you seem to be pretty popular with the baseball team."

I nod, awkwardly.

"Huh," is all I say in response.

"Some people might surprise you."

I'm tempted to dismiss Will's words, but he's the third person to tell me that. Maybe there's some truth to it.

"We only have a month of high school left, so now's the time to make new friends, right?"

Will gives me a small side glance that makes it clear he caught my sarcasm.

I'm distracted from our conversation when the popular contingent passes by our row. None of them bother with a second glance, but the first one I catch suggests Caleb might not be thrilled with my choice of seat companion.

I look away, out the window, and keep staring outside for most of the trip. It's a three-hour drive; most of it through the Kentucky wilderness. Landry might be a small town, but it is *a* town. The winding road we're on takes us past the occasional farm, but then it will be fifteen minutes before we encounter another.

When we finally arrive at the campground, the sun has just begun to set, painting the sky with streaks of yellow, orange, and pink. Groves of pines surround the cabins situated on sandy lake shore. The air is still; the surface of the water peaceful.

Mr. Tanner's booming baritone breaks the tranquil atmosphere as he calls out the cabin assignments. I'm the first name in cabin five, and to my relief, I hear Julie and Shannon are assigned there as well. Just as important, Madison is not.

We're assigned to tables in the main dining lodge based on our cabins, which solves one dilemma for me. Caleb doesn't make any attempt to talk to me during dinner, which resolves another.

There's a massive campfire blazing next to the lake when we walk back to our cabin after dinner. I spot a few classmates darting off into the woods, but most people seem to be actually heading into their cabins. Most everyone is probably biding their time by trying to lull the chaperones into a false sense of security, but I couldn't care less either way. I don't have to pretend like this is my usual bedtime, because it actually is.

I've just exited the cabin's small bathroom in my pajamas when Shannon approaches me. "We're sneaking out in a bit," she tells me. "Do you want to come?"

I'm surprised—and touched—she's including me, but it doesn't change my answer. "I'm really tired," I reply, giving her a smile I hope conveys how much her offer means. "Rain check? I'll go tomorrow night."

Shannon shrugs. "Okay. Night!"

She slips out of the cabin with the other girls right behind her. I climb the rungs of the ladder to my top bunk bed.

Everything inside the cabin is decorated in soothing tones of off-white, honey wood, and light green. We're so close to the edge of the lake I can hear the water lapping against the shore, and the sound lulls me to sleep.

∼

When I descend the ladder the next morning, it's to a disaster zone. There's nowhere to step. Clothes, magazines, and makeup cover the floor. Our cabin looks like the aftermath of a middle school slumber party.

I clear a path to my duffle bag by sweeping most of it toward the side of the cabin with my bare feet. I get dressed, use the bathroom to brush my teeth, and then step outside.

It's early. I didn't bother to check the time on my phone, but I'm guessing my internal alarm clock ensured I was up no later than usual. The sun has barely begun to rise.

Each cabin has its own front porch, but I don't stay on mine. I walk over to the fire pit. Charred remains sit in the center of the stone circle. There's a long bench on each of the four sides, a thick tree trunk that looks like it was cleaved in half. I expect the surface to be rough, but my fingers skim across it without encountering a single splinter.

I take a seat on the one that faces the lake. Mist hovers across its surface, obstructing my view of the smooth water.

"Had a feeling you'd be up."

I look behind me, although I don't need to. I recognize his voice immediately.

Caleb's walking toward me, hands shoved into the front pocket of his *Landry Baseball* hoodie, and sleep still visible in his blue eyes.

"Habit." I shrug.

He takes a seat next to me. My body hums from the proximity. It seems like the amount of time I've spent this close to him lately should have built up some immunity to his presence, but my body is excruciatingly aware of the short distance between us.

Caleb seems oblivious.

"Want to do some actual sight-seeing?" He nods toward the lake.

"What? Now?"

"No. In three hours when everyone else wakes up."

I ignore his sarcasm. "I don't really think we're supposed to…" In fact, I'm certain we're not supposed to leave the campground by ourselves. And we're definitely not supposed to go out on the lake by ourselves. I imagine the only reason none of the chaperones have mentioned it yet is because they didn't think anyone would be up this early.

Caleb stands and walks toward the shore. "Come on, Matthews. What are they going to do?"

I stand, following his steps to the edge of the lake. "I'm more worried about you getting us lost."

"It's a lake, Lennon. We'll hit shore, eventually." Caleb grins, and it's dangerous. Not because it's the practiced one I've seen him give a lot of girls. Because it's a secret one I've only ever seen him give me.

I cave like a poorly stacked house of cards as soon as a dimple appears. "Okay. Let's go."

Caleb hauls a bright yellow canoe from behind some ferns and slides the very front into the blue-gray water. "Get in," he instructs.

I step inside tentatively, grabbing both sides when the canoe rocks unpredictably. I'm certain I hear Caleb chuckle, but when I glance back, his face is as smooth as the water I'm suddenly surrounded by.

In one graceful shove, he jumps in the small boat and pushes us away from shore. Shifting water gurgles as we move forward, until I can barely tell if we're moving at all. Everything around us looks the same. As in, I can't see anything. I can hear the dip of Caleb's paddle and the occasional slosh, but there's no scenery passing us by. Just gray mist everywhere.

I spin around on the small seat so I can look at Caleb. "Do you know where you're going?"

"Oh yeah, I paddle through mist all the time," he tells me, then rolls his eyes.

"We're lost, right?"

"What do you consider being lost?" Caleb counters.

"Not knowing where you are?"

"I know we're on a lake, Lennon."

"Okay, fine. But do you know when we'll *no longer* be on the lake? If we'll ever make it back to Landry?"

"No."

"So, you admit we're lost?"

Caleb chuckles. "No."

"How big is this lake?" I ask.

"No idea," Caleb responds.

"Did you go out last night?" I focus my attention on a small ant creeping along the side of the canoe. If it falls, it'll drown.

"Just played cards with some of the guys in our cabin. You?"

I shake my head, focusing out on the lake. There's a small shadow in the mist that I squint at.

"Duck!" I shout.

Immediately, Caleb leans forward. I do too, reflexively. The canoe rocks precariously. The paddle Caleb was holding slips off the side and into the water. Our slow momentum comes to a halt, giving the mallard enough time to move out of the path of our incoming canoe.

"What...how—" Caleb glances between the green-helmeted bird and the wooden paddle slowly drifting away.

"There was a duck."

He blinks, glances at the bird, and then starts laughing. Loud, husky sounds that echo across the surface of the lake. "You've got to be kidding me."

"You can see it. Right there." I point toward the duck, who's rapidly swimming away. I kind of wish I could do the same. Something tells me Caleb's amusement is heading toward annoyance.

"All I see is our way of getting back to shore disappearing." Caleb points in the opposite direction, toward the floating oar.

"Won't we just like, I don't know, drift toward it? Or paddle with our hands?" I lean down to demonstrate, attempting to drive the currents with the sheer force of my palms. We angle slightly to the right, and then move back to the left.

Caleb bursts out laughing again. Despite the fact we're currently stranded, I smile.

"Please tell me you didn't think that would work."

"Not now, I don't," I reply.

Caleb shakes his head before he stands, pulling off his *Landry Baseball* sweatshirt in one smooth motion.

"What-what are you doing?"

"Getting us back to shore. I thought that's what your hand paddling was trying to accomplish."

His sweatpants disappear next. I swallow and look out at the lake. All three feet of it I can see in front of me.

We've shared plenty of heated moments, but this is the most I've seen of Caleb. Ever.

There's a quiet splash, then a dark head bobs to the surface of the lake beside the canoe.

"Fuck, it's freezing," he informs me.

"Not surprised," I reply.

"I didn't hear you offering to jump in, Matthews," Caleb responds, before he swims toward the wayward oar.

"Here." Caleb's back beside the canoe, holding he paddle. He holds it up to me.

I stretch over to grasp the wooden handle, and I don't realize that was a mistake until I feel the canoe follow my movements. It tilts to the left. All of a sudden, lake water is pouring inside. Caleb was right. It's cold.

I yelp, and then jump ship. Literally.

When my head emerges from the lake, Caleb is treading water beside me. "Didn't you get an A in Physics?"

"Of course I did," I respond through chattering teeth. "You have a plan to get us out of this, I hope?"

"Yeah," Caleb replies. Then he smiles, which I'm not expecting. We're treading water in what feels like an ice bath. Why does he look so amused?

"What?" I ask.

"I'm glad you came, Matthews." The warm feeling his words elicit chases away a bit of the water's chill.

"I just capsized the canoe."

"Yeah, you did," Caleb agrees. Then he kisses me. Familiar heat spreads through me, like a frozen flame.

Kissing in the water is difficult. It's a challenge, staying afloat and remaining close enough to Caleb to kiss him. We manage to do it, though, until my arms are numb

"We should probably deal with the canoe," I tell him.

"Yeah, probably," Caleb agrees. After one final kiss, he swims over to the canoe. He flips it over in one smooth motion, then tows it toward' me. The wayward paddle gets tossed inside, followed by our clothes.

Caleb literally has to haul me up and over the side of the canoe. Somehow, I adjusted to the temperature of the water, and the air is cold and unpleasant now that I'm wearing wet clothing. I wrap my arms around myself, trying to retain some body heat.

Caleb makes climbing into the canoe look easy. He gets dressed, and we finally start moving again. The mist is beginning to clear. I can see at least a dozen feet ahead now.

"So your grandfather is managing everything himself this weekend?" Caleb asks.

"Some of his old track buddies are coming over to help, but for the most part, yeah." I look around at the scenery slowly emerging through the vapor lingering mystically in the air. "I'm worried about him."

"If you're worried about a weekend, how are you going to handle leaving him in the fall?"

I exhale. Part of me is surprised this possibility hasn't occurred to Caleb already. Maybe it has, and this is a test. "I'm not leaving in the fall, Caleb. I'm staying in Landry."

His face is completely blank. Nothing. "Why?"

"You know why."

"Did you apply anywhere?"

"No," I admit. "College is crazy expensive. That's money we don't have. And even if I got a scholarship someplace, I can't leave the farm. Leave Gramps."

"You could sell the farm. That land is worth millions."

He says it like it's easy. Like it's nothing. Spoken like someone with no attachment to this town.

"Matthews Farm has been in my family for generations. Gramps has lived there his whole life. So have I. I've known this is what would happen ever since—ever since my dad died. Gramps can't manage things by himself. I'm all he has left. He's all I have left."

"You've known since freshman year." The words sound flat. Delivered more like he's talking to himself than to me.

"I didn't think it...mattered."

Caleb shakes his head. "Great. That's just...great."

"I don't get why you're mad," I say. "Surprised, yeah. But why do you care if I'm here? You'll be gone."

"Did you listen to a damn word I said at the field that day,

Lennon?"

"Caleb...we both knew this was temporary. I mean, you're... you. I figured this would have ended a while ago." I pause. "I'm glad it didn't. Hasn't. But I know it will."

Caleb laughs, but it sounds totally different than before. It's a hollow, sad sound. "I don't know where you got the idea this was temporary from, but it wasn't from me. It's good to know that's what *you* think, though."

Unease trickles through me, paired with the sinking suspicion I just messed up. "What did you think this was, then?"

"It doesn't matter. I can't keep doing this."

"Keep doing what? I thought we were just, you know, having fun. Messing around."

"Having fun and messing around," Caleb repeats.

"I mean...I enjoyed it." I squeeze the excess water out of the hem of my shirt, wayward drips falling on my legs and the bottom of the canoe. "I know you're more experienced."

When I gather the courage to glance up, Caleb is rubbing a palm across his face. The canoe isn't that big. When his hand lowers, I can see the freckles on his nose and the droplets clinging to his eyelashes. "You think this is about sex for me?"

"I've heard the stories. I saw you kissing Madison."

Caleb's jaw tenses. "Have you been kissing other guys?"

I laugh; I can't help it. "Of course not." Aside from Noah, a sandy-haired surfer who spent a couple of weeks in Landry visiting family the summer after my sophomore year, Caleb is the only guy I've kissed since Ryan James in middle school. The suggestion I'm juggling multiple boys is honestly funny.

Caleb's expression only darkens. "Don't do that."

"Don't do what?"

"Don't act like it's ridiculous."

"Well, it is. You know how people act around me."

176

Now, Caleb laughs. But it's not really an amused sound. "I know Masterson sat next to you on the bus yesterday. And last night, I learned James is planning to ask you to prom."

"I...what? Where did you hear that?"

"Where do you think? James had a lot to say about you during cards, actually. Heard all about eighth grade and the conversations you have at your locker."

"Conversations? It was *one* conversation, maybe two. He asked me to hang out, and I said no. The end."

The canoe hits the shore, lurching me forward. Caleb climbs out immediately and I clamber to follow him. He pulls the canoe all the way onto shore, stashing it in the same spot among the ferns.

Then, he keeps walking.

It takes me a second to register he's really just walking away. And not at a slow pace, either. I have to literally run to catch up with him. "Caleb!"

At first, I think he's not going to stop. But he finally slows, then turns around. "What?"

"Where are you going?"

He raises his eyebrows, then glances deliberately down at his soaked clothes. "To change."

"We were in the middle of a conversation!"

"The conversation is over, Lennon. And so are we. Although, according to you, we never even started. So we're just back to being nothing, I guess."

"I..." I don't know what to say. I made a lot of assumptions about me and Caleb, and I guess the saying about that is true. I do feel like an ass.

"We're fine, Lennon," he says. "Don't worry about it."

But Caleb doesn't *look* fine. He looks disappointed and upset. And it twists something inside my chest, knowing it's because of

me. I was so focused on protecting myself—on managing expectations and not getting attached and not losing sight of reality—
that it never occurred to me I might have the power to hurt him.

"Where are you playing next year?"

I don't follow baseball, and I've spent years trying to tune out
any mention of Caleb. But I know he's a big deal. Know he
should have announced his college choice a while ago and that he
hasn't is a source of speculation.

If he's surprised by the random question, he doesn't show it.
"I haven't committed anywhere yet."

"You-you haven't? Weren't you supposed to, a while ago."

"Yeah, I was."

"Why haven't you then? You want to play in college, right?"

"Yeah. I wanna play."

"You got offers…right?"

He exhales, one corner of his mouth turning up reluctantly. "If
you'd ever come to a game, you wouldn't have to ask me that."

My fingers twine anxiously as I chew on the inside of my
cheek. It never occurred to me to go to one of Caleb's games. I
figured he wanted to relegate any association with me to the
periphery of his life. But Caleb has never acted ashamed of me.
Those insecurities are all me.

"Hey, Winters!" I don't turn toward the voice behind me, but
Ryan edges into my sight anyway. He glances at me, surprise all
over his face. "Hey, Lennon. Didn't realize that was you."

"Hi, Ryan." My voice is wooden as he glances between me
and Caleb with a questioning look. Everyone always seems
surprised to see us together. It's hard not to assume it's because
of me.

"There you are, man." Jake's voice joins the conversation.

I shift uncomfortably. If Jake and Ryan are up, that probably
means other guys are too.

"Why the fuck are you all wet?" Jake asks Caleb, then glances at me.

Caleb ignores the question, turning and continuing toward the row of cabins. Jake looks between me and Ryan, shakes his head, and then follows after Caleb.

"See you later, Ryan."

I spin and head in the direction of my cabin.

"Lennon! Wait."

I sigh before stopping. "Ryan, this really isn't a great time." I gesture toward my sopping appearance.

"What, you forget a suit?"

"Not exactly."

Ryan raises his eyebrows, then drops the subject. "Look, you have every reason to hate me. I was a stupid shit back in freshman year."

"Freshman year? Don't you mean freshman year, sophomore year, junior—"

"Yeah, yeah, I get it." He smiles, then tilts his head. "People change, you know?"

"I don't hate you, Ryan."

"Great. Wanna go to prom with me?"

Damnit. Caleb was right. "I told you we were over. We've been over."

"You just said you don't hate me. So…there's hope."

He gives me a grin most girls would consider charming.

"No. If I hated you, then there would be hope."

Twin lines appear between his eyes. "Uh, what?"

"Thank you for asking. But the answer is no. And it isn't going to change, Ryan."

"Because of Winters?"

"What? Your ego can't handle I'm just not interested in dating you? There has to be another guy?"

"Nah, I just thought you were less of a cliché. The whole town is in love with Winters. And since you hate the whole town, I figured Winters would be on that same list."

"Ryan, I'm sorry if—Actually, you know what? I'm *not* sorry, about anything. I've made it very clear I don't want to date you. And since you fell in line with everyone else after my dad died, I'm not really interested in being friends with you, either. Leave me alone, and leave Caleb out of it."

Ryan shakes his head. "You're awfully defensive, Lennon. Just don't say I didn't warn you. I'm friendly with the baseball guys. Winters goes through a lot of girls. At least I've been upfront with you. He'll break your heart and then walk away. Dude doesn't care about anything but pitching."

There was a recent time when I would have believed every word coming out of Ryan's mouth. Nodded along and agreed. But now? I'm not so sure. "I liked you better when you were ignoring me," I tell Ryan, then head in the direction of my cabin.

Thankfully, he doesn't follow me. And I'm grateful to discover all my cabin mates are still asleep, meaning I can avoid answering any questions about where I was or why I'm drenched.

After showering and changing into dry clothes, I head to the main lodge where we ate dinner last night. The broad spread of breakfast food—bacon, eggs, waffles, pancakes, quiche, omelets, and fruit parfait—is impressive. I normally wolf down a banana and sometimes a granola bar before heading out to the barn for chores.

I take a random assortment of food and head toward my cabin's table. Seconds after I've sat down, Mr. Tanner stands up to announce the day's itinerary. The two options are canoeing or hiking. With this morning's misadventure fresh in my mind, the choice is an easy one for me.

By the time I leave for the hike, I've realized more stares and whispers than usual are following me around. I don't know if they're related to Caleb or Ryan or something else. Since Cassie isn't here, I have no insight into what exactly is being muttered under my fellow seniors' breaths.

By the time we return to the campground, it's dinnertime. In what's become a familiar ritual, I eat with my cabin mates. Following dinner, there's a movie screening. It turns out to be the same spy thriller I saw in the theater with Caleb and his friends. I wonder if the memory is as bittersweet for him as it is for me.

As soon as we return to the cabin from the approved evening activities, things switch to the unapproved. Clothes are tossed around, makeup artfully applied, perfume sprayed.

"Aren't you coming tonight, Lennon?" Shannon asks.

"Right, sure," I respond, hiding my surprise. I read last night's offer as more of an obligation than a serious invitation.

I trail after the rest of the girls, still in my jeans and sweatshirt. Once we're off the porch, half the group splits to the left and darts toward the woods.

"Where are we going?" I ask Shannon.

"Lee found a clearing in the woods. We're supposed to meet everyone there."

I relax a little. Lee Joseph is friends with Will, along with a handful of other people I don't mind. As far as cliques go, it's one I can handle socializing with.

There's not a chaperone in sight, but we stick to the periphery of the campground as we head toward the woods just in case. Eventually we reach a point where we have to dart across the middle of the campground to reach the direction in which we apparently need to head.

We're halfway across when I make the mistake of looking to my right. There are about a dozen figures huddled around the campfire, silhouetted by the dancing flames and starry sky.

I make direct eye contact with Madison. She smiles wickedly. I look away.

"Lennon! Don't you want to play?" Shannon and the rest of the girls all stop, so I have no choice but to pause too.

If Madison is inviting me to participate in something, I have no doubt there's a hidden agenda. But everyone around me is behaving like moths, inching closer and closer to the campfire. Leaving isn't really an option.

"Play what?" I ask as I walk over to the group gathered around the flickering flames. The group, that I realize with a start, includes Caleb.

"Truth or Dare," Madison responds. She tosses her hair, shooting me a challenging smirk.

"We can stay for a bit." Shannon answers before I have a chance to decline, plopping down in an open spot.

The lull in the game turns out to be because of Jake's current dare. He returns to the fire less than a minute after we've sat down, a jar of pickles in hand.

"Couldn't have been easier, Adams." Jake tosses the glass container to Colt. Jake challenges Poppy Tisdale to dance for a minute without music next. I stare in the general direction of the lake instead of watching, cringing from secondhand embarrassment.

Maybe the uncomfortable judgment is obvious on my face, but I'm pretty sure Poppy singling me out has more to do with impressing Madison. "Truth or dare, Lennon?" Poppy asks.

"Dare."

Poppy smirks, then leans back on the bench. "I dare you to kiss Jake."

Not a challenge I saw coming. A small gasp next to me comes from Shannon. She's reacting to the fact I was just dared to kiss one of the most popular guys in school. I'm more concerned with his status as Caleb's best friend.

I stand and take my time walking across the dead pine needles to where Jake is sitting. Right next to Caleb.

As I walk, I weigh my options. There are only two, really. One that will cause harm—irreparable harm—to my ambiguous, strained relationship with Caleb. That should make my choice easy, but I consider it could be easier—better—to take the option away.

I reach the opposite side of the campfire. Caleb is stone-faced and impassive. But as I near the spot where he's sitting, a muscle jumps in his jaw.

A tiny, barely discernible, involuntary motion. And it decides for me.

I stop in front of Jake and lean forward. He's wide-eyed, and I can tell he's resisting the urge to look over at Caleb.

"Don't move," I whisper to him.

His Adam's apple bobs as he hastily swallows. I lean forward. And kiss him on the cheek.

Before I stand back up, I hear a quick exhale to my left, and that's how I know I made the right decision. That Caleb wasn't as indifferent as he seemed.

"You call that a kiss?" Poppy laughs, but I hear the edge of nervousness in her voice as she glances over at Madison.

"Next time you should specify where." I smile at her sweetly. "I'm going to find Lee," I tell my wide-eyed cabin mates, continuing toward the woods instead of sitting back down. They follow me, and it feels like a show of support I haven't experienced in a long time. Maybe ever.

"That was *crazy*!" Shannon whispers to me as we walk away from the campfire. "I can't believe you did that."

Awe saturates her voice.

I don't respond. I'm distracted by the eyes I can feel searing my back. If I turned back around, I know they'd be blue ones.

The clearing Lee discovered looks a lot like a stretch of forest that just has slightly fewer trees than the rest of the forest, but at least it's filled with friendlier faces than the campfire was surrounded by.

I spot Will standing with Marcus and some of the other senior players on the basketball team. He gives me a small wave. I smile back before following Shannon toward a huddle I recognize as containing most of our usual lunch table, Julie, and…Andrew. He looks even more uncomfortable than I feel.

"What took so long? Did you guys get lost?" Eliza asks.

"Nope," Shannon responds. "Lennon had to kiss Jake Barnes."

"Wait, what?" Tina gasps, and everyone looks at me. I shoot Shannon a dirty look.

"It was one dare, and I didn't even do it," I explain. "Not really."

"It was amazing," Shannon interjects. "You guys should have seen Madison Hebert's face."

Joe stumbling over saves me from having to field any more commentary. "Hey, look who it is!" He slings an arm around Andrew's wiry shoulders. "Our esteemed editor…my favorite co-worker…" He nods to Julie. "And our star writer!" He grins at me. "Have you always been this hot, Lennon? Or is it just the vodka?"

Tina squeals. "You have vodka? I thought they searched everything?"

Joe smirks and pulls a flask out of his pocket. "All it takes is a little imagination."

Pretty soon, I'm in the midst of a lot of drunk teenagers. Laughter and jokes fill the night air that's tinged with the scent of the pine needles carpeting the forest floor. There's a sense of community, of belonging, that I haven't felt in a long time. Sometimes, getting lost in a crowd is nice.

I haven't acted any differently. Nothing about my past or my popularity status has changed. But I came on this trip. I opened myself up a little, and I wonder if both Caleb and Cassie were right about me isolating myself. It's a depressing thought, since we're now only a few weeks away from graduation. My high school years are about to end, and I don't feel like I have much to show for them.

"I'm going to head back to the cabin," I tell Shannon, who's sitting on the rock beside me. It's been a couple of hours, and I'm struggling to keep my eyes open.

"Okay," she replies. "Do you want me to walk back with you?"

I'm touched by the offer, but shake my head. "No, I'll be fine. I remember the way."

"'Kay. See you tomorrow," Shannon says, turning to face Lee.

I stand up and head back toward the cabins. The glow of the campfire is easy to see from a distance. As I grow closer, the silhouettes surrounding it come into focus. There are fewer than before, but at least ten still. Caleb is one of them.

I have about twenty feet to decide if I'm going to say anything when I pass by.

My impulses regarding Caleb Winters have always been warped. I took comments I wouldn't have thought twice about from anyone else like a personal attack. And now, I'm stuck with an uncomfortable, heavy lump in my throat that reminds me of this morning.

So, I stop.

"Can I talk to you?" I ask Caleb. My voice is clear. Confident. Impossible to ignore.

At first, he doesn't say anything. Finally, he turns his head to look at me. "I'm busy," he answers, then returns to looking at the fire. His voice drips like bored honey.

"Fine, we can talk here. I—"

With lightning-fast reflexes I'm not expecting, Caleb stands and yanks my hand, hauling me away. He obviously isn't interested in an audience.

We don't get very far, though.

"Hey! You two. Stop!" I turn to see Mr. Tanner, of all people, chasing after us, clearly on chaperone duty. An ineffective one, if the fifty kids drinking in the woods are any indication.

He comes to a panting stop in front of us. "Well, this is a surprise." Mr. Tanner looks between us, and then down at our clasped hands.

My cheeks burn, knowing what assumptions he's probably making right now. "I just need to talk to Caleb for five minutes," I blurt.

"Is it related to your English project?" Mr. Tanner questions. I almost, *almost* think I see a glimmer of a smile in his normally dour expression.

"Tangentially," I respond. As in, I probably wouldn't need to talk to Caleb if not for that project.

"Fine. Five minutes," Mr. Tanner allows.

I'm not expecting his agreement, but I don't hesitate to take advantage of it. "Thank you!"

"What do you want to talk about?" Caleb asks flatly when we stop about sixty feet later, just on the periphery of the woods.

"I'm sorry about earlier," I tell him. "I was just trying to make things easier."

"Easier for who?" Caleb shoots back.

"For *both* of us. I shouldn't have assumed anything, but I just figured you were thinking the same way I was."

"And how's that?"

"That we're on two different roads, and they're about to get a lot farther apart. Making more of this will just complicate everything else…and it'll end the same way anyway."

Caleb grasps the back of his neck with one hand, looking down so I can't see his expression. When he glances at me again, the shadows still block most of it. But what I can see appears resigned. "You know, I always planned to go to Oakmont."

"Oakmont? That's in California, right?"

He nods. "Yeah. Get the hell away from my parents, decent weather, girls in bikinis everywhere…"

I flinch. "Did you not get in?" I ask. My tone is snide, and it has everything to do with the jealousy coursing through me.

"They offered me a full ride and a starting spot, actually. I should have accepted on signing day back in February."

"So why didn't you?"

"That's a damn good question." That's all he says. But if I squint at the subtext—the tightening around his mouth and the way his hands are clenched—I'm worried his lack of an answer says a lot.

"Look, Caleb. It's not just the money or the farm. Gramps is forgetful. I don't know if it's just…age, or something else. And—whatever it is—I can't leave him alone. He took care of me after my mom…and then my dad…now it's my turn. Maybe that's part of why I never tried to change anyone's mind about me. I knew it would be harder, when they left and I was still here." I swallow. "Maybe that's why I never let myself consider this"—I gesture between us—"because I knew you would be the hardest to see leave."

Caleb rakes a hand through his short hair. The strands are barely long enough to make the effort worthwhile. "What the hell am I supposed to say to that, Lennon?"

"You don't have to say anything," I tell him. "I just wanted to…explain." Caleb doesn't say anything. "We can still, uh, you'll be around all summer, right?" I don't even know what I'm offering, or trying to say, but I'm suddenly aware my feelings for Caleb are far from superficial.

"I'm spending the summer in Georgia," Caleb states. "At a baseball camp there. I leave the day after graduation."

I should congratulate him, but instead I accuse. "You didn't tell me."

"I just found out I got in. Why do you even care?"

I glare at him. "You—"

"Matthews! Winters!" Mr. Tanner's deep baritone pierces the night air like a bullhorn. "Time's up!"

In more ways than one, I guess.

I turn to head back for the cabins, but a hand grabs my forearm before I can take a single step. "We'll be right there, Mr. Tanner," Caleb calls back.

There's barely any light that's crept all the way to the perimeter of the campground, but there's just enough for me to see the jaw muscle that kept me from actually kissing Jake pulsate a couple of times. His thumb traces a circle on the inside of my wrist, sending shivers through my whole body.

"You know I'm in love with you, right?" Caleb asks me.

There are some moments in life when you have a premonition something epochal is about to happen. You can prepare for it. Maybe savor it. Take note of all those subtle details your brain might otherwise skip past like the grooves on a scratched record.

This is *not* one of those moments.

I'm stunned.

Flabbergasted.

Nonplussed.

I freeze the second he says the words, but I don't let them sink in. I *can't* let them.

"No, you're not," I choke out. The world is spinning around me, but Caleb is perfectly in focus.

A single, dry laugh slips through Caleb's terse lips. "Right. Yeah. Of course you would know how I feel better than I would."

"I don't—it's not—we're too different, Caleb," I stutter.

"Only in the ways that don't really matter."

I sigh, letting the air escape slowly, like I'm a deflating balloon. "We're different in an 'I'm staying here, you're leaving' way. I don't have the time or the energy to be in a long-distance relationship."

Caleb opens his mouth to speak.

"I don't *want* to be in a long-distance relationship."

Without asking permission, my heart got way more invested in Caleb Winters than it had any right to. If I said those same words he just told me back, I think I would mean them. But letting him in? Letting myself rely on the phrase he just uttered? Letting myself love him and then remaining in a town filled with reminders of him while he goes off to bigger and better things?

I can't do it.

Caleb's mouth snaps shut. I hate the hurt I can see swimming in those blue depths. But he's leaving. Moving on from this town. Moving on from me. Off to a fancy baseball camp and then to an elite university to meet new people with backgrounds as privileged as his.

I'm just the girl he bickers with constantly and occasionally kisses.

He's about to leave me behind, and selfishly, I'd rather walk away first.

Although Caleb's the one who spins and strides back toward the cabins before I have the chance to.

CHAPTER SIXTEEN

LENNON

When I wake up in my sleeping bag the following morning, I'm disappointed. I was hoping the past day and a half didn't happen, and that the sloped eaves of my childhood bedroom would be there waiting to greet me when I opened my eyes. But no, it's the rough boards of the cabin's roof that I'm staring at instead. I sigh and fling the covers away.

Considering how I woke up wanting to flee, I'm surprised by how much I enjoy the day. The chaperones are too exhausted from yesterday's activities to plan anything constructive for today, so it's essentially a free-for-all.

Almost everyone ends up on the lakeshore, including me. I perch on a rock between two massive pines and sunbathe while reading. Shannon joins me for a bit, but everyone else leaves me alone.

It's the first full day in a long time where I haven't *had* to do anything, and it's nice. Really nice.

There's no schoolwork, no farm chores, no responsibilities.

Just the pit in my stomach while I surreptitiously watch Caleb playing football on the thin stretch of sand with his friends. After our canoe ride, I didn't think it was possible for things to get any more tense between us.

I was wrong.

After dinner, I wander out to the campfire. Along with daytime activities, the attempt at evening entertainment seems to have also ceased for the final night here.

Unlike last night, the split logs surrounding the stone circle are all empty. I take advantage of the space to stretch out along the length of one and stare up at the stars. Someone already built a fire, which provides pleasant warmth and a comforting crackling sound.

The snap of a stick warns me of someone's approach, but I don't bother to sit up or look over. "Want to make another bet?" a voice I recognize as Colt Adams's asks.

"No."

There's a soft chuckle. "Well, I'm betting you know why Winters has been in such a shitty mood all day." I make a point not to react and just keep tracing patterns in the stars overhead.

I definitely don't betray the surprise his words elicit. Caleb has looked perfectly carefree all day, joking and laughing with his friends.

Colt laughs. "Refusing to talk about it. Maybe you guys *do* have something in common." Plastic crinkles. "Want any?"

I finally sit up and see he's offering a water bottle filled with clear liquid. But I doubt it's actually water.

"Sure." I surprise us both by accepting. Colt hands me the bottle, and I take a large sip. Eyes watering, throat burning, I hand the bottle back to Colt. "What is that?" I choke out. I've never liked the taste of beer, but at least it's never made me feel like this.

He grins. "Tequila."

I cough. Fire is scalding my system as the alcohol works its way through my body.

"Seriously, Adams?" Luke appears, a heavy frown on his face.

"What?" Colt replies innocently, although I know he's perfectly aware of the reason there's disapproval in Luke's voice. They're obviously not supposed to be socializing with me. Or sharing alcohol.

"Isn't this nice?" Madison asks, appearing and taking a seat directly across from me.

She's changed since earlier, just like me. Only aside from donning leggings, she's wearing a pair of jeans tight enough to appear painted on and a suede jacket that would be more appropriate to wear to a club than a campfire.

"It was until you showed up," I comment.

There's a cat sound to my left, courtesy of Jake, who's walking over toward us. I'm suddenly surrounded by people I don't want to be around.

"Then why don't you leave?" Madison retorts.

Now that Caleb's three best friends are all here, I'm tempted to do exactly that. But my insides are still burning from the tequila. And I'm too proud to let Madison think she scared me off.

"I'm good," I reply.

"Guess you don't have any friends to go hang out with," Madison comments, her expression full of mock sympathy.

"Do *you*?"

She waves a hand toward Colt, Jake, and Luke. "You're looking at them."

I've never really understood the dynamics among Landry

High's popular crowd beyond knowing I'm not a part of it. But I realize it's probably true.

Jake speaks, surprising me. "No need to fight over us, ladies. There's three of us and only two of you."

I scoff before lying back down on the log. Maybe that will keep me from feeling like I might vomit.

I recognize a few more voices as they join our circle. Poppy and some of Madison's other friends slash followers. Ryan James, who thankfully makes a point to ignore me. Then Will, which is a surprise. He's the first newcomer to address me.

"Uh, Lennon, are you all right?"

I suppose me appearing passed out on a log would look a bit concerning to an outside observer. Nice of Will to notice.

"Yeah, I'm good," I reply, moving back into a sitting position. "Just doing some stargazing." My stomach has finally begun to settle, and the burning has abated, leaving behind a pleasant buzzing warmth that reminds me an awful lot of the way I feel around Caleb. Or used to, before dread and uncertainty took its place.

"Really?" Will looks amused.

"Yeah. Just was looking for some peace and quiet. So I think I'm going to head…"

My voice trails as soon as I see him.

Caleb walks between two of the logs on the opposite side of the campfire, taking a seat beside Madison. I got distracted talking to Will, and I missed his approach.

Caleb's expression is impassive, but he's exuding an annoyance that's palpable through the flickering flames separating us. I don't know if it's because I'm talking to another guy, or if it's because I'm among a group that's mainly comprised of his friends. I'm sure the way we ended our last conversation is also playing a part.

I look back at Will to find he's studying me with a bittersweet smile. I'm pretty sure he realizes who just stole my attention for the last thirty seconds, and why.

I scramble to find a new topic of conversation. "Uh, so is basketball still going?"

Will sends me an indulgent smile. "No. It ended about two months ago."

"Oh. Sorry." I laugh, awkwardly.

"Hey, you came to a game. That's more interest than most people show."

I manage a small smile. *If you'd ever bothered to come to a game, you wouldn't have asked that*, echoes in my head.

"Okay, I'll go first!" Madison's exclamation is obnoxiously loud, obviously meant to draw the attention of everyone gathered around the campfire. Which is quite a lot of people, all of a sudden. I spot Shannon, Julie, Marcus, and several others from the group in the woods last night. "Time for Truth or Dare," she announces.

Everyone's quieted, so my scoff echoes loud and clear.

Madison's eyes narrow in on me. "Truth or dare, Lennon?"

"Never said I was playing," I reply.

"You did last night."

"And it didn't exactly make me eager to repeat the experience."

"Hey!" Jake calls, his voice filled with fake offense. At least, I think it's false.

I ignore him as I vacillate between my two options. Well, three, really. I could just leave. But I don't.

"Truth," I finally decide.

Madison was obviously hoping I'd say dare. It takes her a while to come up with a question. "Who was your first kiss?"

I tilt my head and lean back on my palms, a bit disappointed by her lack of originality. "Ryan was. We played Seven Minutes in Heaven at your thirteenth birthday, remember?"

"Whatever." Madison looks away, and I get the distinct impression something's bothering her. Maybe she's just as uncomfortable about our shared history as I am.

Through the trial, I reap the rewards.

"Truth or Dare, Ryan?" I ask.

He's not expecting me to pick him, that much is clear. We have a brief stare-off that ends when he answers. "Dare."

"I dare you to take a dip." I tilt my head in the direction of the lake. "You can choose one piece of clothing to keep on." I know from experience that water is *cold*.

Ryan narrows his eyes, but complies, stripping off everything except his boxer briefs. He's fit from football, but seeing him mostly naked doesn't affect me. There are a few muffled laughs around the campfire as he wades into the lake.

I relax in my seat, relieved my role in the game is officially over. I'll stay for a couple more rounds to make it clear I'm not being run off and then head to bed.

We're leaving early tomorrow morning and I know there will be a long list of things to get done once I'm back at the farm.

"Truth or dare, Winters?" Ryan returns, fully dressed and visibly annoyed.

Caleb only hesitates for a few seconds. "Dare."

"I dare you to kiss Lennon." Ryan pauses for dramatic effect. "On the mouth." He's learned from Poppy's dare.

The challenge is followed by a triumphant look at me. This is Ryan's way of getting back at me for his dare. He doesn't think Caleb will do it.

One glance at Caleb's hard features makes it clear kissing me isn't a welcome prospect. I know it's because of yesterday. But everyone else here knows about the years of animosity between us. All of them—especially Ryan—are waiting and expecting for Caleb to laugh and say I'm the last girl he'd ever touch.

Caleb leans forward and glares at Ryan. Firelight dances off his features, which look carved from stone. "You're a real dick, James," he accuses evenly.

Ryan rolls his eyes. "Fine. I'll do something different. How about—"

Whatever else he was going to say gets lost in the whispers as Caleb stands and walks toward me.

I took my time approaching Jake last night, mostly to give myself time to figure out what I was going to do. Caleb doesn't hesitate. He's directly in front of me in seconds, holding one hand out.

Blood rushes in my ears as I take it, realizing what's about to happen. The hostility radiating off of Caleb has me bracing for a harsh yank, but his grip is gentle as he pulls me to my feet. He drops my hand once I'm standing, but it's only to wrap his arm around my waist and pull me against his body.

I stumble on nothing but pine needles, unprepared for the close contact. I thought this would be a quick, impersonal peck, at most. The bare minimum. I'm shocked he's doing this at all.

His fingers slide beneath the hem of the sweatshirt I'm wearing and ghost along my lower back. Sparks of heat shoot through me.

"You smell like tequila."

"I'm trying new things," I whisper back.

Caleb's response is kissing me. And I rapidly lose all sense of where I am, of the few dozen people watching us, of all the reasons why kissing Caleb Winters is a bad idea.

It's a slow simmer that builds to an inferno. This is probably the last time I'll ever kiss Caleb, so I pour everything I have into it. I don't know if he's thinking the same thing, responding to my passion, or trying to get back at Ryan, but his lips are fierce as they move against mine.

His hands slide higher on my lower back, almost reaching the strap of my bra. I weave my fingers into his hair, tugging the strands lightly. Caleb groans, and it vibrates against my tongue.

Our motions are hasty, but they're practiced. Synchronous, like a choreographed dance. It's possibly obvious to everyone watching this is not the first time our tongues have tangoed.

Caleb pulls back slowly, the cool air chilling my skin once his hands drop. It all filters back: the people, the place, the *game*.

"I didn't think you'd do it," I tell Caleb quietly.

"Yeah, me neither." He turns and heads back toward his seat, past more than a few gaping mouths and Ryan's sullen expression.

Caleb dares Luke to steal a pair of socks from Mr. Tanner's cabin, and the game continues on from there.

After two more dares and a truth pass, I swing one leg over the wooden log so I can slide off the back. "I'm headed to bed," I tell Will, who has stuck dutifully by my side. "Good night."

"Night, Lennon," he replies, smiling.

I return it, before I stand and head toward my assigned cabin. It's empty when I enter it, which is a relief.

I'm guessing the girls I'm bunking with will probably have a lot of questions about Caleb's dare. I only saw Shannon and Julie at the fire, but I'm far from naïve when it comes to the inner workings of Landry High's gossip mill. There won't be a senior on this trip who doesn't hear some mention of it.

I take my time brushing my teeth and washing my face, before I change into pajamas and then snuggle into bed.

There was lots of grumbling about how early we're leaving tomorrow, but I couldn't be more thrilled. It's later than I would otherwise get up, and I'm eager to leave the emotional turmoil of this weekend behind.

Caleb kissing me like that, in front of all his friends…

It doesn't matter, I tell myself.

It doesn't change anything.

CHAPTER SEVENTEEN

LENNON

I never hated Caleb before, I realize.

There were times I couldn't stand being around him, but it never felt like *this*. And I don't hate him now. It just hurts, both when he's around…and when he's not.

Exactly one week after he kissed me because of Ryan's dare, he texts me.

Caleb: *I'll do the introduction and imagery. You can do the rest?*

Although he had the decency to include a question mark, I know it's not really up for discussion. We'll be finishing our English project separately.

He never replies to my agreement. At least we did most of the work weeks ago. Cassie and her partner are meeting every day after school to get it done.

The last week of classes sneaks up on me. One minute, all six hundred and eighty days of high school were stretching in front of me. Now? There's only five left, and they're filled with nostalgia. The last paper meeting. Emptying out my locker. A final assembly.

Events I looked forward to until they arrived.

When I walk into English the day Caleb and I are set to present, I don't pay close attention to any of the pairs that go before us. We haven't practiced. Haven't talked, aside from those two texts, since that night at the campfire. He's ignored me entirely, and I've done the same.

I don't know what to say to him.

When Mr. Tanner calls our names, I startle before standing and walking toward the front of the room on autopilot. I'm here; I'm present, but my mouth is just spitting out the words it knows it needs to say, with little input from my brain.

The presentation ends, and I return to my seat next to Cassie.

"Nice job," she whispers to me.

I manage a weak smile before zoning out again.

Only two more partners have time to present before the bell rings.

"If you didn't present today, be ready next class," Mr. Tanner calls. "And everyone who's already presented, it isn't time to slack off just yet. Make sure you're preparing for the final." Rustling starts, everyone shutting books and grabbing their backpacks. "Caleb. Lennon. Stay after, please," he adds.

I gulp. Our presentation was perfect. Well, almost perfect. It was a little disjointed.

But I'm less worried about what Mr. Tanner is going to say, and more concerned about having to stand next to Caleb while he says it.

"I'll see you at lunch," Cassie says, before heading into the hallway with the rest of our class. Except for Caleb, who follows me over to Mr. Tanner's desk in the front of the classroom once the room clears.

"It seems like you two could use another five minutes to talk," Mr. Tanner states.

Not what I was expecting. And *way* worse than a lecture. If I wasn't so horrified, I'd be shocked Mr. Tanner, of all people, seems to be trying to play matchmaker.

"That's okay," I'm quick to say.

At the same time, Caleb speaks. "Not necessary."

Our rushed voices mingle, creating a cacophony of urgent sound.

"Maybe ten," Mr. Tanner amends, with a hint of a smile.

Our project is done, so his motivation for helping us get along can't be academic. It's sort of sweet that he cares. But I can't appreciate the gesture. Talking to Caleb is *not* something I want to do.

"Five's plenty," Caleb says.

Mr. Tanner's lips quirk before he grabs his bag and leaves the classroom. The door shuts behind him, and then there's total silence.

I stare at Mr. Tanner's spotless desk, all the books we've read this semester stacked in alphabetical order in one corner. I look at the smudge of marker that wasn't erased from the whiteboard. A robin flitters between tree branches outside the window, so I track its flight closely.

Anything to avoid looking at Caleb.

I'm a coward, waiting for him to walk out first.

The silence between us builds and expands until I can't take it any longer. "The presentation went well," I finally say.

There's a low, annoyed scoff. "Don't, Lennon. Just…don't."

"Don't what? You'd rather stand here in silence?" My tone is petulant.

"Actually, yeah. I would." His is hard.

"Mr. Tanner is gone. You can just leave."

"Why haven't you?" he counters.

An excellent question I have no answer to. "We haven't talked since…" I clear my throat.

"What's left to talk about, Matthews?"

I flinch. I got used to him calling me Lennon. Or saying Matthews in a teasing, flirty tone. Not this flinty one.

"I—"

The classroom door opens, and Andrew walks in.

He comes to an abrupt halt as soon as he sees me and Caleb. "Oh. Hey. Sorry to interrupt. I'm, uh, early for class."

Any other time, I would smile at that. But it turns out he's not all that early. Other people start to enter the classroom, and then one leaves.

I stare after Caleb's retreating back.

"Um, Lennon, while you're here…" Reluctantly, I shift my gaze to Andrew. "You know we normally publish a list of where everyone's headed in the fall as part of the graduation issue. I don't have anything down for you…" Andrew lets his voice trail off, looking incredibly uncomfortable.

My shoulders square. "There's nothing to put down. I'm not going to college in the fall."

"Right, okay." Andrew still looks awkward. "And also, well, we usually publish the valedictorian's speech in there, too…"

"What does that have to do with me?"

"I met with Principal Owens this morning. You're ranked second in our class."

"Meaning I won't be valedictorian."

"Not if you do better on your finals than the classmate ranked first." Andrew gives me a *look* that suggests he knows exactly who that is.

Mrs. Clemens enters the room to teach her class and gives me an odd look, obviously wondering why I'm in her classroom and not in her class.

"Anyway, if you end up moving into first, I'm going to need a copy of your speech," Andrew says.

"Fine," I agree. Then, something else occurs to me. "Why didn't you say anything to Caleb? He was just in here."

"I've got more faith in you, Lennon."

Those words should kindle a competitive fire. I know I'll be one of the only graduates without a college listed next to their name. The opportunity to show everyone I'm more than my parents' mistakes and that I'm *choosing* to stay in Landry should be my main focus.

But there's not even the slightest spark.

I give Andrew a small smile, nod, and then head toward the math wing. After Calculus, I walk to the cafeteria for lunch.

Without permission, my eyes dart to Caleb's usual table in the corner as soon as I enter the cafeteria. He's seated with his back to me, talking with Colt, who's across the table from him. Madison is next to Colt. She glances up, catching me staring.

I quickly look away and cross the linoleum to my table.

"What did Mr. Tanner want?" Cassie asks as I drop down on the bench seat beside her.

"He, uh, he liked our presentation," I answer.

I feel badly for lying. But I'm not in the mood to discuss the real reason.

Cassie nods. "Not surprised. You and Caleb are his favorites."

"I guess."

"Hey, Lennon," Shannon calls, from a few spots down the table.

I glance at her. "Yeah?"

"Do you know who Caleb is taking to prom?"

My stomach sinks, but I steel my expression. "No. I don't know."

"You know, some people thought he might ask you, after *the kiss*."

I pick at my sandwich. "It was just a dare."

"But you guys are friendly now, right?"

I glance at Caleb's back. Shannon's nonchalance makes me feel a little better, actually. It'll be easier if no one even suspects anything going on between me and Caleb. "No. Not really." Worried I'm giving too much away, I add, "Maybe he hasn't decided yet. Prom isn't until…" I grasp for a date, and can't come up with one, earning me an eye roll from Cassie.

"It's on Friday, Lennon. You'd better be at my house by four."

"I wasn't planning to go," I say.

"You should come, Lennon," Shannon says. Eliza and Tina chime in with their agreement.

"I don't have anything to wear." My wardrobe is all fleece and denim. The only dress I own is the one I wore to Caleb's grandfather's funeral.

Cassie waves my words away. "No need. I have tons of dresses that you can wear. I bought three dresses for prom last year that ended up being too long."

Sometimes I forget how wealthy Cassie, and almost everyone else I attend school with, is. The only person I'm always aware of it around is Caleb. He's the starkest example, and also the person I most wish was on more equal footing with me. It would be a lot easier to believe what he told me on the camping trip if there wasn't such a glaring inequity between us.

Not only with money. Opportunities. Possibilities.

"Okay, I'll go. Thanks," I tell Cassie. She bounces in her seat.

And just like that, I'm going to prom.

CHAPTER EIGHTEEN

LENNON

I wave goodbye to Gramps, then knock on Cassie's front door. He insisted on driving me over to her house, claiming he needs the truck later.

Oftentimes, that's how Gramps and I communicate. He pretends to have an appointment later instead of saying he wants to drop me off for senior prom. I stop setting a third spot at the kitchen table, instead of telling him Caleb and I ended our...whatever we were.

"Don't forget to take photos!" Gramps calls through the rolled-down passenger window as he backs the truck up.

"I won't! You've reminded me twenty times!" I call back.

The front door opens and Cassie appears in the doorway. Her hair is in curlers and she's wearing a pink, shiny robe.

"You actually showed up!" she teases.

I roll my eyes before stepping inside. Truthfully, part of me is excited for tonight.

The foyer is quiet and empty when I step inside. No sign of Cassie's parents or brothers.

I follow Cassie up the stairs and into her colorless room.

Except it's not entirely white the way it was last time I was here. There's a rainbow of colored fabric flung across her bedspread.

"Any color preference?" Cassie asks, heading straight toward her bed.

"Not really. Which one are you wearing?"

"Mine's hanging up there." Cassie gestures toward her closet door, where a light yellow dress is hanging. Tiny crystals are sewn to the fabric, making it sparkle. "These ones are all for you."

I figured I'd be looking through one or two choices. There are at least a dozen dresses laid out on the bed. One is a muted shade of pink with a flower pattern, which I decide against. The next option is purple and lacy, which I also skip past. Red, shiny fabric catches my attention, but I decide against that, too. I'm not sure I can pull such a bold color off.

The fourth dress is a darker shade of blue, almost navy. It's strapless, made of a soft, silky material than I can't help but touch. The bodice is covered with lace the same color as the rest of the dress.

"I like this one."

"That's the one I would have picked for you," Cassie tells me. "Come on, let me do your makeup before the rest of the girls get here."

She leads me over to her vanity. I don't protest this time. If ever there was a night to wear makeup, this feels like it.

I lose track of time as Cassie rubs and paints and sprays my face.

"Okay, you're done," she finally announces.

I open my eyes. They widen when I catch a glimpse of my reflection. "Wow."

My under-eye circles have disappeared, along with every

blemish. She lined my eyes, making them look greener than usual. My lips look shiny and pink. Kissable.

"Thank you, Cassie."

Cassie smiles as she hands me a tube of lip gloss. "Keep this. You'll have to reapply after we eat dinner." Her smile turns sly. "Or after a certain guy sees you."

"You heard about that, huh?" I knew it was naïve to think Cassie wouldn't hear about the camping trip dare. But she hasn't mentioned it, up until now.

"The whole school heard about it, Lennon."

I rub a finger against the side of the lip gloss. Ironically, the shade is called *Never Been Kissed.* "It wasn't the first time."

"What?"

"Kissing Caleb. I'd kissed him before then. Kissed him a lot, actually."

Cassie gapes at me. This might be the only time I've seen her speechless. "Didn't see that coming," she finally says.

I huff a laugh. "Yeah. Me neither."

"So, you like him."

"It doesn't matter."

"Of course it matters." Cassie pauses. "He stares at you in English, you know. I noticed it all year."

I say nothing.

"So…what happened? Why'd you *stop* kissing him?"

"He's leaving. I'm staying here. That doesn't equal us working out."

"You never know, Lennon."

"I *do* know. I'm not enough for him to come back to, Cassie. And I know that sounds pathetic. I don't mean it like that. I don't think *anything* is enough for Caleb to come back. He hates living here. He's going to go off and become a famous baseball player,

207

and that's what he should do. That's not the life that I want. If we actually tried, it would just hurt us both more in the end."

"Or you could end up married with kids one day."

I shake my head. "Not going to happen."

"Just talk to him tonight. Ask him to dance. Kiss him, if there's a moment. You never know what might happen."

My fingers tighten around the tube of lip gloss. "I *can't*, Cassie."

She tilts her head. "Why not?"

"Because he told me he was in love with me, on the senior trip, and I didn't say it back."

Cassie drops the makeup brush she's holding. I wait. One second. Two. Three. Still, she's just staring.

"Things are bad between us. Talking will only make things worse. He's leaving the day after graduation, so I just have to make it until then."

"*Lennon*. Back way the fuck up. Caleb Winters told you he's *in love with you*?" The end of the question comes out like a squeal. "What did *you* say?"

I exhale. "Honestly, I don't totally remember. I was… shocked. He was already annoyed I didn't tell him I was staying in Landry for college. We were arguing, he just said it, and then I said I didn't want a long-distance relationship."

"Oh my *God*." Cassie leans against the edge of the vanity, still looking stunned.

The *ring* of the doorbell suddenly echoes through the house. Cassie straightens. "That must be everyone else."

I reach out and grab her arm before she leaves to answer the door.

"Don't say anything about this, to them. Please."

She nods. A couple minutes later, she returns, with Shannon and Eliza right behind her.

"—some sort of shoe crisis," Eliza is saying. "She said she'd be here soon." Since Tina's the one missing, I assume they're talking about her.

Both Eliza and Shannon say hi to me. Cassie starts on Eliza's make-up. Shannon offers to curl my hair. Since it's something I've never had the time or patience to do myself, I agree.

It's a long process as Shannon winds section after section around the hot barrel, letting each spiral fall after a couple dozen seconds. After she's finished with the iron, she brushes through the curls and coats my hair in a spray that smells like coconut.

Tina arrives just as Shannon is finishing my hair. "Hot damn, Lennon." She whistles. "You're going to need to walk in after me, okay?"

I laugh off her compliment, but secretly I'm pleased. I rarely put any effort into my appearance. The horses don't care what I look like, and until recently there was no one I was trying to impress. Gramps isn't full of fashion tips and I've spent most of high school with no female friends. After years of messy buns and ripped jeans, the fanciness is fun.

Everyone else finishes their hair and makeup, and then it's time for dresses. I change into Cassie's blue dress in her attached bathroom. The tiled floor is cold against my bare feet, but I barely notice after I get a glimpse of myself in the mirror. Between the dress, the curls, and the makeup, I hardly recognize myself.

After gushing over my appearance, Cassie talks me into wearing a pair of heels. They're too small on me, but at least it makes them a little easier to walk in.

Once everyone has changed, we head downstairs as a giggling, glittery group. Cassie's parents are waiting in the living room. They take a series of photos of us striking ridiculous poses. I send three of them to Gramps, though I know I'll have to remind him how to look at them tomorrow morning.

We walk outside, and there's a shiny black limousine sitting in the front drive. I'm the only one who falters; everyone else seems to be expecting it.

Cassie, Tina, Eliza, and Shannon all clamber inside. I follow after them, glancing around the plush interior in awe. The nerves that have been swirling in my stomach all day make a rapid return, mingling with the anticipation that's lingered ever since I saw my full reflection.

Following years of taunts about my worn jeans and jokes about hay in my hair, it will be satisfying to see what my class-mates say about my formal attire. But truthfully, there's one person in particular I want to see react to Cassie and Shannon's handiwork.

We've barely made it to the end of her street when Cassie pulls a bottle of champagne out of the chiller hidden beneath her seat. Tina produces flutes from some other secret compartment. After popping the cork with a shriek, Cassie pours the frothy liquid from glass to glass until the bottle is empty.

Once we're all clutching the thin glass stems, Cassie raises hers in a toast. "To…"

"Prom?" Eliza finishes.

"The rest of our lives?" is Tina's suggestion.

"The Ladies of Landry!" Shannon trills, barely making it through without laughing.

Mostly because it sounds so fun to say, we all echo Shannon's words before clinking our glasses together.

Prom is being held at Landry's country club. I've only been here once before, for a birthday dinner back when my mom was still alive. The building looks just as pretentious now as it did then, but it's also stunning. The decorations inside don't disap-point either. Twinkling lights, candles, and flowers are everywhere. We walk across the marble lobby to the inside of the ballroom, and I feel like I've stepped inside a fairytale.

"Whoa," Shannon breathes, looking around.

We head for one of the open tables. I eye the two plates, three forks, and multiple glasses a bit apprehensively. I'll have to follow everyone else's lead on etiquette once dinner is served.

More and more seniors continue to trickle in until all the tables around us are filled.

It's not until uniformed waiters start serving the first course that it occurs to me: he might not be coming. None of his friends are here, either. Nor Madison and her usual crew. Maybe they're having their own private get-together?

I should be relieved. It should make tonight more enjoyable. Less trepidatious.

Instead, there's a sinking disappointment.

Dinner is possibly the most delicious thing I've ever tasted. Aside from special occasions, Gramps and I eat a rotation of the same five or six meals. Tonight, there's a salad with zesty dressing, pepper-crusted filet mignon, lemony green beans, and crisp potatoes.

After the dinner plates have been cleared, a spread of desserts is set out along with coffee, tea, soda, and water. The piano music that's been playing in the background stops, and a DJ takes the stage. Pop music starts as soon as some of the tables have been cleared, revealing a dance floor.

A few people begin dancing. But most everyone remains seated, talking or eating dessert.

Not long after, Tina sits up straighter in her seat. "Here comes the cool crowd."

She's looking toward the door. I twist my head before I can stop myself.

He's here. Walking toward one of the open tables amidst a

group of his friends, baseball teammates, and an awful lot of girls. Including Madison.

I look away quickly, before anyone can catch me staring.

Cassie gets a bunch of desserts from the buffet. I take a brownie when she offers the plate to me and listen to the gossip about the couples dancing. More and more people are beginning to head out to the dance floor.

My eyes stay on the front of the room, but my gaze wants to look to my left, over where Caleb went. Eventually, my empty glass provides me with an opportunity to scan the room and preserve my pride.

"I'm going to get some more water," I say. "Anyone else want anything?"

Suddenly, there's silence.

"*Alright*, then." I laugh a little as I stand. "I'll be ba—"

I turn, the word dying in my throat when I realize someone is blocking my path.

He's wearing a tux. That's all I register at first. A whole lot of black and white fabric. Then my gaze travels up, until it reaches blue eyes. My heartrate accelerates to a rapid, uneven rhythm.

After holding my gaze for a few seconds, his drops, looking at my dress. He's close enough I can see his throat bob with a swallow.

"Hey." That's all Caleb says. No compliment. But he's still looking, and maybe that says more.

I know I'm not unattractive. Guys have shown interest in me. But none of them have ever looked at me the way Caleb Winters is looking at me right now: like I'm oxygen and he's just run out of air.

"Hey," I echo, not sure what else to say. I never thought he'd come over here. Not after everything. I'm sure people are staring, but for once I genuinely don't care. They can say or think whatever they want.

Caleb shoves his hands into his pockets. "Do you want to dance?"

I nod, then clear my throat. "Sure."

He nods back as he steps to the side, allowing me to pass by and walk in the direction of the dance floor. Halfway there, his hand settles on the small of my back. I can feel the heat radiating from his palm, sinking through the thin fabric of my dress and spreading across my skin.

The DJ is already in the middle of a song. Caleb guides me toward one corner with some open space. The melody is upbeat and fast, suited for grinding or gyrating. But we stand like we're waltzing, my hand on his shoulder and his on my waist.

"I wanted to ask you," I admit.

Somehow, Caleb became the more vulnerable of the two of us, but it doesn't make me feel powerful. It makes me feel inadequate.

One corner of his mouth twists cynically in response to my confession. "Sure," he says easily.

"I didn't know…if you'd want me to. I wasn't even sure if you were coming. And I was worried you might say no."

In response, he says nothing.

"You look good." I half-smile, so he'll know I mean the compliment. Although, I doubt I'm the first girl who's told him that tonight.

"You look beautiful, Lennon." Embarrassingly, those four words, delivered in an earnest tone, make my eyes prick.

The next song begins playing. We weren't quite in tune with the last melody, but this beat is slower. I stop moving, fully expecting Caleb to drop his hands and return to his friends.

He doesn't.

He tugs me closer.

I can't see his face anymore, just the starched black fabric of his tuxedo jacket.

The song is melancholy, making it perfect for this moment. It's one I've heard played dozens of times before on the radio when I'm cleaning the barn. But I don't focus on the familiar words or the haunting melody. I'm fixated on the weight of Caleb's hands resting possessively on my lower back.

I love him, I realize. I'm in love with him.

Instead of weakening my resolve, it strengthens it. We're close—so, so close—to the end of high school. Despite staying here, it will be a fresh start. No school. No responsibilities, aside from Gramps and the farm and hopefully, the *Landry Gazette*.

Caleb might think he loves me. But that will fade, once he's left Landry. I want to ask if he's committed to Oakmont yet, but I know it'll probably hurt to hear the answer.

The music ends, and his hands drop. We stare at each other.

I muster a smile. "Thanks for the dance."

"I wouldn't have said no, Lennon." Caleb holds my gaze, watching those words sink in before he walks away.

I can't stand out here alone, and I'm not ready to return to my table. So, I head toward the dessert table. I fill a fancy glass with sparkling water and take a couple of long sips. Bubbles tickle my throat as I drain the glass, set it on a tray, and then continue to the bathroom.

The marble restroom is empty when I enter it. My heels create a foreign echo as I cross the glassy surface. It's a challenge to go to the bathroom in the long dress, but I finally manage.

When I exit the stall, I'm no longer alone. Madison is standing at the mirror, carefully painting her lips red. Her dress is a bright shade of teal that would probably look terrible on anyone else, but on Madison, it's just audacious enough.

"Lennon," she acknowledges, lowering her hand and adjusting her dress so the daring back dips down a bit further.

"Hi, Madison," I respond, walking to the sink next to her so I can wash my hands.

"You're looking less like a farm girl than usual."

Instead of replying, I ask, "Why did we stop being friends?"

Madison drops the lipstick in her clutch and snaps it shut before turning toward me, eyebrows raised. "What?"

"You heard me. We were friends. *Good* friends. You've spent the last four years acting like we never were. Just because of my dad?"

"At first, yeah."

"At first?"

"Caleb Winters was moving to town. I wanted to distance myself from you, because I knew that the Winterses care about appearances. Reputations. Money. Even before Caleb got here, he was the most popular guy in town. He and I made sense. I was obsessed with boys and being popular back then. You know that."

"And that's changed?" I tease.

A reluctant smile forms on Madison's face. "Not really."

"So it was all because of my dad."

"I didn't want to be associated with you, because I thought it would drive away Caleb." She shakes her head, pursing painted lips. "And then you turn out to be the one girl he gives a shit about. I thought he'd get over it, honestly. I mean, he's Caleb Winters. Every girl has a crush on him. And you, you barely acknowledged him. But any time someone would say something about you, he'd defend you. Until no one would say anything about you, around him. I kissed Ryan in front of him once, trying to make him jealous. Ryan mentions talking to you at your locker? Caleb hasn't spoken to him since. *That's* why we're not friends, Lennon. Because I'm in love with Caleb. And he's in love with *you*."

I blink at her. "That's not—"

"Save it, Lennon." Madison holds a hand up. "You asked me a question. I answered it. But a little *friendly* advice? As far as I can tell, you're making things a lot harder than they need to be."

With one last knowing look, she walks out, leaving me wondering what it means that the last person I ever thought I would take life advice from seems to be making an awful lot of sense.

CHAPTER NINETEEN

LENNON

The bell rings, drawing my attention away from the back of Caleb's head to the half-scrawled sentence I should have been focused on. Hastily, I finish it, then tuck the sheet with my multiple-choice answers inside the booklet as Mr. Tanner moves down the row, collecting everyone's exams.

He takes mine, so I lean down to grab my backpack so I can depart. It feels strange leaving school in the morning, but now that we're in the midst of exams it's a daily occurrence. I'm back home by eleven.

"Caleb, I'm missing your essay." Since Mr. Tanner has never been one for subtlety, he announces this in front of the entire class. Classmates who were already headed for the door slow, sucked into the drama like motorists passing a car crash.

"I ran out of time," Caleb answers.

"You didn't *write* the essay? *Any* of it?" Mr. Tanner is paging through the blank booklet, like maybe Caleb started writing on page ten for some reason.

"No."

"Not even an outline? I can give you partial credit for that."

"I ran out of time," Caleb repeats.

Mr. Tanner shakes his head before moving onto the next desk to retrieve Ellie Nash's final.

Drama concluded, everyone rushes for the door, eager to leave school and maximize the time before having to return tomorrow for the last day of finals. But no one exits faster than Caleb. He's out the door before I've even risen from my desk.

"I'll meet you at your car, okay?" I tell Cassie. We made plans to go get coffee and cram for tomorrow's tests after the English final.

I catch her nod out of the corner of my eye as I head for the door, jostling a few classmates as I hurry toward the front entrance. I spot Caleb as soon as I'm outside. He's already halfway down the sidewalk.

My strides quicken, giving up on a brisk walk and literally running after him. My heavy backpack bounces against my back with each step and my rubber-soled sneakers slap the cement. People are staring, but I don't stop until Caleb hears me approach and spins around.

"What the hell did you just do?" I accuse Caleb between pants.

"I don't know what you're talking about," he replies.

"You *ran out of time* on a two-hour exam? You *chose* not to write that paper. It's twenty percent of our grade! You'll be lucky to end up with a B. I have no idea why you—"

"You want to be valedictorian, right?" Caleb demands.

Realization trickles in like a melting ice cube, cold and steady. I chased him because I wanted him to convince me he didn't purposefully bomb the final. Instead, he just confirmed he did.

"Not because you handed it to me. I can earn my own accomplishments, Caleb. I *want* to earn my own accomplishments. You didn't do this for me."

"Then why did I do it, Lennon?"

He spins back around and continues walking in the direction of his truck without giving me a chance to answer, which is good.

I'm not sure what I would say.

CHAPTER TWENTY

LENNON

My palms are damp with perspiration, both from the sunshine bearing down on me and my own nerves. I fiddle with the notecards I'm gripping, resisting the urge to bounce my knee.

You can do this. You can do this. You can do this, I chant to myself.

Surreptitiously, I wipe first one palm, and then the other, on the green silk skirt of the new dress Gramps insisted I buy when I told him I'd be the class valedictorian. I can see his beaming face perfectly from the spot onstage where I'm seated. He insisted we arrive ridiculously early so he could snag a seat in the first row behind the graduates. Gramps is confident I can deliver this speech and not make a fool of myself.

I wish I were as certain.

I switch the notecards to my right hand so I can wipe my left palm. The top notecard flutters to the ground next to my folding chair.

I freeze.

Crap.

I'm literally on display, seated in what's meant to be a position of honor at the center of the stage, right next to the podium where Principal Owens is currently speaking.

After three days of endless edits, I know every word of my speech by heart. But relying on my memory while delivering a speech in front of almost every person I know is a daunting prospect.

I contemplate how to manage an awkward shimmying slouch or pretending to itch my foot so I can retrieve the notecard. Before I can act, Mr. Evans, who was chosen as the faculty speaker, leans down and grabs it for me.

"Thank you," I whisper when he hands it over.

Gym is no longer my least favorite class. An easy change to make, since in about ten minutes I'll be a high school graduate, forever free of Kentucky's mandated class curriculum.

Principal Owens mentions my name, and I realize he's introducing me. There's applause—loud applause—not just polite clapping, and then I'm standing at the podium staring out at a sea of expectant faces.

"Principal Owens, faculty, friends, family, and my fellow graduates. This is a day I've looked forward to for a long time. But when I was writing this speech, I also came up with a lot of things I am going to miss about Landry High."

I keep talking and talking, until suddenly I'm down to the last notecard. Something I dreaded and I'm surprised is suddenly about to end. Kind of like high school.

"There are two people I wish could be here today. But I want to acknowledge the person who's the reason *I* am. Gramps, you might be a terrible cook and a worse mechanic, but you've never allowed me to believe there's anything I can't do. You are the only person I've always been able to rely upon. You make me proud to be a Matthews. To be your granddaughter. I hope I've made you proud, too." I swallow a couple of times to clear the lump that's formed in my throat. "And to my fellow graduates: no matter where you're headed next, I know you'll soar. We survived three days in the Kentucky wilderness, so basically, we can survive anything." There's a ripple of laughter. "Congratulations, graduates!"

I flip my tassel, and it's over.

I'm not expecting the swell of noise. There's applause, cheering, and then a wave of navy as all the seniors—now graduates—toss their caps toward the cloudless sky.

Principal Owens comes over to the podium to hand me my diploma, and then makes some parting remarks. The school band plays "Pomp and Circumstance" again as the rest of my class files out along the aisle that's been cleared to the open stretch of the football field just beyond where the ceremony is being held.

Families follow suit, abandoning their seats to congratulate their children, grandchildren, siblings, nieces, nephews, neighbors.

My steps are shaky as I descend the stage's stairs, stunned it's suddenly over.

Gramps is waiting for me off to one side. He beams when he spots me, and I see the faint trail of some salty residue on his weathered cheeks when I draw closer.

"I'm so proud of you, Lennie," Gramps's smile is wide enough it threatens to overtake his whole face. "You were wonderful up there. Really wonderful."

"Thanks, Gramps," I whisper as he pulls me into a hug.

"Your mama would be so proud of you, darling," he continues. Salty tears burn my eyelids. Gramps rarely mentions Mom. Losing her still hurts us both. "Your pops, too," he adds, which is an even more selfless gesture.

Gramps never got along with my father. The only reason he

allowed him to come stay at Matthews Farm after Mom's death was for me.

I say nothing, just squeeze him a little tighter.

Gramps insists on taking me out for lunch to celebrate. When we return to the farm, he heads inside to watch the Jays play.

I hover on the front porch, still in my graduation dress, trying to figure out what to do with myself.

For the first time in a long time, I don't have anything I *have* to do. There's no school assignment. No tests to study for. The horses don't need to be brought in for another few hours. I don't start working at the *Landry Gazette* as a research assistant for another two weeks.

And there's nothing I *want* to do.

Dropping into one of the two rocking chairs, I kick off my shoes and rest my bare toes on the porch banister, staring out at the grazing horses.

The bright sun pulls out the distinctive blue shade Kentucky grass is known for, rolling off in the distance as far as the eye can see. I gaze at the serene sight and admit the truth to myself.

There is one thing I'd like to do right now. Or more accurately, one person I'd like to see. But I'm sure he's in the midst of the fancy graduation party his mother was planning the color scheme for months ago. And then he's leaving tomorrow.

I fall asleep at some point. Nerves kept me up most of last night, and the relief about having my speech over with is relaxing.

When my eyes blink open, it's dusk.

Gramps is talking to someone on the farmhouse's old rotary phone when I walk inside.

My room is a mess, evidence of my hasty departure this morning strewn everywhere. For having exactly one outfit option, I did an impressive job emptying most of my closet.

I change back into my usual jeans and T-shirt before heading out to the barn for the evening chores. Once the horses are fed and watered, I return to the house to help Gramps prepare dinner.

In the middle of eating, my phone begins to buzz.

Without looking at the screen, I know what the messages are going to be about. Much like the senior trip, the graduation night party is a Landry High legend. Only the graduates are allowed to attend, meaning there's just one chance to.

Since I ended up attending both the senior trip and prom—the two other rites of passage—I know Cassie is expecting me to go tonight.

There are several reasons I'm not sure if I should. I ended up being the only senior listed without a college in the graduation program. I'm also not sure what people made of my speech. And the main reason: seeing Caleb one final time before he leaves will be more than a little bittersweet.

Cassie ends up deciding for me. A long series of honks sounds outside as I'm washing the dishes. I know it's her even before I pull aside the curtain that covers the window.

"Go celebrate, Lennie," Gramps tells me, taking the plate I was washing. "I promise not to throw a rager while you're gone."

I roll my eyes as I head to the door to let Cassie in.

"Is that not what they're called?" he calls after me.

I'm grinning as I open the door. "Get in, we're—" Cassie stops talking. "What are you wearing?"

I glance down at my rattiest jeans. My navy sweatshirt has a smear of horse slobber across the chest. And there's a dollop of dish soap on my sleeve.

"Clothes?" I offer unhelpfully.

Cassie lets out an exasperated sigh, but her lips quirk as she steps over the threshold. "Howdy, Earl!" she calls as she passes the kitchen and heads upstairs.

She's never been inside the farmhouse before, but doesn't

have any trouble navigating her way into my bedroom. I follow, intrigued by what she thinks she's going to conjure up from my closet. All she's going to find is clean versions of what I'm wearing.

Based on the perplexed look on her face when I enter my bedroom, she's thinking the same. "No offense, but—"

"Funny how people only say *no offense* right before they're about to offend you."

Cassie laughs. "Fair. But is this your *whole* wardrobe? *All* of it?" She waves at my closet.

"Yeah. My clothing allowance is going toward feeding the horses, at the moment."

Cassie pauses flipping through my hangers and whirls around. "Lennon, I didn't mean—"

"It's fine," I assure her.

She bites her lip, then moves to the dresser and starts rummaging through drawers.

"Here." She tosses me a pair of faded jeans I hardly ever wear because they're too tight to ride in. "Put these on." A minute later, she holds up a V-neck T-shirt I'm not sure if I've ever worn. Definitely not since I got boobs, and I recall why when I pull the shirt over my head.

"Perfect," Cassie proclaims, with an approving nod.

I glance at my reflection in the mirror. Both the shirt and jeans are snugger than what I was wearing. But they're still cotton and denim, which I'm comfortable in.

I pull my hair out of its braid, say goodbye to Gramps, and then we're headed to Jake's house. Thanks to homeroom rumors, I know he hosts most of my classes' parties throughout high school. It makes sense he would have the honor of holding the final one.

The house is packed when we walk inside, which isn't all that shocking based on the number of cars outside and the level of noise.

Jake lives in a luxe development close to the high school. The interior is the opposite of where I live. No creaky floorboards or worn furniture or temperamental heating. Everything—the furniture and the appliances and the wallpaper—looks new and fancy.

As Cassie and I walk through the house, I'm surprised by how many people stop to talk to us. Both of us.

A few classmates bring up my speech, but most of the conversations are just idle chitchat. Pleasantries.

Endings have a way of bringing people together, I suppose.

Once we're in the kitchen, I head for the island covered with almost every drink imaginable. The temperature in the house is about twenty degrees warmer than outside, making me glad I decided against wearing a jacket. Or more like Cassie refused to let me bring one.

I reach for the stack of plastic cups, at the same time as another hand. When our fingers brush, a shock of electricity shoots up my arm.

I freeze; Caleb doesn't.

He grabs two cups and hands one to me.

"Thanks," I mutter.

"Stay away from the punch. It's full of all sorts of shit."

"Cal—" He's already walking away.

I end up with soda, although I'm definitely tempted by the bottles of alcohol. I could use some liquid courage.

Somehow, an evening I thought would drag starts to fly by. My unprecedented popularity lingers. I talk with people I've barely exchanged two words with since elementary school. I dance. I mingle with peers I now consider friends: Shannon, Tina, Eliza, Julie, Joe, Will, and Marcus. Even Andrew, for all our head-butting at the paper.

And I enjoy it all, because I don't have to worry about it ending and everything returning to what used to be normal.

Everything is ending anyway.

Eventually, the night winds down. The crowd thins and the music stops. I have no idea what time it is, but the exhaustion I'm experiencing assures me it's a lot later than I usually stay up.

Not that that's saying much.

Cassie is almost finished with her soda. She's close to being ready to leave, and that's terrifying.

Because there's one thing I need to do. One thing I can't *not* do. One thing I've put off until the last minute.

Until the last minute became now.

"You about ready to go?" Cassie asks me, yawning.

I'm so, so tempted to just nod. To run out of here. But the only thing that's scarier than doing this is living with the regret of *not* doing it.

"Yeah," I respond. "Just give me one minute."

I purposefully lost track of him earlier, but it's not hard to find him now. A usual crowd is nearby, hovering around the popular crowd like bees buzzing around honey.

Cassie follows my gaze, and hers turns knowing.

I don't enjoy being the center of attention. And I hate being the center of attention when I'm doing something that could completely backfire.

As I approach Caleb, people are already staring. If it involves Caleb, it attracts attention. And between his dare at the lake and our dance at prom, I'm sure there's some gossip about us.

But this isn't about anyone else. Over and over again, Caleb has put himself out there. In response, I've mostly been too shocked to really react.

I want him to know those moments mattered to me, though.

That *he* matters to me. Since words seem to fail me around him, I'm relying on actions.

He sees me coming. He's wearing a baseball cap, with the brim pulled low, and it shields most of his face. But I note how his shoulders tense when I push past Colt and enter their little circle. Probably a bad sign.

His voice is wary when he speaks, expecting I intend to stop and exchange syllables.

"Lenn—"

I don't give him a chance to finish saying my name.

I knock his cap upwards, and then I kiss him. *Really* kiss him. The way I would if we were alone, rather than surrounded by a crowd. The way he kissed me next to the campfire. And I pour everything I am into it. My hopes. My fears. My dreams.

Because somehow, when I wasn't paying attention, while I didn't know to stop it, Caleb Winters became all those things to me. Someone I hoped to see. Became afraid to lose. Dreamed about. He mixed with everything else that makes me Lennon Matthews, and is now so knotted with the rest of me I don't know how to untangle him.

I savor the soft friction of his lips against mine until I can't anymore.

Until the pleasure turns to pain.

Until I start to worry I might do something even stupider than kiss him. Like beg him to stay.

I pull away and look up into those hauntingly blue eyes, filled with heat and confusion.

"Don't get lost," I whisper, before I turn to walk away.

He grabs my arm before I take a step, spinning me back around to face him. Thankfully, he doesn't look mad about the kiss. "I'm coming back, Lennon. This isn't goodbye."

"Don't make promises you can't keep, Caleb."

"I'm not." Fierceness fills his expression. "I mean it."

I nod once, but I don't let myself believe it. "Goodbye, Winters."

He knows I don't believe him. It's obvious in the long, frustrated breath he blows out before he nods back. "See you, Matthews."

Cassie doesn't say much on the drive home. We're both tired after a long, draining day, and she knows me well enough by now to get that if I wanted to discuss what happened with Caleb, I would bring it up myself.

She parks in front of the farmhouse, and I'm surprised to see the porch light is on. Even more surprising, Gramps is sitting in one of the rocking chairs. He's usually asleep before me, which makes this about six hours past his usual bedtime. It's almost three.

I say goodbye to Cassie and climb out of the SUV, back into the humid night.

"You're up late, old man," I tease, climbing the rickety front steps and leaning against the porch baluster.

"You're out late, young lady," Gramps shoots back with a wink.

"Yeah... I guess so." I scuff the toe of my sneaker along some of the peeling paint coating the floorboards. "Had more people to say goodbye to than I realized."

More like it took me four hours to muster the courage to say goodbye to one.

"Ah," Gramps responds knowingly. He uses the arms of the old rocking chair to push himself upright, and then comes and stands next to me. The comforting weight of his arm settles across my shoulders. "People have a tendency to come back home, Lennie."

"Like birds?" I quip, trying to lighten the mood and lessen his worries. I know Gramps still feels guilty about college.

"Or baseball players," Gramps responds. "It's the whole point of the game, after all."

An unexpected lump appears in my throat as I look away from the sage, shrewd eyes that are the same hue as mine to survey the farm I've grown up on.

"We'll see," I reply softly.

"Good night, Lennie." Gramps hands me a pamphlet. It's the graduation program from the ceremony. "Thought you might want to take a look at that."

"I already did." Long enough to see I'm the only senior staying in Landry, at least.

"You saw where the Winters boy is going to school then?"

Reluctantly, I shake my head. I skipped over his name on purpose. Honestly, I'd rather not know. Then I can't picture him someplace else.

"You should look," Gramps tells me.

The door shuts behind him as he heads inside.

I stare out into the darkness for a minute, then sigh and open the program. Caleb's at the end of the list, since it's alphabetical.

Caleb Winters. Clarkson University.

I pull in a surprised breath.

Oakmont College is in California.

But Clarkson?

Clarkson is in Kentucky.

CHAPTER TWENTY-ONE

CALEB

The familiar green sign flashes neon in the light cast by the car's headlights. I'm surprised by the nostalgia the sight of it sparks.

Crossing into Landry, Kentucky at the start of the summer used to be an event I dreaded. Time spent away from my friends and baseball camp that would instead be filled with stuffy parties or at the racetrack.

I threw one hell of a fit when I found out we were moving here in time for me to start school at Landry High. But my father couldn't ignore my grandfather's health issues, and I didn't exactly have the option to stay behind alone at age fourteen.

Landry looks exactly the same.

There was a time when that would have bothered me; the way this tiny town in the middle of nowhere stands like a time capsule. So certain every other place on earth is envious of its timelessness. Its pedigree.

I used to think it was ridiculous. Who measures a state's importance by one tiny postage stamp in the heart of it? Turns out a lot of people do.

I lost track pretty quickly of the number of people at Clarkson who would ask eager questions after learning Landry is my adopted hometown, wondering what it was like to live in such a hallowed place.

I was half-tempted to tell them the truth: that Landry is small, and conceited, and doesn't live it up to the hype.

But something stopped me. *She* stopped me.

Because anywhere Lennon Matthews lives can't be any of those things.

I climb out of the car to type in the code at the front gate of my family's estate. The imposing metal doors open slowly, revealing the long, curving drive that winds through the property.

The house is dark and quiet when I park in front. My father's gone, like usual. My mother won't be back for a couple more days. I might have told her my exams ended two days later than they actually did.

It's close to ten, but I head straight for the kitchen when I enter the house. I didn't have time to eat dinner after my last exam, and I'm starving now.

I pull out my phone to call Colt as I eat the turkey sandwich I hastily threw together.

"Winters! Wassup?" he answers.

"You free tonight? I just got back."

"Wait, back as in *here*? You're in Landry?"

"Yeah," I reply. "Are you free, or what?"

"Uh, yeah, sure. I'm at Jake's. Come on over." There's a strange, almost uncomfortable note in Colt's voice. Someone starts talking in the background before he hangs up.

I change into clothes that don't smell like fast food and recycled air, then head back out to my truck.

I'm not surprised to see there are at least five cars in the driveway when I reach Jake's. His house was always the de facto gathering place in high school. Mainly due to the fact he's the kind of guy who's universally liked with the added benefit of his house being only a couple of blocks from the high school.

Unlike me, Jake doesn't live on a massive estate. His parents' house is part of a gated community of residents who appreciate the elite status of Landry's zip code but aren't interested in dealing with the hassle of participating in the horse industry.

I park and walk up the front path.

The front door's unlocked, so I don't bother knocking, just stroll inside like I've done many times before.

"Winters!" Jake calls when I enter the kitchen, drawing the attention of the dozen or so other people huddled around the kitchen island. "What are you doing here?"

"Great to see you too, Barnes," I say dryly, walking over to the fridge and helping myself to a bottle of beer.

Friendships shift in college, I guess. I've spent the last several months making new friends and practicing with new teammates. But I didn't think things would be weird with Colt, Luke, and Jake. They were my best friends basically from my first day in Landry.

Jake ambles over to my side. "You said you wouldn't be back for a couple more days."

I open the beer and take a long pull. "You sound like Colt. Didn't know you guys were so interested in my travel plans. I'll send you both an updated itinerary next time."

I look past Jake at the rest of the kitchen. There are more people here than I initially realized. Far more than the number of cars out front indicated.

"You're the one who showed up at my house out of nowhere." Jake's trademark easygoing grin appears, but there's that same undercurrent of *something* in his voice that was in Colt's on the phone earlier.

I return my attention to Jake and narrow my eyes at him as I take a sip of the cold beer. "I called Colt and told him I was coming."

"Hey, you made it." Colt appears in the kitchen and gives my shoulder a punch in greeting.

"Hey," I reply. "Jake was just about to tell me why the two of you are acting so weird." I raise my eyebrows and glance between the two of them.

Jake rolls his eyes. "Luke!"

The fourth member of our crew pokes his head into the kitchen. "Wassup?" Then his gaze lands on me. "Winters!" He bounds over to bump fists.

I would be much more pleased to see my three best friends for the first time since August if I wasn't becoming increasingly aware there seems to be something they were all keeping from me. "Hey, man. Are you going to explain why these two are acting so strange?"

Luke glances between Colt and Jake, looking lost.

"We were thinking Winters might like a heads-up about the guest you invited," Colt finally prompts.

Luke sucks in an audible breath. "Oh shit, yeah." He turns to me. "Uh, yeah, so I ran into Cassie Belmont over Thanksgiving break," he says.

The words are innocuous enough, but then he glances at Colt, then Jake, making me think they actually aren't.

"Cassie Belmont," I repeat, trying to figure out why that name sounds so familiar. And then it clicks. "Cassie. She moved here senior year."

"Yeah, so, she seemed interested, so we hung out over Thanksgiving a bit. She's friends with…they came over here one night. Both of them."

I take another sip of beer, trying to act casual.

Probably too casual. Everyone in the kitchen is paying attention to us, likely wondering why we're huddled next to the fridge.

I should shrug and put them all at ease. Reassure them I'm not bothered. But I'm too curious. I can only hold the words back for so long.

"You saw her?"

Jake doesn't bother to hide his smirk. I'm pretty sure he figured out I had a thing for Lennon before I did.

"Uh, yeah." Luke replies.

"And you didn't tell me?" There's a dangerous note in my voice, and I know Luke hears it.

I'm fairly certain I hear Jake mutter "wonder why," but I'm too busy waiting for Luke's response to pay attention to Jake's sarcasm.

"She didn't stay long," Luke replies.

"Did you talk to her?" I press, eager for more information.

I'm well aware I'm sounding a little more pathetic with each question. I also know I'm going to visit Matthews Farm at some point during this trip home. Might as well be as prepared as possible.

"Uh, no. She spent most of the time talking to Masterson, actually."

I say nothing, even as my chest tightens. She wasn't interested in him before. Has six months changed that?

"She wasn't flirting back," Colt tells me.

It's embarrassing—but convenient—that he can read me so well. Colt's a straight shooter. He wouldn't say that if he didn't mean it.

"Okay," I respond. Acknowledging I care.

Which isn't a surprise to any of my best friends.

They all know Lennon is a touchy subject, so they tend to avoid it. Jake and Colt telling Luke to mention it makes no sense.

"Wait...why are you telling me this now?" Luke glances at Colt, and that's when I realize. "You invited Cassie again tonight."

Luke nods.

"And you think Lennon will come too."

Another nod.

I take a longer sip of beer. Luke, Colt, and Jake all study my expression, but I know it's not giving anything away.

I'm good at hiding my true feelings. Very good. *To succeed in life, always know what others want*, my grandfather would tell me. *And never let them know what you really want.*

It's usually easy to tell what people want.

Except for Lennon.

I could never tell what she wanted. And ironically, she never seemed to believe *I* wanted *her*.

Seeing her tonight shouldn't matter to me. I know I'm acting nonchalant, but I can't convince myself I actually am.

I don't ordinarily need to feign being confident. I just am. I know what to say, how to act. But something about Lennon Matthews has always disarmed that ease.

"Fine. Whatever," I finally say, because they're all waiting for me to say *something*.

Jake rolls his eyes, but that's the end of the discussion as far as the rest of us are concerned. Luke and Colt start asking me questions about college ball, and Jake jumps in eventually. Our group expands as other friends and old teammates join the huddle.

I move into the living room when the kitchen gets too crowded. It reveals a whole new wave of people wanting to talk to me. I've been mostly silent on social media for the past few months, and everyone wants to catch up now that I'm back in Landry. There are lots of inquiries about baseball from the guys.

Lots of not-so-subtle inquiries regarding my relationship status from the girls.

I'm talking to Brett Michaels when I see her.

Lennon Matthews appears in the doorway, and I forget where I am. Forget my own name. A pickup truck could drive into this living room right now, and I'd still be focused only on her.

She's cut her hair since graduation. The light brown strands only fall a few inches past her shoulders now. She's wearing a pink fleece and jeans. Most of the girls here are in tank tops. A few are even wearing dresses or skirts, despite the December weather. Lennon's outfit heats my blood in a way the bare skin doesn't manage to.

Her mouth is curved into a subtle grimace as she scans the people scattered about the living room, her freckled nose slightly wrinkled. It's fairly obvious she's not here of her own volition. She whispers something to a blonde girl I recognize as Cassie Belmont, who giggles in response.

Then Lennon spots me. And she freezes.

Relief hits me like a wave. Because if she didn't care, if she were totally over me, Lennon wouldn't be looking at me like I'm a ghost.

Seconds suspend in time as we stare at each other. There's no music on, and I don't think it's my imagination that the room around us quiets, exacerbating the fact that neither of us are saying anything.

People pay attention to me. And to Lennon, even if it's for reasons she hates. Add in the fact we argued throughout high school then ended senior year with a series of private moments in public, and I'd guarantee there's still gossip circulating town about us.

I don't move any closer to her. Don't say anything.

It's childish, but I want Lennon to be the one to speak first.

Her poker face is almost as good as mine, but her words give a lot away. I could really use that insight right now.

So, of course she doesn't give it to me.

She stays silent and still. Cassie is a bit slow to realize what's caught Lennon's attention. Once she sees me, she glances between me and Lennon with wide eyes.

I watch her whisper something to Lennon I'd bet my trust fund is an offer to leave. When Lennon shakes her head, I'm certain I'm right.

She wouldn't risk me, or anyone else, thinking I'd run her off.

Jake appears in the doorway behind Cassie and Lennon. "Drinks are this way, ladies." He takes on the role of host and ushers them toward the doorway that leads to the kitchen. Toward where I'm standing with Brett.

Luke and Colt choose this moment to exit the kitchen. I'm a bit suspicious about the timing. They find my awkwardness around Lennon hilarious.

"Surprised to see you here, Lennon," Luke calls out as he approaches.

It's a practiced move. Talk to the friend, or girl, you're not interested in, so you can see how the one you are interested in reacts. Cassie doesn't appear affected by his lack of attention, but I don't think Luke cares either way.

This time he's not trying to bait Cassie.

He's trying to bait me.

Lennon ignores him and addresses me instead. I'd be lying if I said that didn't give me a secret thrill. "You're back."

"What tipped you off?" I tease her for stating the obvious, and I'm rewarded by the sight of a slight flush in her cheeks.

I don't know what else to say, though. Don't know how to broach into any of the heavier topics dangling between us. The last time I saw her, she kissed me and then walked away.

"The kitchen is just through here," Jake says, cutting into the silence that's fallen.

Lennon heads in the direction of the kitchen without saying anything else to me, with Cassie right behind her.

I drain the end of my beer. "I'm going to the bathroom." I stalk down the hallway to the restroom. Miraculously, there's no line.

After I wash my hands, I stare at myself in the mirror for a minute. Six months, and she still affects me. Maybe I'll never get over her.

With an impatient sigh, I shove away from the sink and leave the bathroom to head back down the hallway.

Even more people have arrived in my absence. I have to maneuver my way through them to reach the kitchen for another beer. I finished my first, but that's not why I'm in here. I'm looking for Lennon. And she's standing by the sink. Talking to Ryan James, of all people.

I grab another bottle of beer and slam the fridge door shut harder than necessary. My gaze stays fixed on nothing but the condensation dripping down the side of the brown glass as I head back into the living room, taking a seat on the couch to the right of the fireplace. After a couple minutes of solitude, Colt makes his way over.

He sinks down beside me. "Reunion not all you were hoping for?"

"I don't know what you're talking about," I lie, taking a long swig of beer.

"We can skip past this shit, Winters. It's pretty fucking obvious how you feel about her."

"Whatever," I mutter, drinking more beer.

"You planning to do anything about it?"

I make a purposefully unintelligible sound, and Colt sighs

before standing and leaving the living room.

It only takes a few seconds for Poppy Tisdale to fill his empty seat. She asks me a few questions about college, and then launches into a long description of the sorority she joined, clearly thrilled to have what appears to be my undivided attention.

I'm paying attention, but I'm definitely not focused on her. Especially once Robin Jones joins us on the small couch and jabbers away about her own sorority experience.

But I sure act focused on them when Lennon enters the room. I'm not proud of it. But my pride is still smarting from watching her in the kitchen with Ryan, and it's a hell of a lot easier to pretend I'm listening to what Poppy and Robin are saying than facing why it bothered me so much.

By the time I finish my third beer, which Robin helpfully provides, I'm feeling pretty damn good. The turkey sandwich I wolfed down is no longer absorbing much alcohol, if any, and I've hit that sweet spot where colors seem a little brighter and jokes a little funnier, before the world turns hazy and anything anyone says sounds amusing.

The crowd around me has grown, hanging on to my every word as I describe the slip and slide set up during the first week of classes for the entire baseball team.

About halfway through my story, Jake appears. "Caleb, I need to talk to you. Right now."

His serious tone is enough to capture my attention, but his use of my first name ensures it.

I stand up immediately and follow Jake into the front hallway. "What's going on?" I ask urgently.

"Not here," he replies, veering to the right. Jake slides open a glass door, and steps out onto the back deck that overlooks the expansive backyard. There's about ten people standing on it, and several more standing on the patio that melds into the covered pool.

"What is it?"

"I need one more person for pickup," Jake responds.

I stare at him for a minute, slowly registering there's no serious problem. "You're joking."

"Nope." His serious exterior falls away. "Come on, Winters," he pleads. "Your fan club will still be around later."

"This doesn't have anything to do with my fan club," I reply. "I took a three-hour exam this morning and then drove for a few hours. I don't want to play baseball right now."

"Excuse me," a familiar voice says. "You're blocking the door."

I keep my gaze straight ahead, but know the grin spreading across Jake's face means he's recognized the voice as well. "Lennon!" He turns to face her. "Any interest in a ball game?"

"You just said there was only one spot," I point out.

"You just said you weren't going to play," Jake replies.

Lennon ignores our side commentary. "I'll pass," she replies. "I was just leaving."

"Bummer," Jake responds. "I thought you liked party games. Or was it only Truth or Dare?"

I send him a warning glare for that comment, but Lennon beats me to a verbal response. "I'm sure you can convince Caleb to play. Although he doesn't seem to be very *daring* tonight."

I forget about Jake, my attention immediately snapping to her. "What is *that* supposed to mean?"

Lennon shrugs, sending me an infuriatingly serene smile. "Awfully easy to just sit on the couch and get fawned over all night."

"Jealous, Matthews?"

"You wish, Winters," she scoffs.

I do. I'd love to know she cares.

"I should have known that's exactly how you'd act," she continues. "Enjoying the attention."

"Well, we can't all be like you, Lennon. Not needing anything. Or *anyone*." Yeah...that was the wrong thing to say. Lennon's expression hardens into a glare.

"Come on, Winters. Let's just head to the field. We can't play without you." I'm fairly certain Jake is regretting lulling me out here under false pretenses by this point.

"Maybe I didn't want to need someone who was about to leave for who knows how long," Lennon retorts, ignoring Jake.

"Yeah, how dare I go to college," I snap.

Lennon breaks eye contact with me and looks at Jake. "Actually, I will play."

I know Jake's serious expression isn't faked this time. He looks to me, panicked, and I know Lennon catches it. She snorts and strides back inside the house.

"Fuck," I curse. "Let's go."

The couple dozen guys Jake already drafted for the game are waiting on the lawn to head over to the field, but once it becomes clear I'm playing, the house pretty much empties out.

It's only a five-minute walk to the high school, and I'm hit with another powerful wave of nostalgia when we arrive at the baseball field.

I haven't been back to Landry High since graduation. The sight of the brick building brings back a lot of memories. Not all of them involving baseball.

Jake designates himself one captain, and I'm offered up as the other. I pick Colt first; Jake picks Luke.

Almost everyone from Luke's house made the trek over to the field, meaning the pool of prospects has grown with the number of spectators. Jake gives me five chances before he picks Lennon.

I'm sure that's her preference, and I've already experienced enough rejection from Lennon Matthews.

We grab equipment from the shed tucked between the bleachers and the school, and then the game begins. My team takes the field first, and I'm automatically designated as pitcher.

It's strange, stepping on to the mound I've spent so much time atop. Like coming home, only to realize it's a place I've outgrown.

Robin Jones is the first one up at bat for the opposing team, her eyes as wide and inviting as they were on the couch. "I just swing and hit it, right?" she calls to me.

I nod, chewing on the inside of my cheek to hide the smirk that wants to form when I see Lennon roll her eyes.

Robin swings, but she doesn't hit the ball I send flying her way. Colt is playing catcher, and I know he's capable of handling anything I throw at him.

They're nowhere near what my arm is capable of, but I lob two more pitches fast enough I know Robin won't be capable of connecting with them. She flashes me a disappointed yet sultry smile before handing over the bat to Ryan James.

Normally, I'm ambivalent toward Ryan. I've sometimes gotten the sense he's envious of me. But this time is different. *I'm* jealous of *him*. I'm not about to pass up the opportunity to make him look like a fool after watching him chat Lennon up in the kitchen like they're old friends.

The first pitch I throw isn't quite my top gear, but it's close. Much closer than a late-night pickup game warrants. Colt notices, raising one eyebrow before tossing the baseball back to me.

Ryan swung two seconds too late on the first throw. I can tell he's a bit wary of my next pitch based on the way he takes his time setting up his stance. He's a decent athlete, but I'm better. And we're playing *my* game.

Rather than pitch another fastball, I send the curveball I spent junior year perfecting over home plate. Ryan's reaction is faster this time, but his angle is wrong. The ball whizzes past the bat and lands in Colt's glove with a satisfying smack. The most beautiful sound in the world.

Ryan's angry now. It's obvious to me. And it's obvious to everyone else watching. I allow myself a small grin behind the shield of my glove before I toss another fastball his way. Not my top speed, but almost. And more than enough power to ensure he doesn't have a chance to connect.

"Guess you did earn that scholarship, Winters," Ryan spits out.

I don't reply to him, because I'm preoccupied by the fact that he's handing the bat to Lennon. *Shit.* I was hoping two straight outs would push this back one inning. Maybe two. Maybe never, if we grew a commanding enough lead, which I'm certain we will. No one here is going to be able to hit off me.

Right now, I'm quite annoyed with Lennon Matthews. But I still experience a rush of pride as she moves to stand at home plate. Because she adopts a stance identical to the one I taught her during our baseball lessons senior year.

Once again, I'm grateful for the cover my glove provides. I don't have a lot of time to decide how I'm going to play this.

People paid close attention to me striking out Ryan, but it was nothing compared to the scrutiny I can feel on me now. This is primetime entertainment.

The longer I hesitate, the worse it will get.

I'm irritated with Lennon, but I can't make myself throw the ball much harder than a gentle toss. It's a throw Ryan would have knocked a couple hundred yards. That Robin probably would have at least made contact with. Lennon comes close, but she doesn't tap the baseball. Her hazel eyes narrow at me, as she realized I took it easy on her.

Colt tosses the baseball back into my glove.

I know I could hurl it whizzing past Lennon before she even batted an eye. But I can't do it. I want her to have a chance to hit it.

So I lob her another softball, one she doesn't even attempt to hit. "Are you fucking kidding me, Winters?" she yells, loud enough for every outfielder to hear.

Anyone who wasn't already paying attention to us sure as hell is now.

"I could ask you the same thing," I call back. "You can't hit the ball if you don't even bother swinging, Matthews."

"I can't hit a ball that takes ten minutes to reach home plate, either," Lennon retorts.

"Here, let me help." Ryan steps forward and crowds next to Lennon. He whispers something to her as I grind my teeth. She doesn't encourage him, but she sure doesn't push him away either.

Fuck it.

I throw the third strike as soon as she looks at me, poised to hit the ball. But unlike the last two, she doesn't have a prayer of doing so. I don't check my speed or force; all I bother to do is ensure the ball is as far away from her as possible while remaining in the pocket.

The sound of leather hitting leather resonates around the field. I give Colt an apologetic look. Even with the glove, I doubt his hand is feeling too great right now. That was at least ninety-five. Maybe a hundred.

Lennon looks stunned.

She asked for it, but I don't think she expected for me to deliver.

I drop my glove on the mound for the next pitcher, then walk toward the dugout. I skirt the edge of the field, so I don't encounter anyone on the other team.

"I'm going to have a bruise tomorrow," Colt mutters to me, shaking his right hand.

"Sorry. Didn't mean to throw that hard."

"Yeah, you did."

I don't deny it as our first batter heads to hit Jake's pitch.

The game proceeds, but it's lopsided. The teams are pretty evenly matched, aside from me. No one on the opposing team can hit a single ball I throw, not even Luke or Jake, which means we score run after run, while the other team can't manage one.

Luke has had his fill after three innings. "Let Adams pitch, Winters!"

Normally, I would resist being replaced. But right now? I could not care less.

I lost my pleasant buzz a while ago, and most of the people watching and playing are oblivious to the fact I'm throwing pitches that college players would have a hard time hitting. It's the only outlet I have for my anger at the moment.

"Fine." I stride toward home plate, barely pausing to toss the baseball to Colt as we switch places.

"Matthews! You're up," Jake yells.

She's not. Robin Jones is next in the batting order. I glance over at Jake. He grins at me. I don't know whether to be grateful or pissed about his interference.

Lennon's long, denim-clad legs approach me, and I promptly forget about Jake's meddling.

She's close to me. Really close. Closer than we've been for six months. She realizes it, too. Lennon's lips are a terse line and her shoulders are tensed.

She misses Colt's first two pitches, the second of which is an obvious ball. I call it, and he rolls his eyes.

Lennon readjusts her position, and I can't help myself. "Drop your right shoulder."

She does, along with her left. So she can lower the bat and glare at me. "You're giving me pointers?"

"You didn't seem to mind last time." Lennon's cheeks are pink, but I'm not sure if it's in response to the cold or my comment. It's just occurring to me, now that the alcohol and adrenaline are wearing off, that it's fairly chilly out.

"Speak for yourself," she responds.

"Fine. I didn't mind giving you pointers last time." I stand, abandoning my position so I can move behind her. I shift slowly, giving her time to move away if she wants to.

She doesn't, and it prompts a powerful flash of déjà vu as I adjust her grip on the bat and then reluctantly step away.

It's the first time I've ever been happy to see an opposing player hit the ball, and I don't hide the stupid grin on my face watching her jog to first base.

Despite the other team managing to hit some of Colt's pitches, the game winds down pretty quickly after that.

It's getting late. I don't know exactly what time, but I fight back a yawn as I massage my right shoulder. I'm going to feel those pitches tomorrow.

People depart in waves, but Lennon's not one of them. She leans against one of the posts of the dugout, not even pretending to talk to anyone.

I help Jake return the baseballs, bats, and gloves back to the equipment shed before returning to the field. It's almost empty now; just a few stragglers still here.

Mostly my friends. And hers. None of them are oblivious to

social cues, so they disappear quickly once it becomes clear we're both waiting on purpose.

Even once we're alone, she still doesn't say anything.

"It's nice to see you," I finally state. Lame, but true. And what I should have led with, as soon as she arrived at Jake's. "How are you?"

"I'm in love with you." Her response is matter-of-fact.

I experience a little sympathy for how Lennon must have felt when I dropped the same declaration on her. I know I surprised her then, but *surprised* doesn't really cover how I'm feeling right now.

It takes me at least a minute to regain the ability to speak. Once I do, I say the first thing that pops into my head. "Absence really does make the heart grow fonder, huh?"

"I felt this way before you left, Caleb." Another shocker.

"You did?"

Lennon nods, then bites her bottom lip. "I know you said you were going to come back. I believed that you believed that. But…" *She* didn't believe I was coming back. It's so apparent, the words might as well be written across her face. "You lived here for four years, Caleb. Your grandfather is gone. Your parents are hardly ever here. You don't even like horses! There's nothing pulling you back here."

"There's you."

"I thought you'd meet lots of girls and that anything you felt for me wouldn't matter for very long. I don't have the best track record of people choosing to stick around. And, you're *Caleb Winters*. You have everything going for you. I was scared to find out what it would be like to compete against all that."

"And all that's changed? Just because I came home for winter break like I thought you knew I would all along?"

"No," she says softly, shaking her head. "*Nothing* has

248

changed. That's the problem. I thought your feelings would go away. And…I thought mine would too. I thought I'd be busy enough with everything here—that it would be a relief when you were gone. But not telling you how I felt and doing nothing about it…didn't make any difference. So, I figured I would at least be honest with you, since you were always honest with me."

"What are you saying, Lennon?"

She looks away, out at the field. "Nothing's changed, Caleb. Landry is my home. I have Gramps and the farm. I don't know if —or when—I'll ever leave. And you have this whole other life now." Her gaze meets mine again. "I mean, I don't even know if you're single."

"I wouldn't have flirted with you earlier if I wasn't single, Lennon."

"There wasn't a single time tonight I thought you were flirting with me, Caleb." There's a clear challenge in her expression, revealing a glimpse of the girl who kept me on my toes for four years.

I can't help it; I laugh. "Oh, really?" I take a step closer to her.

"Really," she confirms, pushing away from the post.

One more step, and she's inches away. "I'm going to kiss you," I tell her. "But you have to agree to something first."

"I don't think Ryan would make any demands—"

"Don't be a smart-ass," I inform her grinning face. She obviously noticed my jealous behavior earlier. "You have to agree to give me a chance. Give *us* a chance."

"And then what?" Lennon asks.

I shrug. "I don't know. I don't have all the answers. But I want to try, Lennon. That's all I've ever wanted from you: a chance."

She searches my face, giving no indication of what she's thinking on her own. "Okay," she finally says.

I'm not expecting the rush.

It's a release, like finally letting out a breath I didn't realize I was holding. Reaching the end of a journey when I thought I still had a long trek ahead.

I kiss her, and I forget we're standing on a high school baseball field in the small, snooty town I used to dread visiting.

Lennon kisses me back, alongside the patch of grass I spent most of high school on, and for the first time, Landry feels like home.

CHAPTER TWENTY-TWO

CALEB

Three Years Later

"Hey, Caleb."

I glance up from the bucket of baseballs, already knowing exactly what I'll see. Sophie St. James is leaning against the chain link fence. Either her practice must have just ended or she stayed late like I did, because she's wearing a spandex tank top and soccer shorts.

"Hey." I straighten and swipe my forehead with my arm, brushing away the sweat that's collected there before tugging the brim of my hat back down.

"Why am I not surprised you're the last one out here?"

"Probably because I always am." I shoot her a small smile before uncapping my water bottle and taking a long pull. The ice in it has long since melted, drops of condensation all that remains. They fall to the dirt as I set my water back on the bench, forming tiny puddles.

"Came to see if you want to get dinner later. There's some Mexican place downtown that just opened."

"I'm good, thanks."

"Come on." Sophie leans over the fence, offering up a prime view of her cleavage. I quickly look down at the bucket, grabbing a ball and rubbing my thumb along the red laces. "You've been out here all day. Carrie and Lexi are coming. And Brian said he'd round up a bunch of the guys."

"Of course he did." I shake my head. In the three weeks I've known Brian, I've learned he is physically incapable of turning down a drink. Or a hot girl. "We only have five days left."

"*Exactly*. Summer is almost over. Have a little fun, Caleb."

I toss the ball in the air and catch it. "Fine. I'll be there."

"Yay! Okay, I'll see you later." Sophie smiles, then jogs off toward the cabins.

I pick up the bucket before trudging back out to the mound. Even Zach is gone. He begged off an hour ago, leaving me without a catcher.

That's fine. I don't need one.

Baseball is a team sport. But this little patch of earth in the center of the diamond can often feel like an island. And I'm marooned with the responsibility of controlling the score of the game.

I raise my leg and draw my hands into my chest, preparing to pitch. My arms follow my stride as I push off from the mount and let the ball fly. It's a perfect strike, rattling the chain of the back-stop with its force.

I keep practicing until the sun starts to sink, finally providing some relief after a sweltering day. I clean up all the equipment and then head toward the cabins.

When I enter mine, the three guys I'm bunking with are all

lounging around in the air conditioning. Hugh is sprawled out on the couch, sipping a beer.

Brian looks up first. "Tell me you're not just getting back from the field, Winters."

"I'm not just getting back from the field."

Brian swears, then shakes his head. "Man, you're a machine."

"Isn't your arm dead?" my fourth roommate, Charlie, asks.

I flex my shoulder. "Nah. It feels good. I'll ice it, after I shower."

"Hurry up. We're headed to dinner soon." Brian straightens and stretches. "Sophie told you, right?"

"Yeah, she told me."

"I'll bet she did."

I roll my eyes, then head into the bathroom to shower.

Brian basically shoves me out of the door as soon as I'm ready, eager to get going. My stomach grumbles as we drive along the long road that leads to downtown.

Mayfair is considered the best baseball camp in the country. It's located on a huge complex that hosts a bunch of other training programs, including football and soccer. The only upside of the relentless heat is that Kentucky feels cooler by comparison.

The downtown section is larger than I expected the first time I came here, the summer before starting college. It's supported by a nearby college in the colder months, and by the hundreds of athletes that attend Mayfair camps in the summer. Lots of new places pop up regularly, like the Mexican place we're headed to tonight.

My stomach grumbles as soon as we walk inside the restaurant. I haven't eaten since lunch, and burned a few hundred calories since. I'm starving.

Sophie is already sitting with a large group in one of the corner booths.

A loud cheer goes up when they spot us. Brian has the big personality that makes him the life of the party. And, as conceited as it sounds, I've always been popular without trying. I used to think it was my last name. But no one here aside from Sophie associates it with anything but the season. So I guess some of it is just…me.

I end up wedged between Brian and Hugh. At least arriving last means we're at one end of the circular table, but it's still a tight fit. There are already pitchers of margarita on the table. I ignore the cocktails and fill a plate with chips and salsa instead.

"You guys were outside all day?" Joel Maguire asks Brian. He's here for football, not baseball.

Brian groans dramatically. "Yeah. You?"

"Nah, we lifted weights inside for a while."

"Lucky." Hugh grumbles to my left.

The waitress appears to take our orders. I glance over the menu, deciding on a chicken burrito. After enough ribbing from Brian, I order a beer too. He means well, but he doesn't love base-ball. Not the way I do. He—and most of the other guys I've played with—leave the game on the field. I've never been able to do that.

My phone buzzes in my pocket. My mom and Lennon are the only two people who call instead of text, and my mom is in Paris right now. It's the middle of the night there.

I elbow Brian, who's blocking me in. "Move."

He sighs, dramatically. "We just got here."

"Lennon is calling. I mean it, man. Move."

"She is? Let me say hi."

It took one phone call for Lennon to charm my three room-mates with her sarcasm and lack of baseball knowledge. Charlie answered my phone one time when I was in the bathroom, and it got passed around the guys. Brian hasn't shut up about talking to her again since.

"No. Get your own girlfriend."

"Wouldn't be fair to all the ladies who want some of this." Brian gestures to himself.

I pretend to vomit as my phone continues to buzz. I'm worried the call is going to go to voicemail, so I pull it out of my pocket and answer. "Hey. Hold on, Brian is being…himself."

"Hey!" Brian protests, as I forcibly shove him out of the booth. I've got a few inches and several pounds of muscle on him.

The front of the restaurant is crowded with people waiting for tables, and the music is loud. So I head back out into the heat, crossing the street and sitting at a bench in front of the local library.

"Sorry about that."

"It's why I keep calling you. I never know what to expect."

I laugh, running a hand through my hair and wishing it wasn't still so damn warm out. "That's the reason, huh?"

"I guess it helps that you're hot, too."

I sweat off the sunscreen, no matter how many times I reapply. My cheeks hurt when I smile, but I do it anyway. "At least you can admit it without freaking out, now."

"I didn't *freak out*, that's a massive exaggeration."

Sometimes, Lennon and I feel a long ways from who we used to be in high school. But there are also times I miss it, when Lennon sitting across from me with peanut butter and a scowl on her face doesn't feel that long ago.

"Whatever you say, Matthews."

"I ran into Colt yesterday."

I lean back against the bench. "Oh, yeah?"

"Yeah. He has *big* plans for Saturday."

"I'm sure he does. Jake's influence, probably."

"He said to answer his texts."

"I've been busy."

"He said you'd say that, too."

I huff a laugh. "His family has a place on Palsky Lake. He wants to go up there, after his party, and stay a couple of nights."

"That sounds fun."

Long-distance relationships are hard. But by far the worst part about being in a long-distance relationship with Lennon is she's hard to read. I have a difficult enough time telling what she's thinking in person. Over the phone, it's almost impossible.

"I don't have to go."

"He's one of your best friends, Caleb."

"Yeah, so he'll understand if I don't go."

"You've been gone most of the summer."

"Exactly. I miss you, Lennon."

"I miss you too. But you can still—"

"Will you come with me?" The question spills out without thinking.

"To Colt's family's lake house?"

"Yeah. It'll be fun."

"I can't leave Gramps."

"Yes, you can!" I hear called in the background. I smile automatically. Earl Matthews is one of my favorite people on the planet, and not only because I'm in love with his granddaughter.

"I thought you were asleep, Gramps. Stop eavesdropping!"

There's some rustling in the background that makes me think Lennon moved to a different part of the farmhouse. "You were saying?" I tease.

"Miraculous, how his hearing is perfect when I'm on the phone with you but the baseball games have to be blasting for him to follow the innings."

"Did he watch the Jays game last night?"

"Did you forget who you're talking to?"

I snort, then sober. "I know you worry about him. But it's only two nights, Len. You. Me. Our own room…"

My attraction toward Lennon has never just been physical. Even when I met her as a hormone-filled fourteen-year-old, I was just as interested in talking to her as I was in anything physical. But I miss sex. Brian sneaks a different girl into our cabin most nights.

"Isn't it supposed to be a guys' trip?"

"They'll all prefer if you're there. Trust me."

"Okay. I'll talk to Gramps."

Just like that, my mood soars.

We talk for a few more minutes, catching up on each other's days. I'm tempted to ask Lennon if she's heard back from Clarkson. But she doesn't mention it, so I don't bring it up. We've made it two and a half years attending different schools. I have no doubts we'll make it through another.

As soon as I step back inside the restaurant, I hear my name called. Sophie is standing at the bar, waving me over. "They're slammed, so I came over here to get the next round," she explains when I reach her.

"Did the food arrive?" I ask, glancing at our table. "I'm starving."

Sophie doesn't answer. She steps closer, bringing the smell of lime and tequila with her. "I'm really glad you came tonight, Caleb."

I step away, some of the relaxation following my call with Lennon evaporating. "This is getting old. I have a girlfriend, Sophie."

She licks some salt off the rim of her margarita. "I was so excited when my parents said you'd committed to Clarkson, you know. You were pissed about moving to Landry. Figured you'd never look back at that town, once you left for college."

"Things change."

"My parents expect us to get married. *Your* parents expect us to get married."

I don't react.

"Yeah." Sophie exhales. "I figured that wouldn't happen when every girl on campus—including me—threw herself at you and you didn't look twice at anyone. Even when you *were* single."

"You'll meet someone special, Sophie, and it'll make sense."

Sophie scoffs and sips her drink. "I hope she knows how lucky she is."

I grin. "I think she's more resigned to being stuck with me at this point."

As soon as she agreed to try, I pursued Lennon with a tenacity I'd only ever applied to baseball. For weeks, I called her every night at seven p.m. sharp. Every free weekend, I drove back to Landry. She told me she was scared of not being a priority, and I was hell-bent on proving her wrong. Still am, honestly. Part of the reason I've been the last player to leave the field each day is that I'm not going to do any training once I'm back in Landry. My plan is to do nothing but spend time with Lennon until I have to leave for Clarkson and start senior year.

Sophie shakes her head. "I was sure you'd turn into some massive player. People cheat, Caleb. They fight and change and get bored. You know that as well as I do."

"We're not our parents." Mr. and Mrs. St. James's marriage is about as happy as my parents' is. That is to say, not at all. Maybe why they're all such good friends.

"Not yet," Sophie predicts darkly.

"You're drunk."

"Yep." She smiles and takes another sip of margarita. "You should have tried one. They're good."

"No, thanks."

"Should I hook up with Travis or Carter tonight, do you think?"

I roll my eyes. "No comment."

Sophie huffs. "So, when did you know?"

"Know what?"

"That you loved Lennon."

I sigh. "Sophie…"

"I'm being serious!" she insists. "You're the only guy I know in a long-term relationship. The only guy I know who *wants* to be in a long-term relationship."

When I look over, her expression is earnest. Like me, Sophie grew up with a terrible model for romantic relationships. Maybe she really is curious. Maybe this will finally end her flirting. I'm not sure her interest even has all that much to do with me. Sophie just likes a challenge.

"I don't know when I was sure I loved her. My feelings just grew and grew to a point when I knew I did. But I knew I *could* love her the first time we met. Something about her just…stuck. Remember that telescope I got in seventh grade?"

She slaps a hand on the counter. "God, yes! I forgot how much of a nerd you were when you got hot."

I snort. "*Anyway*, it was kind of like that. My life was like a constellation I'd memorized. I knew where everything was, what everything looked like. Had the whole path memorized. High school, then college, then pros. And Lennon was like a shooting star, dimming everything else. Impossible to ignore. She changed the way everything else looked. There was suddenly a before I knew her, and an after." I shrug. "Like I said, you'll get it one day."

"A guy who describes me as a shooting star? I'm more likely to discover a unicorn." She scowls.

I laugh and shake my head. "Do you need help with the drinks?"

"No. It was mostly a ploy to get you over here and see if you guys broke up just now?"

I stare at her, brow raised. "I know, I know. She's an eclipse. I got it. Food arrived a while ago, you should go eat."

I nod, then head for the table.

CHAPTER TWENTY-THREE

LENNON

"Lennon!" There's an urgency in Gramps's voice that makes me abandon Gallie in the cross-ties and sprint out of the stallions' barn, grooming brush still in hand.

Gramps is standing out on the front porch of the farmhouse, leaning against one post that has the important task of keeping the railing upright. My heart rate slows when I see he's standing and smiling. Relief swamps me.

It's not until I reach the bottom stair and spot the white piece of paper he's holding that I regret running over so quickly.

Some more time to figure out what I'm going to say to him about this would be nice. Although, I've had a week to come up with the words to tell the other person I really need to show that paper to—or at least share its contents with—and I've still got nothing. A few extra seconds now probably wouldn't accomplish a whole lot.

"You got in?" Gramps shakes the sheet of paper in front of me, as though I didn't memorize every word it says the day it arrived.

"Yeah, I did," I confirm unnecessarily. I can read the bold *Congratulations!* from here.

Gramps scans my face. "Look a little less enthused, huh?"

"Gramps..."

I weigh how to play this. Caleb's going to be a tougher conversation for several reasons, but at least I can be honest with him about exactly how worried I am to leave Gramps alone. Telling that to my grandfather's face is a whole other matter. Even if stubbornness isn't hereditary, I most certainly inherited it from him.

"You're going, Lennie."

"And how are you going to take care of the farm by yourself?" I challenge.

"I'll figure something out."

I scoff. "That's what you *always* say. I'm not going to leave you here when I'm perfectly capable of helping out. RCC's been fine for the past few years. One more won't make any difference."

"You belong at a school with more than one faculty member in the journalism department, Lennon," Gramps informs me. "Where you couldn't get A's in your sleep."

"I work hard for those A's," I reply, scowling.

Gramps smiles. "I know you do, darling. But you deserve to be at a college where everyone else in your classes are, too."

I kind of regret telling him about the humorous anecdotes involving some slackers who attend Richardson Community College with me now.

"I'm happy at Richardson," I insist.

"Then why did you apply to Clarkson?"

I look away from his knowing gaze. "You know why."

"What did Caleb say?"

"I haven't told him yet," I admit. "That I got in, at least. I told him I applied. Honestly, I didn't think there was a real chance I'd get in. They hardly ever accept senior year transfers."

And that's *exactly* why I applied. A gesture I wouldn't have to follow through on. Except now, I could.

"Why haven't you told him?"

I scoff. "Stop asking me questions you already know the answers to."

"Because you know he's going to be thrilled about it?"

I keep studying the peeling paint of the porch. "Plenty of couples make long distance work. We see each other when we can."

"It's been almost three years, Lennie."

"I can't believe you're telling me to chase after a boy. Read a parenting book."

Gramps laughs. "I'm telling you to chase your dreams. I know you love this farm, but there's a lot more out in the world than just Landry. And there's more to college than just classes, too. It's a life experience you're missing out on by driving three towns over twice a week to take a few classes."

"You're telling me to go to Clarkson, specifically. Not just a good college."

"There's a reason that's the school you applied to, right?"

I look back over in time to catch his knowing smile. "He has a whole separate life there. Friends, teammates, classes. I don't know how I'd fit in there. *If* I'd fit in there."

Gramps gives me a reassuring smile. "You will."

"What if things don't work out between us? What if I transfer and we break up? He's going to get drafted next summer or end up at some fancy job like his dad. At least if I stay in Landry, I'll have my life here to focus on. If I uproot everything for him, I'll have nothing."

"That boy doesn't love a thing in this world anywhere near as much as he loves you, Lennie."

A lump the size of Kentucky forms in my throat.

"Maybe," I whisper.

The truth is, Caleb's *never* given me any reason to doubt his feelings for me. He's proven how much he loves me over and over again ever since I agreed to give us a chance.

It doesn't change the fact our lives are wildly incompatible.

Unless one of us makes some major sacrifices, that's not going to change anytime soon.

I'm the obvious option between us; Caleb is at Clarkson on a full athletic scholarship. And he's a big deal in the baseball world. But I'm not sure how I can justify choosing a boy over my only living family and the farm that's been in my family for generations.

"I wouldn't be pushing it if I thought you really didn't want to go, Lennie. But I think you do want to, and I don't want to be your excuse. Nothing would make me happier than seeing you spread your wings."

"I'll think about it," I promise. And I mean it. I've thought of little else since the paper Gramps is still holding arrived in the mail a week ago.

"And tell Caleb," Gramps advises.

"You just want to be able to gang up on me with him," I accuse. Most of the time, I love that Gramps thinks the world of Caleb. Not so much when the two of them join forces against me.

Gramps grins, not denying it. "Well, he managed to get you to apply, and that's more than I've been able to do."

I roll my eyes. "I'm headed back to the barn."

"I'm proud of you, Lennie," he tells me, and the love over-flowing in his voice makes tears prick my eyes. "No matter what you decide, I'm always proud of you."

"Thanks, Gramps," I manage.

"What time are you leaving tonight?"

"Cassie's picking me up at six."

"All right. I'm heading over to Mike's shortly. Mary will probably convince me to stay for dinner, so I doubt I'll be back before you leave."

"Okay." I'm worried about leaving Gramps on his own for the next two-and-a-half days, but after the conversation we just had, I know better than to raise my concerns right now. The knowledge he'll have company tonight is somewhat reassuring. "Have fun at Mike's."

I close the distance between us to give him a hug. The familiar scent of leather and tobacco surrounds me, and I inhale deeply. Gramps gave up his evening pipe years ago, but the clove smell still permeates most of his clothing. Probably because he hasn't added any new clothes to his wardrobe in just as many years.

"Have fun at the lake. But not too much fun, all right? I'm too young to be a great-grandfather."

"Leaving now!" I announce, making a show of covering my ears before I turn back in the direction of the barn. It was embarrassing enough when Gramps would make those sorts of comments when Caleb and I first started dating. It's even more mortifying now that I have a sex life to speak of.

Gramps's deep laugh follows me back to the barn. Gallie is tossing his head impatiently, clearly unhappy about the prolonged time in the cross-ties. I pat his smooth neck before running my left hand down to his rump and continuing to groom him from where I left off.

I'm picking his hooves when I hear the old farm truck start, sparking to life with a loud roar that gradually quiets to a rumble. Gramps honks twice as he passes the barn. I wave, watching the dust raised drift off toward the training track and then disappear into nothingness.

The clock hanging in the tack room reads 5:20 by the time I'm finished in the barn. I speed walk back to the house, shower, and then stand dripping in the center of my room, surveying my limited outfit options.

I'm confident Cassie is not going to drive me to Colt Adams's twenty-first birthday party wearing my standard uniform of jeans and a T-shirt. I survey my three dresses, two of which she let me borrow last summer and refused to let me return. I settle on the most casual of the three: a blue cotton one with thin straps that reveal the new freckles dotting my shoulders. It's been too hot to bother with sleeves lately.

Gramps left the letter from Clarkson on my bed. I study it for a few minutes before tucking it inside a book on my bedside table.

I pull my old duffel bag out from underneath my twin bed once I'm dressed, tossing most of my wardrobe inside. Caleb is returning tonight from baseball camp in Georgia. He's only back home for five days before heading to Clarkson for yet another baseball camp that will lead into the start of senior year.

After Colt's birthday party tonight, we're going to Colt's family's cabin for two nights. Ironically, it's on the same lake we traveled to for the senior trip in high school.

This is the first time I'm returning to it since that disaster of a weekend. I'm just as apprehensive about leaving Gramps now as I was then, but he assured me he could handle it.

Cassie's voice echoes through the house just as I'm zipping up my bag.

"Coming!" I call back, grabbing my phone off the charger and heading for the stairs.

Cassie is leaning against the wall that separates the kitchen from the entryway when I descend the steps. She smiles approvingly when she sees my choice of attire, which is a first. For once, we're dressed similarly. Cassie is wearing a pale pink sundress that pulls out the lighter shades in her dirty blonde hair.

"Damn, girl," she tells me. "You look *hot*."

I laugh. "You sure you don't want to rifle through my collection of fleeces before we go? For old times' sake?"

Cassie rolls her brown eyes. "You ready?"

I hike the strap of my duffel bag up on my shoulder. "Yup. Let's go."

"Is Caleb back yet?" she asks as we head outside.

"I don't think so. He said it'd probably be closer to seven."

"Excited for your weekend getaway?"

"Yeah, I am," I reply honestly as we climb into her car and start down the driveway.

Time with Caleb is a limited, precious thing. Basically the polar opposite of how I viewed interacting with him for most of high school.

"Is Kyle coming tonight?" I ask. I'm not the biggest fan of the guy she's been dating for the last five months, but I tolerate him for Cassie.

"Nope." She pops the P.

"Everything going okay between you guys?"

"Things aren't *going* at all. We're on a break that's headed for a break-up."

"I'm sorry, Cassie."

"It's fine. College is a time for exploring new things, right? Meeting new people."

"Right," I reply dryly, and she catches it. College hasn't been either of those things for me.

"I didn't mean…"

"I know. It's fine," I assure Cassie.

I haven't told anyone about applying to Clarkson, except for Caleb. And now Gramps. The more people who I tell, the more I'll have to let know I'm staying put after all.

I know some people judge me for the decision I made senior year of high school. Who see staying in Landry as giving up or being lazy.

But it was my decision to make, and I made it. I'm two semesters away from earning a degree. Not at an Ivy League institution like most teenagers I graduated alongside, but labels and reputations are things I've always done my best to disregard.

I'm at peace with my decision to stay in Landry.

I just didn't expect to fall—and stay—in love with someone who means just as much to me as the fifteen acres of dirt that contain everything else in the world that matters to me.

"Only one more year," Cassie tells me, in what I know she means to be a comforting manner.

"Yeah," I agree, although the statement isn't much of an assurance. Things between me and Caleb won't magically become less complicated next year. The exact opposite, actually.

If Caleb pursues baseball professionally, he could end up anywhere in the country. If he opts for a business career, he'll end up in some big, busy city that is not Landry, Kentucky. Living three hours apart doesn't sound all that terrible compared to either of those two scenarios.

Cassie seems to sense my discomfort with the topic, because she lets the subject drop as she parks outside Colt's house. Like most of the residences in Landry, it's obnoxiously large. The circular driveway is packed with cars.

It takes Cassie ten minutes to maneuver into a spot that ensures neither the car in front nor behind will be able to leave until she does. I open my door over a flowerbed and sigh. Even if she wanted to, I don't think Cassie could shift spots. I pick my way through daisies and mulch, finally ending up on the brick walkway right behind Cassie.

As we approach the front door, some nerves appear in my stomach. I used to dread social events because of the surreptitious glances and whispers that would follow me. They still do, but it's no longer gossip about my parents' drama and the falling-down collection of buildings known as Matthews Farm.

I'm pretty sure I could count on one hand the number of people who thought Caleb and I would last when we started officially dating. Since then, most of the town seems to have accepted we're not a couple on the cusp of breaking up.

The novelty of me dating Caleb Winters may have worn off somewhat, but interest in Caleb has far from waned. Since I'm now viewed as a reliable source of information when it comes to him—maybe the *most* reliable source of information—that means I've remained newsworthy by mere association.

Cassie and I step inside the house, and I'm shocked by the number of people here. The few gatherings I've attended this summer have all been around twenty people at the most. There are at least fifty in the living room alone, and this is supposed to be a backyard barbeque, meaning the bulk of the attendees are outside.

"Wow," Cassie comments, glancing around as well. "Big turnout."

"There must not have been anything else to do tonight," I reply, and Cassie laughs. It's a remark only someone who's fully settled in small town life would appreciate. Because there's *rarely* anything to do. Let alone multiple options.

Cassie follows me toward the back of the house. Because of his close friendship with Caleb, I'm quite familiar with the layout of Colt's home, even when it is packed with people.

We enter the kitchen, and I'm relieved to see it's not as

crowded as the rest of the house.

Cassie makes a beeline for the island. I trail after her, glancing around to see who I recognize. Unfortunately, the person I make eye contact with would not have been my first choice of conversationalist.

I send Madison a small smile, anyway. "Hi, Madison. How are you?" I ask politely, halting a couple of feet away from her.

"I'm good, Lennon. You?" she responds, fiddling with a strand of her hair.

"All right, thanks."

We've made progress from high school, but not much. I spent most of the four years believing she unceremoniously dumped me as a best friend in response to my father overdosing at the racetrack just before the start of our freshman year. I learned at senior prom it had more to do with Caleb Winters's arrival in town. Apparently, Madison sensed his interest in me three and a half years before I had the slightest clue, and held a grudge for the same length of time.

"Lennon!" Cassie calls from the island, finally realizing I'm no longer right behind her.

Madison gives me a small smile. "See you." She heads for the deck door that leads to the backyard before I can reply.

I amble over to Cassie, who hands me a can of beer.

Drinks in hand, we walk out into the backyard. The smell of roasting meat permeates the humid air. The sun is rapidly dropping behind the tall oaks that line the Adams' backyard, with only the faintest glimmers of golden light visible between the broad trunks.

There are a few unfamiliar faces I'd guess belong to those here with their families to enjoy Landry's main summer attraction: the racetrack. But the bulk of the people gathered around are familiar ones.

I doubt anyone could say I was social in high school with a straight face, but I grew up here. Most everyone in the backyard has played some small part in my life.

Cassie and I head toward Shannon, Eliza, and Tina first. I saw all three of them at Cassie's house two nights ago, but they greet us like it's been years, in the enthusiastic manner of people feeding off boisterous energy and enjoying the buzz of booze. Larger gatherings like this are rare in Landry.

"Caleb's not here yet?" Tina asks me.

I figured the news he'd be here tonight was public knowledge based on the turnout. I wasn't the only person who thought Caleb Winters would leave Landry and never look back. The fact that he hasn't, that he spends every free minute not tied up by baseball commitments here, has largely been attributed to me. So was his choice to attend the university with a Division I baseball program closest to Landry.

I love him for proving me wrong about his commitment to us.

I hate that him doing so has increased interest and envy regarding our relationship.

How people are blown away by the fact Caleb Winters is voluntarily choosing to return here even though his grandfather is gone and his parents only stop by a couple of times a year. Despite not growing up here and only having roots of the tangential kind.

How his dedication has raised eyebrows about how I've never so much as made the three-hour trip to Clarkson University to visit him or watch him play.

I shrug in response to Tina's question. "Not sure."

I avoid talking about Caleb with other people, even among the group of girls I'm standing with, who I consider close friends. Being the recipient of envy is something I find both uncomfortable and unfamiliar.

Even though they've all accepted our relationship, no one I know seems capable of looking at Caleb without hearts in their eyes. He's not the uncaring player I once pegged him as, but he's not perfect. And as someone who is fully aware of her imperfections, it's uncomfortable standing so close to someone under a constant spotlight of attention and adoration. It feels like flying too close to the sun.

Cassie sets off on a tangent about her woes with Kyle, the frat guy she's been dating on and off since junior year.

I listen intently along with Shannon, Tina, and Eliza, keenly aware of how they all keep glancing toward the back porch whenever anyone exits the house.

Sick of holding the rapidly warming can of beer and eager for a cold soda, I excuse myself as soon as there's a lull in the conversation. Being legally able to drink has only further diminished my interest in doing so. There's not even the allure of the forbidden anymore.

"Hey, Lennon."

I halt my progress toward the coolers to glance to the left. Andrew is standing next to the collection of trash cans, clutching a bottle of water. Out of everyone at this party, he's probably the only one who could give me a run for Most Antisocial. I'm shocked he's here.

"Hi, Andrew." I give my former editor a friendly smile, feeling a twinge of nostalgia as I watch him shove his glasses up his nose in a familiar motion. There was a time when I didn't think there was any part of high school I'd miss. Turns out there are lots. "How's Yale?"

"Good! Good!" Andrew informs me eagerly, launching into a detailed description of the journalism courses he's taken and the newspaper internships he's done without any prompting.

Guest lectures from world-famous reporters and visits to *The*

New York Times aren't at all how I've spent the past three years, and it elicits a pang of resentment I fight to ignore. That could have been me in another life. I have the writing talent, the drive, the ambition. I just…have had to reallocate them.

"What about you? How is the *Gazette*?" Andrew asks when he finishes his update.

"The *Gazette* is good," I reply.

The truth is, it's been an endless slew of grunt work with little pay or opportunities to write. But it's been something. A little piece of my life that's just for me.

Andrew listens intently as I describe some of the few more exciting tasks I've received. I'm touched by the way he acts as though my anecdotes are just as interesting as his. It makes me feel a little bad for all the times I gave him sass in high school.

I'm halfway through describing the paper's plan to cover the upcoming Landry Cup when I feel the shift. It ripples through the whole backyard.

Caleb Winters is what an unbiased observer would call a ridiculously hot guy. He had girls falling over themselves to talk to him in high school, and the past three years haven't made him any less appealing. More so, it seems.

His hair is shorter than it's been in months—an attempt to combat the Georgia heat, I'm guessing—and all it does is show off his symmetrical bone structure.

He must have come straight here from the baseball camp he's spent the past month at, because he's got a duffle bag slung over one shoulder. The strap pulls the cotton of his T-shirt taut, revealing how he has the musculature of an elite college athlete to go along with good genes.

I keep talking to Andrew, forcing my attention to remain mostly on him as Caleb stops next to where Colt is standing, saying something to his best friend. I don't mind Caleb knowing

I'm insanely excited to see him, but I've never been able to shake the compulsion to act more aloof when we're in public. I don't enjoy appearing vulnerable, especially around people who used to taunt me in the halls.

And, it's only been a month since I saw him. There's no need to act like a clingy girlfriend. We'll face stretches longer than this once Caleb returns to Clarkson for his senior year. There may not be as much geographic distance between us then, but we're both busy enough weekend visits more than every six or eight weeks are impossible.

"You should think about doing a trainer feature, too," Andrew suggests. I focus back on him and our conversation about the *Gazette*.

"That's a good idea," I reply. "They don't get much coverage. If I had any say—"

"Hey."

I let my eyes fly to where they want to go, relieved I'm no longer having to fake any indifference.

"Hi," I breathe.

Caleb stares at me, and I do the same to him. I soak in the satisfying sensation of being in the exact place where I want to be. When Caleb's in Landry with me, things feel perfect.

Too bad it's an exceedingly rare occurrence.

"Hey, Andrew," Caleb greets, looking away from me for the first time since he approached.

"Uh, hi—hi. Caleb."

I smile as Andrew stutters. I know he cares about baseball about as much as I do, so his obvious nerves are more a testament to Caleb's universal appeal. Probably also has something to do with the fact most of the backyard is looking at us now. Andrew and I are the two people here least appreciative of attention.

"See you guys," Andrews blurts, then takes off.

I stare at the spot he was standing for a few seconds, then slowly let my eyes drift over to the guy standing next to me. I allow the joy I'm experiencing to break through as a wide smile when our gazes meet, re-memorizing his features from up close.

The blue eyes I love to get lost in.

The dark hair now too short to flop on his forehead.

The smirk as he watches me ogle him.

I think I fall in love with Caleb a little more every time I look at him.

"You missed a spot." I touch the tip of his nose, where the skin is peeling in response to intense sun exposure. New freckles dot his nose and cheeks as well.

Caleb sighs. "I was wearing a hat. And sunscreen. I just sweat it off."

"It was that hot?"

"Ridiculously so. High nineties every day. Hit a hundred a couple of times. Each year I say I'm not going to go back…"

"And yet each year you go again."

"It makes Landry summers feel cool in comparison," Caleb tells me.

"Right. Because you spend *so* much time in Landry during the summer."

The sentence slips out before I filter the words, and I watch them register on Caleb's face. Guilt. He looks guilty for going to the best baseball camp in the country, and the same emotion swamps me.

"I'm sorry," I whisper. "I just missed you."

"I missed you too, Matthews." He tugs me to him, and I sink into the first kiss we've shared in twenty-seven days.

"It was the last time," he says when his lips leave mine.

I know the words are meant to be a reassurance, but they're the exact opposite. Caleb won't be returning to the baseball camp in Georgia he's attended since graduating high school because next summer he'll either be at a professional team's training camp or done with the sport for good.

That may mean he's not spending a month in Georgia, but it won't mean he's spending it here in Landry instead.

"Good." I don't let any doubts leak into my voice.

We only have five days together before he heads back to Clarkson. I'll have plenty of time to stress about the future after he's gone.

Right now, I just want to soak up his presence.

"Did you eat?" Caleb asks me.

I shake my head. "I was waiting for you."

Caleb kisses me again. This time, it's more than a quick peck of greeting. It's heat and tongue and urgency. I melt against him, not caring that people are probably watching us. Lust leeches away any inhibitions.

"Damn. I missed you, Matthews," Caleb tells me when we finally break apart. Hunger is clearly reflected in his blue eyes. Along with some sadness. Because we say those words way too much to each other.

Missing someone can be interpreted as a gift. It means it's someone you care about enough to. It's also an awful ache with no easy remedy or cure.

"Doesn't seem that way," I tease, turning my head so I'm pressed up against the hollow of his throat. He smells the same as always. Like spearmint and woodsy cologne and Caleb.

I feel his lips press against my hair before he pulls me over to where Colt is grilling.

"Did I mention how much I like this dress?" he asks as we walk across the grass, flashing me a cheeky grin.

"Not with words, but I kind of got the sense you liked it just now."

He laughs. "I like the dress."

"It's one Cassie gave me."

"I figured, since you're not wearing jeans."

I punch his arm for that comment. "You try riding a horse or cleaning the barn in a dress."

We fix burgers from the array of toppings that have been spread out. Caleb takes a seat in one of the lawn chairs on the patio. There are plenty of seats available, but he pulls me onto his lap. I let him, happy to pretend like we're the only two people here.

Most of the people here are ones I see more frequently than I'd like to.

Caleb Winters is one of two people in this world I feel like I'll never be able to spend enough time with.

He chats with some guys from his high school baseball team while I eat, describing new plays and drills from the camp he was at that I couldn't care less about.

I've absorbed some knowledge of the sport through osmosis, both from Gramps blasting game commentary from the living room and Caleb talking about it, but any affection I have for the sport is purely based upon Caleb's love of the game. I also harbor some appreciation for the uniform he wears while playing it. I'm not sure who decided the pants had to be *quite* that tight, but I'm certainly not complaining.

We must radiate the same nauseating air that a couple who makes out in a movie theater does, because after Caleb catches up with his old teammates, almost everyone leaves us alone.

I finish my burger and hand Caleb my drink before leaning against his shoulder.

"Bad?" he asks.

"If you like warm beer, probably not."

I watch the tendons of his throat contract as he takes a sip. "Not great." He grins.

"Make sure to tell Colt."

Caleb sets the can on the ground and then leans back in the chair, pulling me against his body. His fingers trail up and down the bare skin of my thigh, and I shift in his lap.

"Caleb…" I warn. He smirks but doesn't stop the motion.

Heat simmers in my veins.

"Did you hear back yet?" Caleb asks abruptly.

I don't need to ask for clarification on what he's wondering about.

"No," I lie, glad he can't see my face right now.

I need to tell him. I know I need to tell him. But I haven't decided how to. Haven't decided what I'm going to say when I do. I'm running out of time on both.

"They hardly ever admit new students just for senior year," I add, even as I know it's unnecessary.

I may be withholding the truth from him right now, but I know I'm not going to lie and tell Caleb I didn't get in. When I decide not to go, I need to be completely honest with him about why. Not take the easy way out. If such a thing exists in this situation.

"I know," Caleb replies. After a pause, he adds, "Thank you, Lennon."

His words burn with an earnestness that makes it clear he's not belatedly thanking me for the lukewarm can of beer. But I act as though it's nothing more than a casual statement of appreciation. Because acknowledging the fact Caleb knows the sacrifice even applying was for me makes this a thousand times harder.

"Yeah," I whisper.

We sit in silence until Jake and Luke approach. "Ready, lovebirds?" Jake teases. "Colt's packing up the car."

"I left my bag in Cassie's trunk," I say, breaking out of

Caleb's grip and standing. "Let me go grab it."

I catch Jake's nod before I walk away. He and Luke stay by Caleb's side as I head over to where Cassie is standing with Ellie Nash and a few other girls from our graduating class.

"Look who finally remembered Caleb's not the only person here," Cassie teases.

There's no malice in her voice, but there is a hint of jealousy. Coming from her, I know it's based on how unlucky in love she's been. But it's reflected tenfold in the gazes of the other girls near us, and it makes my insides twist unpleasantly. This is one aspect of being with Caleb I know I'll never grow accustomed to. The never-ending interest. It's not like I don't see his appeal, so maybe it's hypocritical of me. Doesn't make being blasted with blatant envy any more enjoyable.

"Can I have your car keys? I've got to grab my bag."

Cassie nods, pulling them out of her pocket. "You're leaving already?"

"Soon, I think. It's a three-hour drive."

Cassie tosses the keys to me, and I fumble a catch. Hand-eye coordination is still not a strong suit of mine.

"Thanks."

I weave through the crowd and head into the house. It's practically empty now, either the allure of food or of Caleb's arrival drawing almost everyone outside. I find Cassie's car among the maze of them and then realize I'm not going to be able to get the trunk open.

Huffing out a sigh, I unlock the car and climb over the backseat, tossing my duffle bag into the middle and then rolling over the seat. I land in a heap.

When I emerge from the car, Colt is standing in his driveway, grinning.

"What the hell are you doing?"

"The hordes of people you invited to this party blocked Cassie's trunk in," I explain, shoving some hair out of my face and straightening my dress.

"Talk to your boyfriend about it. I invited like forty people. Caleb draws a crowd."

"Yeah." I sigh. "I know."

Colt eyes me curiously, but says nothing else as he holds a hand out to me. "Here. I'll put this in the trunk. Through the back, like a normal person."

I roll my eyes and hand it to him. "Thanks. I'll be right back. I've got to give Cassie her keys back."

I head back into the house, emerging out onto the back deck seconds later. Things seem to be winding down outside. There are still plenty of people milling about, but all the food and drinks have disappeared. Colt planned for the party to end at ten, and it's nearly eleven now. I find Cassie and hand her keys back.

"Have fun." She winks at me before giving me a quick hug.

"Thanks," I reply. "I'll see you soon."

Caleb's easy to find; he's in the midst of the largest crowd of people. I don't attempt to approach him, just stand on the periphery until he spots me and walks over. He takes a while.

"Why do you look all...rumpled?" he asks, wrinkling his brow when he reaches me.

"Rumpled? What do you mean?" I reply, as though I have no idea what he's talking about.

"You look like you were just making out in the backseat."

"Funny. That's exactly what I was doing," I reply, smirking.

Caleb looks completely unconcerned. Despite the distance that usually separates us, fidelity has never been a concern of mine. I don't think it's one of his, either.

"Did you fall or something?" Caleb persists.

"Of course not."

"You're not the most coordinated, Lennon."

I gasp. "How dare you?"

"If you don't tell me, then I'm going to assume it's super embarrassing. Like the time you spent fifteen minutes trying to hit a baseball in gym."

"It was ten! Half the class couldn't hit the ball!" I protest.

Caleb just raises both eyebrows.

I sigh. "Cassie's car is boxed in. I had to climb across the rows and into the way back to get my duffel bag out of the trunk. In my dress," I admit.

Caleb's laugh is loud and genuine. It both eases the fist around my heart and tightens it. The sound of his amusement settles me. It makes me believe what we have is special and solid and worth fighting for. It also makes me worry that a long-distance relationship can't last forever and that some other girl will be listening to his laugh one day.

I force both extremes out of my head as we exit the backyard and approach the SUV loitering outside the front door.

"Finally!" Luke bemoans when we appear.

"Where's Jake?" Caleb asks.

"Looking for you two," Colt responds, rounding the back of the car and hauling himself into the driver's seat.

I make a beeline for the door behind his. I'm eager to depart, both tired and excited. Caleb climbs in after me, and Luke snags shotgun. I snuggle against Caleb as soon as he settles in the seat beside me, and he chuckles.

"What chance is there I'm not going to have to carry you into the cabin when we get there?"

"Nonexistent," I mumble, already closing my eyes.

Jake's voice joins the din of Colt and Luke arguing about what music to play in the car, and that's the last thing I register before falling into a deep, dreamless sleep.

I wake up slowly, blinking at the darkness as I try to figure out where I am and what woke me.

I roll over, squinting at the sliver of light as it grows in the doorway.

"Yeah, okay," Caleb is saying.

Someone responds, too quietly for me to hear. I think it's Colt.

Then there's more light, as the door opens wider.

I sit up in bed. "Hey."

Caleb grins lazily at me, leaning against the doorframe. "Hey."

"What time is it?"

He steps into the room, shutting the door behind him. "Late."

After a few seconds of rustling, the mattress dips. My arm reaches out, searching until I encounter warm skin. "We're here?"

"Uh-huh." His hand lands on my hip, tugging me closer into his body. "Sorry I woke you up."

"Are you?" I whisper.

Caleb rolls over me, supporting his weight with both elbows. My eyes have adjusted to the lack of light, so I can see his lips curve upward. I feel his chest rumble with a laugh. "Not really."

His lips land just above my collarbone, brushing a light kiss against the sensitive skin. My breathing becomes rapid and my heartbeats quicken. No matter how many times Caleb touches me, I always react like it's the first time.

It's a sensation I can't become accustomed to.

Caleb's mouth moves higher, up the side of my neck and along my jaw. All I can hear in the dark room is our breathing and the quiet rustle of the sheets.

I moan when his lips finally land on mine, the blankets slipping off the bed as I wind my legs around his waist. I don't even notice the loss of warmth, just appreciate the new freedom of movement.

Caleb continues kissing me until my lips are swollen and my breathing is ragged. I can feel his erection growing against the inside of my thigh, teasing me with the promise of pleasure.

"Caleb…" I run my hands up his shoulders and into his hair, pulling gently at the strands as I wriggle impatiently. The persistent, heavy throb between my legs is impossible to ignore.

He tugs up the dress I'm wearing, running a warm hand across my stomach and up to cup my breast. I gasp as his mouth lowers, his tongue tracing tantalizing patterns across the newly revealed skin. My stomach clenches as a flush works its way across my overstimulated body.

We both groan as he pushes inside of me. I can't see more than the shadowy outline of his body, and it feels like my other senses are all heightened as a result. His skin feels warmer and his cologne smells stronger and the stretch as he fills me is consuming.

"Fuck." The husky rasp of his voice as he thrusts is an aphrodisiac. Low and intimate and a little shaky. A tone I've never heard him use with anyone else.

The rest of what he whispers is lost in the meeting of our lips and the movement of our bodies. Pleasure builds to an almost unbearable pressure and then finally shatters, crashing over me in powerful tremors. I feel him swell inside of me as he finds his own release.

I'm tired and satisfied, sinking into the soft mattress beneath him. Caleb doesn't move away, running his hands across my bare skin like he's trying to rememorize every inch of me.

"I love you," I whisper.

"Love isn't a big enough word, Len."

CHAPTER TWENTY-FOUR

CALEB

The total lack of sound wakes me. I'm used to shouts and yells in the morning. Whistles and gongs. Brian was not a morning person, and he made sure the rest of us shared in his misery.

Consciousness slowly trickles in with the sunlight, and it's the absence of any obvious indication I need to wake up that makes me do so. Well that, the fact I forgot to draw the blinds when we arrived late last night, and how there's the foreign warmth of a body pressed against me.

I open my eyes, slowly registering the unfamiliar surroundings of the Adams's lakeside cabin. A red quilt, cream-colored walls, and matching mahogany furniture decorate the room. I came here with the guys once in high school, but memories of that trip are hazy.

I turn my attention to the girl sprawled out beside me. The sheets cover her from the waist down, but there's still a whole lot of skin on display. She teased me about my new freckles, but there are just as many additions on her arms and shoulders.

"Len," I whisper. "Lennon." She groans, tossing an arm over

her eyes and almost whacking my left one in the process. I smirk as I lean down and kiss her neck. "Wake up."

"What time is it?" she mumbles from behind her elbow.

"Early. No one else is up yet."

"Why are you?" Pragmatic even while half-asleep.

"I want to go canoeing." Not what I planned on saying, but a thought that's been circulating around in my head ever since I saw the small boats stacked by the garage when we arrived here late last night.

"That's a terrible idea," Lennon mutters. I chuckle.

"All you'll have to do is sit there while I paddle," I promise her. "Preferably *not* unexpectedly yelling."

Lennon slides her arm off her eyes, finally giving me an unobstructed view of her face. She squints up at me, an adorable pink flush spreading across her chest once she realizes we're both naked and her boobs are on display.

I lean down to kiss her, unable to help myself. We hardly ever wake up in bed together, and mussed hair and sleepy eyes is one of my favorite looks on Lennon Matthews.

"Come on," I cajole when my lips leave hers. "For old times' sake."

Lennon lifts her head off the pillow to kiss me again. "How about we just do this?" she suggests, sliding her hand down my stomach. My body instantly reacts, blood rushing south so fast it's painful. I catch her palm before she reaches my hardening dick, weaving our fingers together.

"Please?"

She groans but throws the covers the rest of the way off and climbs out of bed. "I can't believe you're turning down *sex* to go *canoeing*."

I grin as I roll out of the now-empty bed to pull on a sweatshirt and a pair of basketball shorts.

"We can have sex in the canoe."

"Hard pass," Lennon replies as she pulls on my old *Landry Baseball* hoodie. With nothing underneath.

If I wasn't so eager to get going before Colt, Jake, and Luke wake up, I'd push her right back into bed and fuck her while she's wearing it.

In high school, I never participated in any of the silly traditions most of the other guys did. I never gave a girl my letterman jacket or asked her to decorate my locker on game days.

Because there was only one girl I wanted—*this* girl—and for most of high school she wanted nothing to do with me. I wish I could go back and tell my younger self there are better ways to get a girl's attention than antagonizing her every change you get, but the logic made sense to me at the time.

We were never a real couple in high school.

For a long time, I thought we'd never been a real couple, period.

So every time I see Lennon in my favorite sweatshirt—the one she stole from me when we started officially dating—I experience a satisfying, possessive thrill.

Lennon Matthews has always been hard for me to read. Maybe because I'm twice as desperate to know what she's thinking as I am with anyone else. The fact she wears an article of clothing with my name on it nearly every day gives me some much-needed reassurance.

I'm in deep with her.

Deeper than I ever imagined being with a girl at just twenty-one. I planned my life out a while ago, centered around baseball. High school, college, pros.

I didn't factor in dating, much less a serious relationship. But I know, with absolute certainty, that if it ever comes down to choosing between baseball and Lennon, I'd pick her and walk away from the sport.

And that's…kind of terrifying.

Once we're both dressed we head down the hallway, past the shut doors to the bedrooms where Luke, Jake, and Colt are passed out. Through the massive kitchen Lennon's eyes widen at. I carried her in fast asleep when we arrived, so this is the first she's seeing of the cabin besides our bedroom.

Cool, damp air greets us as we step outside, tinged with the scent of pine and grass. Lennon shivers at the cooler temperature. I pull her into my side as we walk along the dirt path that leads down to the shore of the lake.

I drop my arm once we reach the canoe rack so I can pull a green one down and haul it down to where the water laps against the sandy shore.

I gesture to the front of the boat.

Lennon sighs, shakes her head, and then steps inside the canoe.

"You're the only person I would do this for," she tells me.

I chuckle. "Love you too."

She pauses and glances back at me, a soft small on her face that's totally different from her reaction the first time I said those words to her, less than a mile from where we are now. This trip feels like a do-over from the one we took as seniors, which is part of why I'm trying to recreate it.

"You good?" I ask, after she's crawled through the canoe to the front seat.

"Uh-huh." Lennon settles in the seat and lets her hair out of the messy bun she pulled it back in. The cool morning breeze blows some of the light brown strands off to the right.

I climb into the back seat, pick up a paddle, and shove away from the lake's shore. The wind picks up as we move away from the sandy stretch, the trees no longer providing any measure of shelter.

Unlike the last time we were on this lake together, there's barely any mist. I paddle along the shoreline, passing floating docks and the occasional duck. Lennon catches my eye after the first mallard we pass, and we share a bittersweet, secret smile. Aside from that moment, she seems lost in thought.

I know she's stressed about the future. About *our* future.

Lennon Matthews and I have little in common, at least at first glance. Probably after a second look, too.

We have different families, dream, expectations, and opportunities.

Most of all, I thought that our feelings for each other would never be comparable.

Ever since we got together, I've been worried Lennon's waiting to tell me it isn't worth it. For her to decide she wants a guy who's around for more than just a weekend once every couple of months. Who doesn't spend most of the summer in Georgia and all of the spring traveling around the country to play at different colleges.

"Okay, this isn't terrible," Lennon finally admits, twisting around to smile at me.

"Told ya." I smirk back as I continue to paddle along. "Just wish I'd paid attention to which direction we came from."

"You had better be joking, Caleb, or I swear this is the last time you're going to get me in a canoe with you."

"That's what you said last time," I tease.

Lennon sticks her tongue out at me before turning back to look out at the lake. "Guess I'm a sucker for baseball players."

I chuckle, because we both know she's the furthest thing from a groupie. The girls who flirt with me at Clarkson parties and hang around the bleachers after our practices know nothing about me aside from the fact I can throw a baseball pretty damn fast. Lennon knows me better than anyone else in the world.

"Good to know," I tease her.

Lennon scoffs as she leans back on her palms. "So…are you excited to go back to Clarkson next week?"

I look away, out at the smooth surface of the water, any amusement slipping away as things turn serious between us. "Yes and no."

I'm excited to be reunited with my teammates and friends.

I'm eager to prepare for the next season—for my final season of college ball.

I'm dreading leaving her.

"I'd be more excited if I knew you'd be there this fall." I can't help but add the words, even knowing it will pull the sudden tension between us tighter.

Lennon says nothing.

She might not have heard back yet, but I'm not harboring any doubts she'll get into Clarkson. I doubt she is either. She was our class valedictorian at Landry High, which is the best school district in the state. And, as far as I know, she's gotten nothing but A's at Richardson Community College.

We both know the chances of her attending Clarkson this fall will be decided by her attachment to Matthews Farm and to Earl rather than the whims of the Admissions Office.

It would be a lot easier for me to resent her indecision if I didn't get just how hard of a choice it is.

I've spent a lot of time at Matthews Farm since my first visit there, over four years ago. With Earl. With the horses. I know what those acres of grass signify to her.

"It's fine, Len," I assure her when the silence continues to stretch between us. "Whatever happens, we'll be fine."

Lennon likes to challenge me. It's one of my favorite things about her. She's not one to shirk from a problem or pretend every-thing is fine when it's not. The fact that all she says in response is, "Okay," gives me a clue of just how worried she really is.

"I mean it."

"What is it with you and serious conversations in canoes?" Lennon asks me, spinning around fully so she's looking at me, not the lake.

I'm relieved to see she's smiling. The sun is rising, back-lighting her hair and pulling out tints of red in it.

"We've had plenty of serious conversations on dry land," I reply.

"Yeah, I guess," she concedes.

We have a lot of serious conversations, period.

"I like having you to myself," I tell her. "I feel like I hardly ever do."

Most of the time I spend with Lennon is at Matthews Farm. I'm closer with her grandfather than I ever was with either of mine, but it never feels like we're totally alone there. And when-ever we're not at her farm, it's around my friends or Cassie or worse, random people from town who stare at us the whole time.

I feel like I'm often on eggshells, not wanting to appear too desperate for her attention. Not wanting to get into an argument about anything when we probably won't have time to come to any sort of resolution before I have to leave again.

"I like it too," Lennon tells me before tilting her head back to catch the sunbeams filtering down from the sky.

The only sound is the splash of my paddle as we glide along the glassy surface of the lake, topped with a light layer of mist that's quickly disappearing. A bird's call echoes in the distance, reverberating across the empty, open space.

"Must not be many early risers living around here," Lennon

comments, looking around the lake we appear to have to ourselves. "Guess none of *them* got dragged out of bed."

"You would have been up by now anyway," I retort.

She doesn't deny it. "Yeah, the curse of growing up on a farm. If I ever do leave, that's going to take some getting used to."

I catch how she says if, not when.

It's not news to me that Lennon's life plan has never not included remaining in Landry. Or that I'm really the only complicating factor.

We keep drifting along the surface of the lake until the sun truly starts to shine, burning away any lingering mist and bathing the surface of the lake in sparkles.

"We should probably head back," I tell Lennon.

She nods in agreement, so I paddle to the left. The green hull of the canoe slowly spins around to face the way we came from.

I'm distracted by maneuvering the canoe around a floating dock, so I miss the moment Lennon takes my sweatshirt off. I glance over in response to the movement I catch out of the corner of my eye and watch as she shimmies out of the shorts she's wearing as well.

"Wh—" I clear my throat, taken totally off guard. "What are you doing?"

She grins unexpectedly, as she tosses her clothes in a heap on the floor. "Exactly what it looks like."

Before I have the chance to blink she's in the lake, her brown hair looking black when her head emerges from the water and she bobs beside the canoe.

"Come on, Winters." She leans back so she's floating on her back. "Water is warm this time."

I glance around. There's still no one else in sight on the lake. We're close to a small cove with a rock outcrop that will keep motorboats away. And the shoreline here is densely wooded, no houses visible.

My eyes return to Lennon floating.

I smile at the sight.

Lennon is serious and responsible and often inscrutable. A playful, joking Lennon is rare. A version of herself I hardly get to see, and have never seen her show anyone else besides Earl.

I stand, the canoe rocking slightly as pull my hoodie off. Lennon shifts so she's treading water. Her hazel eyes are focused on me and filled with heat. I pull down my shorts, and after a moment of hesitation, add my boxer briefs to the pile. Wearing them back wet under dry clothes will suck.

When I break through the surface of the water, she's right next to me. "It's nice, right?"

"Definitely warmer than last time." When we came here in high school it was spring, not summer.

Now that I've adjusted to the initial shock, the water feels refreshing. I'm way more focused on Lennon than the temperature, though. She's close enough I can see every freckle on her face. Study the droplets of water clinging to her eyelashes. Watch the pulse of her heartbeat thrum beneath her jawline.

A line of water streaks down from her darkened hair to her cheek, and I brush it away with my finger.

"You know," she starts. "Since *I'm* naked, and *you're* also naked…"

I groan, having no trouble figuring out what she's suggesting. "Len, there's no way I can keep us both afloat and actually move once I'm inside of you."

"Thought you were *so* athletic, Mr. Hotshot Baseball Pitcher."

I smile and shake my head. "Not that athletic. We'll drown."

She floats closer, winding her arms around my neck and wrapping her legs around my waist. "What a way to go, though," she whispers.

I manage a laugh before her lips are on mine. Our bodies fit together like two puzzle pieces. Her hands travel up my back and across my shoulders, slipping into my hair. I got it cut recently, so there's not much to pull. But her fingernails graze my scalp, and it feels so good I don't care.

My hands slide down to her hips, the water adding a slipperiness that's surprisingly erotic. The last—only—time I kissed a girl in the water, it was her.

Things were uncertain between us in a different way back then. Every time I kissed her, I was worried it would be the last time. I'm not worried about that now. And I'm no longer a fumbling teenager either. Just because sex seems logistically impossible doesn't mean we can't do other things.

Lennon gasps when I pull her right on top of my erection, severing the connection between our mouths. "Make yourself come on me," I whisper, moving my lips down the side of her neck.

"Here?" she murmurs back. I can't see her face from this angle, but I'm sure she's looking around our surroundings. Even if someone has showed up, it doesn't matter. They'd have to be right beside us to see what's going on beneath the water.

"Yeah. I want to watch."

"What about you?"

"Len, we both know that even *when* you get into Clarkson, we'll still be separated for another year. I get it; it's okay." I press another kiss against her wet skin, right in the curve where her shoulder meets her neck. "I have an excellent memory. I might not get off right now, but I promise I will. Many times, probably."

Lennon bites her bottom lip, a blush working its way across her skin despite the cool water.

Her hips begin moving. Slowly, at first, then faster and faster. Her breathing quickens as she rubs against me, chasing pleasure.

Sexy.

Shy.

Mine.

I never experienced jealousy, until I met Lennon. My whole life, everything has been handed to me. Other people wanted to be me. Be around me.

So it took me a little while to figure out what the tightness in my chest was when I'd see her walking out of Biology, laughing with Will Masterson. Why it pissed me off so much when someone would make a joke about the grass stains in her jeans or the hay in her hair. And once I admitted it to myself, I kind of wished I was still in denial. Because nothing changed between us for a long time. I spent years knowing I had absolutely no claim on her and hating that fact. Even if we do break up one day, if she decides long distance isn't worth it, the way she once told me, I'll always be hers. And I'll never forget this moment, seeing her fall apart and knowing I'm the reason her lips are parted and her eyes are hazy.

Lennon pulls my lips back to hers when she finishes. We stay like that a while, laughing like little kids every time one of us has to splash to stay afloat.

It's the happiest I've felt in a long time. Staring down a player with a bat has never given me this feeling.

Just her.

"You know the canoe has been floating away this whole time?" she asks me.

I wince and look around. Sure enough, the green canoe is a couple hundred feet away from us. I'd probably care less if I had any clothes on. Getting arrested for public indecency isn't on the itinerary for this trip.

"I'll race you," Lennon challenges, following my gaze to the boat floating further and further away.

"Deal. Loser makes breakfast."

Lennon doesn't reply. She starts swimming at a much faster pace than I'm expecting. I'm a decent swimmer and in great shape, but I've got more bulk and muscle than she does, and it means I arrive at the canoe at least five seconds after her.

She grins when I grab the opposite end of the boat. "I'd like eggs and toast, please."

"When did you get that good at swimming?" I ask, between heavy breaths.

"I did swim team in elementary school," she replies.

"You did?"

"Uh-huh." Lennon is studying the boat. "Should I get in first?"

"Uh, yeah. Hang on." I swim to the opposite side, directly across from where she is. "Okay. Climb in."

Lennon pulls herself over the rim of the boat and lands in a heap on the floor. Once she's dressed, I tell her to lean to the right. Hopefully, it'll be enough to counteract my weight.

I haul myself up and over the left side. The canoe doesn't remain as steady as it did during Lennon's return, sloshing side to side precariously, but it doesn't capsize.

I pull on my shorts and hoodie, then grab the paddle to turn in the direction of Colt's place. The sunshine warms my damp hair and wet clothes, but neither of us are dry by the time we reach the spot we started from.

Lennon helps me pull the canoe onto shore, and then we walk along the path back toward the house.

"This place is really nice," she comments as we pass the four-car garage.

"Yeah, it is," I agree.

"You've been here before?"

"Once, in high school. The four of us came up back in junior year."

"What did you guys do?"

"Stupid stuff you do when you're sixteen and there's no parental supervision," I reply.

Lennon rolls her eyes as we enter the house. Colt, Jake, and Luke are all in the kitchen. Colt is fiddling with the coffee maker, Luke is surveying the contents of the fridge, and Jake is slumped on one stool at the kitchen island, looking half-asleep.

"Morning, guys," I greet.

My three best friends all look over, wearing matching expressions of confusion.

"We thought you two were still in bed," Colt says.

"Why the hell are you all wet?" Jake asks. "*Again*."

I forgot he saw us after the last canoe trip we took together, too.

"We took a canoe out," I answer, heading for the fridge and reaching around Luke to grab the orange juice. "Lennon wanted to go swimming."

"You went canoeing?" Luke questions.

"Yeah."

"You should've taken the speedboat out instead," Colt comments. "Way more fun."

"There's a speedboat?" Lennon asks.

"Uh-huh. We can go out after breakfast," Colt tells her.

"There's a speedboat," Lennon informs me.

I nod, smirking. "Yeah, I know."

Lennon huffs out an annoyed sigh. "I'm going to change. Breakfast will be ready when I get back, right?"

I turn back toward the fridge. "Yeah, yeah. I'm working on it."

"'Kay." She smiles at me before disappearing down the hall.

"Sweet. You're making breakfast, Winters?" Jake finally perks up.

"Not for you."

"You're cooking for Lennon! Just make extra!"

"I'm making her breakfast because she's my girlfriend. And because..." If I don't tell them now, Lennon will probably mention it later. "I lost a bet."

Colt laughs. "What was it?"

"Swimming," I grumble.

"Is that code for something else?" Jake asks, wagging his eyebrows.

"No, you idiot. I literally mean swimming. She beat me back to the canoe."

"Are you sure there's not a third reason you're on kitchen duty?"

I pull a carton of eggs out of the fridge and glance at Jake. "What?"

"I got a *really* good night's sleep last night. Seems like a sad effort on your part, Winters."

I shake my head. I've never discussed my physical relationship with Lennon before, and I'm not going to start now. That stays between us. "Why the fuck were you *listening*?"

"I've never vacationed with a couple," Jake says. "I was expecting some noise, that's all."

"We're crashing at Colt's for two nights. I wouldn't call that a vacation," I respond, cracking and mixing the eggs.

"Whatever. If you need some pointers to spice things up, I got you."

I pick up a banana from the bowl on the counter and throw it at Jake. "Talk to me when you get a girlfriend. Far as I can tell, no girl wants to fuck you on a regular basis. That's hardly a ringing endorsement."

He grins at me. "I don't have a girlfriend because *too many* girls want to fuck me on a regular basis."

"Keep telling yourself that, Barnes."

"I really should have spent longer changing." I glance at the doorway, watching Lennon walk across the kitchen to the island and take a seat on the stool next to Jake. "Put a sock on the door next time, you guys."

It's almost comical, watching Jake sit up and the tips of his ears turn red. "Sorry, Lennon. I'm just…tired."

Lennon reaches over, grabbing the banana Jake caught off the counter and peeling it. "Thought we didn't keep you up?" She pops a piece of fruit into her mouth.

I don't hide my grin as I pour the eggs in the pan.

"I—that wasn't…"

"Maybe you should just stop talking, Jake," Luke suggests.

"Don't act like you're not single too," Jake replies.

I look at Luke. "You and Amanda broke up?"

He shrugs. "Yeah. She got super serious. Wanted to know my plans for next year. Said we should be figuring it out together. I told her I don't even know what I want myself, never mind factoring in another person. That was pretty much that."

"I'm sorry, man," I say. When I look at Lennon, she's studying the empty banana peel on the counter.

Luke and Amanda were together for a few months.

Lennon and I have been dating for almost three years. We've known each other for seven.

The two situations aren't comparable.

At least, I hope they're not.

~

After breakfast, we all head back to our rooms to change into bathing suits. Lennon remains in the kitchen, loading the dishwasher.

"I'm glad you brought Lennon this weekend," Colt tells me as we walk down the hallway toward the bedrooms. "It's nice seeing you so happy, man."

"Thanks. I am."

"Luke's break-up didn't freak you out?"

"Me and Lennon are nothing like that. I'm serious about her. Always have been."

Colt laughs. "Yeah, I know. I'm the one who tried to get you to just tell her you were crazy about her and got a lot of shit for it, remember?"

I don't deny it. "I never saw it going well. And I was right. It didn't go well when I finally *did* say something. But I always—I just... I don't know. I knew, you know?"

"Not really," he replies, and I chuckle.

I think Colt's longest relationship has lasted a week.

"Yeah, I guess you wouldn't."

"I'm glad it worked out for you two. Every other guy in Landry is not."

I side-eye him. "What's that supposed to mean?"

"You know what I mean, Winters. Ryan James looked like he'd sucked on a lemon when you showed up at my place last night. And you know Will Masterson is single again. Plus there are probably lots of guys at RCC who—"

"Are you *trying* to get punched in the face?"

Colt laughs. "She's crazy about you. I almost want to consider a serious relationship, after seeing you guys together. And I knew why you were in such a foul mood, the last time we were here. Even if you wouldn't talk about it."

I don't deny it. The summer after junior year was when I

really started to give up hope of anything changing between me and Lennon.

"I'll meet you down at the dock." Colt punches my shoulder, then heads into his room.

By the time I head outside, all traces of the early morning chill Lennon and I were met with at dawn have disappeared, replaced by a heavy blanket of heat.

The shiny motorboat Colt talked about for most of the drive here last night is tethered about thirty feet offshore, the white paint blinding in the sunshine. I wish my parents had bought a place here instead of the ski chalet in Aspen I've only been to once.

I made no secret of my distaste for Landry when I was a kid. Or how much I hated the idea of moving there for high school. I'm positive my parents assumed graduation was the last time I would spend any time in the small town.

Instead, I've spent every possible second there I could.

Neither my mom nor my dad were supportive of my relationship with Lennon when we first started dating. And they both assumed it would be a brief fling.

Two and a half years later, the comments about spending time at one of the other properties they own besides the Kentucky farm have increased in number significantly.

If my parents thought I wasn't serious about Lennon Matthews before, they most certainly know I am now.

"Swim or row?" Colt asks, nodding to a rowboat lying next to the canoe Lennon and I took out earlier.

"Swim," Lennon answers, pulling her shirt over her head and revealing a dark green bikini underneath.

I'm not the only one looking. I glare at Luke when I catch him glancing at Lennon as well. I know none of my friends would make a move on her, but the direction of his gaze makes me question the wisdom of bringing my girlfriend on a trip with three single guys.

Jake and Luke shuck their shirts as I wade into the water. I didn't bother with one. Lennon's already halfway to the boat, and Colt's rearranging stuff on shore.

Lennon's climbed aboard the speedboat by the time I reach it. She's studying the array of dials and gauges behind the wheel when I climb the ladder, lake water pouring off my body and dripping from my swim trunks. The bright sun immediately starts to dry me.

"Do you think Colt knows how to drive this thing?" she asks.

"No idea. I don't think boats are all that complicated, though. You just turn it on and go, right?"

Lennon rolls her eyes. "Yeah. Sure."

A quick glance behind reveals Colt is still on shore, and Luke and Jake are just entering the lake. I stalk forward, caging her against the side of the railing.

"Jake was just talking shit earlier. I didn't say anything."

"I know."

"I don't talk about that stuff, Len. Not with anyone. It's just between us."

"I know," she repeats, then rises up on her tiptoes to kiss me.

I move closer to her; tightly enough, the water coating both our bodies doesn't have a prayer of sliding downward.

It's been a long time—years—since we first kissed at the baseball field I spent high school playing on. Up until that moment, I wasn't sure if she had the slightest attraction toward me.

I thought that was why kissing Lennon Matthews felt different than kissing any other girl. But it's been three and a half years since Lennon Matthews first kissed me. And the feel of her lips against mine is still a sensation I know I could never replicate with anyone else. There wouldn't be this rush of love, along with lust.

"Get a room, you guys." Jake's on board, Luke right behind him.

"The room next to yours, you mean?"

My cheeks stretch with a grin in response to Lennon's comment as she slips out of my arms, leaving me leaning against the side of the boat to watch Colt swim toward us.

We spend the day driving around, disturbing the pristine surface of the lake: swimming, tubing, and water-skiing. Drinking and joking. By the time we return to the dock, we're all sun-kissed and exhausted.

Jake and Luke collect sticks for a fire in the stone pit set up in the yard, while Colt and Lennon head inside to grab hot dogs to roast for dinner. I contribute nothing, stretching out on one of the benches that surrounds the fire pit and staring up at the rapidly darkening sky.

I know my future holds a lot of options and question marks. I also know I'm fortunate to have the choices I do. But this is one of those meaningful moments in time not resulting from any accomplishment or dedication on my part

I'm at his family's lake house right now simply because I wasn't a dick when Colt asked me if I wanted to sit with him at lunch on the first day of high school. There's been no investments of blood or sweat to get to this peaceful spot in the woods. But I feel the same sense of accomplishment and contentedness I do when I throw a perfect strike anyway.

It makes me wonder if I might be happy living in Landry. If

settling in a small town might not be so bad if I get to stare up at the stars every night the way I'm doing right now.

"Up for some Truth or Dare?" Jake asks loudly, disturbing the peace.

Without looking over, I can tell he and Luke managed to light the fire. The air temperature has risen thanks to the dry heat cast by roaring flames.

I sit up, turning my gaze to catch the grin Jake's aiming my way. Luke is looking at the freshly lit sticks, barely interested in our teasing. Like usual. Of the four of us, he's usually the most mature.

I narrow my eyes at Jake, not rising to the bait dangling in front of me. Guess I'm not the only one who's been recalling our senior year trip today.

"Wrong approach, Barnes." Luke opts to get involved, after all. "Just get Lennon to play."

"Yeah, that'll be easy," Jake replies, settling back in one of the Adirondack chairs with a huff.

I smile.

The sound of Lennon's laugh echoes through the pines, and I turn to see her stumbling down the path to the fire pit, giggling at something Colt is telling her. They reach us. Colt takes a seat across the campfire, next to Jake. Lennon plops down in my lap, dropping a package of hot dogs on the dead pine needles that litter the ground.

"Feel like roasting me one?"

"Are you admitting you always burn them?"

"Once. It happened *once*, Caleb."

"Hey, Lennon," Jake calls. I shake my head as I grab a roasting stick and stuff it through the raw meat. I know what he's going to ask. I also know what the answer is going to be.

"What?" she replies.

"Feel like a game of Truth or Dare?"

Lennon laughs. "No."

I shoot Jake a triumphant smirk. He pouts. "Why not?"

"I don't feel like it," Lennon responds as she opens the bag of hot dog buns and fishes a couple out.

"Not even if you get to kiss Winters during it?" Jake persists.

"Caleb is pretty amenable to kissing me even when we're not playing childish games," Lennon tells him.

I chuckle as I hold the stick out to the open flame. Jake lets out a resigned sigh, then sets about roasting his own dinner.

The hot dogs disappear quickly, as do the marshmallows Colt runs back to the house to grab. Jake heads inside as well, returning with a guitar I've seen him strum before. I know for a fact he learned how to play as a way to get girls, but he's actually pretty decent now.

He starts off with a couple of country songs, then transitions into a Mumford and Sons one I've heard before but don't know the words to. Lennon does. Her soft soprano mixes with Jake's deeper baritone, adding to the bird calls and lap of lake water that were our only soundtrack before.

Like swimming earlier, singing is something I randomly discovered Lennon is really good at. I'd heard her hum along to the radio in the barn, but it wasn't until we were driving in my truck one day and she started singing along that I realized she's better than average.

She and Jake duet for another few songs before Lennon's head droops on my shoulder. I hide a smile. I'm pretty sure the one time I called her after ten p.m., she was already asleep. It's nearing midnight now, and neither of us got a full night's sleep.

"Bed?" I murmur.

Lennon groans as she snuggles closer.

"We're headed in," I announce, standing with her in my arms.

"Cool," Colt replies. "I'll be ready for bed in like fifteen minutes, if you could come back to carry me in then."

I can't flip him off while I'm holding Lennon, but I'm pretty sure my face conveys the message.

Climbing a dirt path in the dark carrying someone is a challenge, but I manage to make it to the door. Lennon groans again when we reach the bright lights of the cabin. I walk through the living room and down the hall into our bedroom, closing the door with my foot before lying her down gently on the bed. When I start to stand up, she doesn't let go. Her hands are clasped behind my neck, clinging to me like a monkey.

"Len," I whisper, pulling back enough to see her face. Her eyes are wide open, her lips curved up mischievously.

"I don't want you to go anywhere," she murmurs, tightening her grip. I could easily break through her hold, but I don't.

A lump forms in my throat. I know she's not just talking about right now. She means next week, when I'm supposed to be back on campus. Next month, when I'll still be at Clarkson. Next year, when I'm not sure where I'll be.

"I'll always come back, Lennon."

"Do you promise?"

The vulnerability in her voice pierces right through the center of my chest. I shift so I'm supporting my weight on one arm while my other hand brushes across her cheek. "I promise. You're the one thing I'm sure about. You're my home. All the other stuff, it doesn't matter. We'll figure it all out."

She gnaws on her bottom lip. "It's your senior year. You shouldn't be wasting time driving back to Landry and—"

"Len. Stop it. It's what I want to be doing. If I could, I'd drive back every weekend."

The anxiety on her face finally recedes. "I'm in this, Caleb.

You're better at saying how you feel and you're making more sacrifices and—"

"Le—"

"Wait. Let me say this. I was wrong, back in high school. I didn't believe you. I didn't believe in us. And I'm so grateful…" Her voice breaks in the middle of the word, and she inhales before continuing. "I'm so grateful that you did. You're the best thing that's ever happened to me, Caleb Winters. I want you to know, whatever happens this year, or next year, I'm *in* this. I'm all the way in. You could get drafted to a team that plays on Mars, and I'd wait twenty years for you to get back from space."

I didn't think it was possible to love Lennon any more than I already do. But the warmth in my chest is more powerful, more consuming, than anything I've experienced before. "Only twenty? What if the spaceship took a wrong turn and it took me twenty-one years to get back? I'd come back and find you with another guy?"

She rolls her eyes and shoves my shoulder. Since it's holding up all of my weight, I quickly drop my other elbow so I don't crush her. "Way to ruin the moment."

My smile mirrors her reluctant one. "I think you're pretty good at saying how you feel."

"Roll over," she whispers. "I'll show you too."

And I know that's the end of any serious conversation.

CHAPTER TWENTY-FIVE

LENNON

We leave the lake early on Monday morning. Colt drives. Luke rides shotgun. I'm squished between Caleb and Jake in the middle seat, but I don't really mind.

I rest my head against Caleb's shoulder, taking advantage of the opportunity to lean against him. His hand rests on my knee, occasionally drawing circles on the bare skin.

I feel closer to him than I have in a while. Not just physically, although there's a pleasant ache between my legs that reminds me we had more sex in the past two days than the last six months.

Caleb hasn't mentioned me attending Clarkson again since our canoe trip, but I know he's probably thinking about it.

I am, too.

I'm completely conflicted about what I really want.

He told me I'm his home last night.

Home can be a lot of things, I'm learning.

Landry is home.

Gramps is home.

But Caleb is my home now, too.

And I can't have all three at once besides these small snippets of time when Caleb comes back.

This trip is longer than we've spent together in nearly a year, and he's leaving in two days for a baseball camp back at Clarkson before senior year starts.

I *could* go with him, but I'm not sure if I can.

If I should.

I don't know who a Lennon Matthews, who doesn't live in Landry, Kentucky, is. I've never been her.

Throughout the loss and upheaval I've experienced, my home address always stayed the same.

I spent high school knowing I wouldn't be able to leave for college. I made my peace with missing out on that experience years ago. Part of me was relieved, honestly. I'm comfortable taking care of Gramps and the horses. They need me. Rely on me.

Caleb doesn't. He already has far more than I could ever offer him.

I stare out the window at the countryside flashing past, dreading the upcoming conversation I need to have with him. I still don't know exactly what I'm going to say, but I have to tell Caleb I got into Clarkson.

Purposefully keeping it from him isn't fair. I don't need to tell him to know how he's going to react, though. He'll say he understands why I'm not going, and that we'll make it work.

There's no other option to change our current situation besides me transferring. I know hardly anything about baseball, but I know Caleb is good. Really good. I know he will be able to play professionally if he wants to. Clarkson is a three-hour drive, but it's the closest school to Landry with a decent baseball program. I can take journalism classes anywhere. What I can't do is take care of the farm and look after Gramps.

I'm disappointed when the green Landry sign flashes by,

meaning we're back in the town limits. Not only because I'm happy leaning against Caleb in the close confines of the backseat, but because I'm dreading the coming conversation.

We drop off Luke first, Jake next, then head toward Matthews Farm. There's more room to spread out now, but I remain pressed against Caleb.

I stare out at the lush green fields as Colt drives up the familiar pothole-ridden lane that leads to the farmhouse, studying the trees that need to be pruned and the sagging fence rails that need to be replaced.

Sometimes—a lot of the time—it feels like I'm failing on all fronts.

I'm an absentee girlfriend.

An underachieving granddaughter.

An abysmal farmer.

Repairs take time and money, both of which are limited resources. Having horses that are fed and sheltered and exercised is the highest standard I can strive for. Attending community college rather than the highly ranked one Gramps wants me to allows me to meet that low bar.

We pass the start of the east pasture, and I look for Dusty in her usual spot under the massive oak.

She's not there.

A chill that has nothing to do with the air conditioning blasting from the car vents spreads across my skin.

Caleb feels me tense. "What's wrong?"

"Dusty's not under the tree."

To most people—to anyone except him—that sentence would make absolutely no sense. I catch Colt's puzzled look in the rearview mirror.

Caleb realizes what I'm saying immediately. He's helped me turn the horses out. He knows Dusty should have been let out in the east pasture along with the rest of the mares several hours ago, and the fact that she isn't there is strange.

We keep driving along.

Neither of the stallions are in the west pasture, either.

Caleb's hand tightens on my knee.

We round the final bend in the driveway, and there's my worst nightmare, spread out before me like a pop-up book. There's an ambulance, a police car, and a pickup truck I recognize as belonging to Mike Foreman, one of Gramps's old racing buddies who often stops by. But there's no sign of my grandfather. And, suddenly, I just *know*.

I know that I've lost the only living family I had left.

I don't remember how I found out my mother had passed. I only remember Gramps holding me when I got home from school that day, telling me everything was going to be okay.

I do recall how two Landry police officers came to our door one July morning to tell us my father's body had been found at the racetrack. I also recall how Gramps told me I still had him— how I would always have him.

Colt slams on the brakes. It jars me back to the present tragedy.

Horror is appearing on Caleb's face as he absorbs the scene before us.

I slide out of the opposite side of the car and walk straight up to Bob Everett, Landry's chief of police. He fiddles with his belt buckle as I approach, dread filling the lines of his weathered face. This is a small town. He knows how many losses I've already faced. Knows this one will be the hardest to recover from.

Grief isn't something you become accustomed to.

Each time, it hits differently.

"He's gone?"

Chief Everett nods, slowly. "I'm so sorry for your loss, Lennon. Is there anyone we can call?"

"No." I laugh, but nothing about this moment is the least bit funny. "No. There's no one."

He nods again, already having known the answer to the question he was obligated to ask.

I'm barely cognizant of anything happening around me as I sink down onto the bottom step of the front porch stairs and rest my forehead on my knees. Voices swim around me in a distant din of noise. The fire truck departs. Two paramedics talk quietly as they walk about our overgrown front yard.

I've thought about this moment.

Gramps's health has been bad for years. There were days he barely dragged himself out of bed. I imagined him falling on the stairs one morning or calling out to me in the middle of the night. Pictured having to rush him to the local hospital for an emergency procedure. Decided who I'd call to help with the horses while I sat in the waiting room.

But this outcome never occurred to me. I never thought I would leave and return to find him gone.

If Gramps had any choice in the matter, I know this is the way he would have wanted to go, though, and that's just about the only thing holding me together right now.

Someone takes a seat beside me. I know that it's Caleb before he even speaks. "They're ready to go. Do you want to see him?"

His words are matter-of-fact. No pity or devastation. Caleb is good in a crisis. He's reliable and steady, always there when I need him.

"No." I don't have to think about my answer before speaking.

I want to remember Gramps smiling down at me from the porch before I left for Colt's birthday party. Telling me he's proud of me.

Not cold and still and no longer breathing.

My gaze is still aimed at the ground, but I hear Caleb stand to tell the ambulance to leave with Gramps's body.

Tires roll aways a few minutes later. I don't move, trying to reconcile what my life will look like with such a central component of it missing for good.

There's a distant whinny a few minutes later, and that's what finally sends a jolt of direction through me.

Gramps wasn't the only one here who relied on me.

I raise my head, taking in the surroundings. The front yard looks normal, and it's worse than having the emergency vehicles out front as a beacon of bad news. The stretch of grass that's more weeds than blades looks the same as always. As it did when Gramps was about to walk out of the barn or drive up in his old truck.

Colt's SUV is still here, closer to the barn than it was when I climbed out of it. He must have moved it to let the other vehicles leave. Colt is leaning against the driver's side door, talking intently with Caleb.

They both glance over as I stand and walk toward the barn. Colt's expression is somber. I don't look at Caleb. I'm worried I won't be able to keep it together if I do.

I know this must be hitting him hard. Not only were he and Gramps close, but I'm sure it's occurred to him by now this means he's all I have left.

I head straight into the tack room, grabbing halters from the row of hooks just inside the door. Impatient hooves clang against wood panels as the horses realize someone is finally paying attention to them.

Her stall is furthest, but I walk to Dusty's first. She nuzzles me as soon as the door is open. I'm tempted to bury my face in her mane and cry. But if I let myself fall apart right now, I won't be able to pull myself back together for a while.

I slip Dusty's halter on and lead her out into the aisle, pausing to put Stormy's halter on her as well. Stormy tosses her head, making her displeasure about being cooped up all morning known. She is blissfully unaware of how badly I wish Gramps had woken up this morning to let her out.

I'm struggling to buckle her halter in place when I hear Caleb's voice. "What are you doing?"

"What does it look like?" There's a bite to the words that I don't mean to include but can't seem to curb. Shock is ebbing away, leaving behind a whole host of ugly feelings swirling inside of me like a tornado.

"You don't have to. I can…"

"It's fine."

I tug at the lead lines, and the two mares follow me eagerly. Past Caleb, who's watching me with a concerned expression that's probably merited but only annoys me more. Past Colt, who obviously just heard me snap at Caleb and is now looking at me like I'm a bomb that might detonate. Past the skid marks that tell me the ambulance arrived too late.

It takes me an hour to let all the horses out and muck out their stalls. I can hear the quiet murmur of Colt and Caleb's voices outside the barn as I work, but I can't distinguish anything they're saying.

Probably for the best. I'm sure they're talking about things I'm not ready to think about yet. Decisions will have to be made. Arrangements too.

When I emerge from the barn, they're still standing next to Colt's SUV.

"I'm so sorry, Lennon," Colt says as soon as I appear.

"Thanks." I give him a small smile, then keep walking.

Up the porch stairs, through the front door, past the kitchen, up the stairs to the second floor, and down the hall to my room. I don't stop until I reach the twin bed tucked beneath the eaves.

I collapse on top of my comforter, not caring I'm in clothes that are damp with sweat and smell like manure. I lie face down, inhaling the familiar scent of laundry detergent and cotton.

Quiet footsteps sound on the stairs, drawing closer and closer to my bedroom. I flip over onto my back to watch Caleb cross the room and stop beside the bed. He's pale beneath his tan, eyes worried and jaw clenched tight.

I scooch over, until the cool drywall is pressed against my arm. Caleb takes the silent invitation, lying down beside me. The bed is way too small for both of us. It's barely big enough for me.

"Steve Fisher came over around eight to drop a program for this weekend's races. He noticed the horses hadn't been turned out, so he came inside to check on Earl. Found him on the couch and called nine-one-one. They think it was a stroke. It was... quick." His voice wavers a little, but I don't react. "After the autopsy, they'll transport him to the funeral home. You'll have to decide about the burial then. Steve had to leave to take his granddaughter to school. He asked Chief Everett to pass along his condolences and to let him know if he could help with anything."

I manage an "Okay."

"What can *I* do, Lennon?"

I roll, so I'm half-lying on him. We woke up in a similar position just a few hours ago, but it feels like days have passed. "You're doing it," I tell him.

And then...the tears come.

∼

The next five days pass in a daze of wandering around the farmhouse wearing cut-off jean shorts and a ratty tank top while fielding endless phone calls with the funeral home, church, and cemetery.

Kentucky is experiencing a record heat wave, and the farmhouse only has one wheezing window unit. It's almost as miserable inside as it is out in the barn.

I watched Gramps do this twice, for each of my parents. But in many—most—ways, he was more a parent to me than either of my actual ones. Their deaths were defined by the mistakes they made while living. Gramps's is just...sad. The farmhouse is too quiet and empty without his work boots clomping up and down the stairs or his baseball games blaring from the living room.

Caleb has barely left my side since we returned from the lake. He's worried about me. And he feels guilty. Guilty I wasn't here. Guilty he wasn't here. But the coroner confirmed Gramps's death was quick and painless and there's nothing anyone could have done, even if he hadn't been alone.

And as much I wish I'd been here for Gramps's final moments, I'm equally glad I wasn't. He knew I loved him, and I know he loved me. I wish he could have been here for more of my life. But there was nothing left unsaid between us. No regrets are haunting me now.

"Can I help?"

I don't glance up from the old jackets I'm sorting through, just keeping making piles of wool and denim to donate to charity.

"I'm almost finished."

There's a pause as Caleb decides how to respond. I've spent the past week doing an accurate imitation of a zombie. Barely eating. Hardly sleeping, though that's partly because of the heat.

I wouldn't blame Caleb if he left to go stay at his family's estate. It has air conditioning and a private chef. But every morning he's asleep on the couch when I come downstairs, since neither of us want to sleep in Gramps's bedroom. Every meal, he makes food he knows I probably won't eat more than three bites of.

It's so tempting to sink. To stop thinking and stop caring and just ignore everything around me. Gramps's friends keep coming over to help with the barn chores, so I've barely had to do anything lately.

Caleb is keeping me afloat. And that scares me, because he's leaving soon. He should have already left. If I let myself lean on him now, I'll fall over once he's gone.

"The horses are all set," he tells me. "Tim Wilson came over and helped."

I look up and nod.

He shoves his hands into the pockets of his shorts. "Len…"

"I know, Caleb," I cut him off. "Today, right?"

He sighs. "I pushed it back as far as I could."

"I know. It's fine. I'll be fine." I finally glance up at him.

"You could come with me."

It's a relief he's finally saying the words. The strongest string tying me to Landry has been snipped.

I'm no longer tethered to this farm. To this town. But the lack of a link only makes me want to hold on tighter.

I stayed here with the horses I helped Gramps raise and train after my mother died. After my father died. After Caleb left for college. It feels right I remain here after Gramps is gone, too.

"My place off-campus is nice. The guys won't mind if you stay with us for a while. And if you liked it, we could get our own place."

Anxiety tightens in my chest. Not at the thought of living with Caleb. That part sounds wonderful. But about leaving Landry. It feels like losing what little I have left.

"I can't." I want to shove the words back in my mouth when I watch Caleb's face fall, but I can't bring myself to take them back. Or to explain them.

To Caleb it must seem like I'm still picking a falling-down farm over him, after almost three years of barely being together. He still doesn't even know I got into Clarkson, and I feel guilty about that too.

"He's gone, Lennon," Caleb says softly. "And he wouldn't want you to be sitting here, making piles."

"I know he's gone. And since he's gone, I don't know what he'd want."

It's a lie Caleb doesn't call me out on.

He's right. If he could see me now, Gramps would call me a coward and push me out the front door in the direction of Clarkson. He wanted me to go. He *told* me to go.

I gather up the pile of jackets and stand, picking my way past Caleb and down the hallway.

The entire farmhouse is in shambles. I was worried I wouldn't be able to bring myself to change anything, so I've gone to the opposite extreme. I've emptied bookshelves, strewn clothing, removed paintings from the walls. Anything and everything to stay busy.

There aren't any empty boxes left in the hallway, so I head into my room. Caleb follows, studying me as I dump the jackets into a cardboard box and neatly label the side with a marker. I stay in motion, moving to my bed to fold the load of laundry I did at two a.m. when I couldn't sleep.

Caleb takes a seat on the mattress next to the pile of clean clothes. I should have known he wasn't going to drop this so quickly.

I didn't ask him to stay, but he has. I knew it wouldn't— couldn't—last forever. He has a life to get back to.

I only heard Caleb's end of the conversation, but I know his baseball coach is not pleased with the delay of his star pitcher's attendance at a mandatory team camp.

"I'll come back next weekend," he tells me.

"It's fine, Caleb. Really. I'm a big girl." I force a smile, but he doesn't look convinced.

"I'm worried about you, Lennon."

"What do you want me to say, Caleb?" I ask as I fold my favorite T-shirt. "I'm sad and upset and I don't see either of those things changing anytime soon."

"Exactly why you shouldn't be alone right now."

"I have the horses."

He doesn't reply right away. At first, I think it's because he's trying to come up with a way to tactfully tell me he meant company of the non-equine sort. But he's no longer looking at me. He's staring the piece of paper he pulled out of the book I stupidly left out on my bedside table.

"You got in."

I bite my bottom lip hard enough to taste blood. "Yes."

"You got in *weeks* ago."

"Yes," I repeat.

Caleb looks up at me. I watch him visibly push the anger away to keep his voice even. "Were you ever going to tell me?"

"You think I'd lie to you about this?"

He stands. "You *did* lie to me about this, Lennon! I asked you if you'd heard back from Clarkson, and you told me that you hadn't!"

"I know. I'm sorry." I toss the T-shirt I'm holding back on the bed. "I didn't know what to tell you, okay?"

"You should have told me what we both knew all along: that you were never going to go." He shakes his head, dropping the letter onto the mattress.

"It was complicated, Caleb! I didn't know what to do."

"I told you we'd be fine if you stayed here, Lennon. I don't understand why you wouldn't tell me. It didn't need to change anything."

"It would have, though," I reply. "It would have been a choice, that *I* made. It would have been me choosing this farm. And I was worried it would seem like *not* choosing you."

"It doesn't have to be one or the other, Lennon. You don't have to stay here to keep the farm. I could hire staff, or we could move the horses down the road to my family's stables."

"I can't let you do that, Caleb."

"Because of the money?" I can tell he's fighting it, but more anger trickles into his expression.

"That's part of it," I admit. I was raised to work hard. Not accept hand-outs.

"I have plenty, Lennon! I could easily—"

"I know you have plenty," I interrupt. "*You*, Caleb. It's *your* money."

"To spend how I want."

I open my mouth.

"Just think about it, Lennon." He walks past me, headed for the doorway. "I'm going to change for the funeral."

"Caleb."

He stops, but doesn't turn around. "I *am* sorry. I should have told you as soon as I got the letter."

Blue eyes meet mine as Caleb glances over one shoulder. "I should have told you congratulations, Lennon. I never doubted that you'd get in."

Just that I'd go. Neither of us say the words, but I'm certain we're both thinking them.

As soon as he's gone, I push over the stack of folded cloths and curl up in the center of my bed.

CHAPTER TWENTY-SIX

CALEB

The first person I see when I step inside the church is Colt. He's standing to the right of the curved wooden doors that mark the entrance to the nave, tapping the pamphlet that lays out how the next hour will proceed against his thigh.

"Hey," I greet.

"Hey," he repeats, giving me a grim smile. "You doing all right, Winters?"

"Hanging in there," I reply, grabbing a paper program from the basket.

It's nice to have something to fiddle with when you're nervous. Makes me glad I play baseball, not soccer.

"Is Lennon?"

"I think so."

I actually don't.

Lennon is far from fine. She shouldn't be. No matter when it happened, losing her grandfather would be awful. He was the one who raised her. The only blood relative she had left.

I have no idea how she acted in the immediate aftermath of her parents' deaths. It was before we met. But right now, there's no sign of the girl I know intimately. Who I've shared memories and swapped love declarations with. Lennon has shut me out—almost completely—and it's far more heartbreaking than holding her for four hours while she cried was.

It's also terrifying.

I thought the days of worrying how she felt about me were gone. But that's exactly how I feel right now.

Lennon didn't tell me she got into Clarkson. That stings. Because I thought we were totally honest with each other, and the fact that she lied has me second-guessing. And I found out right before her grandfather's funeral, which I have to head back to Clarkson from.

"It's got to be really tough for her," Colt comments, watching the stream of people entering the church.

Understatement. I had to fish the suit I'm wearing out of a cardboard box because Lennon sorted the clothes I brought over from my parents' right along with her grandfather's things. She hasn't stopped moving in days. Stacking, sorting, cleaning, piling. The bags beneath her eyes suggest she isn't sleeping. And I know she's hardly eating.

"Yeah," I agree.

"You're headed back today?"

I nod.

I don't know what else to do. Staying this long was risky. If I wait much longer, I'll be jeopardizing my spot on the team. You don't miss training camp. Not as an inexperienced freshman, and most definitely not as the starting pitcher and team captain.

The days I've already missed required me to stare down a couple of ultimatums from the coaching staff. I'd stay—for her. Lennon is more important to me. But she doesn't want me here. She's made that clear. So I'll give her space, if that's what she needs to grieve.

Colt is silent as I watch more people walk by. Most of the pews are already full. I hope Lennon notices the large turnout. Landry may have its share of snobs, but Earl Matthews was a good man. He spent his whole life in this town, racing horses and raising his daughter and granddaughter.

"I should head in," I tell Colt. Reluctantly. I'm dreading the service. And how I'll have to leave, right after it ends.

"Yeah, okay," he replies. "Luke and Jake are almost here. We'll see you after."

I nod, then start down the central aisle. Lennon is up ahead, standing just to the right of the altar. Her face is blank as she listens to something Eliza Gray is saying. Cassie Belmont is next to her.

Cassie spots me first. Her eyes widen, prompting Eliza to look over as well. Neither says anything as I reach them. Lennon's friends clamming up around me used to be amusing and some- what flattering, but right now it's the last thing I'm thinking about.

"We'll see you later, Lennon," Cassie says, then pulls Eliza away.

I'm guessing they think this is a reunion of sorts, not that we've only been separated for the last half hour. While her grand- father's friends have come by to help with the horses, Lennon hasn't had anyone over since Earl died. She's shutting everyone out, not just me.

We stare at each other for a few seconds.

"I'm sorry." Lennon surprises me by speaking first. "For leaving without you. For lots of things."

"I'm sorry, too," I reply. Now isn't the time or place for a deeper conversation.

"You don't have anything to apologize for, Caleb," she tells me, right before she steps forward into my chest.

322

I freeze at the unexpected contact, the first she's initiated between us in days. I bend my head to kiss the top of hers, inhaling the familiar scent of her shampoo.

Rich organ music suddenly bellows through the church, putting a stop to any of the soft chatter that's been taking place.

Lennon pulls back but grabs my hand. I follow her to the front pew and take the seat next to her. There's no other family to sit alongside, but a few older men I recognize from stopping by Matthews Farm fill in the rest of the row.

One of them is Tom Stradwell, the owner of the local paper where Lennon has worked for the past few years. He gives me a nod of acknowledgement, which I return.

Lennon's staring straight ahead at the minister climbing the few stairs to the altar. She's still holding my hand, and grips it tighter once he starts speaking.

I listen to the sermon, but I'm not absorbing any of the words being spoken. My knowledge of what is planned during this service is limited to the little I overheard on Lennon's end of phone calls over the past few days.

I have yet to open the pamphlet I'm clutching in the hand Lennon isn't holding. Instead, I'm thinking about the conversation I had with Lennon at my grandfather's service. When she told me what she had or hadn't contributed at her parents' funerals, I never imagined I would be the one sitting beside her at her grandfather's.

As a teenager lusting after Lennon Matthews, I pictured the easy moments. Taking her to prom and getting to second base at one of Marcus's field parties. Not the hard ones, like watching her say a final farewell to the man who raised her.

Lennon's fingers slip free from mine, and she slides out of the end of the pew. Her spine is straight and her steps sure as she heads straight for the pulpit.

I'm not sure what she's doing.

I get my answer as soon as she reaches the microphone.

The familiar strains of Kentucky's most famous melody pour out of the organ, soaring through the air to collide with the sloped ceiling and stained glass. Nostalgic notes vibrate the wooden pews and floor as Lennon starts to sing, her clear voice blending and weaving with the instrument's accompaniment.

I've heard this song dozens of times. Most of them, I was slouched in a seat in my family's private box at the track, counting down the minutes until we could leave and I could take off a stiff suit.

This time, I'm listening the girl I love pour her heart and soul into the sound. The lyrics hit differently as I picture Earl in his rocking chair on the front porch of the farmhouse each time Lennon sings *my old Kentucky home*.

I don't see a dry eye in the church.

Mine aren't.

The last note dies. Lennon descends the steps to return to my side. As soon as she's back in her seat, she grabs my hand again. The action loosens the fist that's been squeezing my chest ever since I saw that ambulance. Assuages some of the fear that things between Lennon and me might never be the same.

A few words from the minister concludes the service. Our pew is the first to empty. I follow Lennon to the back of the church and outside into the heat.

Free from the echoey interior of the church, conversations pick up as attendees exit the building. Earl's friends are the first group to reach Lennon. I step away, giving them space to talk to her alone. A middle-aged couple I don't know are the next to exit, followed by one I *do*.

"What are you guys doing here?" I ask my parents when they reach me.

I told my mom about Earl's passing when she called me a couple of days ago, but it never occurred to me she'd come to his service. Never mind my father. I think it's been a full year since he's set a foot in Landry.

"We wanted to pay our respects," my mother replies, sweeping a hand across her brow to catch any stray blonde hairs. People are staring as they leave the church, and my mother's worst nightmare is being seen looking anything but her best.

"Why?" I know my parents too well to think this is a selfless gesture. With them, there's always an ulterior motive.

"We were visiting Landry for the Cup next week anyhow," my father says. "Your mother suggested we move our arrival up. Louis tells me the filly has a real chance."

I scoff. My father is a lot more interested in the money Winters Stables rakes in than the horses that garner it. He lets Louis, the trainer my grandfather held in higher regard than any of his blood relatives, handle everything related to the thoroughbreds.

"Lennon has a nice voice," my mother states. I know what she's doing, trying to shift the attention off the tension that's swirled in almost every conversation my father and I have had for the past decade. "I had no idea she could sing so well."

"Maybe if you'd ever put any effort into getting to know her, you would," I reply.

"Caleb. Don't speak to your mother like that."

My jaw clenches to the point it's painful.

"When are you leaving for Clarkson?" my mother asks, breaking the stiff silence.

"Soon. I have a weight session at four."

"I can't believe your coaches were all right with you staying in Landry after camp started," my father comments. "It could look very irresponsible, Caleb."

My mother jumps in. Probably sensing how close I am to losing my temper. "It was very thoughtful. Your father and I are just worried about how rash decisions might affect your future."

My father doesn't dispute her words, although we all know his definition of *future* is different from the one my mother's referring to.

There are two clear paths waiting for me after graduation next spring: baseball or business. My mother wants me to play. My father wants me to join his company.

"Her grandfather *died*, Mom."

"I know," she replies, patting her hair again. "And I understand you felt obligated—"

"It didn't have anything to do with obligation. I *love* her."

She sighs. Neither of my parents are well-acquainted with the concept of love. "You're both *so* young, Caleb."

"That's what you said when I told you we were dating. It's been almost three years. We're only a year younger than you and Dad were when you got married."

My mother swallows, then looks away. "It was a different time," she states.

It's a more passive response than what she'd really like to say. But she's wary of pushing me on this topic. If it comes down to Lennon or my parents, my mom knows which side I'll choose.

My father has no such qualms. We're already at odds. He doesn't have any desire to protect the happy family image my mother is so intent to curate.

"Don't be an idiot and tie yourself down, Caleb," he tells me. "There are plenty of women out there. Not to mention, that girl is a sinking ship. We passed Matthews Farm on our way here. She must be swimming in debt by the look of that property. Elaine always said—"

"Who's Elaine?"

My father looks annoyed. With me, with being here, who knows. "Earl's daughter. We were in the same year at school."

"Lennon's mother?"

My mother interrupts before my father responds. "We came to show our support, Caleb."

There was a brief moment, when I saw my parents here, where I thought their presence was an olive branch. That they were finally acknowledging how much Lennon means to me. Now, I see it for what it really is: calculated optics. There's not a single person in Landry who won't hear about how Austin and Abigail Winters attended Earl Matthews's memorial service.

It's their way of cloaking true intentions.

Public support covering private meddling.

"You should go, Mom."

That's all I say. They're not going to change their views, and neither am I. I know we'll have more arguments that come to the same conclusion, but I'm too drained to engage in one now.

My mother nods. "Tell Lennon we're sorry for her loss." She steps forward to give me a hug and a kiss on the cheek. Expensive, flowery perfume surrounds me in an invisible cloud.

They're not even going to acknowledge Lennon directly. It doesn't surprise me; it does piss me off.

All I manage in response is a stiff nod.

My father holds out his right hand in farewell. I stare at it for a long moment before I give it a firm shake. Before I've fully turned around, they're swept up in a conversation with Luke's parents, making plans to have dinner tomorrow evening.

Lennon's still surrounded by well-wishers, so I don't approach her. I head over to where Colt, Luke, and Jake are standing, next to the rose bushes that line the front path of the church.

"Your parents are here," I tell Luke.

"Yeah, I know. They asked why I was coming, and I

mentioned you, and then it turned into this whole thing about how if your parents might be here, they needed to be too."

I shake my head. I can't stand social posturing, and Landry is overflowing with it.

"Did you know *your* folks were coming?" Jake asks me, nodding to where my parents are still conversing with the Evanses.

"No," I reply. "Their attempt to soften the blow of warning me off Lennon again."

"Oh," Jake replies. He doesn't need to ask how I feel about that. Or if I want to talk about it.

I glance at my watch. "I have to head to campus. I've got a weight session at four." It's just past noon now and I've got a three-hour drive to Clarkson.

I say goodbye to my friends, then head toward the lone figure standing at the edge of the parking lot.

Lennon speaks first, which is good. I have no clue what to say to her.

"How soon do you have to leave?"

I search her face, trying to figure out if this is just a simple inquiry or something more.

"Soon-ish," I reply vaguely.

If she asks me to stay, I will.

Lennon nods, staring away at nothing. "I need to pick up his ashes. They've been ready for a couple of days, but I haven't..."

My eyes close for a second, trying to block out the lost expression on her face.

"Lennon..." I'm at a complete loss for words. My heart bangs painfully against my ribs as I'm confronted with the impossible situation of watching someone I love struggle and being power-less to help.

"I don't know what to do with them," she admits, still looking at the line of cars departing from the church's parking lot.

I swallow. "You could spread them on the farm."

She nods once. "That's all I could think of. But... I don't know. It doesn't seem like enough."

"I think it's what he would have wanted," I tell her, praying I'm not overstepping.

She nods again. "Yeah, you're right."

"I can come..."

Lennon shakes her head. "I need to do this myself. And I know you have to get back."

"Okay."

"I wish I'd been there, but I'm also glad I wasn't."

I nod. "I know."

There's a stretch of silence, long enough I think this might be how we say goodbye: five feet apart. But then Lennon turns toward me and closes all the distance between us. I can taste the salt of her tears on her lips before she buries her face in my neck.

"I love you, Matthews," I whisper. There's a lot more I want to say. About Earl and about Clarkson and about the future. But I'm not sure if she's ready to hear any of it. If she needs time and space to adjust to everything that has suddenly changed in her life, I'll give it to her.

"I love you too, Winters," she replies. "Drive safe."

Lennon walks away first, leaving me standing here.

I head for my truck and hoist myself into the driver's seat. The moments right after leaving her are always the worst. When I can still see her, but know I need to add to the distance between us.

This time is especially tough, for obvious reasons.

I know she's grieving.

I know the rug just got pulled out from under her feet.

I know more change probably seems like the most unappealing thing in the world right now.

But I also know Earl wanted Lennon to go to a good college. If he were still here, nothing would have made him happier than seeing her thrive at a school that challenged her.

The harsh reality of his death—one I know Lennon doesn't want to face yet—is that she has more options. Horses and land don't have a fraction of the hold on her that Earl did. She spent every moment with him she could, and now there aren't any left to share.

If she still stays in Landry, it will feel less like familial obligation and more like lack of love. That's probably not fair, especially in the wake of the three words she just told me. And since I haven't given up anything for her.

The night we got together, she told me she was scared to compete against other parts of my life.

Now, I'm experiencing the same fear.

Because I feel like I'm losing.

The brick house I've lived in since sophomore year is in total chaos when I open the front door.

"Hey! Winters!"

I turn to see Drew Maxwell, one of my teammates and housemates, strolling up the walk behind me.

"Hey, Maxwell." I bump his fist when he reaches my side.

"Cutting it a little close, aren't you?"

"Could say the same to you," I reply.

Drew grins. "Blame Jessica Oxford." I roll my eyes. Drew's smirk fades, as he studies me. "Everything good with you? We were all worried."

I was vague with the guys about the reason for my delayed return to Clarkson. They all know I have a serious girlfriend, but I've kept Lennon and my life in Landry almost entirely separate from who I am at Clarkson. And it didn't feel right to mention Earl. Doing so would seem like passing Lennon's loss off as my own.

"I'm good."

Drew nods. "Glad to hear it. Anderson's arm sucks."

"He's better than you could throw," I retort.

"Yeah, but I'm not the back-up pitcher," he replies, heading for the stairs. "Nice monkey suit, by the way," he calls over one shoulder.

As he disappears upstairs, there's a pounding sound that suggests Elliot's descending them. Sure enough, he appears seconds later, dragging a hand through his shaggy brown hair.

"Thank fuck," he breathes when he sees me. "Dude, I thought you had some sort of injury and couldn't figure out how to break it to us."

"Nope. I'm healthy as a horse," I reply, heading for the stairs myself. "Going to get changed."

Out of all the guys I live with, Elliot is most likely to ask questions. Part of me would love to get the perspective of an unbiased observer, but I also know it would never do what Lennon and I have justice. Most of our history is woven in moments and memories impossible to explain. Telling someone my girlfriend's grandfather died and she's been mostly distant since doesn't describe the situation accurately.

"All right," Elliot replies as I pass him. He eyes the suit I'm wearing, but doesn't comment or ask why I'm dressed up.

My room is the last one on the second floor. It overlooks the big oak behind the house. It's also the largest, which I learned when Drew took it upon himself to measure each bedroom. Unfortunately for him, I'd already chosen this one.

I change quickly, then check my phone. I skip past all the messages except two. The first is from my mom. It's a paragraph explaining she didn't mean to upset me earlier. At least, that's what the first two lines are about. I skim them, then skip to the end. It's a request to let her know when I've arrived on campus. I'm certain she's got my phone on a tracking app but I respond anyway, letting her know I have.

The other text is from Lennon.

Lennon: *You back?*

I reply to let her know I have, then gnaw on my bottom lip as I consider what else to say. Asking how she is won't go over well. Neither will inquiring if she's eaten.

Caleb: *I miss you.*

There's no immediate response, so I shove my phone back into my shorts, pull on my sneakers, and head downstairs. My other two housemates, Garrett and Jamie, are already downstairs. They pause to welcome me back, then continue rushing around, grabbing everything they need for our weight session.

We all pile into Garrett's Explorer to head to campus. The guys fill the short trip by complaining about the hundred-yard shuttles and sled pulls during practice this morning.

I "uh-huh" and "hmmm" along to their complaints, more focused on the weight of the phone in my pocket. Waiting— hoping—for it to buzz.

It doesn't.

There's an audible stir when the five of us enter Clarkson's athletic complex. A few guys from other sports teams stop to slap hands. Girls wearing tight spandex slow as they pass us. Drew and Jamie engage most of them, rolling their eyes at me when I don't pause.

Aside from baseball, it's the main thing I'm known for on campus. Even at the start of freshman year, when I was technically single, I didn't hook up with anyone. It's well known that I have a girlfriend, but since Lennon has never so much as visited campus, plenty of people pretend not to.

My phone buzzes in my pocket right as we enter the weight room. I whip it out so quickly it's a miracle I don't tear the mesh material. And it's not a random news alert or social media notification. It's from her.

Lennon: *I miss you too.*

Air leaves my lungs in a much-needed exhale. It's not that I doubted she did or would. It's that I needed her to say it.

"Winters!"

I turn to see Coach Thompson approaching. Hastily, I tuck my phone back into my shorts. He hates technology and I'm already on thin ice.

"Hi, Coach," I greet.

His shrewd gaze looks me up and down. I know evidence of Lennon's recent sleepless nights are clear on my face.

"You good, son?"

"Yes, sir," I reply.

I was just as vague with him about my whereabouts as I was with the guys, which I know is a large part of the pushback I received. I told Coach Thompson there was a personal matter I had to take care of, and my reliability in the past and importance to the team is the only reason I'm not being asked to pack up my locker right now.

"I trust you had a damn good reason for your absence?"

I swallow. "I lost someone I cared about, Coach. The funeral was this morning."

His expression softens into a sympathetic one I've never seen before. "I'm sorry to hear that." He keeps studying my face. I'm guessing the lines of exhaustion and lingering sorrow are saying a whole lot more than our conversation over the phone did. "If you need to take more time, let me know."

"Thanks, Coach."

He nods. "Nice to have you back, Winters."

"Thanks," I respond. Coming from Coach Thompson, that's basically the equivalent of a bear hug.

We set up our usual circuit around the weight room. All the teammates I hadn't seen yet give me warm greetings and relieved smiles. I wonder how many of them thought I was absent due to a serious injury, like Elliot.

Once our weight session ends, the whole team heads to Maloney's. The local pizza and wings joint is already buzzing with activity that significantly increases in volume when the team appears.

Baseball is Clarkson's most popular sports team. Mainly because we *win*. The last time Clarkson's football team had more wins than losses was before I was born. In the three years I've played on the baseball team, we've made it to playoffs every season.

We fill up three booths along the side of the restaurant that faces the street. The town Clarkson is located in doesn't hold much of a draw to anyone but college students attending school here, but there are a few younger families walking along the sidewalk outside. Probably here to camp in the surrounding mountains.

I end up smushed in a booth between Drew and Elliot, impatiently tapping the table. I'm starving. Aside from the eggs I burned this morning before choking them down, I haven't eaten anything. Lennon didn't eat anything at all. My table drumming quickens as I battle the urge to text her again.

Before I can fully talk myself in or out of a decision, our waitress appears.

"Hey, boys," Jessica greets.

Her attention bounces between Drew and Jamie, who's seated across from me. Unlike most of the girls who hang around the team, Jessica has divided her attention between my two housemates since freshman year.

Predictably, the love triangle—lust triangle would be more accurate—has generated lots of drama. When guys tell me I'm wasting my college years in a serious relationship, I wonder what they make of this mess. The other side of casual hook-ups is not all that sexy.

"Five large cheese pizzas," Elliot orders. "Actually, make it six. And two pitchers of beer. No, three. We're celebrating having *our* pitcher back!" He claps my shoulder. "Get it?"

"Yeah, I got it," I assure Elliot.

"Coming right up," Jessica replies.

A few of the guys here aren't twenty-one yet, but Maloney's popularity has more to do with its generous carding policy than its greasy pizza. "I might need one of you guys to help me carry it all over."

"I will," Jamie immediately offers.

"All right." Jessica departs with a coy smile, while Drew stares daggers at Jamie.

Elliot sighs next to me.

I'm not the only one fed up with their drama.

"Why don't you guys find someone else? *Each* find someone else," Elliot stresses.

"Like who?" Jamie scoffs. "A freshman?"

"Make a move on Sophie," Elliot replies.

"She's still holding out for Winters," Jamie replies, glancing at me.

I take a sip of water, pretending I didn't hear that comment. Maybe after our last conversation at Mayfair, the dynamic will be different.

"Surprised Sophie isn't here, asking where you've been the past few days," Drew comments.

I don't reply. Truth is, she texted me asking just that. It's one of many messages sitting unread in my phone right now.

"Here's the beer." Jessica sets two pitchers down on the table in front of us. Foam fizzles atop the amber-colored liquid. "I'll be right back with the third one and some cups."

She's back within thirty seconds, then Jamie jumps up to help her fetch the pizzas. We've all devouring hot slices and cold beer within minutes. But the food and familiar company isn't enough to distract me.

I'm worrying about her.

CHAPTER TWENTY-SEVEN

LENNON

Sunbeams creep across the hardwood floor slowly, turning shadows into honey-colored wood. Normally, this is when I'd roll over to slip back into the haze of sleep until my alarm goes off.

Instead, I keep watching the light expand, illuminating the clothes strewn across my bedroom floor.

I toss one leg to the side, wincing when it hits the plaster wall. This bed is too small for me. Has been for years. But now that there's a larger one available, I can't bring myself to use it.

I hoped turning the house upside down would help me move forward, but all it has accomplished is ensuring I have to spend an extra ten minutes looking for anything.

I slide out of bed, not bothering to change out of the oversized T-shirt I'm wearing. It's either Caleb's or Gramps's. I discovered after Caleb left that half the clothes he brought over made it into cardboard boxes along with Gramps's.

The morning light has reached the edge of the bed, revealing the white cotton I'm wearing is free of any stains or rips. Caleb's, then. It's probably designer.

I yank on a pair of jean shorts and stumble into the hallway, almost tripping over the stack of books I told myself I'd move last night. *Tonight*. Maybe. I amble down to the kitchen, picking my way through the rest of the scattered belongings I now own.

The sun that woke me hasn't fully risen. Mist hovers over the grassy fields that surround the farmhouse. I look out the window above the sink, at the peaceful scene. I know it's impossible, but I can almost define the sloped shape of an equine form out in the field. All the horses are still in their stalls, though, unless I've really lost it and left one out last night.

The quiet gurgle of the coffee maker is the only sound in the silent house. I should get a dog. Or a cat. Or just start sleeping in the barn. The total absence of sound is peaceful.

It's also really lonely.

I eye the plastic bag sitting on the counter. It's almost empty. Each morning since the service, I've spread some of Gramps's ashes on my trip out to the barn. It makes me feel like he's here with me, slamming pans or about to hobble down the driveway to fetch the paper like he did most mornings. But even that sliver of solace is nearly gone, disappearing as fast as the mist evaporating off the grass.

The few days that have passed since the memorial service have been hard. I'm not someone who struggles with isolation. I don't mind being alone with my thoughts most of the time. The sting of loss has started to ease.

I miss Gramps—I'll always miss Gramps—but I don't have regrets. I didn't leave freshman year and miss the past three years with him. I'm not sure if I believe in any cosmic power, but my last conversation with him was exactly what I wanted him to know. I'm grateful he knew I got into Clarkson. Glad he knew I'd have Caleb.

Now, I just need to decide where I go from here. The simplest

—easiest—path would be to change nothing. To continue living in this farmhouse, attending RCC, and taking care of what remains of my family's racing legacy.

I'm not under any illusions about my financial situation. I've been snooping around bank statements for years now. When a lawyer came over yesterday to hand me the deed to Matthews Farm, the little else I've inherited didn't surprise me. Money is tight. But it's manageable. I could make staying here work with the paltry savings, my income from the paper, and the stallions' stud fees.

I just...don't know if I should.

The coffee maker shuts off, returning the kitchen to total silence. I fill a mug with a healthy helping of caffeine, grab the bag of gray dust, and head out onto the front porch.

I'm tempted to take a seat in one of the rocking chairs, but as much as I want to prolong this, I also want to get it over with. Like the memorial service, I know this is something I need to get through. And hope like hell it looks better on the other side.

Hot coffee scorches my tongue as I walk the familiar path from the farmhouse to the main barn. There's no hint of the heat I know will blanket the farm later today. The cooler weather makes me dread the sun's full rise. I'd rather it stays like this, just on the precipice.

Another searing sip of coffee burns my throat as I watch the final physical remains of Earl Matthews drift away toward the towering oak that shades the barn.

I'm left holding an empty plastic bag. The woman working at the funeral home was definitely judging my refusal to purchase an urn, but I didn't know what I would do with it after spreading Gramps's ashes. Now, I'm left to ponder what I do with this bag.

Keep it?

Toss it?

It's the type of ridiculous, morbid predicament Gramps would have been in stitches about. The memory of his booming laugh prompts a smile to tug at the corners of my mouth for the first time in over a week.

The flicker of amusement is what causes me to flick the radio in the barn on for the first time in weeks when I walk inside. I even sing along to an old Billy Joel song as I mix the grain and supplements that make up the horses' diets.

There's a dusty piece of paper affixed to the bulletin board above the bins of grain, covered with Caleb's scrawl. It's hard to recall the time when I thought Caleb Winters was selfish and entitled as I study the notes he made about each horse's diet so he could help me feed them.

Resentment mixes with gratefulness. He's making this choice a hard one. Accepted or not, I know I wouldn't be even considering Clarkson if not for Caleb.

I distribute the pails of grain throughout the mares' stalls, then set about mucking out the manure while they eat. The mares get turned out in the east pasture, then I repeat the process in the stallions' barn. Summer days are long enough I've switched to riding at night, during the sweet spot where the sun is retreating but the bugs haven't come out yet.

After showering and changing, I hop into the truck and head down the driveway, smiling when Stormy trots along the fence line to keep pace with me. It's not until I turn on to the main road that she spins and canters back to join the rest of the mares.

I'm halfway to town before I realize I never ate any breakfast. I haven't had much of an appetite lately, and I know it's not only attributable to grief. I'm also stressed. The heavy, omnipresent sort of anxiety that sits in your stomach no matter what you do, like a dark cloud. The kind of worry that accompanies a big decision with no perfect outcome.

340

Since I'm ahead of schedule, I stop at the local coffee shop where Cassie and I used to spend Sunday mornings.

There's no line at this hour. Most of the summer tourists are likely sleeping in. Most of the locals probably have espresso machines in their state-of-the-art kitchens.

The sleepy teenager at the counter surprises me by greeting me by name.

"Hi…" I squint at the nametag affixed to his apron. "Charlie."

The boy beams at me. He can't be older than sixteen. "What can I get for you?"

"Iced latte, please. Extra shot of espresso," I reply. "And…a blueberry muffin," I tack on reluctantly.

I'm still not hungry, but the bowl of cornflakes I ate last night weren't much of a dinner.

Charlie nods, then grabs a pair of tongs and sets to work, fishing a muffin out of the pastry case.

"How is Caleb liking camp?" he asks, giving me an expression that's akin to an overeager puppy.

"Uh, I think it's fine," I respond.

"This is going to be his best season yet," Charlie predicts, as he tosses a muffin dotted with blue spots into a bag and hands it me. "Seriously. That's what the guys on TV last night were saying."

Caleb's ability to throw a baseball being discussed on television is news to me, but I don't say that. I never know *what* to say when people bring up Caleb and baseball.

I have nothing to do with that part of his life. His athletic accomplishments are his and his alone. I've never even seen him pitch in an actual game.

But that's not what people want to hear. They want the inside scoop. The team drama. The professional prospects.

"That's great."

Charlie nods. "Coffee will come out at the end of the counter. And…uh, I'm sorry, Lennon. About your grandfather."

"Thanks," I reply, pairing it with a smile. It's not the kid's fault he just went two for two on topics I don't want to discuss.

My latte appears in minutes. I sip on the cold coffee slowly once I'm back in the truck. The amount of caffeine I've already consumed today is probably burning a hole in my stomach. Until I start sleeping, there's no other option.

It's a short drive to the brick building that houses the *Landry Gazette* from downtown. The newspaper offices are perched above a real estate office, just one block from the racetrack. I whistle under my breath as I pass the listings posted in the window. Land in Landry isn't depreciating. The least expensive property is listed for just under seven figures.

Cold air smacks me in the face as I open the glass door that reads "Landry Gazette." Wooden stairs creak as I climb them to the second floor. The stairwell muffles sound, so it's a shock to step into the hustle and bustle of the newsroom.

"Lennon. A word," my supervisor, Alex, tells me as he breezes by and heads for his office.

I trail after him immediately. I'm well aware he sees his role in coming up with and overseeing my assignments as a massive waste of time.

Most of the paper's permanent staff members are in their mid-thirties and live outside of Landry. My impression is they've ended up here because their spouses wanted to live outside the big cities where most reputable papers are located.

Alex's office is the total opposite of the messy farmhouse I picked my way through this morning. A couple of framed articles hang on the wall, but aside from that the space is spotless. A neat row of red pens is the only decoration on his desk.

"Good to have you back, Lennon."

"Thanks," I respond. The words are genuine, but I'm guessing Alex wouldn't have been upset if recent events meant I didn't return to the paper for a few more weeks.

"Now, for the summer—"

Emily, one of the other research assistants, pokes her head in from the hallway. "Sorry to interrupt…"

"Then why are you?" Alex asks, grabbing a pen and spinning it between two long fingers.

"Mr. Stradwell is here. He'd like to speak with Lennon. Immediately."

"Right." Alex's face looks resigned, like he was expecting this.

I can't say the same. Tom Stradwell, the *Gazette*'s owner, attended Gramps's funeral, but aside from that, I can't recall the last time we spoke. He focuses more attention on his golf game and grandkids than at the many papers he owns.

Since he's almost a decade past the traditional retirement age and the sole reason I've had a reliable paycheck for the past three years, I judge his time management less harshly than I know many of my co-workers do.

"Let him know—" Alex starts.

"No need to send a messenger, Alex-boy. I'm right here."

Alex's jaw clenches. If I had to guess, I'd say being called "boy" by your boss while you're in your early thirties is not the greatest feeling.

"Hello, young lady." Tom's gaze has shifted to me.

Unlike Alex, I'm expecting the greeting. It's what Gramps's friends have always called me. It started when I was a toddler jumping into puddles and has stuck ever since, despite the fact I'm a "lady" often scrubbing water buckets or dumping manure when they stop by. Maybe because of it.

"Hi, Mr. Stradwell," I respond.

"Tom, Lennon. Always Tom." He smiles at me. The corners of light blue eyes crinkle, forming creases that work their way down his aged face. "Can we have a minute, Alex?"

We're in his office, but Alex doesn't point that out. "Yes, of course, Mr. Stradwell."

There's no name correction this time. Alex's jaw tightens before he shoos Emily out of the room, shutting the door behind them.

Tom rounds the corner of Alex's spotless desk and takes a seat in the swivel chair, leaning back as far as the springs will allow. They let out a squeak of protest, and that's the only sound in the small room for several seconds. Tom folds his fingers under his chin, surveying me closely. I shift under the scrutiny.

"You doing all right?" he finally asks, kindly.

I knew venturing out into the world would probably involve some obligatory sympathies, but I didn't expect to end up in a conversation with one of Gramps's oldest friends.

"I'll be fine," I answer.

It's not exactly what he asked, but he lets it slide with an understanding "hmmm."

"I know Earl felt like he would likely leave you with an awful lot to worry about."

"I'll manage."

"If you need money—"

"I'm good," I reply quickly, then soften my tone. "Thank you. But I'm good."

Tom's lips quirk. "That Matthews pride is still a force to be reckoned with, I see."

I acknowledge his observation with a small smile.

"I want you to know you'll always have a place here. Full-time position is yours once you graduate, if you'd like. Course, I'd imagine you may end up someplace else once you and the

Winters boy make things official. Earl seemed to think it was just a matter of time."

"Official?" I echo. "We're just dating."

Tom grins. "I follow Clarkson baseball closely. Caleb Winters risked being benched his senior year to stick around town. You've got a good man there, young lady."

"Um, thanks."

I'm not sure what else to say.

That boy doesn't love a thing in this world anywhere near as much as he loves you, Lennie. I can recall Gramps's voice perfectly. Did Caleb risk his baseball career to remain in Landry, or is Tom exaggerating?

Tom raps the desk twice, then stands. "If you need anything—anything at all—you let me know, okay?"

"I will," I promise.

I may be stubborn and proud, but if I need money, I'll take it from Tom. With him, it would merely be a loan. With Caleb, it's complicated. Even considering—because of—the implication Tom just made.

Tom hears the honesty in my voice. "Good. Now, it's off to the links for me. Here's hoping the grandson can manage to hold on to his club this time." He winks at me, then heads out the door.

Alex returns seconds later to walk me through my assignments and schedule for the summer. He doesn't ask what Tom and I discussed, but sends me a series of curious looks that make it clear he'd like to. I pretend not to notice as I scribble notes on research topics and deadlines.

"Uh, one last thing." Alex's voice has shifted from commanding to uncomfortable, and it makes me look up. "I've—I've heard you're in a relationship with Caleb Winters?"

"Um, yes," I reply, startled.

Alex is not the sort of supervisor you confide in about bad

dates in the break room. He makes it clear to every member of the staff that if it's unrelated to work, he doesn't want to hear about it. A mindset I appreciate, and one I did not expect him to break out of.

"There's some interest from the sports staff about doing a feature on him." Some scorn follows the words.

Alex is clearly not a baseball fan.

Suddenly I'm back in high school, staring Andrew down in the glorified closet where we had our paper meetings. The only difference now is that I know I hold some sway over Caleb's choices. That if I ask him to do this, he will.

"What does that have to do with me?"

"They're wondering if you think he'd be...amenable," Alex replies, looking very much like he'd love for a member of the sports staff to be talking to me about this instead. I'm surprised he even agreed to mention it.

"That seems like a question for him," I respond.

Alex nods. "Understood. That's all, Lennon. Thank you."

I nod. Based on his expression, I actually might have elevated his opinion of me with my response.

Just another unexpected part of today.

I spend the next seven hours doing research for the politics editor, Alice. The primary this fall is for Landry's seat in the state legislature, one previously occupied by a familiar name: Richard Winters. Caleb's grandfather. He was already representing Kentucky at the national level by the time I was born. It's hard to picture the distinguished looking, stern man I'd occasionally see in town ever concerning himself with any of the issues listed on the current candidates' websites.

Everyone has to start somewhere, I guess.

I leave the paper just before dinnertime. When I reach the end of the driveway leading to Matthews Farm, I discover the rusted mailbox has chosen today to topple over.

I pull into the driveway and hop out of the truck to straighten it. Unfortunately, the post itself has rotted through. No matter how many different angles I try to prop it up from, it refuses to stay upright.

"Fine," I mutter, yanking the box clean off the post and plopping it in the dirt. *Sorry, mailperson,* I think, as I add *buy new mailbox post* to my mental to-do list.

I should probably get a new mailbox as well. The peeling letters that spell out Matthews Farm are barely visible. The outline from where the sun has altered the rest of the paint is the main reason it's even possible to read what was initially displayed along the side of the metal mailbox.

The horses all head for the gate as soon as I park outside the barn. They know what my arrival home means. I walk into the tack room first to mix their grain, depositing a bucket in each stall before returning to the gate.

I grab Stormy and Dusty's halters first, buckling them in place and then leading the two mares into the barn. I repeat the process with the rest of the mares, then make my way over to the west pasture to fetch the stallions. I grab Geiger first. Unlike the mares, I never lead the stallions in at the same time. They're ornery and unpredictable on a good day.

When I return for Gallie, he's trotting back and forth along the fence line. I whistle, and he bolts for me. I grab his halter and put it on as efficiently as I can with him constantly tossing his head.

Rather than start toward the barn, I close the pasture gate behind me, containing us both inside the couple of acres the stallions graze on every day. I knot the lead line around the ring I clipped it to, forming a makeshift set of reins. After guiding Gallie over to the fence, I climb the lower two rungs. I'm still a foot below his broad back, but it's enough I can pull myself up with a mixture of determination and exertion.

It's Gallie's day to be exercised, but I would be on his back tonight even if it wasn't. This isn't how I usually ride him. Ride any of the horses.

But I'm feeling tired. Lazy. Reckless.

Even at age six, Gallie could give the horses set to race in the Landry Cup this weekend a run for their money. Riding him without a bit or saddle is similar to standing on a plane during take-off.

I slide onto rippling muscles anyway. Gallie's figured out what's going on. He's dancing in place, tossing his head in excitement. Before I second-guess this decision—before I grab my makeshift reins, even—he takes off, eating up meters of grass at a breathtaking pace.

I knot my fingers in his black mane, weaving them between the rough strands in a desperate attempt to stay on his back.

The speed is jarring.

My stomach got left back by the fence.

Adrenaline streams through my veins. For the first time in days, I can't think. I'm focused on the immediate, on ensuring I don't end up beneath the hooves trampling the ground with a rhythmic series of resounding thuds. On the strides churning up divots of grass at a startling speed.

I relax atop shifting muscles, making a grab for the rope that's been swaying in time with Gallie's strides at the exact wrong moment.

A bird flies out from one of the oaks that lines the pasture. Gallie spooks, turning to the right with a pivot that would make a barrel racer proud. I'm not one, and my reflexes are too slow. My vantage point shifts as I fly through the air and then land in a heap on the hard ground.

My shoulder takes the brunt of the impact. I roll onto my back, staring up at the clear sky as I readjust to being on the grass, rather than flying along above it. One by one, I shift all my limbs and muscles. Aside from my shoulder, the only bruise is to my pride.

If Gramps were here, he'd be bent over laughing as soon as he realized I was all right. He always preferred to watch others ride than hop aboard a horse himself.

I love riding. It's been a part of my life for longer than I can remember. But the number of hours I've racked up on horseback were more a product of necessity than pleasure. One of many tasks I took on a long time ago simply because there was no one else who could, or would.

All of a sudden, I have a chance to drop all of them. To decide if they're chores I still want to do now that I have a choice not to.

A terrifying, exciting prospect.

My view of the dusky sky is interrupted by a black muzzle. Gallie has returned to my side, realizing I was left behind.

I stand slowly, both to avoid startling the massive stallion and because hitting the ground at that speed felt like I imagine being smacked by a speeding train would.

I don't bother trying to climb back on his back. I hobble back toward the barn. Gallie is happy to amble alongside me. He kept running for several minutes after dumping me, and it appears to have been a more effective form of exercise than the controlled canter around the training track that's his normal running routine.

After depositing Gallie in his stall, I head inside for my second shower of the day. The water pressure feels heavenly against my tired muscles. I dress in jeans and a T-shirt, then pad downstairs to the kitchen.

A quick glance inside the fridge reminds me why I ate cold cereal for dinner last night. I heave out a sigh and pull a loaf of bread from the freezer.

Two slices pop out from the toaster a few minutes later, ready to be slathered in peanut butter. I take a seat in my usual chair at the kitchen table, slowly munching on the glorified snack. I finish eating but keep sitting. Today's checklist is complete. Horses, work, horses, eating. All done. I could read. I could watch television. I could continue sorting through piles.

There's only one thing I want right now. Rather than shove it to the back of my mind, I embrace it. And the same reckless energy that made me climb on an animal weighing more than a ton with nothing more than a flimsy rope makes me stand, grab the truck's keys, and head out the door.

The truck wheezes to a stop outside 52 Edgewood Drive. I sit for a moment, staring at the house Caleb has spent the past three years living in. It's larger than I expected it to be; a three-story brick structure with a neatly trimmed lawn out front.

Every light in the house looks like it's on, so I won't be waking anyone up. I shouldn't be surprised. Pretty sure I'm the only person in the state of Kentucky under the age of forty who goes to bed at ten p.m. on a regular basis. It's almost midnight now.

I climb out of the car, grabbing the bag of clothes I hastily threw together and slamming the door shut behind me. The sound echoes on the empty street. I walk toward the brick house, startling when a loud *clang* comes from the right.

"Sorry!" I glance over at a guy who looks to be my age, with sandy blond hair and a friendly smile, who's standing with two overflowing trash bins. The lid for one is now lying on the cement sidewalk. "Didn't mean to startle you."

"It's fine," I reply, loosening my grip on the bag I'm holding. "Here, let me get it." I approach him, grabbing the fallen lid and plopping it back atop the bin.

"Thanks." He gives me a wide grin.

"No problem." I turn to leave.

"Are you coming back to campus early?"

I spin back to face him. "Uh, no. I'm not a student here. Just visiting someone."

"That makes more sense. I *definitely* would remember seeing you around."

Friendliness turns flirtatious. I smile, awkwardly. This is what I get for being a good Samaritan, I guess. I'm out of practice when it comes to dissuading flirting. Guys weren't exactly swarming me in high school, and there's not a single person in Landry unaware I'm dating Caleb Winters.

"Good luck with those." I nod to the bins.

He smiles before continuing to the curb. "Hope to see you around."

I walk up to the front door of Caleb's house and knock.

"Yeah?" The door swings open, revealing a shirtless guy with dark blond hair chewing what looks like a stick of jerky. He looks me up and down, then smirks.

"Is Caleb home?" His truck is in the driveway, but I suppose he could have gotten a ride with someone. I probably should have texted him a heads-up, but I liked the idea of surprising him.

"It would be great if you could spread the word around campus that other people live here, too," the guy replies. "Not *just* Winters."

"If I went to school here, I'd definitely consider doing that," I reply.

His face crinkles in confusion. "Where do you go to school?"

"Could we have this conversation while I'm not standing out on the street?"

"Uh, yeah. Sure. Come on in." He pulls the door open, and I step inside.

The outside of the house may not look like it's inhabited by a group of college guys, but the interior definitely does. Sports equipment is hung on pretty much every visible surface: railings, doorknobs, and a couple of chairs. A pair of socks are flung on the floor and the walls are bare.

I'm not sure why Caleb was bothered by me turning the farm-house topsy-turvy. Seems like it would have just felt the same as living here.

"Guys are through here." The blond guy whose name I probably should have asked for heads down the hall and disappears to the right.

I swallow my nerves and follow. I've only met two of Caleb's college teammates. They visited him in Landry last summer, and we got lunch. They were both perfectly nice, but the one meal didn't establish any of the rapport I have with Colt, Jake, and Luke. No one at Clarkson knows anything about me and Caleb's past: good or bad.

"Winters! Some chick for you," I hear called out just before I reach the opening.

I enter what is obviously the living room. Four guys are sprawled out around the large space. There's a massive sectional couch holding two of them; the third and Caleb are in bean bags.

Unsurprisingly, there's a baseball game playing on the flatscreen television.

I *am* surprised to see a bunch of girls parked on the couch between the boys. A few are sitting on the floor as well. I do a quick count, registering there's eight of them. A couple take note of my arrival, but the others are distracted, talking with the boys.

"Who?" one girl asks the blond who announced my arrival. "Sophie said she couldn't come tonight."

Caleb glances over, sees me, and freezes.

Then, a broad smile spreads across his face. Every second of the dark, three-hour drive here from Landry is suddenly worth it. He stands and strides over to me.

I'm expecting a hello, or for him to ask what I'm doing here.

Instead he kisses me, pulling me tight to his body and wrapping his arms around my waist. I melt into him, not hating the fact he's greeting me so enthusiastically in front of his friends and teammates. And especially the other girls here.

"Hey," I whisper, when we break apart for air.

"Hi." He grins, but the humor leaves his face as he studies mine. "Is everything okay?"

"Yeah, everything's fine. I just wanted to see you."

Caleb's smile returns. "You left after the night feeding?"

"Uh-huh. Mike's going to take care of things in the morning."

Gramps's friend seemed thrilled by the prospect when I called from a gas station an hour ago, especially when I told him I was going to visit Caleb.

"I'll have to head back tomorrow afternoon."

Caleb's smile dims a little when I reveal just how brief a visit this will be. He recovers quickly, though, turning so he's no longer blocking the rest of the room.

Everyone's staring at us, ignoring the game on the screen.

"Guys, this is my girlfriend Lennon. Lennon, you've met Garrett and Jamie. That's Drew." Caleb nods to the blond guy who let me in the house. "And Elliot." He nods to the other guy on the bean bag.

"Nice to meet you all," I say.

He doesn't introduce the girls, and I wonder—hope—that means he doesn't know their names.

"See you guys tomorrow," Caleb says, then pulls me from the room and toward the stairs.

"Maybe I wanted to watch the end of the baseball game," I tease.

Caleb laughs. The warm, husky sound of it warms me from the inside out. "We can watch it in my room if you're really that invested."

Once we're upstairs, he leads me down the hall and into his bedroom. I glance around. I've seen glimpses of it on video calls, but never in person. It's more tastefully decorated than the one in his parents' house in Landry. The walls here are white rather than red. His comforter is navy, rather than lime green.

Textbooks and more baseball equipment litter the room, but aside from that, there isn't much in the way of decoration. There are a few baseball posters up on the walls. There's a framed photograph on his desk, and it's one of us. I smile when I see it.

"Do you want anything to eat? Drink?" Caleb walks over to a mini fridge tucked in the corner.

I shake my head as I let my bag drop to the floor and kick off my shoes. "No, thanks. I'm good."

He pulls a sports drink out for himself. I watch his throat contract as he drinks some of the red liquid.

"Want to watch something?" He misreads my eye roll. "It doesn't have to be baseball, Len."

I walk over to him, not stopping until I can feel the heat radiating from his skin. "I don't want to watch anything, Caleb."

"Oh." Understanding dawns as he studies my face. "You could have just said this is a booty call."

I tug at his T-shirt. "This is a booty call."

Caleb yanks the cotton material off in one smooth motion and then walks forward, forcing me backward. I giggle as he pulls my shirt off impatiently, leaving me in just a bra and jeans. "Don't think I don't want to, because I *really* do, but are you sure that you want to?" he asks as we tumble down onto his bed.

"I'm sure."

I'm sick of feeling sad, of experiencing nothing but grief and uncertainty. But most of all, I want to reconnect with Caleb. To show him how much his support after Gramps passed meant. To reassure him that while everything else in my life might have changed, my feelings for him have not.

"I *need* you, Caleb."

Hunger replaces uncertainty as he pulls my mouth to his. Lust condenses in my stomach and spreads throughout my veins as he rolls above me, his tongue skillfully stroking mine. I feel *alive*, a mass of emotions and desires. My hands explore the corded sinew of Caleb's bare back, savoring how the muscles shift and tense.

I can't get close enough to him, only moving away to pull down my jeans and tug at the gray sweatpants he's wearing. His mouth moves to my neck. I arch upward, moaning his name and not caring how needy and desperate I sound.

Anticipation tumbles through me like a waterfall when I feel his cock press against my entrance. My heart races and my breathing quickens.

"Fuck," Caleb groans, as he slips the rest of the way inside of me.

I stop thinking and just feel, letting myself get lost in the sensation of being completely consumed by Caleb Winters.

And hope the way I'm clutching on to him is telling Caleb everything I haven't found the words for yet.

CHAPTER TWENTY-EIGHT

LENNON

Caleb is already awake when I wake up the following morning, which rarely happens. I'm usually the early riser of the two of us.

He walks into his bedroom as I'm pulling on his old *Landry Baseball* sweatshirt, giving me a warm smile and a soft kiss. "How'd you sleep?"

"Pretty good." I smirk. He grins back before kissing me again. I'd rather he thinks it was his bedroom skills that made me pass out immediately after sex than the fact I've barely slept in days.

"I've got practice in twenty minutes," he tells me.

I glance at the alarm clock. It's just past seven. "This early?"

Caleb shrugs. "It's too hot later in the day."

"Okay."

"It's only an hour. I can come back and pick you up after. Or you can come?"

"I'll go with you." I'm ambivalent toward baseball, but I love Caleb. For him, I can sit through a practice. After all the times he's helped me with the horses, it feels like the least I can do.

Caleb's smile tells me that's the answer he was hoping for. "There's a diner we can go to for breakfast after."

"Do you have coffee?" I slept well last night, but I'm running on a major deficit overall.

He grabs a travel mug from his desk and hands it to me. "Way ahead of you, Matthews."

"Wow. I could get used to this treatment." I take a sip of the coffee, smiling when I taste my usual creamer in it.

"You could," Caleb responds.

I take my time lowering the mug. I wasn't under any illusion the topic of me attending Clarkson wouldn't come up during this visit, but I'm not ready to seriously discuss it yet.

"I need some more time, Caleb."

"Fine," he agrees easily, but a muscle in his jaw jumps.

We both know time is a finite resource. The Admissions Office was understanding when I informed them of Gramps's death and requested an extension on accepting or declining their offer, but that leniency is limited. The fall semester starts in just over a month.

After I finish getting dressed, I follow Caleb downstairs. The rest of his housemates are rushing about, grabbing sports equipment and eating granola bars. All of them give me curious looks, a couple of them smile. Caleb grabs two breakfast bars from a kitchen cabinet and waves at the rest of the guys.

"See you guys at the field."

They all stare at us as we walk into the hallway and out the front door.

"I guess you don't have a lot of girls spend the night?" I tease.

Caleb gives me my favorite grin. "Just you, Matthews." He tosses me one of the bars, and I manage a catch. His smirk turns to an overdone look of surprise.

I laugh as we climb into his truck. "Shut up."

He turns the key in the ignition and then looks over at me. "What?" I ask through a mouthful of granola bar. It's a small miracle crumbs don't spray everywhere.

"It's just weird that you're here, going to practice with me. Good weird," he clarifies, catching my raised brows. "Really good weird. The best weird."

"*The best weird*? No wonder I beat you out for valedictorian based on your English grade."

Caleb grins. "What can I say? You make me less articulate, Matthews."

I smile, then sober. "I'm sorry, Caleb. I…" My eyes drop to the footwell, embarrassed by the sting in my eyes. "I'm a mess right now, and I didn't want you to see me like this. Because it's *scary*, how much I love you and how much I want to rely on you. The fact that you stayed… I talked to Tom and he said you risked your whole season to stay, and I'm worried you'll hate me for—"

I stop talking when Caleb's lips hit mine. He kisses me twice. Fiercely. "I could *never* hate you, Lennon. Never." His voice softens. "Do I wish you'd talked to me instead of yanking paintings off the walls? Yeah, that was a little concerning. But you could have decided to go sky-diving and I would have strapped in right next to you."

"Now you tell me," I joke.

Caleb smiles. He shifts the car into reverse, then looks over at me again. "I've experienced scarier things."

He turns to back out of the driveway before I have a chance to study his expression, but I'm pretty sure that was his way of telling me that his feelings for me might be just as terrifying as mine for him are.

∼

I thought Landry's athletic complex was impressive. I suppose it is, for a high school. But Clarkson's is *massive*. A series of bulky buildings surrounded by a lot more activity than the rest of the campus we drove by.

Caleb parks next to the baseball field. Bleachers surround it, unlike the couple sprinkled around Landry's.

"Wow. How many people does the stadium hold?" I ask. Caleb looks over at me and starts laughing. "What?" It's not like I can count the number of seats.

"This is our practice field. The baseball stadium is on the opposite side of the pool."

"Your practice—"

Caleb's already out of the truck. I open my door, sliding down onto the asphalt. The looming buildings look even taller now. I stare up at them as Caleb unloads his gear from the back. A couple of guys wearing football jerseys walk past on the sidewalk. They both call out greetings to Caleb.

"I'm going to go get changed," Caleb tells me, coming back around with a duffel slung over one shoulder. "You good?"

"Yeah," I reply quickly, not wanting to be an imposition. "I'll just…look around." I wave a hand vaguely through the air.

Caleb chuckles. "Sure. I'll meet you at the bleachers after and we can get breakfast."

"Okay," I agree.

He leans forward and kisses me before heading off toward one of the many brick buildings. I quickly lose sight of him. Baseball isn't the only sports team already back on campus. There seem to be people wearing *Clarkson Athletics* apparel everywhere I look.

I head toward the tennis courts, looping around a running track and past a lacrosse field. This place is huge. I gain a new appreciation for why people gush about how Caleb received a full athletic scholarship here.

When I reach the tennis courts there are two girls hitting balls back from a machine that's spitting them out at an alarmingly rapid velocity. I turn around, heading toward the football stadium instead. Guys in jerseys begin spilling out of one side of it. A few give me looks as they pass by.

I hurry back toward the baseball field. There aren't any players out on the diamond yet, but the stands have started to fill. With a few guys, but mostly with girls.

I take a seat on the far edge of the bleachers, slouching and tilting my head back so I can stare up at the sky. It's a perfect, cloudless blue. A shade that is nice to look at but bodes for another hot, merciless day of heat.

I wish I'd remembered to grab my mug of iced coffee from Caleb's car. By the time we leave, it'll be watered down and warm. I pull off my sweatshirt and drape it on the bleachers next to me as the temperature continues to rise.

Excited chatter sounds to my right, and that's how I know the team must have arrived. I shade my eyes, watching as guys enter the dugout in pairs and trios. Caleb isn't in any of the groups. Finally, I spot him walking toward the field, talking to an older man in a polo shirt who looks like the head coach. An assortment of trainers trail behind them.

I don't think I'm imagining how the level of noise in the stands corresponds with Caleb's arrival. But I tune out the chatter and focus my attention on the field.

My eyes stay in place, but my brain roams. I'm on a college campus. And not just any college campus, a school that sent me a letter offering a place here.

It was one thing to consider that in the abstract, another thing to *be* here. It wasn't just the logistics of Gramps and the horses that kept me from visiting Caleb until now. I was apprehensive about what visiting a college campus could be like.

I didn't tour any universities when I was in high school. I'm completely out of my element, but there's a flicker of excitement, of interest, about imagining what it would be like to be a Clarkson student.

"Excuse me. Where did you buy that sweatshirt?"

My head turns to the right as soon as I register the question. A redheaded girl seated one row behind me is leaning forward, her focus aimed my way so there's no mistake about who she's talking to. The three girls seated beside her are also looking at me. I glance down at the sweatshirt next to me. "Um, I didn't buy it. It's from my high school."

"It's got *Winters* on it. I've never seen it in the school store. They only carry his jersey, not sweatshirts."

Up until this exact moment, I had no idea you could buy clothes with Caleb's name on them. And I wasn't aware girls *wanted* to buy them. Learning that's the case throws me for more of a loop than seeing how many of them were in his living room last night did. "It has his name on it because *he* gave it to me."

The redhead's eyes widen. She glances at her friends, who look equally stunned. "You *know* Caleb Winters?"

Hearing people say Caleb's name with awe and admiration isn't new. The need to stake my claim, or mark my territory, or whatever you want to call it, *is* new. I've never had to explain our relationship to a stranger.

"Yes." I nod, then quickly stand and grab the sweatshirt.

Leaning against the metal fencing that surrounds the baseball field sounds more appealing than continuing this conversation. The team has gathered by one of the dugouts. I hope that means their practice is almost over. I'm starving.

"Wait!" the girl practically shouts.

Everyone in the immediate vicinity glances over, so I can't pretend I didn't hear her. I glance back.

"How well do you know him?" the redhead asks.

"What do you mean?" I know exactly what she means. I want her to say it.

"Are you two friends, or…"

"We've been dating for three years." My back-the-hell-off tone registers, but she doesn't look affected by the warning in it. Instead, she looks me up and down, then says, "Okay."

I continue down the bleachers, not bothering to say anything else. I've never been worried about Caleb cheating on me. But this is my least favorite part of being Caleb Winters's girlfriend: the attention.

The interest.

I didn't have to deal with it in high school. I've been protected from most of it since we officially got together. It's not that I didn't think girls here would be interested in him. It's just different, seeing it for myself.

I reach the chain-link fence and lean one shoulder against it, hoping that girl doesn't think she chased me off. I pull out my phone and text Cassie.

Lennon: *Did you know you can buy clothes with Caleb's name on it?*

Less than a minute later, my phone begins to buzz. When I answer, Cassie is laughing. "Did you seriously *not* know?"

"How would I know? Half the kids in my classes wear pajamas every day. Not sports stuff." To be fair, the community college I've taken classes at for the past three years doesn't even have any sports teams to represent.

"So, you're at Clarkson?"

"Yeah." I scuff the toe of my sneaker in the dirt. "I missed him. And…I got in here. Figured I should take a look at the campus."

"You got into Clarkson? Congrats, Lennon! That's a big deal."

"Thanks, Cassie."

She pauses, so I know what question is coming before she speaks. "Are you going to go?"

"I don't know. Part of me really wants to. Not only because of Caleb, although it would be nice to not be in a long-distance relationship, for once. Tom Stradwell told me I have a permanent position waiting for me at the *Gazette* after I graduate from RCC. But a degree from Clarkson would open up a lot more opportunities."

It bothers me that's the case, but I know it's true.

"What's holding you back, then?"

"I'd have to sell Matthews Farm. Clarkson gave me some financial aid, but I can't afford to pay someone to take care of the horses and look after the property. But if I do that, I won't have anywhere to stay during breaks."

"You know you could stay with me. Or Caleb. Or apply to stay on campus. It's a much bigger decision than that, Lennon."

I exhale. "Yeah. I know."

"I'm sure Caleb would..."

"He offered. But I...I can't."

"Why not? You know how rich his family is. Then you don't have to pick one or the other. You can graduate from Clarkson and then decide if you want to keep the farm or not. See where Caleb gets drafted. Really think it through, before making a choice you can't take back."

"I don't care how much money they have. This isn't him buying me dinner. Horses are crazy expensive. We're talking about hundreds of thousands of dollars."

Cassie isn't as shocked by the amount as I'm expecting her to be. "That's probably the interest his trust fund makes in a month."

I'm not sure if it's a joke or if she's being serious. Caleb and I have never discussed exactly how much money he has.

"Are you worried you'll break up? Is that why you don't want to take money from him?"

"No, I'm not worried about that. Things are good between us." I think back to last night and this morning. "They're really good, actually."

"You should think about taking him up on it, then. It's okay to accept help."

"Yeah."

I *have* accepted help from Caleb. Many times. Money is different. To me, at least. Cassie's family is nowhere near as wealthy as the Winterses, but they're more than comfortable. She has a different perspective on it than I do.

"Text me when you're back in Landry so we can hang out."

"I will," I reply, before hanging up.

When I glance at the field, I'm surprised to find it empty. Players are trickling out of the field house carrying bags and water bottles. I was talking to Cassie for longer than I realized.

"Hey." Caleb smiles when he reaches me.

"Hey," I reply, suddenly feeling shy. None of the crowd in the bleachers has dispersed. It feels like we're on display, like *I'm* on display.

"Who were you talking to?" Caleb asks.

"Cassie," I reply. "I texted her about something and she called me back."

"What did you text her about?"

I'm saved from answering by an unfamiliar voice.

"Never seen you leave practice on time before, Winters. Now I see why." A tall, skinny guy with cropped blond hair has paused a few feet away from us, a wide grin stretching across his face.

"Your RBI could use some extra practice, Davis," Caleb retorts.

Impossibly, the blond—Davis—grins bigger. "You gonna introduce me?"

Caleb sighs, but he's smiling. "Lennon, this is Nick Davis, our third baseman. Davis, this is my girlfriend, Lennon."

Davis—or Nick, I'm not sure what to call him—holds a hand out for me to shake. "Nice to meet you, Lennon. Don't worry, I've heard all the jokes before."

"All the jokes about—oh." I realize.

Nick chuckles, probably in response to my blush. "We were sure Winters was making you up."

I smile, but there's a spasm of guilt in my stomach. Selfishly, I never really considered things from Caleb's perspective.

Aside from having to make the three-hour trip to Landry, I figured me never coming to Clarkson didn't bother him. I'm anti-social on my best day and bored by baseball. Now, I'm realizing how unfair that was. Caleb would come to Landry to fit himself into my life—spending time with Gramps and taking care of the horses—while I've never made any effort to step into his.

"Hey, Torres," Nick calls out. "Come meet Winters's girl."

Instead of just one guy, five amble our way.

"We've gotta head—" Caleb starts.

I shake my head at him. "I want to stay."

He studies me, clearly surprised. But in a good way, I think. There's a warmth in his eyes that turns my insides to goo before I turn to meet more of his teammates.

Eight hours later, I park beside the barn. After breakfast, Caleb took me on a walk around campus. And then I had to leave. Come back to my responsibilities here.

Touring Clarkson's campus, I could see it. I could picture

myself there. I finally understand why people say college is more than an academic step. At RCC, I go to class and come home. It's never felt all that different from high school. But Clarkson felt like a whole other world. It *is* its own world.

And that appeals to me more than I thought it would. But being back in Landry, stepping out of the truck to survey the familiar acres that make up Matthews Farm?

My feelings are all snarled up again.

I head inside the farmhouse to dump my overnight bag and grab a snack. My appetite seems to have finally returned. I swap out my sneakers for a pair of paddock boots and walk out into the field to fetch Geiger. Gallie isn't thrilled about being left behind, racing back and forth along the fence line as soon as the gate clangs shut behind his pasture-mate.

I tack Gallie up and head in the direction of the training track. Then come to a sudden stop.

Caleb's truck is parked next to mine.

I blink at the black vehicle, certain I'm imagining it. I've barely been home a half hour. Caleb would have had to leave Clarkson just after I did.

No matter how many times I blink, the truck is still there.

"Caleb?" I finally call out, feeling foolish.

No answer.

I continue toward the training track and there he is, leaning up against one of the few posts still standing. Caleb straightens and smiles when he sees me, unknotting the fear he's here because something is wrong.

"Uh, what are you doing here?"

He drops my gaze, looking down at the dirt track. My eyes focus on the white papers he's tapping against his thigh.

"Caleb?" I prompt.

He sighs. "I was just going to have the bank send these to you, but I decided it would be better to give them to you in person. The mail wasn't delivered until after you'd already left, and I wasn't sure how to tell... It doesn't matter. Here."

Caleb closes the few feet between us and holds the papers out to me.

"What is it?" I ask, transferring the reins to my left hand so I can take the papers in my right. Geiger snorts and tosses his head.

"Money."

Breath leaves me in a *whoosh*. "Caleb..."

"I know, Lennon. I know you don't want it. But I can't just sit back and not do anything. I have the money. Let me help. You would do it for me."

I swallow and look away. He's right. I would, if our roles were reversed. But he's the one who's *actually* doing it. That's different from a hypothetical handout.

"It doesn't have to be for college," he continues. "The account is in your name. Spend it however you want. Fix the farm up. Buy new yearlings to race. It's yours."

"It's too much." I haven't looked at the dollar amount yet, but I'm sure it's an obscene amount of money.

"It's *not*," Caleb replies. He glances down at the ground again, then back at me. One hand rubs the back of his neck. "I'm fucking serious about us, Lennon. If you say yes when I ask, a lot more than what's in that account is going to be yours one day."

Shock spreads through me. Marriage isn't a topic that's ever been broached between us. I had no idea it's something Caleb has thought about.

"Oh," is my brilliant response.

Caleb laughs. "Did I freak you out?"

"No. I just...we've never talked about it."

"I know you're not ready. I'm not ready either. We have a lot of other stuff to figure out first. But one day..."

"One day sounds good," I tell him. God, if my freshman year self could see me now. When I dropped that form off, I never, ever would have imagined having the last name Winters one day.

Caleb steps forward and presses a kiss to my forehead. I close my eyes, absorbing his presence. "I've got to go. I have a film session tonight."

I can't believe he drove all this way, just to give me a packet of papers.

"*Tell* me what you're thinking, Len," he says. "Don't shut me out."

I hold his gaze. "I promise."

"Okay. I'll call you tomorrow."

One final smile, and he turns to leave. I grab his arm before he can take a step and kiss him. It's more than a peck. I loop my arms around his neck and bite his bottom lip. Caleb pulls me flush against his body, returning my passion.

Gallie whinnies impatiently, pulling on the reins I'm holding. I'm surprised I didn't accidentally drop them.

We're both breathing heavily when Caleb reluctantly pulls away. "I really have to go, Len."

"Yeah, I know." Now would be the obvious moment for him to remind me that if I transfer to Clarkson, our relationship wouldn't be this series of rushed moments anymore. But he doesn't mention it. Doesn't push me. "I love you, Caleb."

His face softens into my favorite smile. "Love you too, Len."

They're words we've exchanged plenty of times before. But I'll never take hearing Caleb Winters tell me he loves me for granted. It doesn't have anything to do with the fact he's the only person alive who *I* love.

Caleb has the world at his feet. He's choosing to include me in it. He makes me feel safe and adored, and to me that's far more valuable than the contents of the bank account the papers I'm holding declare me the new owner of.

He kisses me again, the pull between us almost magnetic. We're rarely completely alone like this. We're at a lake with his friends or at a house filled with his teammates. When he stayed at the farm until Gramps's funeral, I was too dazed to really register it was just the two of us here.

I fist the soft cotton of his shirt, trying to keep him here. To tether him to me. My reservations about attending Clarkson have nothing to do with not wanting to spend every possible second with him, and I hope he knows that. I try to tell him with each swipe of my tongue against his.

Caleb looks pained when he pulls away for a second time. Gallie has started stamping the dirt with one hoof. "I really, *really* have to go now," he tells me.

"I know."

He smiles, kisses me once more, then turns and heads in the direction of his truck.

"Caleb!"

He spins back toward me. "Yeah?"

I hold up the papers. "Thank you. It's way too much and I'm not sure if I'll ever spend a penny of it. But *thank you*."

He's given me options. Choices. *Thank you* doesn't seem like enough, but it's all I have to offer him.

Caleb nods, then keeps walking. I remain in place. He doesn't glance back before he disappears around the corner of the farmhouse, and I'm glad.

I know indecision is written all over my face.

CHAPTER TWENTY-NINE

CALEB

C oach Thompson catches me sneaking into the room where we hold film sessions five minutes late. I hold my breath when our eyes connect. I've seen him make an example out of tardiness before—calling guys up to the front of the room or making everyone stay late. But when I mouth a *Sorry*, he just nods.

He's trusting me, assuming I have a good reason for being late even after missing whole days of camp. I'm not sure he'd consider driving six hours roundtrip to spend fifteen minutes in Landry a good one. It was irresponsible and selfish.

But I didn't feel like I had a choice. I was planning to travel to Landry this weekend to give the papers to her, then she unexpectedly showed up last night. As soon as they arrived this morning, I started driving. It felt like a conversation we needed to have in person. I mean, I basically proposed to her.

After our film session ends, I end up at O'Reilly's with a bunch of the guys. It's an Irish pub close to campus that serves three-dollar pints on weeknights.

Our large group takes up an entire corner of the pub, but none of the other patrons seem to mind. It's a mix of other Clarkson students and a few older guys who must live here year round.

"Jessica's coming," Drew announces to my left, dropping his phone on the table. Jamie scoffs. The rest of us exchange looks. "Sounds like Sophie and Maggie are coming, too."

Now I'm the one getting side glances. I realize I never responded to Sophie's text last week. I'm assuming she's probably heard about Lennon's visit, adding to the incoming awkwardness. Jamie confirms when he adds, "I'm sure she's heard about Lennon's visit by now. Maggie met her at morning practice, apparently."

"She did?" I ask.

"Yeah, she said there was some chick with your sweatshirt there."

I take a sip of beer. I figured Lennon noticed all of the girls in the stands, but she didn't say anything to me. It's something we've never directly discussed, aside from the few teasing comments she's made after her friends acted differently around me. Cassie Belmont still clams up around me, and she's Lennon's best friend.

Lennon hates being the center of attention, which I often am. And the amount of money I have makes her uncomfortable. In the span of one day, I put her on the spot and handed her a six-figure check.

"Is Lennon visiting again soon?" Jamie asks.

"I don't know. She's got a lot going on at home right now." I leave it at that.

Jamie nods. "I hope she does. You're funner to be around."

I snort and take another sip of beer.

"I always figured you were full of shit when you said you don't resent not being able to hook up with other girls," Elliot says.

"You've obviously never been in love," I reply.

"Nope," Elliot replies. "Not interested."

"Incoming," Drew mutters.

Sophie reaches us first, wearing a low-cut top that has every guy looking at her. I rub a finger along the rim of my pint glass as she takes a seat on the stool next to mine. I keep my gaze on the table.

"Hey, guys," Sophie says. There's a flurry of responses from the guys.

When I look up, she's staring straight at me.

I smile because it's that or make this even more awkward. "Hey."

"I'm the one who invited you, not Winters. Spread the love, St. James," Drew teases.

Everyone at the table besides me and Sophie laughs. Sophie is clearly not thrilled about being called out for her fixation on me. I can sympathize but I'm also thinking if she were a little less obvious, there would be nothing to say.

Conversation shifts to discussing some Greek-themed frat party happening this weekend.

"How was practice earlier?" Sophie asks me, since neither of us are participating in the conversation.

"Fine," I reply. "It wasn't too hot this morning, and then we just had a short film session tonight. Easy day, all things considered."

"More like the best fucking day of Winters's life." Jamie joins our conversation. "Three years, and he finally got his girl to come visit."

"Fastest I've ever seen him leave practice," Drew chimes in with.

"He didn't even stay downstairs to see if the Jays won last night," Elliot adds. "Wonder why."

"He dragged Lennon upstairs to watch the end of the game," Jamie tells Elliot with a smirk.

They're purposefully trying to be dicks, but I'd rather endure their joking than make small talk with Sophie

I shrug. "I like her more than you three idiots."

Elliot grabs his chest like I've wounded him.

"Maggie mentioned Lennon was at practice this morning," Sophie says.

"Girl's got some sass, Caleb," Maggie tells me from her spot across the table.

I grin. "Yeah, I know."

Sophie studies my expression. "She didn't stay for very long."

"She had to get back to Landry."

"Her grandfather died, right? Your parents mentioned it. They went out to dinner with Mom and Dad a few nights ago."

I tense at the mention of Earl, and I'm sure it shows on my face. "Yeah," I reply, taking a long sip of beer and hoping Sophie gets the hint this isn't a topic I feel like discussing.

She doesn't. "That was really nice of you to stay in Landry. I'm surprised she let you, though, knowing you had camp."

There's some judgment in her words—judgment of Lennon. It turns my next ones curt.

"She didn't have a choice."

Sophie smiles, registering my annoyance and trying to temper her words. "Like I said, nice."

It feels like the conversation we had at Mayfair never took place. Maybe she was drunker than I realized, and doesn't remember it. Maybe I underestimated how much she likes a challenge. Maybe it's her parents' influence. No matter the reason, it's annoying.

"Who needs another round?" Drew asks.

"Me," I reply, standing. "I'll help you grab them."

Elliot and Jamie both request fresh beers. The girls all ask for cocktails. I hope Drew is listening to their orders, because I'm not really paying attention.

I lean heavily against the wooden counter as we wait for the bartender to come over.

Today has been a lot. Mostly good. Waking up with Lennon this morning, having her come to practice, introducing her to my teammates. But I worried about what she'd say about the money the whole drive to Landry. And then stressed about running late the whole trip back to Clarkson.

I'm exhausted.

"I'll stop inviting Sophie out," Drew says quietly.

"It's fine. She's your friend."

She's my friend too, which makes this more complicated. Before I moved to Landry for high school, Sophie and I were close. Our parents were—are—best friends. When we were younger, there were a few times when I thought about making a move. But I never did. And then I met Lennon. Sophie and I are never going to happen, and I wish she'd accept it.

"I'm not going to pick a girl over you, Winters. No matter how hot she is."

The bartender comes over to take our order. Thankfully, Drew remembers everything. Between the two of us, we're able to carry the bottles and glasses back over to the table.

"Caleb!" Maggie calls as we return. "We were just talking about you."

"Oh, yeah?" I ask, a little wary.

"You're from Landry, right?"

"Right." I smile but no one else catches the joke, the way anyone *from* Landry who knows me would.

There was a time when I never would have claimed it as my hometown. Landry is tied up in a lot of complicated feelings for me. Resentment toward my grandfather. Annoyance toward my parents. Special memories shared with Colt, Luke, and Jake. Love of Lennon.

"I've heard Landry is amazing," Maggie gushes. "Like some sort of posh resort town?"

I shrug. "Yeah, sort of."

"I'm going to Landry this weekend for the Landry Cup," Sophie says. "You can come with me, Maggie. See it for yourself."

I look over at Sophie, surprised. "You're going to the Cup?"

She nods. "Your family invited mine. I've never been, and Coach gave us this weekend off. You should come."

"Not my thing."

"Doesn't your family have horses running?" Sophie asks me.

"I think so," I reply, shrugging. "I don't really follow any of the racing stuff, honestly. My grandfather had a whole team of people running it all for him, and my dad has kept them on to manage everything related to the horses. I'm not involved."

"You grew up in Landry and you don't follow horse racing?" Jessica asks incredulously. She's the only fellow Kentuckian at the table.

"I didn't *really* grow up there," I respond. "I just visited in the summers and went to high school there."

"Still. You know it's basically Horsetown, USA, right?"

I nod. "That's what Lennon calls it. What little I know is thanks to her."

"Her family has racehorses?" Jessica asks.

"Yeah." There's no family now, though. They're Lennon's.

"Are any of them racing on Saturday?" Maggie asks.

"No, they're not," I reply.

I don't know if revitalizing her family's racing legacy is something Lennon wants. Most of the responsibility involving the horses was foisted on her. I don't know if she wants it to remain part of her life.

I guess I'll add it to the list of things we still need to figure out.

~

Everyone rushes to leave practice Friday afternoon. It's sweltering out and we only have one weight session this whole weekend. After hours of practice this past week, that sounds like a mini vacation.

I finish getting dressed and say goodbye to the few remaining guys in the locker room, leaving through the side door that leads right out into the parking lot. I'm halfway to my truck when my phone rings.

I pull it out of my pocket.

Mom is flashing across the screen.

I sigh, then answer.

"Hi, Mom."

"Are you in some sort of trouble?" she demands.

"What? No."

"Don't lie to me, Caleb. Your father and I can help. There's a private investigator who—"

"Mom. I'm not in any trouble. I swear." I reach my truck and toss my baseball bag in the back.

"Why did you transfer half a million dollars out of your trust fund, then?"

And…there it is. I kick the back tire as I pass it, annoyed but not surprised. "You and Dad weren't supposed to have any access or control over that account after I turned eighteen."

"Our financial manager does. A transfer that size raises flags, Caleb. Is someone blackmailing you? Is it drugs? Gambling?"

I'm disturbed and amused those are the first assumptions she's making. And dreading the truth. Naively, I guess, I thought she and my dad wouldn't find out.

"I told your father you shouldn't have access to that trust fund until you were twenty-five. Did he listen to me? Of course not."

I keep silent. I'm guessing she knows exactly where the money went. Knew before she called.

"You gave money to *her*."

I stay silent.

"Is *she* in some sort of trouble? There's—"

"It was a gift."

"A *gift*? Your father gave me diamond earrings while we were dating. He didn't write me a check for *five hundred thousand dollars*. I mean really, Caleb, what were you possibly thinking?"

"I was thinking that she needs money and I have money."

"Plenty of people need money, Caleb. Are you going to start passing out hundred-dollar bills to strangers on the street, too?"

"I'm not planning to spend the rest of my life with *plenty of people*, Mom. Just her."

Silence. It's the farthest I've gone, when defending Lennon to my parents.

"You don't even know where you'll be living next year, Caleb" she finally says. "I know she matters to you right now, but things change. People change."

"I'm going to marry her, Mom. You—and Dad—can flip out about it all you want. It won't change anything. Except your involvement in my life, going forward. I'll stop answering the phone."

"There's no need to react hastily, Caleb."

"Hastily? We've been dating for almost three years, Mom. When are you going to get over it?"

She sighs. "Will you be in Landry this weekend? It's the Cup; the St. Jameses will be visiting."

"I can't come back this weekend."

Another sigh. "I'm planning to host Thanksgiving at the chalet this year. Will you be able to come to that?"

"I tell you I'm busy Saturday and you want to make plans in *November*?"

"We have to plan ahead. There's—"

"Is Lennon invited for Thanksgiving?" I ask.

"I—yes, of course."

There's no *of course* about it, since my mother has purposefully excluded Lennon from everything else. But I decide to choose my battles. "Fine. I'll ask Lennon."

"If you change your mind about this weekend, let me know."

I exhale and shake my head, even though I know she can't see. I know exactly why my mom wants me to come home this weekend. And I'm not interested in playing my part in the perfect family façade.

"I have to go, okay? I'll let you know about Thanksgiving after I talk to Lennon."

"Fine," she says. My mother hates not getting her way.

"Fine," I repeat, then hang up.

I crank the air conditioning and drive home.

CHAPTER THIRTY

LENNON

I'm mucking out Stormy's stall when I hear gravel crunching. I lean the pitchfork against the wall and head outside. I'm not expecting anyone.

There's a delivery truck stopped in the driveway. A middle-aged man hops out of the open driver's side, wearing a brown shirt and matching shorts.

"Matthews?" he asks.

"Yes," I reply.

He shoves his hat up to scratch his forehead, then lowers it. "You know your mailbox is on the ground?"

"Yeah." I sigh. "Sorry. It's on the to-do list."

"All right, well, this has gotten sent back a couple of times. Other guy couldn't find the place." He walks toward me and hands me a navy plastic bag. "Have a good one."

"Thanks. You too," I call after him.

I start back toward the barn, glance down, and stop in my tracks.

The package I'm holding is addressed to Earl Matthews. It's postmarked the day after Gramps died.

I hold my breath as I tear the plastic open. The sound of an engine fades as the truck traverses down the driveway toward its next stop.

I drop the bag to the ground and hold up the cotton material that was inside.

It's a gray *Clarkson University* sweatshirt.

I stare at it. Then stare some more.

At some point during the three days between when he found out I'd been accepted and before he passed away, Gramps took the time to order this. He meant what he told me from the porch. He wasn't pushing me to transfer to Clarkson out of obligation, it's something he really wanted for me.

I wonder if Gramps would have given this to me before I decided. He always made his opinions clear, but never pressured me into any decision. If I'd returned from the lake to him in one of the rocking chairs on the front porch, he would have brought Clarkson up again. Pushed me to tell Caleb.

I glance between the shingled barn and the gray sweatshirt I'm holding. And then, I finally make the decision that's been hanging over me ever since the white envelope with the Clarkson University emblem appeared in the mailbox almost a month ago. Back when the mailbox was still standing.

Caleb answers on the second ring. "Hey."

"Hey," I reply.

"Is everything okay?"

"You can stop asking me that every time I call," I tell him wryly. "I could just be calling because I want to talk to you, not because something is wrong."

Caleb laughs. "Fair enough. Is that why you're calling?"

"No. I called to ask why you're not at home."

"How do you know I'm not at home?"

"Because your truck isn't in the driveway."

A rapid inhale echoes across the line. "You're here?"

"I'm here."

"The spare key is under the front mat, if you want to go outside." Muffled voices come through on his end. *Now anyone could steal...What, your jockstrap?* There's laughter, then Caleb's voice cuts through. "I'll be there in ten minutes."

I don't go inside. The summer heat isn't terrible today, so sitting outside actually feels pleasant. I take a seat on the tailgate of the truck, tipping my head back to feel the sun warm my face.

Less than ten minutes later, I hear a car door slam. Caleb walks toward me, wearing a backward baseball cap and an adorably confused expression.

I don't tease him with my decision. It's been drawn out enough. "I enrolled this morning."

Caleb stares at me, his face frozen with shock. He really didn't think I would transfer. Nothing in his expression suggests this as an expected outcome. "You did?"

I nod. "And then I called a real estate office. The farm is going on the market first thing tomorrow. The realtor thinks it'll sell fast."

I know it will sell fast. Land in Landry is hard to come by. There's high demand and low supply. And large properties close to downtown are *impossible* to come by. Those stay in families for generations. There will probably be a bidding war, despite the sad state of the buildings.

Caleb's expression is carefully blank. He's trying to gauge how I feel about this. How he should feel about this.

"What are you going to do about the horses?"

"They have extra space at the track now that the Cup has been run. I can board them there for the time being…then I'll probably sell them. I'll have plenty of money once the farm sells. But they deserve to live somewhere they're ridden regularly. With a big pasture and lots of attention."

Caleb shakes his head. "You love those horses, Lennon. And that farm."

"Yeah. I do." I inhale deeply. "But I love you more." Caleb starts to say something, but I keep talking. "Gramps tried to convince me to sell the farm for years. He wanted me to do this. To leave Landry and go to a competitive college. I had to decide, and now I have. I need to come here without a safety net. To be scared of falling. To push myself out of my comfort zone."

"Why does it have to be one or the other?" he asks. "Don't you want to live in Landry after graduation?"

"I don't know. But I know *you* don't."

Caleb curses and looks away. "Don't put this on me, Lennon."

"I'm not," I insist. "But you said you're serious about us. I'm serious, too. I came to celebrate, not fight."

I slip off the tailgate and stand. "I decided, Caleb."

He closes the distance between us, tugging me close to him. "I didn't think you'd do it," he whispers into my hair.

I half-smile as I recognize the words I told him once, a while ago. "Me neither."

Caleb pulls back just far enough for me to see his face. "Will you move the horses to Winters Stables instead of the track? They'll get ridden daily and go out in a big pasture. And you can think about it more, before you decide."

I nod. "Okay."

There's a flash of relief on his face. Something that won't totally change. If I'm being honest, I experience it too. I don't have regrets about my decision, and I'm determined not to have them. But it was a big decision to make. Knowing I won't have to put on a brave face for the sale of the horses I've known since they were foals is a relief.

"How long are you here for?" Caleb asks.

"Not long. I've got a meeting with the dean, a tour of campus, and then I have to drive back to Landry for the night feeding. I'm working at the paper tomorrow. And I have a lot to do over the next few weeks."

He studies me. "You're sure?"

I don't need to clarify what he's asking about. I nod. "I'm sure."

It's a relief, honestly, to have finally made a decision.

The Dean's Office is cold. A blast of air conditioning permeates my clothes, forming goosebumps on my skin. I step toward the large desk decorated with a vase of daisies. A rotating fan sends their sweet, floral scent straight at me as I approach the stern-looking receptionist.

"Hello. Can I help you?" she asks me, glancing away from her computer screen.

"Hi. Yes. I'm Lennon Matthews. I have an appointment with Dean Williams."

The woman nods, her stoic expression unchanging. "I'll let her know you're here."

"Thank you," I reply.

"Would you like some tea? Water?" she asks.

"I'm fine, thanks."

She nods, then returns her gaze to the computer.

I glance at the paintings lining the walls before taking a seat on the very edge of one of the velvet topped chairs along the wall. I stare at the empty seats across from me and fiddle with the hem of my shirt. I'm wearing a nice pair of shorts with it, but I suddenly worry I should have worn a skirt. Or a dress. My advisor at Richardson Community College would regularly show up for our meetings in jeans and a faded T-shirt. This is much nicer than I was expecting.

"Lennon Matthews?"

"That's me." I stand and shake the hand of the woman who called my name. Her tight bun is paired with a friendly smile.

"Wonderful to meet you, Lennon. I'm Dean Williams."

"Nice to meet you, too," I reply.

"My office is this way."

I follow her down the hallway to a nondescript wooden door. The interior is elegant, filled with more oil paintings complemented by dark wooden accents.

Dean Williams takes a seat behind the desk that takes up most of the space in the room and gestures for me to sit in the chair angled across from her.

"How are you, Lennon?"

"I'm good, thanks. You?" I reply stiffly.

All of a sudden, this is becoming very real. Telling Caleb. Being on campus. Diving so deep into change, my comfort zone is miles above me and far out of sight.

"Good." Dean Williams smiles. "Now that you're enrolled as a student, you'll receive a welcome packet in the mail. That will explain how to set up your student account, register for classes, and should provide you with all the information you'll need to become a full-time student. If you have questions about any of that, I would be happy to answer them. But I really wanted to set up this meeting to check in with you. We like to do so with all of our transfer students, seniors or not. I know you requested an extension on your acceptance because of bereavement. I wanted to offer my sincere condolences and make certain you know there are lots of resources at your disposal to make this as smooth and easy of a transition as possible."

"Thank you," I reply.

"I've looked at your records, and you're an exceptional student. I don't anticipate that you'll have any trouble managing the course load here or adjusting to a new academic atmosphere. The same is true for most of our senior transfers. It's usually the social transition they find most difficult. We hold events throughout the year to provide opportunities for transfer students to meet one another. I hope you'll find the time to attend them if possible. Do you know any current Clarkson students, by chance?"

"Uh, one."

"Is he or she a senior as well?"

"He. Yes. We went to high school together."

Dean Williams glances at a folder on her desk. I'm guessing it's my file. "Landry High School?"

I nod.

"The only other senior student we have from Landry High School is Caleb Winters."

I'm not sure how to respond to that, and it must show on my face. For the first time in this conversation, Dean Williams is the one who looks unsure. "My husband is a big baseball fan," she tells me, looking almost sheepish.

"Oh," I reply. "Well, uh, yeah. I'm talking about him." My nerves have dissipated, but I wasn't expecting either Gramps or Caleb to come up during this meeting.

"I'm sure Mr. Winters will be a great resource for you," Dean Williams states. "Our athletic teams are quite involved in campus life."

I smile, awkwardly.

"All right. Well, let me run through a few logistics with you, and then I'll introduce you to Samantha Bridges. She will be the one giving you your tour today. She's a junior and a journalism major, so she should be able to answer any questions you have from a student perspective."

"Sounds great," I reply.

And just like that, I'm a student at Clarkson University.

CHAPTER THIRTY-ONE

CALEB

Lennon carries two more boxes out of the farmhouse and stacks them by my truck. Most of her hair has fallen out of its ponytail. She swipes some strands out of her face and straightens. "This is the rest of it."

"Okay," I reply, hiding a smile.

When the horses left an hour ago, it was with twenty boxes of supplements, fly sheets, halters, brushes, and who knows what else.

Lennon's belongings barely fill half the truck's bed.

I add the two boxes she just brought out to the few already in the truck. Lennon fiddles with the keys she's holding as she glances around the yard.

"I guess this is it," she states.

Nothing looks different. Her horses are gone, hauled away by one of my family's fancy racing rigs to their new home down the road. But the barn looks the same. The old truck is parked outside it, just like always. And the exterior of the farmhouse doesn't reveal the interior has been stripped. Lennon donated all of Earl's belongings to charity. All her clothes are in my truck. An auction house is coming to collect all the furniture tomorrow.

"Let's go," she tells me, heading toward the passenger door.

"If you want to—"

Lennon doesn't even let me get the whole offer out. "No, I'm ready to go. Let's go."

"All right." I climb into the driver's seat and shift the truck into drive. Lennon fiddles with the stereo. I watch her out of the corner of my eye as she scans through the stations, pausing on one and then flipping forward two more without stopping.

"Do you want to stop and see how they're settling in?" I ask.

Finally, she stops fussing with the radio. Her fingers tap against her thigh; she glances in the rear-view mirror, and then there's a sigh.

"Yeah."

The gate is open when we reach my family's farm, so I continue right up the drive. This is the first time I've been back to my family's Landry estate since I came to get my suit for Earl's funeral. It looks the exact same as always: pristine. This property was my grandfather's pride and joy. Out of obligation more than anything, my father has made sure it's kept up to the same standards.

I stop by the stable rather than driving all the way up to the house.

My mother's Range Rover is parked in the roundabout. I'm surprised to see it. We haven't spoken since she called me about the money missing from my trust fund, but I wasn't expecting her to still be in Landry. The Cup—and all the social events that are all my mother cares about—have passed.

Lennon leaps out of the truck as soon as it stops. I smile as she makes a beeline for the barn.

"I'm going to go get a coffee for the road. Want anything?" I call after her.

"No, I'm good," she says over her shoulder before disappearing inside the main stable.

Landry's solitary coffee shop is quiet and empty when I arrive. It's long past the usual morning rush.

I order my coffee from a high school-aged kid who first gapes at me and then peppers me with baseball questions.

What was meant to be a brief stop quickly stretches into fifteen minutes. The arrival of another customer finally ends our conversation.

Halfway to my truck, I run into Tom Stradwell on the sidewalk.

"Hello, Mr. Stradwell," I greet.

"Caleb! I thought that was you! How are you?"

"I'm good, sir. How are you?"

"Good, good. What brings you to town?"

"Uh, Lennon. I'm helping her move everything to campus."

A smile forms before I've fully finished my response. "I had a feeling," he tells me. "I can only imagine how proud Earl would be if he were still here with us. That young lady was his moon and his stars."

"I know," I reply.

Lennon's bond with her grandfather is one I was always a bit jealous of. God knows Richard Winters never held me in the same high regard. He considered baseball a waste of time.

"I'm sure she'll excel at Clarkson. I hope she'll give the *Gazette* the time of day after the offers pour in." Mr. Stradwell smiles.

"What do you mean?" I ask.

"Lennon is the best research assistant we've ever had at the paper. Hell of a writer, too. I offered her a full-time job after graduation."

"Oh." I do a poor job of masking my surprise.

Mr. Stradwell peers at me. "Lennon was born here. Raised here."

"I know."

"The Winters name runs just as deeply in the Landry archives as the Matthews one does."

"I know," I repeat, trying to figure out what the hell he's trying to tell me.

"I never met a man more loyal than Earl Matthews." He pauses meaningfully. "Some things skip a generation."

"I know this place means a lot to Lennon," I state.

"I wasn't talking about the town, young man." He smiles at me. "Good luck with your senior year, Caleb. I have no doubt you'll accomplish a lot."

"Thank you," I reply.

Tom winks, then continues down the street.

I stay in place for a minute, feeling like I was just spun around in a circle. Not only from the topsy-turvy ride of trying to figure out what Tom Stradwell was talking about, but also from the unexpected revelation Lennon already has a job offer in Landry after graduation.

Eventually, I stop standing on the sidewalk like a fool and walk toward my truck.

There's no sign of Lennon when I park by the barn. I'm not surprised. I'm sure she's looking over feed schedules and exercise charts with Louis, the barn manager.

I climb out of the truck and stretch before taking a long sip of the iced coffee I just bought. The August sun is relentless, beaming down like a spotlight. The cold liquid barely counteracts the heat.

"Caleb?"

I turn to see my mother. She's wearing a floral print dress and a confused expression as she approaches my truck.

I school my expression carefully. "Hi, Mom."

She pauses a few feet away from me. "I didn't know you were in town."

"Just for today. I'm helping Lennon move."

My mother's lips purse. "Move?"

"She's transferring to Clarkson."

"That doesn't explain why you're *here*, Caleb."

I exhale, knowing she'll probably take this about as well as the check I wrote Lennon. "Her horses were moved here this morning. I arranged everything with Louis. Let me know if you want me to pay room and board for them."

Her expression hardens, turning into a cold mask. "When will you be back in Landry?"

"No idea," I reply. Lennon is taking any incentive to return with her.

She nods, realizing the same. "Well, I'll be at the New York penthouse for the next few months."

"Fine."

"What about Thanksgiving?"

"I haven't mentioned it to Lennon yet. We've been busy figuring other things out."

My mother swallows a couple of times, then fiddles with her pearl necklace. "All right. Let me know after you…talk to her."

Voices sound, right before Lennon emerges from the barn. Her face is lit up as she talks to Louis, who followed her outside.

When she turns toward me a second later, her steps stutter. But she continues, walking over to my side and offering my mom a polite smile. "Hi, Mrs. Winters. How are you?"

"Fine, Lennon. I hear you're transferring to Clarkson?"

Lennon glances at me, then back to my mother. "Yes."

"Best of luck. I'm sure it will be an adjustment for you."

My jaw is clenched so tightly it hurts. I can't figure out why my mother insists on acting like this. Why accepting Lennon is some Herculean task to her.

"We won't be at Thanksgiving, Mom," I say, then pull Lennon away.

As soon as we're in the truck, she shoots me a questioning look. "Thanksgiving?"

"In Aspen. My mom keeps bringing it up. I don't want to go. To be around her or my dad."

"She's your mom, Caleb."

"She's conceited and condescending."

"She's still your mom. Don't take having one for granted."

I nod.

The drive from Landry to Clarkson is a familiar one. But this time—for the first time—Lennon is beside me. I watch her stare out at the rolling countryside for most of the trip. She seems lost in thought.

I park outside of Archibald Hall three hours later. It's predominantly a freshman dorm. I'm guessing Lennon was assigned here since she's a senior year transfer.

"Time to see if those muscles are good for anything but looking at," Lennon teases me as she unbuckles her seatbelt.

I smile but then sober, just staring at her.

"What?" she asks, running a hand through her hair.

"Are you okay?"

"I thought we agreed you were going to stop asking me that."

"Okay. The next time we go for a drive and you say more than ten words to me, I won't ask."

Lennon rolls her eyes. "I'm good. Really. This is all just...a lot."

"I know it's a lot. That's why it freaks me out when you shut me out."

"I'm not trying to shut you out," Lennon tells me. "I promise. I just don't want you to think I'm a total mess."

"Life is messy, Len. That doesn't make *you* a mess." I pause. "Although I'd still be here—even if you were."

She smiles. "Thanks, Winters. Not just for all the boxes you're about to carry."

"But mostly, right?" I joke as I climb out of the cab. "You know you packed more for the horses?"

We survey the dozen boxes in the back of my truck.

"Are you complaining I didn't pack more?" Lennon asks.

"No, definitely not," I'm quick to say.

"That's what I thought." Lennon smirks, then grabs the nearest box. I snag two and follow her over to the entrance of her dorm.

Clarkson's campus is busier than I've ever seen it. As a member of a sports team, I was eligible to skip the dorm experience. I don't spend much time on campus, period. Aside from attending classes, all my time is spent at the sports complex or my house off-campus.

There's a folding table set up in the lobby where a few student volunteers and staff members are checking students in.

Lennon reaches the front of the line and gives her name. One girl at the desk is leafing through a stack of papers; the other stares at me.

"All right, just sign here and then you're good to go," the girl says to Lennon.

"Aren't you Caleb Winters?" the other asks.

"Yeah, I am," I confirm. I don't need to glance at Lennon to know she's probably rolling her eyes.

"What are you doing *here*?"

"My girlfriend." I nod to Lennon, then follow her toward the stairs. "What room are you?" I ask.

Lennon flips the folder open. "219."

"Second floor?"

"Great guess," Lennon mutters sarcastically.

I smirk as I trail up the stairs after her. The dorms are air-conditioned, but the frequent opening and closing of every door in the residence hall means the HVAC system is being rendered mostly irrelevant for the time being.

There are a few side glances as we walk along in search of Lennon's room, which is bizarre. I don't interact with many people on campus. It's strange to realize random people recognize me at first glance.

We reach 219. Lennon uses her new student ID to unlock the nondescript wooden door. It swings open to reveal a compact room. The walls are white and the floor is covered by a dark gray carpet. A twin-sized bed, desk, and chest of drawers are the only furniture. I stack the two boxes I'm holding on the desk and glance at Lennon.

"What do you think?"

She surveys the small space. "That I over-packed."

It takes three more trips to transport the rest of her belongings from the bed of my truck into her new room.

My phone vibrates as she begins opening boxes. It's Drew, asking if I want a ride to the team meeting.

I reply, telling him I'll meet them there, then turn to Lennon.

Her expression is knowing. "You've got to go to a baseball thing, right?"

"Right," I confirm. "But the field house is only ten minutes away, not three hours. I'll be back in an hour. Two, tops."

"It's fine. I've got a lot of unpacking and organizing to do, anyway. My advisor wants to meet with me tomorrow, so I need to go over all the Journalism requirements. And also figure out where the school store is so I can get all my books…"

Her voice trails off when she catches my smirk.

"What?"

I shrug. "It's just funny seeing you be all nerdy again. Reminds me of high school."

Lennon manages to blush and look indignant simultaneously. "Nerdy?"

"It was a compliment," I assure her. My phone vibrates in my pocket again. "I've gotta go."

"Okay," Lennon replies.

I step forward to kiss her, then turn to leave. "Oh, wait. I forgot to give you this." I grab one box off her desk, rifle through it, then hold out the plastic bag I snuck into it last night while she was packing. "Here."

Lennon's brow wrinkles as she grabs the bag from me and rips it open.

"Now that we go to the same school again, I thought you might want to wear it," I say as she holds up the *Clarkson Baseball* sweatshirt. "You can still wear the Landry one back home."

Lennon flips the material over, staring at my name and number on the back.

"Some girl told me they don't sell sweatshirts with your name on it in the school store," she tells me, raising one eyebrow.

I grin. "They don't. See you later, Matthews."

CHAPTER THIRTY-TWO

LENNON

I edge through the doorway, glancing around the massive lecture hall in awe. This is the opposite extreme from the cramped, ammonia-scented rooms I've attended college in until now.

Excited chatter fills the soaring space.

Sunlight spills in through windows that line the far wall and overlook Clarkson's football stadium.

I walk up the central aisle and take a seat about halfway up the stadium-style seating.

My phone vibrates as soon as I sit down. I pull it out of my bag to see a new text from Caleb.

Caleb: *Happy first day!!!!*

I roll my eyes—mostly at the *four* exclamation points—but can't help the smile that forms.

Lennon: *You're a dork.*

Caleb: *Takes one to know one, Matthews.*

I respond with an eye-rolling emoji, then shove my phone back into my backpack.

"This seat taken?"

A guy with light brown hair and tortoiseshell glasses is standing to my left. He nods to the chair next to me when our eyes connect.

"Nope, it's free," I reply, watching out of the corner of my eye as he settles in the spot beside me. There are still plenty of other open seats.

He looks up and catches me looking. "I'm Eric," he tells me, holding out a hand and flashing a set of straight, white teeth.

"Lennon," I reply, shaking his hand.

"Nice to meet you, Lennon." Eric bends down and pulls a notebook out of his backpack. "Have you had Glannon before?"

"Glannon?"

Eric smiles. "The professor." He nods to the front of the room, where a man with a graying shock of curly hair is opening up a briefcase and removing stacks of paper from it.

"Oh. Uh, no," I reply, although I'm guessing my first response already answered his question.

"Did you swap majors?"

"No, but this is my first year here. I just transferred."

"Oh, cool. From where?"

"Richardson Community College." I wait for the flash of judgment, but it doesn't appear.

"Well, welcome," is all Eric says. "What do you think of Clarkson so far?"

"It's…nice. A little overwhelming, but I'm sure I'll get used to it."

"Yeah, it's a great school. I transferred here sophomore year, and I've been really happy so far."

"Where did you transfer from?" I ask.

"Lincoln."

I laugh. "Well, if you can fit in here after transferring from Lincoln, then that gives me some hope."

Eric smiles. "Yeah, I'm sure you'll be fine. Although I'm pretty sure the only people here who care about the rivalry with Lincoln are the jocks and their groupies, and I steer clear of that crowd. Are you a sports fan?"

"Um, no. Not really," I respond. It's the truth, but also feels disloyal Caleb.

"You'll be fine, then," Eric tells me.

"Great," I reply, smiling.

"Welcome to Journalism 356: History of American Journalism," the booming voice of our professor says.

He's either speaking into a microphone, or the acoustics in this room are award worthy.

The few students still trickling in rush to open seats.

All conversation ceases.

"I'm Professor Glannon. Most of you have had me before. Please don't take the fact I won't remember your name personally. I'm old, and there's quite a lot of you."

Quiet laughter ripples around the room.

"I don't have many ground rules. The main one is no eating. It's distracting and frankly rude. Especially if you didn't bring enough to share with all two hundred of your classmates. Second, no beverages besides coffee and water in this room. Some professors frown upon encouraging caffeine consumption. Just get enough sleep blah blah blah."

More laughter.

"You all want to make it in the field of journalism, however. Let me tell you now, it's a demanding career that pays terribly. You won't ever make enough to afford a drug habit besides coffee."

Eric chuckles beside me.

"But other than those two ground rules, anything goes. Scroll on your phones, spend half the class wandering the halls, pass notes to each other. As long as you do it subtly enough I don't notice. I'm getting paid to teach you regardless of whether you learn anything or not. Everyone good? Any questions?"

Silence.

"All right. Jane, get those syllabi out, and we'll get started."

A petite, dark-haired woman stands with a thick stack of papers in hand, and my first class at Clarkson begins.

Eric turns to me when class ends an hour later. We're both packing up our bags, along with the rest of the class. I'm going to need to buy more notebooks. I took twelve pages worth of notes on the first lecture alone.

"What did you think?" Eric asks.

"I loved it," I reply honestly. "A lot different from any other journalism class I've ever taken."

"Yeah, Clarkson's program is fantastic. It's the main reason I transferred here."

We both stand and start walking down the stairs.

"You know, I'm going to see a new documentary about social justice journalism with some friends on Saturday afternoon. Would you want to come? They're all journalism majors too, so I can introduce you around a bit. Plus, the film's supposed to be really good."

"That sounds great," I reply honestly. "But I can't do Saturday afternoon, unfortunately."

"No worries. I can switch it to Sunday, if that's better for you?"

"Oh, no, it's fine. I don't want to mess everyone's plans up."

Eric waves his hand in a carefree motion. "It's no problem at all. I'll talk to them and give you all the details in class on Friday. Really nice to meet you, Lennon."

He smiles, then turns to the right and disappears into the crowd of students.

I take twenty minutes to find my next class. Despite being another journalism elective, it's located clear across campus in an almost identical yet slightly smaller version of the brick building my first class was in. Even acknowledging the confusion of navigating the winding walkways that connect the academic buildings, there's a smile on my face the whole time.

The atmosphere on campus is electric.

I pass other students discussing deep-sea trenches and stage lighting. Professors discussing exam formats and comparing lecture halls. Athletes dribbling basketballs or clutching racquets.

I've always loved school. Loved the thrill of discovering new things about the world. The satisfaction of understanding a concept. The positive reinforcement of seeing a red A at the top of a page.

This is the first time I've been somewhere that compulsion feels tangible. I wasn't the only student at Landry High who worked hard. But everyone else was using it as a means to an end.

To *this* end.

There were other students at Richardson Community College who took their studies seriously, but not many. Most of them were taking classes to end up in a slightly better career, not for the love of learning. That mentality is a simple reality for many people. Was for me, until now. And I don't regret my time at RCC. It's made me more appreciative of Clarkson now.

My Multimedia Journalism class is less entertaining than History of American Journalism was, but just as engaging. Once again, I scribble notes as fast as I can to keep up with the professor's words.

I luck out with another friendly seatmate, this time a girl named Anna who explains to me all the journalism classes with a media component are held in this building, while written journalism shares a building with the English department.

"See you next class, Lennon!" Anna says before she rushes off.

She already extensively explained the badminton class she has in ten minutes. The sports center is eight minutes away. I wish her luck before she sprints off.

When I emerge outside, campus is even busier than it was before my last class. It's just before noon, which must be when lots of classes let out. I allow myself to be swept up in the movement, heading in the direction of the campus center but unsure where I'm actually going.

This is only my third day on campus. Not only am I still trying to find my way around, I'm adjusting to setting my own schedule. It's always been set for me. By the Landry educational system. By the horses. By Alex at the *Landry Gazette*.

For the first time, my only obligations are the classes I selected myself. It's freeing. It's also set me adrift. I have two hours until my final class of the day, and absolutely no idea what to do for them.

I pull my phone out to text Caleb, only to discover he's already sent me one.

Caleb: *Lunch?*

Lennon: *Yes!*

Lennon: *Where?*

He responds a few seconds later.

Caleb: *Peterson.*

I roll my eyes.

Lennon: *One of the brick buildings??*

My phone vibrates in my hand.

"This is only my third day on campus."

Caleb laughs. "Peterson is the massive circular building in the middle of campus. I didn't think you could miss it, Matthews."

I can see students heading straight toward a building with a rounded glass atrium in front.

"My floormates brought me to a different dining hall last night," I grumble.

"Are you sure it was a different one? You *are* directionally challenged."

"Shut up."

"You had better comebacks when you got us lost in Landry High."

"I'm hanging up now," I warn.

"See you in the atrium. Call me if you can't find it."

He hangs up too fast to catch my response.

I follow the crowd into air conditioning. It's not quite as hot as the remnants of many Kentucky summers I've experienced, but warm enough, I wouldn't voluntarily choose to prolong my time outdoors.

Caleb is easy to spot. He's sitting on the arm of one of the couches sprinkled through the lobby-like space, typing something on his phone.

I'm not the only one looking at him. But I am the one he smiles when he sees, shoving his phone in his pocket and standing up straight.

"Hey."

"Hey," I repeat, stopping a respectable distance away.

Caleb isn't having it. He reaches out and tugs me closer, so I'm inches from his face.

He grins down at me. "This is cool, huh? Being lunch buddies."

"Super cool," I drawl, tempted to call him a dork again.

But I know what he means. We didn't sit together back in high school. We were part of two very different crowds. And for the past few years, we've missed out on these casual, common moments.

Caleb laughs before releasing me, only to grab my hand and pull me toward the line of people waiting to enter the dining hall.

"So...how was it?" he asks me eagerly.

I'm tempted to mess with him, but I don't. "Amazing," I reply. "You wouldn't believe..." I launch into a detailed retelling of my morning.

I know Caleb isn't the least bit interested in journalism. I've never met a talented writer *less* interested. But he listens to me prattle on and on about every piece of wisdom my professors shared as we move along the buffet to grab lunch.

"How were your classes?" I ask when I finish talking about mine.

Caleb shrugs. "Fine."

"That's it? I just spent twenty minutes telling you about mine."

"Thirty-three actually, but who's counting?"

I stick my tongue out at him. "I was just thinking about what a thoughtful boyfriend you are, and then you ruined it."

He laughs. "I loved hearing about your classes, Len. Business isn't half as entertaining."

I study him. I know Caleb's major is mainly to placate his father. To ensure he can take his place in the lucrative company whose exact function I'm still not clear on. All I know is whatever Mr. Winters does adds to the Winters' substantial wealth and requires a lot of overseas travel.

"You don't like your classes?" I ask. This too, is unfamiliar ground between us. When I was at RCC, he'd never talk about academics here with me.

"They're fine. Means to an end. C's get degrees too, you know."

"Uh-huh. You'd know," I tease.

I'm certain Caleb is at the top of his—actually ours now, I guess—class.

"I can't be smart *and* good-looking, Matthews. It's not fair to other guys."

"It's really not," I agree.

He smiles. "I'm really glad—relieved—you like your classes so much. I was a little worried I was going to have to haul all ten of your boxes back to Landry after a week."

"I'm not going to change my mind," I tell him. "Even if I did hate my classes here—which, considering the fact RCC's journalism department had *one* faculty member, was pretty unlikely—you're here. That alone would have been worth sticking a year out for."

Caleb half smiles, but it quickly fades. He plays with his fork, dragging a stray piece of lettuce across the otherwise empty plate. "I saw Tom Stradwell in town before we left."

"You did?"

"Yeah, when I was out getting coffee."

"Oh." I'm puzzled by the sudden shift in conversation.

"He said he offered you a full-time job at the *Gazette* after you graduate."

"Oh," I say again, this time realizing what he's getting at. "Yeah, he did."

"Are you going to take it?"

"I don't know," I reply honestly. "There's a lot of…factors to consider."

Specifically, the boy sitting across from me.

Caleb nods. "Yeah, I guess so."

He doesn't ask if he's one of them. He knows he is, but I tell

404

him anyway.

"Like you."

He bobs his head. Swallows a couple of times. "Right."

We stare at each other, unsaid things hovering between us.

Along with things we've said and will have to say again.

"I've got practice," Caleb finally says.

Of course.

"It's not even baseball season," I grumble. "I thought sports *had* seasons. Clear starts and ends."

I'm joking, but I'm also not. I admire Caleb's dedication and I know he works hard. I also thought the days of him rushing off to some baseball commitment would cease between summer camp and the actual start of the season. I should have known better by now, obviously.

Caleb gave me a copy of his class schedule, but not his baseball schedule. I'm sure there was a reason for that.

"Not if you want to win," Caleb replies. His voice is teasing, but I also know he's serious. This is an important season for him, and his teammates and coaches obviously take things just as seriously. "We've got a scrimmage on Saturday."

"I know," I respond. "I'll be there."

I wonder if Caleb is aware that this is the first time I'll be seeing him pitch in a game. Ever.

We both stand, deposit our empty plates and dirty silverware in bins, and head back outside.

"You've got another journalism class later?"

"Nope. Pottery," I reply.

Caleb stares at me. "*Pottery?*"

I shrug. "I needed an arts requirement, and I can't play any instruments."

"You can sing."

"Yeah, for fun," I respond. "I don't want to be nitpicked for tone and range and whatever else they're always talking about on those singing competition shows."

"There wouldn't be anything to nitpick, Lennon. I mean, everyone was saying…"

He trails off before he finishes the sentence, but we both know what he was going to say. Neither of us have brought up Gramps's funeral since the August morning it took place.

"You're good," he finishes.

We walk out of the atrium and into the September afternoon. I'm silent; so is Caleb.

"I wish I could call him and tell him everything I just told you," I admit, keeping my gaze on a gray squirrel scampering along the paved path we're walking on. "About my classes and about the fire alarm going off in the middle of the night. About all of it."

"He'd be crazy proud of you, Len," Caleb tells me quietly.

"I know," I whisper.

I'm not just saying it to agree. I know Gramps would be proud. It's just not the same as getting to see the look unfold on his face first-hand. Hearing it in his voice.

"Come here."

I turn and collapse against Caleb's chest, resting my cheek against the soft cotton of his shirt. This isn't the weather where snuggling and sharing body heat appeals as an enjoyable experience, but we do it anyway.

He smells familiar. Comforting.

He feels solid. Safe.

"I love you, Len," Caleb whispers into my hair.

I pull back and give him a wobbly smile. "Yeah, I love you too."

"Text me a photo of your clay creation, yeah?"

Wobbly turns steady.

Caleb's always been excellent at knowing just what I need.

Letting me fall apart.

Helping me hold it together.

"Yeah, I will," I assure him.

He gives me a quick kiss and then strides away toward what I'm assuming is the sports center.

I thought it was the other way, but I definitely won't be telling Caleb that.

I head in the opposite direction. My pottery class starts in a half hour, and it'll probably take me every minute to find the art building.

CHAPTER THIRTY-THREE

CALEB

The atmosphere in the locker room is electric. This is our first scrimmage against another team. Not officially the start of the season, but the start of something.

None of the games we play will count for months, but this game is against Lancaster, one of our main rivals. It's our chance to set the tone for what sort of team we'll be this year.

A championship-winning one, if I have any say in it.

Normally, I close myself off before games. I let the world fade to white noise aside from visualizing exactly how fast and how far I'll throw a sphere of leather-coated cork and yarn.

Today, I let the nerves and excitement roam free. I soak in the atmosphere of my teammates snapping gum and slapping their mitts as I sit on the ledge in front of my locker, bouncing my knee. The scent of leather and mint swirls around with thick anticipation.

Lennon Matthews has never seen me play in an actual baseball game.

Not once, in the seven years I've known her.

In person, at least. The local Landry news station has

streamed some of my games over the past few years, and I know Earl watched. We'd discuss them when I came to visit.

Lennon probably felt an obligation to sit there as well. But she never came to one of my games in high school. The closest she's come to seeing me pitch was the pickup game the night we finally got together. Or the summer practice she talked to Cassie for most of. Neither of those really count.

I don't resent her for it. I know Lennon's only athletic interest is one you have to be aboard a horse for.

She views baseball as a part of my life to put up with, not a selling point. She's never made any attempt to memorize stats or act like she understands the sport just to impress me, and it's one of my favorite things about her.

We don't put on shows for each other. Never have, and it's maybe the only silver lining of our romantic relationship being prefaced by years of antagonism.

Doesn't mean I don't want to impress her.

Coach Thompson steps to the front of the room for his pregame talk. Describing it as including the word pep would be a stretch. It's a dry recitation of the words he's been shouting at practice for weeks. It does its job, though. The man in front of me is the second reason I chose to attend Clarkson, the first being its proximity to Landry. Coach doesn't put on airs or tolerate cockiness. He leads by example and asks for nothing but hard work from his players.

My coach in high school was the exact opposite. He was just as intimidated by my last name as my throwing arm, and I took advantage.

I've grown up since then.

I think.

Our team pre-game ritual ends with a cry of "Go Thoroughbreds!" and then we file out of the locker room toward the field.

Clarkson snagged the mascot every school in the state wanted —for obvious, horse-obsessed reasons—and we rub it in as frequently as we can. I'm sure the cheer will be echoed across the field many times over the course of the scrimmage.

Lancaster's team is already in the visitor's dug-out, eyeing us, as we approach the field. I barely spare them a glance, totally in the zone.

The shouts from the crowd and the sight of the field crew preparing the diamond all fades away.

It's just me and the leather ball I'm holding. I run my fingers along the red stitching, searching for the perfect spot to grip the ball.

I never look for it. I have to feel it.

During her brief foray into sports journalism—my attempt to make her not hate me, which I have to say was a total success— Lennon asked me what my favorite thing about playing baseball is.

It was a question I'd answered many times before. I know Lennon judged my response, but I was more truthful with her than I'd ever been with anyone else.

Lots of things come to me easily. But baseball has always been different. It's always been mine and mine alone.

People may care more about the fact I can throw a baseball because I'm a Winters. But my ability to throw a baseball has nothing to do with the fact I am.

It's wholly my own, and it's part of the draw for me. People who are jealous of my family's status never seem to consider I might not want to be known for someone else's legacy. Ironically, it's one of the few things Lennon and I have in common. It just so happens my family is defined by my grandfather's accomplishments, while hers is by her parents' shortcomings.

I follow my usual warm-up routine, first jogging, then

stretching before I head toward the bullpen. Our pitcher, Reynolds, follows without me asking him to. I rotate my shoulder, take a deep breath, and let the first pitch fly. It smacks his glove with a resounding *snap*. I exhale.

After a few throws, Reynolds backs up to the usual pitching distance. I pitch a few more fastballs, then switch to breaking balls. I end with a few off-speed pitches before returning to the bench. Every one was perfect.

I'm ready. These last few weeks I've been throwing pitches that would—will—make pro scouts salivate. I'm still climbing toward the peak of my college career, and I let that confidence, that superiority, bleed across my face as I head for the mound.

Like all sports, baseball has a mental component.

Lancaster doesn't have a prayer of winning this scrimmage, not while I'm pitching, and I let that show on my face.

Momentum has to be set into motion, and that's exactly what I'm about to do.

I get some double takes when I enter Archibald Hall.

A few people call out "Good game!"

I smile at those. The stands were packed earlier to watch us annihilate Lancaster. Our opponents didn't manage a single run while I was on the mound. A lucky bounce allowed them two runs once Anderson stepped in for the final few innings, but we still won with a comfortable lead.

I sprint the stairs, so it only takes me about five seconds to reach Lennon's floor.

There are more people on the second floor, but I don't stop long enough to register anyone's reaction.

I stop outside of Lennon's door and knock twice.

It opens a couple of seconds later. All the air leaves my body in a harsh exhale.

I've always been insanely attracted to Lennon Matthews. It was there the first time I saw her, standing just outside the principal's office with her chin raised and her shoulders squared. Since that moment, I've seen her in fleeces and flannel. Prom dresses and sundresses. Bikinis and naked.

This look is new.

Sexy and daring.

If I had to guess, I'd say she called Cassie about what to wear. Maybe even went shopping.

"Do I look okay?" Lennon asks me, tugging the hem of the lacy tank top she's wearing. Despite the effort, the shirt doesn't cover any more skin. I'm both grateful for and tortured by that lack of movement.

I have to clear my throat twice before I can respond, surprise and lust garbling my thoughts. "More than okay. You look beautiful, Len. I—*wow*."

She exhales and smiles, relief obvious on her face. "Okay, good. I'm ready to go, then."

Lennon steps forward, but I don't move out of her way.

"I'm not."

Confusion creases her expression as I crowd her until she's forced to take a step back into her room. I shut the door behind us, then spin and press her against the wall. When her head tilts back to meet my gaze, I can see the rapid flutter of her pulse beneath her jawline.

"What are you doing?" she whispers.

Instead of answering, I trail my fingers up her arm. Her breath hitches when I reach her shoulder. Stops when I brush the side of her breast. Quickens as I trail my fingertips down the side of rib cage and settle my hand along her waist.

"Lennon," I whisper.

"Yeah?" she murmurs back. Her hazel eyes are overflowing with emotion that matches that in my voice.

"Thank you," I say. "I know I'm not the only reason you transferred. I know it was an impossible decision for you. But having you here—knowing you're close by, seeing you at the scrimmage today… I can't really tell you what it meant to me. But thank you."

Today was the cumulation of three years of wondering what she was doing during every college game I've ever played in. For the first time, I knew.

"We're going to be…" Her eyes flutter closed, her breath catching as I slide a hand under her skirt. "Late," she finishes, as my fingers tease the top of her thigh.

This is the first time I've ever been grateful for harsh fluorescent lighting. I can see every change in Lennon's face while she reacts to my touch.

"If that's what you're thinking about right now, I must not be any good at this."

Lennon huffs out a laugh that turns into a moan. "You're very good at this, and you know it."

She kisses me first.

I close my eyes, getting lost in the moment. Caging her body between me and the wall as we kiss with an urgency that suggests the world is falling down around us.

I'm hyped up on adrenaline from the game and the rush of winning. Relieved everything between us has stabilized after a stretch of uncertainty. And then part of is it just…Lennon.

I still get this giddiness around her that's hard to explain. It feels like an addiction. No matter how much I'm around her, I always want more time.

That feeling is called love, I guess.

It's hard to define something so intangible, that emerges in so many forms. That changes and grows. That doesn't duplicate and is always different.

Lennon melts against me as I fist the front of her underwear and tug, giving her the friction she wants but not actually touching her.

Our kisses become messy. Wild, instead of practiced. Focused on being as close to each other as possible, not careful tongue strokes.

When Lennon suddenly breaks away, I'm not expecting it. Breathing heavily, I study her, resting one palm on the wall just above her head. Her underwear is soaked through and she was just grinding against my hand.

I wasn't expecting this to be the moment she decided to pull back.

Her lips quirk upward as she registers my confusion. "I'm not a big baseball fan."

"I know," I reply. "You've mentioned it, a few times."

Lennon's smile grows. The sight of it tugs at my chest. Chips away at the fear coming to Clarkson was a choice she might regret. "And I wish it didn't take up so much of your time," she continues.

Both of my eyebrows rise. I have no idea where she's going with this. "Okay…"

She pushes my chest. Not that hard, but I'm not expecting it. I stumble back a step. If I didn't have decent reflexes, I'd probably be flat on my ass right now.

Lennon follows, closing the distance between us again farther from the wall. Her hands are tugging at the top of my shorts, and I think—*hope*—that I figured out what she's doing. My dick jumps as she pulls the material down, basically begging for her attention.

"But you looked damn good pitching."

Suddenly, she's on her knees in front of me, and I can't hear anything over the roar of blood in my ears.

Lennon's hand circles my erection, rubbing the sensitive skin. I'm honestly worried I'll come from the pressure alone before her mouth even touches my cock.

I can see straight down her shirt from this angle. The sight becomes even more erotic when her tongue peeks out, tracing the tip in slow licks meant to drive me wild.

My hips jerk forward, a groaned "fuck" spilling out when the wet heat of her mouth sucks me. The pleasure is indescribable. Overwhelming. So acute it's almost painful.

I know I won't last long, and I'm right.

Lennon ignores my warning, not slipping away until my dick is soft and my head hazy. Pleasure swims through me in lazy trickles.

I move to kiss her, but Lennon pushes me back again. This time, she doesn't step toward me after.

"Do you have any idea how long this took me?" she asks, gesturing toward her appearance. "I already have to redo my lipstick."

I grin, unrepentant, as she grabs a tube off her dresser, fixing my shorts. "Fine. I won't fuck you until later."

The party tonight is at my house, a celebration of our impressive start to the season. It means I won't have to walk or drive anywhere after it ends, and hopefully Lennon will decide to stay over.

"You're sure I look okay?" she asks, swiping a shimmery gloss across her lips that makes me want to kiss her all over again. "This is what other girls wear?"

"You don't need to dress like other girls, Len. Just wear what you want to wear."

"I know." She fiddles with the lip gloss before tossing it back on top of her dresser. "I just want to…fit in, I guess."

I walk over and kiss the side of her head. "You look like other girls. Just hotter."

Lennon is extraordinary. Unique. She has a different perspective on the world than most people our age. While most other college students are focused on grades and who they want to hook up with over the weekend, Lennon has been balancing school and a job. Not to mention the responsibility of running a stable and taking care of her grandfather.

That makes her different. She'll never *fit in*, in a good way.

And even if she did have a similar life experience, she'll be viewed differently tonight. She's showing up with me. Not only am I well-known on campus for baseball, people have a strange interest in my personal life. I don't bring girls to parties and I don't flirt back. Tonight, I'll be doing both.

Lennon flicks out the light in her room and we head down the dorm hallway, side by side.

"You played *really* well today, Caleb," she tells me, purposefully bumping her arm against mine.

I nod, seriously. "I know. Some even considered it blowjob worthy."

When her fist hits my bicep, I don't flinch. I was expecting the hit.

I laugh. "Thanks. I might have been showing off some today."

"Scouts were there?"

"For *you*, Matthews."

"Oh." The short syllable is saturated with surprise. "Really?"

"Really," I confirm.

We walk out of her dorm, into the balmy evening. It's the perfect temperature now that the sun has disappeared, still warm but not hot.

"I'm nervous," Lennon confides, as we walk along the sidewalk toward my truck.

"About what?"

"Tonight. This party. The way everyone pays attention to you, it freaks me out. I want to be off in some corner."

I already knew Lennon feels that way. But her confiding it is new. In the past, it's always been her squeezing my hand when we're at Jake's house or when people stop me on the sidewalk downtown.

"We don't have to go."

"No. I want to go. I just also want you to know if I act weird and awkward tonight, that's why." Before I can respond, she asks, "How late do these parties usually go?"

I glance over after we're inside my truck. "You got a curfew?"

Lennon smirks as she buckles her seatbelt. "A guy in my journalism class invited me to a movie tomorrow morning."

"Oh, yeah?" I pull out of the parking lot and head back toward my house.

"Yeah."

"What movie?"

"I forget the title. It's a documentary."

"Sounds fun."

"It *will* be, actually," Lennon responds, catching my sarcasm. "A bunch of journalism majors are going, so I'll get to meet some new people."

I brake at a stop sign, reaching over and squeezing her knee. "That's great, Len. And this won't be that late. The whole team has practice tomorrow morning. None of the guys want to do ladder drills or sprints hungover and exhausted."

There are twice as many cars on the street as there were when I left to pick up Lennon. And we're located close to Greek Row, meaning most of the people coming tonight walked over.

Loud music reverberates through the night air as we walk toward the open front door.

I watch Lennon fiddle with the hem of her top as we step inside the house. She moves closer to me, so I rest my palm on the small of her back, guiding her forward, then turning her to the right.

"You cleaned?" she asks me, making a show of looking around the first floor.

I laugh. The house has never looked worse, and it's messy on its best day.

We head toward the kitchen. I nod my head at the familiar faces calling out to me, but I don't stop and talk to anyone.

Once we're in the kitchen, there's a little less attention.

"You want a drink?" I ask Lennon, pulling open the fridge door. The pizza Drew ordered late last night is sitting on the shelf in an open box. I shake my head and pull down the lid.

"Sure," she answers, surprising me.

I glance at her. "Alcohol?"

She nods, leaning against the counter in front of the sink. I pull out a bottle of beer for myself and a seltzer for her, mixing the flavored water with a shot of vodka.

Right after I hand the cup to her, I see the glass crack. My right hand flies up reflexively, catching the baseball flying through the air at a speed that makes my hand sting.

Lennon's eyes are huge, glancing between my hand and the shattered window. The ball missed her by inches. Maybe less.

Jamie rushes into the kitchen first. Drew is right behind him, his gaze unfocused. He's drunk.

Elliot arrives next, and whistles. "Nice reflexes, Winters."

"What the *fuck*?" I spit.

Drew raises both hands in a placating gesture. "We can fix the window. I thought Jamie would catch it. It was a good throw, man." That last sentence in aimed at Jamie, who shrugs.

"I'm not worried about the *window*. You almost hit Lennon!"

More people are crowding the kitchen, looking at the shattered glass and the pissed-off expression I'm wearing.

"I'm fine, Caleb," Lennon whispers. Her hand lands on my arm, squeezing once. "I'm fine."

"It was stupid, Lennon. I'm sorry. Glad you're not hurt. Not only because Caleb probably would have never talked to me again."

I snort. Lennon's hand slides down my arm, tangling her fingers with mine.

"Come on outside, guys," Elliot says, in an obvious attempt to dispel the tension. "Lennon, you can play on my cornhole team. Winters is banned."

When I look at Lennon, her expression is pleading. I have to stop imagining how that throw could have just hurt her.

I nod, and her face relaxes before she looks at Elliot. "Why? Caleb has terrible aim."

Laughter fills the room before Lennon pulls me toward the door that leads to the back deck. I toss Drew the baseball as I pass him, accompanied with a warning look. Drunk at a party isn't a good time for pitching. Never mind I've done the same thing myself.

Sandy Peterson is coming up the steps from the yard as we cross the deck.

"Hey, neighbors." He grins at me and Elliot, then his gaze slides to Lennon. Recognition replaces friendliness. "Garbage bin girl!"

"I prefer to go by Lennon," Lennon replies, smiling back at him.

"Right, of course. I should have asked for your name." He

chuckles. Coming from a guy who's never bothered me before, it's grating. "I'm Sandy."

Sandy holds out his hand to shake Lennon's. Elliot shoots me an amused look behind Lennon's back.

"I've looked for you every other night I've been on trash duty, you know. I'd given up on ever seeing you again."

Forget recognition, he's full-on flirting.

"I've only been on campus for a week," she replies. "I ended up transferring here."

"No way! How come?"

Elliot and I might as well be part of the deck.

Lennon nods to me, and Sandy's gaze follows.

"Oh!" He finally puts one and one together, which equals Lennon is off-limits. "You're Winters's mysterious girlfriend. Most of campus thought you didn't exist."

"Well...I do."

Sandy looks to me. "Nice scrimmage, Winters."

"Were you there?" Lennon asks.

"Uh, no. I had an ultimate frisbee thing," Sandy replies.

"Ultimate frisbee? Is that different from normal frisbee?"

Elliot snorts quietly at Lennon's innocent response. I smile.

Sandy chuckles and shakes his head. "Not really." His voice is still friendly, but it's lost its flirtatious undertone. "See you guys later," he says, then continues up to stairs.

Elliot starts down the stairs. Lennon and I follow.

"How do you know Sandy?" I ask, aiming for a nonchalant tone.

Lennon laughs, making me think I missed. "Jealous, Winters?"

I am. But it's not coming from a place of insecurity. It's the fear everyone has: of losing something—someone—that matters to you. And the realization there are guys out there who Lennon wouldn't have had to give up anything for.

"I don't know him," she tells me. "I happened to be there when a lid fell off a garbage can he was carrying, so I put it back on for him. That's the whole *scandalous* story."

I shake my head at her sass. "Okay."

"Lennon!" Elliot calls. "Your turn." He's already waiting by one of the cornhole boards.

I tilt my beer in that direction. "Good luck."

She pecks my cheek, then heads in that direction.

I walk over to where some of the guys are standing around.

"Hey, Winters," Joe Anderson, our back-up pitcher, greets.

"Anderson," I acknowledge.

"That your girl?" He nods to where Lennon is standing, taking two bean bags from Drew.

"Yeah."

He whistles.

"Watch it, Anderson."

Joe grins but wisely opts to change the subject. "You catch the Eagles game last night?"

"Yup."

We chat about their chances of making it to the Super Bowl until I realize Lennon's not standing by cornhole any longer. She's under the oak tree, talking with Drew, Jessica, and Sophie.

I tell Joe I'll see him later and head toward their group. I'm sure it will just be a matter of time before Jamie shows up to fight for Jessica's attention.

"That was a quick game," I say when I reach them.

"Yeah." Drew sighs, which tells me the outcome.

He's a sore loser.

"Still working on that hand-eye coordination, Len?" I tease.

She scoffs before sipping her drink.

I smile, then glance at the other girls. "Hey, Jessica. Sophie."

Both girls are already looking at me. And also eyeing Lennon.

"You guys just get here?" I aim the question at Jessica, because I'm never sure how to act around Sophie now.

"I was just introducing them," Drew says.

"I didn't see you guys come in," I say to Jessica. I don't want to be a dick and ignore Sophie. But I'm also sick of her games.

"We came in through the back gate," Jessica explains. "Maggie said things are getting crazy inside."

"Great," I deadpan, glancing at Drew. I advocated for having the freshmen's house host tonight. "Hope you remembered to lock your door, man."

"I did," he assures me.

"I was wondering when you ladies were going to show up." Jamie joins our circle, right on cue.

Elliot's behind him, rolling his eyes.

Lennon steps to the side to let them join our loose grouping, placing her directly in front of me. I sling my arm around her waist and pull her into my body. She tilts her head back to look at me.

"Can I have some of your beer?"

I glance at her empty cup, then hand the bottle to her. "You hate beer."

"I talked to Cassie earlier. She said I should try new things," Lennon replies, confirming my assumption Cassie was involved in the outfit she's wearing tonight. I'm not sure if I should be grateful or not. The skirt and top are similar to what a lot of other girls are wearing.

But it's different on Lennon.

Partly because I keep picturing her kneeling in front of me while wearing it.

"Cassie isn't the one who's going to have to carry your lightweight ass upstairs," I respond.

Lennon grins at me around the bottle. "Fine by me."

I roll my eyes.

"So Lennon, how are you liking Clarkson so far?"

Sophie's question breaks through the group's chatter. The side conversations cease, everyone waiting to hear Lennon's answer. I squeeze her waist once, knowing the attention is probably making her feel uncomfortable. We're not in Landry any longer, amidst people who Lennon has known since kindergarten. These are all strangers, from her perspective.

"It's great," Lennon replies. She smiles. "So far, so good!"

I squeeze her waist again. Lennon takes another sip of my beer, then hands it back to me.

"It must be a big adjustment, though? Weren't you at a small community college before this?"

My eyes narrow in Sophie's direction. Her tone is pleasant enough, but I never know what her motivations are.

Sophie meets my gaze, smiling serenely.

Lennon is oblivious. "It's been a big change," she replies.

"Brave of you, to make it senior year," Maggie comments.

Lennon glances over her shoulder at me. There's a tangible connection when our eyes connect, something warm and special arcing between us. "Caleb's helped," she says,

"With moving boxes, simple directions, chauffeuring you around…"

"With everything. You help with everything." She sways into me, the heat of her skin managing to sear through two layers of clothing. Her smile is lazy and slow, suggesting the alcohol might be affecting her.

I kiss the top of her head, wishing we could just head upstairs. I'm over this party. Usually, I'll grab a beer, park myself in a chair on the back deck, and talk sports with the guys for a few hours before disappearing.

Tonight, I don't even feel like doing that much. I'm tired after a long day and I can't sleep in tomorrow morning. All I want is to be in my bed with Lennon.

"Do you miss Landry?" Maggie asks. "I want to move there, after visiting for the Cup."

"You went to the Cup?"

I know why Lennon sounds surprised. The Landry Cup is an exclusive event that appeals to a certain niche, mostly horse fanatics much older than us.

Maggie nods, enthusiastically. "Sophie invited me to go with her family. We stayed at the Winterses."

I'm holding Lennon tight enough to feel her tense, but she doesn't react otherwise. "Fun," she comments, grabbing my beer again and taking a sip.

I should have mentioned Sophie to her sooner, I guess. But it's never come up naturally. And purposefully bringing it up never seemed necessary. Like there's something there I need to justify or explain, when there's not. But if I'd found out some guy stayed at Matthews Farm with his family, I'd have questions. So I'm kicking myself for not having mentioned it until now.

Drew asks Sophie a question about her game tomorrow, and then the conversation continues on from there. I don't pay much attention to whatever is being discussed, I just stand holding Lennon.

It starts to get colder and colder outside. Eventually, we all head in. There's a piece of cardboard taped over what used to be the kitchen window that we pass before walking into the house.

The kitchen is more crowded than it was when we went outside. I toss my empty beer bottle in the recycling, ignoring Jamie as he pretends to be a sports announcer analyzing my pitch.

I'm about to ask Lennon if she's ready for bed when she grabs my hand and pulls me into the living room instead. It's packed, pop music streaming from the speakers and vibrating the walls you have to press against to get through the busy space.

Lennon pulls me into the crowd, not through it. A few people glance my way, but most everyone is too occupied to notice.

We dance for three songs before she speaks. "I didn't realize Landry would have so many fans here."

If we weren't so close together, I wouldn't be able to hear her. But despite the loud music, it feels like we're enclosed in our own little bubble. "Surprised me too."

"You've never mentioned Sophie before."

I exhale, even knowing it's inevitable. If she didn't bring it up, I would have. "There's not much to say. Her parents are best friends with mine. They have a unit in the same building in New York, so we spent a lot of time together when we were younger."

"So, basically...your parents love her."

Lennon's voice is matter-of-fact. But I know my parents' derision bothers her, as it should. It bothers me, how they've never made any effort to get to know Lennon or supported us as a couple. Especially since Lennon doesn't have a large support system or massive extended family.

"*I* don't. I've never even kissed her. When I was in middle school, maybe I thought we'd end up together, one day." I slip my hands under the hem of her shirt, splaying both palms across Lennon's lower back and tugging her even closer. "But then I met a girl. I met *the* girl. I walked out of Principal Owens's office and I couldn't get the girl who wanted to be there even less than I did out of my head."

Lennon's lips turn up. "I probably never apologized to you about that. Getting you lost and then blaming you, I mean." She shakes her head. "You must have hated me."

"Actually, I wanted to kiss you."

Her expression goes blank with shock. I know she knows that I love her. But I don't know if Lennon has ever totally grasped how deep my feelings for her are or how far back they run. I've never made a point to emphasize it. It was slightly embarrassing, honestly. How suddenly sure I was. No person until then—or since—captured my attention so immediately and completely.

"Well, what's stopping you now?"

I smile before lowering my lips to hers.

We keep dancing, enjoying being two people in the same place at the same time. And I push away my worries this is just a temporary lull before the next wave rolls in.

Lennon and I have never enjoyed calm waters.

CHAPTER THIRTY-FOUR

LENNON

The loud blare of Caleb's alarm wakes me up—long before I'm ready to be conscious. I roll over, smushing my face against the warm, hard planes of his chest.

"Morning," he murmurs, running his fingers through my hair.

It feels amazing. I groan, both from the pleasure and the realization the rest of me feels awful.

I don't drink and I don't go to bed late. Last night, I did both. Caleb and I didn't come up to his bedroom until after two a.m. I think the last time I stayed up that late was our graduation party. And I only had one drink and half of Caleb's beer. But since my alcohol tolerance might as well not exist, I'm pretty sure my dry mouth and pounding head means I'm hungover.

Caleb slides out from under me and climbs out of bed. I bury my face in his pillow, promising myself I'll never drink or stay up past midnight again.

"Len." Something nudges my elbow a little while later. If I didn't feel so terrible, I'd probably be asleep.

I roll over reluctantly, blinking at the bright sun. Caleb is fully dressed, holding a sports drink out to me.

"It'll help," he promises. "Take this too."

Caleb hands me a small white pill. I sit up to swallow it with the red liquid that tastes like cherries.

"You okay?" He takes a seat on the mattress, watching me with a mixture of concern and amusement.

I lean forward and into him. He smells so good. Like fresh laundry and soap. Clean and masculine. I snuggle into the curve of his neck, my lips brushing his throat.

"Yeah." I sigh. "Just sleepy."

But I'm awake. I suck at a spot on the side of his neck and Caleb goes rigid, like I electrocuted him. I move to another spot, and he exhales a harsh breath. "I have practice, baby. I'm already running late."

I pull back and pout.

He grins. "You know, I was thinking I should never let you drink again. But if this is how you act in the morning, maybe I will."

I finish the sports drink and set the empty bottle on the side table before falling back against the sheets. I'm not wearing anything under the T-shirt I pulled on last night, and I watch him realize that.

Beneath the hangover symptoms, I feel giddy. This feels like such a normal morning, but it's the first time we've woken up in bed together after attending a party the night before. I've experienced a lot with Caleb, but this is a first. And frankly, something I never thought I *would* experience with him.

Caleb takes baseball very seriously. Every time we talked while he was at Mayfair this past summer, he was just coming back from the field, hours after the session had technically ended. I heard the background commentary on his end of the line, the jokes being made about all work and no play.

So, I'm expecting him to kiss me goodbye and head to practice.

Instead, he stands and tugs down his baseball pants, just low enough to free his growing erection. Caleb grins, probably at my shocked expression, then crawls over me.

We both moan when our bodies align, the hard press of him rubbing against sensitive skin.

"I'm already late. So this is going to be hard and fast, Matthews." That's all the warning I get, before he's sliding inside.

Caleb hooks my right knee over his hip, spreading me open and sinking even deeper. Before I've fully adjusted to the new angle, he's withdrawing and then stretching me again, hitting the magical spot that causes my mind to go completely blank.

His thrusts are relentless, building the pleasure higher and higher until it explodes.

I come with a loud cry and then he's kissing me, muffling the moans with his mouth as I feel the warmth of his release fill me.

He keeps kissing me, even after we've both finished. It's not until his phone begins buzzing that Caleb moves away, pulling out of me and climbing off the bed to zip up his pants.

I stay exactly where I am, sprawled on the mattress half-naked and completely content. I need to go to the bathroom and get cleaned up, especially now. But I soak in the sensation a little longer.

After years of feeling like I was letting Caleb down—living three hours away and never visiting, causing problems between him and his parents—I finally feel like I'm enough for him.

Caleb has never made me feel less, and reasonably, I know that it's not my fault I needed to take care of Gramps or that my parents made certain no one in Landry would associate the name Matthews with anything positive.

But it still feels really good, to have Caleb looking at me like I'm his whole world and feel like maybe that's exactly what I am.

He's mine.

"I'll talk to you later." One final kiss, and then he's gone.

I climb out of bed a few minutes later, stretching before I pull my clothes from last night back on. I'm glad I called Cassie for advice. This isn't the outfit I would have picked out myself.

Walking downstairs is strange. I've never been in the baseball house before without Caleb.

Remains of the party are littered everywhere. I toss a few used cups into the trash as I pass through the living room.

My phone buzzes with a text.

Caleb: *Left the truck keys on the counter.*

I smile as I head into the kitchen. It hadn't even occurred to me, until just now, that I had no way to get back to my dorm.

The keys are sitting on the counter, just like he said.

It's still pretty early, but there are some signs of activity when I walk outside. There's a middle-aged man walking a yellow lab across the street and a girl who looks to be my age jogging ahead on the sidewalk.

This isn't the first time I've driven Caleb's truck, but it's the first time I've done so somewhere unfamiliar. All the fancy features that are supposed to make it easier to drive just stress me out. I have to turn on the car to adjust the seat electronically, and an alert begins beeping as soon as I back out of the driveway. I clear out the oil change reminder and continue driving toward campus.

The first thing I do when I return to my dorm room is take a shower. I feel more like myself when I'm back in jeans and a T-shirt rather than a short skirt and lacy top.

Eric texts while I'm brushing my hair, letting me know he's

leaving and asking if he should pick me up. I reply, telling him I'll meet him there.

I've only been downtown a couple of times before, but I find the tiny theater that showcases independent films easily. Eric is standing outside with two girls and one guy when I approach.

"Hey, Lennon!" Eric greets me with a wide grin.

"Hey, Eric. Hi, everyone."

"Guys, this is Lennon," Eric states. "Lennon, this is Amanda, Abby, and Joe."

"Nice to meet you all," I say.

Abby and Joe are holding hands, so I assume they're a couple. Amanda's sporting a friendly smile and a short bob.

"Nice to meet you, Lennon. Although Eric hasn't shut up about you, so I sort of feel like I know you already," Amanda teases, nudging Eric's arm. His ears go red.

"Eric has been great," I say, trying to alleviate his embarrassment. "It's really nice to have someone to ask all my journalism department questions to."

"Good job, Eric," Abby says, grinning.

"The school should pay you for driving around the welcome wagon so well," Joe adds.

I hide a smile. It usually takes me a while to warm up to strangers, but their light-hearted banter is easy to feel at ease among.

"So what made you choose Clarkson?" Amanda asks once we're inside the theater, waiting for tickets. "Transferring for senior year must have been a hard decision."

"Uh, yeah, it was," I reply. "But my old school didn't have a great journalism program. Plus, my boyfriend goes here, so that's helped with the adjustment."

I pretend I don't see the disappointment flicker across Eric's face.

"Oh, cool," Amanda replies. "You should have brought him along."

I'm tempted to laugh at the thought of Caleb sitting through the documentary we're about to watch. If it's not baseball or an action thriller, he couldn't care less.

"Not really his thing," I respond.

"Joe didn't want to come either," Abby says. "I basically dragged him along. Some feminist you are," she tells her boyfriend.

"I *am* a feminist!" Joe insists. "I believe in equal rights. So much so I was going to support a *women*'s sports event."

Abby looks unimpressed. "You were going to stare at Sophie St. James, you mean."

"Sophie St. James?" I repeat.

"She's on the women's soccer team. Looks like a supermodel. I have yet to encounter a guy on campus who doesn't have a thing for her," Amanda supplies.

"Oh."

"It's impossible to keep track of all the sports teams, but there are a few athletes you can't help but hear about. Over and over again." Amanda's voice makes it clear she's not an avid fan.

"Oh," I say again.

We get our tickets and then head inside the dark theater. The documentary is engaging, splicing news coverage and reporter research on issues like healthcare, racial injustice, and voting rights. It's the exact sort of work I'd love to be doing but never thought I'd be able to.

As much as I resent Landry's elitism, I recognize it just represents one microcosm of society. Big, important newspapers hire graduates from big, important universities. I didn't have a prayer of getting hired anywhere beside the *Landry Gazette* with a degree from Richardson Community College. Like it or not—and I don't—that's simply the way the world works.

But now…I will be the graduate of big, important university.

And Matthews Farm sold.

I haven't told Caleb yet. I found out right before his scrimmage yesterday. The realtor called to tell me. It sold for a mind-boggling amount of money. I'm *rich*, by most people's measure. I'm no longer tied to Landry and I have the funds to live in a big city on a journalist's salary.

I have options, and depending on where Caleb gets drafted, I also have decisions to make.

A discussion of the film dominates the conversation as our group exits the dark theater and emerges back on the street. I blink at the sudden sunshine. The painkiller Caleb gave me helped with the headache—and so did the sex—but there's still a dull throb in my right temple.

Abby suggests heading to a pizza place just down the block. I quickly agree, since I'm starving. I didn't have time to go to the dining hall after showering and before heading here.

The pizzeria is clearly a popular off-campus hang-out, judging by the number of college students packed inside.

Despite the crowd, the line moves quickly. We all order slices, managing to snag one of the few open booths.

The steaming pizza arrives, and we all dig into the hot food immediately, continuing to talk about the documentary we just saw. For the first time, my comments aren't being met by bored stares. Aside from Andrew, no one at Landry High shared my passion for journalism. And RCC was known for its business and computer classes. *Useful* skills. I'm pleasantly surprised how Abby, Amanda, Joe, and Eric all seem just as interested and engaged in writing as I am.

"Great. Baseball team is here," Joe drones, right as I'm taking a bite of my third slice.

My head snaps to the left, looking at the entrance. The pizzeria's front door is open, a stream of sweaty guys wearing grass-strained clothes walking in with red faces and joking smiles.

Caleb isn't with them, but both Garrett and Drew are. I glance back at my pizza.

Clarkson is a big campus. I wasn't expecting to see the team here, and I feel awkward seeing them without Caleb around. Most of the guys are ones I met last night.

"And…right on cue. Here come the groupies," Eric laughs, then shakes his head.

All the girls in the booth nearest the door have vacated their spot, approaching the team with hair flips and flirty smiles. They're the girls I would look ridiculous ever trying to imitate. The girls I spent most of high school thinking Caleb would go for. Always knowing what to do and say and wear. Confident. *Cool.*

"They're probably asking where Caleb Winters is," Amanda comments with a scoff.

My eyes fly to her.

"Yet you *also* noticed he's not here," Eric comments, a smile twisting his lips up.

Amanda glances at me. I must look confused. "Caleb Winters is a senior on the baseball team. He pitches, I think?" She glances at Eric, who shrugs. "Throws the ball. Whatever. I don't go for the jock type, but he's stupid hot. And never hooks up with anyone, so getting his attention is kind of a challenge. If he took one look at me and decided to pay attention to anything except baseball… I'm not saying I would take him up on it, but—"

"But you would round some bases," Abby interrupts, laughing.

Joe and Eric both roll their eyes. But I would bet the large amount of money I'm now in possession of that neither of them are anywhere near as uncomfortable as I am.

I assumed Clarkson was too large for everyone to know who Caleb was. I assumed the social structure was like Landry High's, where certain groups kept separate and didn't pay each other much attention.

Wrong on both counts.

I take a bite of pizza to avoid having to contribute to the conversation.

I should tell them who the boyfriend I mentioned earlier is. If we become friends, which I'm hoping we will be, they'll find out eventually.

But I have no idea how to say anything now, without it being incredibly awkward. Maybe I should wait until after we're eating. I can laugh it off right before I leave. If I say something right now, we'll have to spend the rest of lunch in the aftermath of Amanda mentioning she's thought about having sex with Caleb. It sounds like she's never even talked to him. But still, it's weird. For me. And for her, if she knew I had sex with him a few hours ago.

"Hey, Lennon." I glance up from my pizza. Garrett is walking by.

"Hey, Garrett," I respond. I can't ignore him, and I don't want to. He didn't have to acknowledge me, and the fact he did makes me feel more welcome.

"Lennon," Drew greets as he passes by next, shooting me a quick grin before he follows Garrett.

"Hi, Drew," I reply.

Two of the girls with them glance back at me, looking confused. More players pass by. And every single one of them greets me by name. Even the ones whose names *I* don't know. Or remember, I guess. I must have met them all last night.

The four people I'm sitting with are all staring at me with wide eyes, by the time the baseball team has all passed by. Honestly, they're not the only ones. People at other tables are staring too.

"Does your dad coach the baseball team or something?" Amanda laughs. "You're on a first name basis with half the players?"

I pick at my crust. "I barely know them."

"You barely know them?" Both of Eric's eyebrows are raised. "It seems like they know you."

"Just from the party last night," I reply. "Aside from Garrett and Drew, that was the first time I met most of them."

"You went to the baseball party last night?" Abby leans forward. "I'm so jealous. They're super secretive. Invite only. I only find out about them days later. How did you know there was one last night?"

Awkward or not, I have to tell them now. I toss a burned bit of crust to the side, trying to decide what to say.

"Winters!"

I'm the last one at the table to look toward the door. Abby is no longer waiting for an answer. She's focused on Caleb entering the pizza place with Elliot right behind him.

"That's Caleb Winters," Amanda whispers to me.

I nod in response, watching Caleb say something to Elliot. If this wasn't so weird, I'd find it funny.

I know the exact second Caleb spots me. I haven't texted him since I thanked him for leaving his keys. Didn't tell him I was coming here after the documentary.

But there's always been this awareness between us, even before we started dating. I think it happened the first time I saw him, molecules in the air shifting to announce his presence.

Caleb says something else to Elliot, who looks over here as

well. Then he heads straight for me, a move I did not see coming in what has already been an eventful morning.

"Is it just me, or is *Caleb Winters* coming over *here*?" Amanda whispers to our table.

I don't have time to answer before he reaches us.

Caleb leans down and gives me a kiss in greeting, not bothering with words. His lips are warm and his mouth tastes like grape, probably from his sports drink.

"How are you feeling?" he asks.

"Better." I nod toward my empty plate. "I just ate my weight in pizza. And what you gave me this morning helped."

As soon as the words are out of my mouth, I know how he'll interpret them. Caleb laughs, low and husky, as heat floods my cheeks.

"The painkiller," I clarify.

His blue eyes dance. "I knew what you meant, Matthews."

"How was practice?" I ask, in an obvious attempt to change the subject.

"Well, I was late, so there were laps."

"Sorry," I whisper.

He shakes his head once, still amused. "Worth it. You get the truck here without crashing?"

"It's parked down the street." I pull his keys out of my pocket and set them on the table. "You're supposed to take it for an oil change in a hundred miles."

Caleb smiles, then pushes the keys back toward me. "Keep them. I'll get a ride back to the house with Drew, then come over later."

"Okay, sounds good," I say, then remember where we are. When I glance away from Caleb, Abby is the first person I look at. Her eyes are round, her mouth slightly open.

I clear my throat. "Caleb, this is Eric, Joe, Amanda, and Abby.

They all went to the documentary with me." And apparently, they all already know who he is, but I add, "Guys, this is my boyfriend, Caleb," just to be polite.

"Nice to meet you guys," Caleb gives them all a friendly smile, which they all seem too shocked to reciprocate.

He glances to me, one eyebrow raised. I lift a shoulder in response. "How was the documentary?"

"It was amazing," I answer.

"Good." Caleb leans down and gives me another kiss, then straightens and nods to the rest of my table. His gaze returns to me. "Bye, Len."

"Bye."

Caleb leaves, heading toward the booth the baseball team took.

Total silence lurks in the wake of his departure.

"Oh. My. *God?*" Amanda whispers. "Your boyfriend who goes here is Caleb Winters and I…" Her voice trails, eyes still impossibly wide.

"No wonder the team all stopped," Joe says. "Winters carries some serious weight on the team."

"And here I was, thinking maybe they just liked me." I smile, then take a sip of my water.

"Oh, shit. Sorry. That's not what I meant." Joe quickly back-tracks, and my attempt to lighten the mood just made everything weirder.

"It's fine. I was kidding," I tell him.

"You could have mentioned you knew him sooner," Eric tells me.

"I know," I reply. "I had no idea you guys would have any idea who he is. Once I realized, I wasn't sure what to say."

"I'm so mortified," Amanda says. "Did I seriously say—"

"That you wanted to hook up with Lennon's boyfriend?" Abby finishes. "Yeah, you did."

Amanda looks to me. "I had no idea you guys were dating. Claire Olsen told me he was single. I'm *so* sor—"

I start laughing. "I know. It's fine. Really."

There's a stretch of silence, then Abby speaks. "How long have you guys been dating?"

"Almost three years. We went to high school together."

"And you did long distance up until now?"

I nod.

"Wow. That must have been hard."

"It was," I reply. "But it never felt like we were that far apart."

Which is a relief to recall, considering we'll face more separation. Even if we end up living in the same place after graduation, professional baseball players travel plenty.

Eric mentions the spring electives that were just posted, and the conversation moves on from Caleb and me.

CHAPTER THIRTY-FIVE

CALEB

Days fly by, turning into weeks. That's been the case every year I've been at Clarkson. The first few days back on campus pass by at a normal speed. I blink, and a month is gone.

Time is speeding by especially fast senior year because I'm no longer conflicted between here and Landry. Lennon is here with me, so my focus is on nothing but her and baseball.

I scribble the last line on my exam and close the blue book. There are only five minutes left in class, but I'm the first one finished. Everyone else is still writing furiously, but I don't need to be. I'm confident I'm handing in A material.

I stand and shove my pen in my backpack, slinging it over one shoulder before I start down the stairs toward the front of the room.

People glance over as I pass. I'm playing better than I ever have. Despite counting for absolutely nothing in terms of our season, the fact my pitches as of late are better than the current Jays pitchers' have elevated the level of interest in me on campus.

I've always been good. I'm heading toward great, at the best possible time.

I hand my exam to the elderly professor teaching this Business Ethics course and head out of the lecture hall. I've got to be out on the baseball diamond in fifteen minutes. I hurry outside of the building that houses the Business department and head toward the sports complex.

"Hey, Winters."

I turn to see Drew walking just behind me, yawning. Since we share a wall, I'm pretty sure I know why he's so tried today. I seriously considered driving to Lennon's dorm and trying to fit into her twin bed.

"Hey," I respond. "How's it going?"

"Eh, all right." Another yawn. "You?"

I shrug. "Just left an exam."

"Ugh. It go all right?"

"Yeah," I reply. "It did."

"Tell your face that."

I huff a laugh. "Yeah, I know. I'm stressed about other stuff."

"Right. Curse of being talented."

"What are you talking about?" I glance over at him. "You're a great player."

"I'm decent," Drew replies. "I don't know about great. I always knew college would be the end of the road for me. Yeah, maybe I'd be a fifth-round pick. But then what? Bounce around the minors for a few years until a younger, less average guy comes along?"

"You don't know that," I argue.

"Pretty sure I do. Just like I know it won't be like that for you."

"You don't want to play, but you want me to?"

Everyone expects me to enter the draft, but I don't have to. I could put my business degree to good use. Go work for my dad, or really piss him off and choose one of his competitors. I would know where I was ending up. I wouldn't have to deal with the uncertainty of trades or injury or all the other unknown factors in sports.

"Just saying if I had your arm, I'd ride it all the way to the top, man."

I scoff. "I haven't even gotten drafted. I think it's a little soon to be speculating about championships."

"Dream big, Winters. If you don't, you won't get very far."

I don't reply as we head into the locker room and change for practice. But Drew's words keep running through my head on a loop as I change, only stopping to glance at the practice plan before heading out onto the field.

They mowed earlier today, so the scent of freshly cut grass swirls in the crisp fall air as I run a few laps around the diamond and then start my stretching routine.

Unless we're messing around, Coach normally lets us do our own thing for the first fifteen minutes. I follow my stretching with some band work to get my arm ready to pitch as the rest of the guys filter out onto the field.

We move on to catch play next. I pair up with Anderson, focusing on hitting a different target each throw, while he works on adjusting his landing foot. Position-specific drills follow. I work on pitcher fielding for the hour after that: fielding bunts, covering home, and throwing to base.

The whole team comes back together to run through bunt defense and pop-up priority.

I'm sweating by the time we start batting practice. It feels more like early September than late October. I gulp down water, flipping Elliot off after he squirts his water bottle on me. Any feeling of refreshment is counteracted by the fact I know he rarely remembers to wash it.

I hit ground balls to the fielders in between swings for forty-five minutes, and then practice ends.

"Park?" Jamie asks as we pack up our gear and head for the locker room.

"Hell yeah," Drew replies.

"Yeah, I'm in," I say.

We usually go to the swimming hole located twenty minutes away from campus after summer camp sessions, but the weather is warm enough today it doesn't feel any different.

None of us bother changing. We condense into one car and head for the park. A flock of birds startle out of the trees once we start down the path that leads to the water, laughing and joking loudly.

Despite the exhausting practice we all just went through, we're all in good moods. That's the beauty of team sports. It's a bonding experience like no other. You win together, lose together. Celebrate together, cry together. Spend time and sweat and dream. You see people at their best and their worst.

And their most ridiculous.

Elliot sprints for the swimming hole, tossing his baseball gear behind him like a trail of crumbs. Baseball hat. Cleat. Jersey. Other cleat.

"He better pick this shit up," Drew grumbles.

"Better idea. Let's hide it," Jamie suggests. "He can ride back to campus naked."

"Are you forgetting we all drove here together?" I ask.

Jamie ignores me, grabbing each piece of Elliot's clothing we pass, then stuffing the pile behind a log just before we reach the circular pool of clear water that's our destination.

Garrett gives him a surreptitious high five.

I strip off my sweaty shirt and pants, then dive into the cold water. It's colder than it was a month ago, washing away the dust and dirt from practice immediately. I float on my back, staring up at the cloudless blue sky.

My ears bob below the surface occasionally, muffling any sound. It's peaceful. Or it was, until Jamie starts calling my name.

"What?" I call back, giving up on floating and treading water instead.

"Come on, man, we're getting pizza!"

Everyone else is already out. I swim over to the edge and pull myself onto the shore.

"No one brought towels?" Drew asks.

"Did you?" I counter.

"We're going to need to stop by the house before pizza," Jamie decides. "No way am I going out in public like this."

Garrett makes a face as he pulls his sweaty shirt back on. Reluctantly, the rest of us do the same. Except for Elliot, who's looking for his clothes.

"No one say anything," Jamie threatens in a low voice.

Drew snorts as he pulls on his pants.

"Have you guys seen my clothes?" Elliot calls, wandering back toward us. "I swear I left them all on the path. Do birds take that shit for nests? Or deer?"

Garrett looks constipated, he's trying so hard not to laugh.

"I don't think there are any deer around here," Jamie says as we reach him. "You were tossing things off toward the bushes. Just go look around."

"In the bushes?" Elliot replies, looking dismayed. "Guys, I'm not even wearing boxers. No way am I about to climb around in the bushes. What if there's poison ivy and it touches my junk?"

"Get over it and hurry up," Drew says. "Cops hang around here sometimes. You don't want to get arrested for public indecency."

"Yeah, you could end up on some sex offender registry," Garrett chimes in with.

"What the fuck am I supposed to do if I can't find them?" Elliot glances around, wildly.

"No clue. But you're not getting your naked ass in my car," Drew says.

He walks toward the parking lot, essentially a small clearing. The rest of us follow.

Elliot sighs and turns back toward the swimming hole.

Drew starts wheezing as soon as he disappears. "How has he not realized we're fucking with him?"

Jamie doubles over laughing as soon as he's in the car.

The rest of us all climb inside too, waiting for Elliot to emerge from the woods. Hopefully clothed.

"I'm starving," Garrett finally announces after twenty minutes have passed. "Do we leave and come back for him later?"

"I can't believe he hasn't found them," Jamie says. "They're barely hidden."

"Maybe he jumped back in the water," Drew states. "Seems like something he'd do."

Elliot suddenly appears, fully dressed and scowling.

"Going to be a long drive back," Drew says, turning on the car.

We all burst out laughing.

CHAPTER THIRTY-SIX

LENNON

"That's all for today, folks. Grab an application for the Fulright Fellowship on the way out, if you're interested. Keep up the caffeine consumption!"

As soon as Professor Glannon stops speaking, the lecture hall erupts in activity. Laptops are closed. Pens clicked. Backpacks unzipped.

"What's the Fulright Fellowship?" I ask Eric as we pack up our bags.

"It's a grant for continuing study in the field of journalism," Eric explains. "It usually involves placement at an elite newspaper and it's open to every senior journalism major at any school in the country. Clarkson students have won before, but it's hard to do. Super competitive."

"How do you apply?"

"There's an essay prompt. Also, to qualify for consideration, you have to have spent a couple of years working for a newspaper in some capacity."

"Oh." I expected the requirements to be something I couldn't meet. Not being a senior year transfer, for example. But…I could apply, it sounds like. "Are you going to apply?"

Eric laughs. "Yeah, of course. Along with a bunch of other fellowships. Aren't you?"

"I don't know. I only just learned about it now."

"Don't you want to work for a paper?"

"Of course."

"Then you should definitely apply. I'll read your essay for you, if you want. Give you some feedback before you send the application in."

"Thanks," I tell him. "What's the prompt?"

"Can people change?"

"Really? That sounds like a question on a philosophy final, not for a journalism grant."

Eric shrugs as we walk outside. "They're looking for good writers. It's not a research assignment you need sources for or an interview you have to conduct. Just show them you're capable of writing something compelling. If you can write it about a three-word prompt, you can write it about breaking news."

I nod. "That makes sense."

"If you want to talk about it more, we can meet in the library one night this week. I—I'll see you later, Lennon." Eric changes whatever he was going to say once he sees what I've just spotted.

Caleb is sitting on the bench across from the journalism building, talking on the phone as he waits for me. We're supposed to go grab lunch off-campus.

"Thanks, Eric. See you next class."

Eric nods and disappears into the crowd. I met him, Abby, Amanda, and Joe at a local coffee shop last weekend to work on assignments. None of them mentioned Caleb or brought up what happened the last time we all hung out at the pizzeria.

It was nice. It made me feel like I'm finding my own place here, not just fitting into Caleb's world.

He looks up and smiles as I approach. Caleb is wearing a Jays baseball cap, one Gramps gave him for his birthday last year. Gramps mostly loved Caleb because he knew how much I do. But I know it secretly thrilled him I was dating *the* Caleb Winters, baseball star.

And Gramps was obsessed with baseball. He could name every player's hometown and rattle off years of stats at the drop of a hat.

Once upon a time, at least. There were days he couldn't remember what year it was, much less the team's starting line-up.

He's been gone for three months. In some ways, it feels like far more time has passed. My life today looks so wildly different than I ever imagined it being. I've met people and experienced things I never would have in Landry.

In other ways, I'm not sure I've fully accepted he's gone. There are moments when I'll catch myself living in that fantasy world. When I've just woken up, or been focused on something else, and I'll think of something I want to tell him. The split seconds it takes to recall that I can't are some of the hardest ones to get through.

Grief isn't a linear path from loss to rediscovering joy and laughter. It's a trail of zigs and zags, of ups and downs, that eventually leads to more happy days than sad ones. It's a journey that never really ends, just becomes easier to travel.

It also has a way of making some things more meaningful. Others less so. It's a reminder not a single moment we have is guaranteed. That worry about the future takes time away from the present.

"Yeah, okay. Bye."

Caleb hangs up the phone right as I reach him. Stands, so I'm looking up at him instead of down.

"Hey. How was class?" he asks, slipping his phone in his pocket and then pulling his hat off to run a hand through his hair.

I don't think Caleb has any idea how that move affects me. If he did, he'd do it all the time, just to amuse himself.

Sometimes, no matter how well you know a person or how many times you've looked at them, you stare at them the way a stranger would. And Caleb is just...really hot.

"Lennon?"

"Good, yeah. Class was good."

Caleb nods as we start walking along the paved path toward the parking lot. I've taken an elbow to the side or experienced a close call with the skateboarders who love to fly around campus many times before. But Caleb walking beside me is like being enclosed in a bubble. Everyone walks around us, instead of trying to walk through straight.

"Have you heard of the Fulright Fellowship?" I ask.

"No. Why? What is it?"

"It's a journalism grant. I don't know much about it. My professor mentioned it at the end of class, and Eric was telling me more on the way out."

"Are you going to apply?"

"I guess so. Apparently, it's really hard to get."

"I have faith in you, Matthews."

I smile. "Who were you talking to?"

"Colt."

"How's he doing?"

"Pretty good. He wants to plan a winter break trip, since we'll both be tied up with baseball over spring break."

We reach his truck. Caleb tosses his baseball bag from the cab into the bed, and then we're headed downtown. He takes me to a hole-in-the-wall sandwich shop I've never been to before. Gramps and I hardly ever ate out and Landry has a small selection of restaurants. Exploring all of the eating options here has been an unexpected highlight of attending Clarkson.

Caleb pays for my lunch.

It's something he's always done, ever since we first started dating. He's a perfect gentleman when it comes to the tiny details most guys don't seem to bother with—opening doors for me and walking closer to the street when we're on the sidewalk.

When it comes to money, he's never bought me extravagant gifts or flaunted his wealth in any way.

I'm not even sure exactly how much money he has. I know he has a trust fund and I know he inherited a lot when his grandfather died. The only time he alluded to how much was when he brought me the bank account papers.

The bank account I haven't touched. Because now that Matthews Farm has sold, I don't need to. I have money of my own—lots of it.

And I haven't told Caleb that.

I haven't told him the property is gone or disclosed the dollar amount. Caleb hasn't asked. So maybe he's already assumed it sold. He knows as well as I do plenty of people with lots of money want to live in Landry. If there was more property available, working there would be a real estate agent's dream. And the property that is available goes fast.

Once we're settled at a table with our food, I decide to stop putting it off. It's not like he won't find out about it. I'm sure it's a topic of gossip in Landry. I don't think Caleb has talked to either of his parents lately, or they probably would have mentioned it. Maybe now, they'll stop thinking I'm after Caleb for his money, which has been heavily insinuated on the few occasions I've met Mr. and Mrs. Winters.

"There's something I've been meaning to tell you."

He looks up from his turkey sandwich, expression serious. "Okay…"

"Don't look so freaked out. It's good news."

Mostly good news, at least. It's still strange to think someone else will be living on Matthews Farm. People born in Landry rarely leave. Until Caleb, there was never a thought I might end up somewhere else. I pictured getting married in the white church in town. Walking my own kids to Landry Elementary in the mornings the same way Gramps walked me. Growing old in the rocking chairs on the front porch of the farmhouse.

I didn't ask the realtor for any details about the buyer when I signed all the paperwork. I'd rather picture it the way it was when I left for Colt's birthday party. Not empty, the way it was the last time I saw it. And not bulldozed to make room for a larger house, maybe lots of larger houses, which is probably what's happening right now.

"What?" Caleb raises one brow, waiting impatiently.

"I'm rich." I smile, trying to lighten the mood. "Well, maybe not compared to you. But compared to most people, I am."

Caleb's expression doesn't change. "You sold the farm."

His seriousness punctures the happiness I was trying to project. "Yeah. The closing was last week."

He exhales heavily. "Okay."

"Okay? That's *it*?" I wasn't sure how he'd react to the news. But I thought he'd say something more than a two-syllable word with no inflection.

He picks up his sandwich. "What do you want me to say, Lennon? It was your decision to make."

"I wanted you to be happy about it, Caleb. I talked to Louis yesterday to check in on the horses. He said Winters Stables is interested in buying them all to add to the breeding program.

451

Once that's done, I won't have any responsibilities in Landry. After graduation, I can move anywhere."

"Because that's what you want or because you think that's what I want?"

"Caleb! Hey!" A female voice cuts through the tense moment. But Caleb doesn't look away from me. Not right away.

Finally, he leans back and glances to the right. I follow his gaze. Sophie is walking this way, with a few girls behind her. They're all in soccer jerseys, clearly having just come from a practice. Even sweaty and tired, they all look gorgeous. I think one of them was with Sophie at the party, but I can't remember her name.

"Oh. Hi, Lennon." My greeting is substantially less enthusiastic than Caleb's was.

I muster a smile. "Hi, Sophie."

She turns back to Caleb. "I should have known you'd be here. Remember sophomore year? You had lunch at this place almost every day."

I take a bite of my egg salad. I know exactly what game she's playing, and I'm not interested in engaging. So what if they ate lunch together while I was back in Landry, probably mucking out stalls? I'd bet it was with the whole friend group they seem to share.

And even if it wasn't, I don't really care. I'm more annoyed she interrupted our conversation, although I don't know how I would have answered Caleb's question. I don't know where I want to live after graduation. So, I'm trying to open up all the possible options. I thought he'd appreciate that, not act like I'm making mistakes.

I keep eating my lunch, tuning out Sophie's chatter. To his credit, Caleb isn't really engaging. He mostly nods in answer to what she's saying, leaving Sophie and her friends to carry the conversation.

By the time they finally turn to leave, I've finished my lunch.

Sophie spins back around instead of following the other girls over to the counter to order.

"Oh, I forgot. I was texting with Brian earlier. He said to say hi to you, Caleb."

I glance at Caleb. I've only heard him mention one Brian... one of his roommates at Mayfair. It's a common name. Entirely possibly Sophie is talking about someone else. But based on the tight clench of Caleb's jaw, I don't think she is.

"Okay," Caleb answers, then finishes his sandwich in a few bites. He balls up the wrapper and tosses it at the trash can sitting about ten feet away. Makes it, of course. "You ready to go?"

"Yeah." I nod and quickly stand. Between his reaction to the news about the farm and Sophie showing up, this hasn't been the most enjoyable meal. I'd rather be outside, enjoying the fall weather.

As soon as we're out on the sidewalk, I speak. "I thought Mayfair was a baseball camp."

Caleb sighs. "They host soccer and football clinics too. Sophie was there with a few other girls on Clarkson's team."

"And you never mentioned it?"

"Back then, I didn't think you'd ever end up at Clarkson. I didn't think you'd ever meet Sophie."

"So you hid it because you thought I'd never find out?"

Caleb starts to look pissed. "Find out *what*, Lennon? There's nothing to hide. Has she hit on me? Yeah. Have I done anything except make it clear to her I'm not interested? No. I thought you trusted me."

"I *do*. It's just weird that you never mentioned it. Never mentioned her."

"You never said anything to me about that journalism guy you keep hanging out with."

"Eric? What does he have to do with it?"

"He's into you, Lennon."

"He's just friendly," I say, annoyed he's dragging Eric into it. Aside from Caleb, he's the person who's made me feel most welcome at Clarkson. Without him, I wouldn't have even met Abby, Amanda, and Joe. Or gotten advice on journalism electives. "He's never hit on me."

"Oh, yeah? So he's never asked you to hang out, just the two of you?"

I flush, recalling Eric's suggestion after class. "That's different. We were talking about the fellowship I told you about. It was school-related."

"How is it different? Sophie was at Mayfair because she's a student athlete, same as me. It was sports-related."

"Fine." I look away. "Forget I said anything about it."

Caleb grabs my hand and tugs me to a stop, his annoyed expression softening. "I *want* you to tell me when you're upset about things, Len. There's nothing more terrifying than when you shut down and shut me out. It's kind of funny, actually, that you're jealous."

I glare at him. "Funny?"

Instead of flinching from the warning in my voice, he smiles. "I haven't touched another girl since the first time you kissed me. So yeah, it's funny you're jealous."

"You mean since we started dating."

"No. I mean since the first time you kissed me."

"In high school? But that whole summer, and you were here—single—all fall…"

He shrugs. "I was in love with you, Lennon. I wasn't interested in anyone else."

I step closer and kiss him, the sudden rush of love so over-whelming it needs an outlet. Love is a word made up of actions.

The rest of the walk to Caleb's truck is peaceful. We don't argue very often. Maybe that's because we spent the first few years of high school exclusively communicating that way. Maybe because the first few years of college only allowed limited time together, and neither of us wanted to spend it discussing anything unpleasant. This is the closest we've come to a fight in a while, and storms make you appreciate the calm more, when it finally arrives.

"My mom keeps bringing up Thanksgiving." Caleb is the first to speak, once we're headed back toward campus. "I thought she'd back out and decide to stay in New York, but she's still leaving me voicemails about it."

"Oh," I reply. Thanksgiving isn't all that far away, I suddenly realize. "Do you want to go?"

Selfishly, I'm kind of hoping he says no. Caleb's relationship with his parents is complicated. Partly because they thoroughly disapprove of me.

"Only if you want to."

I give him a wry smile. "I'll go if you want to. But Cassie invited me to spend it with her family, so if you'd prefer to go alone…"

"I'm not going without you, Lennon."

"Okay. Then let's go." I have no family members left due to lots of unfortunate circumstances. I don't want Caleb losing his by choice. I'll go and be pleasant, even if I want to hide every time Mrs. Winters looks at me. At least Caleb's father mostly ignores my presence. "Is there skiing?"

"In Aspen?" He laughs. "Yeah."

"I haven't been since I was a kid. Madison's family invited me in middle school."

"It'll come right back to you," Caleb tells me.

"I doubt that. I was never that good. And don't people break their legs skiing all the time?"

"If it happened 'all the time' I don't think anyone would go. You can stay on the bunny hill. We can even get you one of those ropes little kids use if you want."

I snort. "Well, based on how the last few interactions with your parents have gone, spending a few hours at the hospital might be more fun."

Caleb laughs, but then turns serious. "We don't have to go, Len."

Guilt swirls in my stomach. "I want to go."

"Liar."

I smile. "I think we should go."

I expect that to be the end of any heavy conversation. Caleb has other ideas. "About the farm..."

"It's sold, Caleb. Done."

"I thought you wanted to live in Landry, though."

"That's a big decision to make. I thought Gramps would be around for a lot longer. I got used to the idea it's where I would stay. I was waiting to see where you ended up." I raise a shoulder and then let it drop. "Things changed."

"Well, I still have a farm in Landry."

"You mean your parents do."

Caleb shakes his head. "No. I mean *I* do. My grandfather left me the property in his will. As soon as I turned eighteen, it was mine. One final way to piss of my dad, probably. My parents got his townhouse in DC. Took my dad about a week to sell it."

I picture the Winters estate, soaring columns and impeccable landscaping. Everything shiny and state-of-art and brand-new. "You own the farm?"

"Yes."

Based on what Matthews Farm just sold for, I have a pretty good idea what the Winters estate must be worth. "Wow."

"Tom Stradwell told me he offered you a job at the *Gazette*. We can move back to Landry, after graduation."

"But what about baseball? The draft?"

"I don't have to play, Lennon."

"But you want to. You love baseball."

"I love you more," Caleb says. His words twist my insides, in both a good and a bad way.

"You don't have to choose, Caleb. I gave the farm up to come here. I didn't abandon a dream."

"Didn't you?" he replies.

I look away. In some way, I guess I did.

CHAPTER THIRTY-SEVEN

CALEB

L ennon's hand tightens around mine, almost cutting off the circulation.

I glance over, hiding a grin. We're on our way to Aspen for Thanksgiving. This is the first time we've ever been on plane together, and it turns out Lennon is a nervous flier. Or maybe she's more anxious about arriving. "It's going to be fine, Len."

"I know," Lennon says quickly. Her grip loosens, so it feels like we're holding hands instead of her hanging onto me for dear life.

"You do?"

"Yes!"

"We can back out."

"You've been saying that for weeks. And we're already in the air, Caleb. If I was going to back out—which I'm not—I couldn't anymore."

"They're not going to say anything."

They'd better not. I made it very clear to my mother—to both my parents—that there were conditions for accepting their Thanksgiving invitation.

Lennon gives me a small smile, then turns back to her laptop. She's been typing one-handed for the past hour, working on the essay for the journalism grant she's applying for.

I'm glad she is. It makes me feel a little less guilty about everything she gave up to come here. I know it was about a lot more than me, but I doubt she would have ever applied to Clarkson, let alone transferred, if this wasn't where I was.

That comes with some responsibility for her to be happy, it feels like.

And if that happiness doesn't include Landry, if it's a fancy job at an important newspaper, then that's great.

But I'm not convinced it is. The happiest I've seen Lennon was walking around the east pasture with Dusty following her. Wild, windblown hair and grass-stained jeans.

I want her to have choices. I just don't want her to choose something because it's an option now she didn't have before.

When we land in Colorado an hour later, I have to surreptitiously shake my arm for five minutes to get the blood flowing again. We hit some turbulence mid-flight that had Lennon's grip tightening again. Then as soon as the skies quieted, she fell asleep on my shoulder.

Lennon stirs as the plane fills with activity, everyone standing and opening the overhead bins or turning on their phones to make calls.

Once it's finally our turn to disembark the plane, we follow the exit signs through the airport. I've only been here once before, and it wasn't half as packed then it is today. We pass a long stretch of gates and then the baggage claim. I'm grateful Lennon's a light packer. We didn't have to check a bag, so we bypass the huge crowd waiting for the belt to begin moving and another one watching the luggage spin. Lots of people brought snow sports equipment, clogging up the chute with bulk other than suitcases.

It's a shock to step outside. Kentucky hasn't fully transitioned to winter yet, temperatures still hovering above freezing. I didn't check the weather here before we left, but I wasn't expecting it to be this cold. There's even snow on the ground, cleared away from the sidewalk and road in white piles that suggest it fell recently. I was only expecting the artificial kind.

"Wow," Lennon breathes. Her attention is focused on the towering, snowy peaks that make up the distant landscape.

"Just wait until you see the view from the top of one," I tell her.

"Wouldn't that require skiing down from the top afterward?"

I give her a *duh* look, and she laughs. "Yeah, *no*. Hard pass."

A long line of cars is waiting to pick up new arrivals. I guide Lennon over to a black SUV, climbing inside the warm car as the driver loads our two suitcases into the trunk.

When he asks where we're headed, I have to look up the chalet's address on my phone to relay it to him.

Lennon's eyes are wide as she takes in the downtown section we drive through. It's approaching dusk. The lights lining the street are just turning on, casting a golden glow over the shops and restaurants and condos.

The awestruck expression on Lennon's face makes me second-guess what I was thinking earlier. Maybe this is what she wants. New experiences. Different places.

She looks even more stunned when we arrive at the five thousand square foot property. The chalet was a twenty-five-year anniversary gift from my father to my mother. Less romantic and more of an acknowledgment he's not the easiest person to get along with. Now that I'm not living at home and hardly see them,

I never know exactly what the state of my parents' relationship is. Since this is the most ostentatious of the luxurious properties my parents own, I'm guessing not great.

Lennon isn't the only one taken aback by the sight of the chalet. Our driver doesn't attempt to school his amazed expression when he reaches the top of the winding driveway.

The chalet is meant to blend in with the mountain it's built on. It might succeed, if seven-bedroom, seven-bathroom mansions just popped out of rock formations like magic.

Lennon gives me a *Seriously?* look as we climb out of the car and grab our bags. I pay the driver and then we head toward the front door.

"It's bigger than I remember," I tell her.

She snorts.

I've only been here once before, and it was a short trip. I register the exterior like it's the first time I'm seeing it.

The stone and wood construction is covered by a black metal roof barely visible beneath a dusting of snow. Floor to ceiling windows serve the dual purpose of exposing the interior and providing a sweeping view of the surrounding scenery. Tall, proud pines stand between the columns that flank the front door.

Lennon stops once she reaches the front porch, looking off to the right. I pause when I reach her.

This is one part of the chalet I didn't forget. The front side overlooks the town below where we started from. If you look out from any other angle of the house, all you can see is snow-dusted mountains and evergreens.

No civilization, just wilderness.

Whoever the real estate agent was who pocketed the heavy commission on this property had the whole *location, location, location* line in spades. The house itself is gorgeous. The view is stall-your-breath stunning.

"Wow. I didn't realize we were up this high," Lennon says, surveying the drop below.

We're not looking up at the peaks; it feels like we're part of one of them.

"Yeah, the view is nice," I agree.

Lennon laughs. "Nice?"

"Come on. The house is not too bad either," I tell her.

I open the front door and gesture for Lennon to enter first.

The layout is mostly open. The kitchen, living room, and dining room all meld together as soon as you pass through the entryway.

Lennon stops in place as soon as we do. The far wall is completely composed of windows made from glass squares framed by black wood. It has the effect of appearing as though the wall is covered by a photograph collage of the same breathtaking view we were admiring outside, pieced together in perfect scale.

"You're here!"

I turn to see my mother descending the staircase that curls around the far side of the gourmet kitchen.

"I sent you our flight number so you'd know exactly when we were arriving," I reply.

Based on her tone, you'd think we dropped out of the sky unexpectedly, rather than the fact that the only reason we're here is repeated badgering. It doesn't bode well for the rest of this visit.

"Right." My mother lets out a nervous laugh. "Well, come on in and get settled. The other guests should be arriving shortly."

"Other guests?" I ask, flatly.

"The St. Jameses are staying with us for a few days."

I close my eyes briefly, so, so tempted to just walk back out the front door. I should have known she was incapable of not pulling this kind of shit. It shouldn't even matter that she doesn't know how persistent Sophie has been and she's only hoping throwing us together will spark interest.

"Why?"

Another nervous laugh, paired with a hair pat. "I was talking with Eloise, and she said they didn't have any plans. So I thought it would be nice to include them."

"Why didn't you tell me you were including them? Or better, ask me before you did?" I pretend to think about it. "I think I know why. Because you knew I wouldn't come." I shake my head. "The manipulation is getting really old, Mom."

I'm not harboring any delusions my mother invited Sophie and her family for any reason besides a distraction from getting to know Lennon and another attempt to shove me in Sophie's direction.

"There's plenty of room, Caleb. It looks like this place could sleep twenty."

Lennon surprises me by speaking. After the way she reacted to learning Sophie was at Mayfair with me, I figured she'd be just as upset about this development.

But when I look over, her expression is pleading. Silently asking me not to make more of a scene.

I exhale, and my mother jumps on the pause. "Let me show you to your rooms."

"We're staying in the same room, Mom." I drop the words with a clear note of finality. I don't care if it makes my mother uncomfortable or messes with her wholesome family mindset. "Which one?" I ask.

"First one on the right."

I nod. "We'll go get unpacked."

I head for the stairs without another word. Five minutes here, and I already need a breather.

The house is silent aside from the crackling of wood in the

fireplace, some soft jazz playing from invisible speakers, and Lennon's footsteps following me.

As soon as we enter the bedroom, I start pacing the room and ranting. "Unbelievable! I can't believe she—"

"You're overreacting," Lennon tells me, lifting her suitcase on the bed and unzipping it.

I turn toward her, surprised. "I'm overreacting? You realize this means Sophie will be here?"

"So? You told me not to worry about her. So...I'm not worried. She can show up and flirt with you all she wants."

I study her. Lennon looks truly unbothered. "She still should have told me."

"That, I agree with. But she didn't, and we're here now. Maybe it will make the trip better, having them here as a buffer. And it doesn't matter. I don't want to fly again before I have to, so we're stuck here."

"We could drive."

She rolls her eyes. "Caleb, come on. They're your parents. If you don't want to spend future holidays with them, that's fine. I'll be completely on board with that plan. But we're already here for this one."

I pull her to me, brushing some of the hair away from her face. Her ponytail didn't fare very well on the trip here. Lennon's hazel eyes teem with amusement as she watches me study her. There's no sight in the world I know better than Lennon Matthews's face.

I keep gazing at her, even as her cheeks flush with self-consciousness.

"You're pretty fucking amazing, you know that?" I whisper.

Lennon scrunches her nose, wrinkling the constellation of freckles. "Yeah, I know."

I move even closer, my lips ghost against her jaw.

464

"Caleb…"

"Mm-hmm?" I murmur against her skin.

"We should unpack."

I slip my fingers under the bottom of her puffy coat and am greeted by an endless stretch of warm, smooth skin. "Yeah, we should," I whisper.

Then I kiss her, easing my tongue inside the warm heat of her mouth the same way my fingers are creeping under her jacket. Lennon melts against me, closing the small distance between our bodies.

"Here are so—oh!"

Lennon pulls away, and there's my mother, standing in the doorway holding a stack of white towels and wearing a shocked expression. The arm not clutching towels is still extended from pushing the door open.

"Oh!" my mother says again. I don't think she's ever seen us kiss before. She hasn't spent enough time around us to know that if I had my way, that's how I'd spend the majority of the time.

"You could have knocked," I say.

Lennon elbows me in the ribs.

My mother tracks the movement. Her eyebrows rise higher. She thinks Lennon encourages antagonism toward my parents, not that she's the main reason I'm even here.

"I was just dropping off some towels. There are extras in the hall closet if you need them."

"Okay," I state.

"Okay," my mother repeats. "I'll let you two…" She quickly turns and leaves the room without finishing the sentence.

I glance at Lennon and smirk. She rolls her eyes.

We unpack, which doesn't take long. I try to talk Lennon into hiding out in our room until dinner, but she ignores me and heads back downstairs. I follow with a sigh.

My father has appeared in our absence. He's settled in the leather armchair by the fireplace, sipping bourbon and studying a packet of papers I'm certain are business-related.

He rises when we walk down the stairs, flashing his most charming smile. I don't think he approves—actually I know he doesn't approve—of Lennon any more than my mother does, but at least he doesn't act like it around her.

Austin Winters thrives on being well-liked. On being the easy-going guy who just happens to be wealthy and powerful. He rarely lets that mask slip, and he most certainly doesn't allow it to around anyone besides me and my mother.

"Lennon! So glad you could join us."

"Hi, Mr. Winters," Lennon greets politely. "Nice to see you."

"Austin, please." He gives Lennon his trademark, charming smile, then turns his attention to me. "How are you, son?"

"Fine, Dad," I reply.

"Classes going well?"

"Yes."

"George Coleman sent us an article about your last scrimmage, honey," my mother says, appearing from the kitchen with a glass of wine in hand. "Seems like it will be a great season."

"Yep." I take a seat on the couch facing the wall of windows. Lennon sinks down beside me.

I could have predicted my father would ask about academics and my mother would bring up baseball before we came downstairs. Add in my mom's meddling and my dad pretending our last conversation at Earl's funeral never happened, and this is following the same pattern of every other interaction I've ever had with my parents.

"Did you hear about the scrimmage, Lennon?" my mother asks politely. She seems to be on her best behavior now, but I don't trust it will last.

"Uh, yes. I was there, actually," Lennon replies. "Caleb's pitching was very impressive."

"Oh, I didn't realize. Caleb said you didn't make it to many baseball games," is my mother's response.

I send her a sharp look for that comment.

"It's easier to go to his games now that I live ten minutes away from the baseball field, rather than three hours," Lennon says.

"Ah, yes. I heard that you transferred. How are you liking Clarkson so far?" my father asks her.

"It's been great," Lennon responds. "I'm really enjoying all my classes. Richardson's journalism department didn't have anywhere near the same amount of resources."

"I would imagine not." My father chuckles. "Have you given any thought to what you might do with a journalism degree?"

I grit my teeth. "People typically become *journalists*, Dad."

"Difficult industry to get a foothold in," he comments, taking a drink of bourbon.

"It is," Lennon agrees.

"Long hours. Horrible pay," my father continues.

"The same is true for many career paths," I state. "I think it's more important to pursue something you're passionate about."

"Passion doesn't pay bills, Caleb."

Rich, coming from a man who inherited most of his wealth.

"Can I get you two anything to drink?" my mother asks, clearly sensing the fire isn't the only reason the temperature in the room is rising. My temper is climbing with every comment my father makes. "The St. Jameses should be here any minute. Their flight was supposed to land at six."

"Great," I mutter.

"You must have met Sophie, if you're at Clarkson now," my father says to Lennon.

"I have," Lennon replies.

"Her father is an old business school buddy of mine," he continues. "Quite an eye for investments he's got."

Lennon nods. "It's nice that you two have stayed in touch."

"I'm grabbing a drink," I announce. "Do you want anything?" I ask Lennon.

"Just some water," she replies.

"Okay." I stand and head into the kitchen.

The fridge is filled with prepared meals and plenty of alcohol. I grab a beer for myself and fill a glass of water for Lennon.

When I approach the couch again, they're discussing Earl. My grip tightens on the beverages I'm holding.

"—such a loss," my mother is saying. "Must be especially difficult with the holidays approaching."

"My grandfather wasn't one for giving certain days more significance over others," Lennon replies. "But it's certainly been difficult, not having him around."

I return to my seat on the couch and hand Lennon her glass of water, giving her knee a quick squeeze once I have a free hand.

"Caleb said you both came to the service. That was very nice of you."

"Of course. We were coming to town for the Cup anyway. We wouldn't have missed it," my mother replies.

I drown my scoff with a gulp of beer.

"We drove past Matthews Farm while we were there," my father states. "Quite a chunk of land there. What is it, nine acres? Ten?"

"Fifteen," Lennon replies. "And it's not Matthews Farm any longer. I sold it."

This is news to both of my parents, based on their shocked expressions. I guess enough of their friends in Landry are strictly summer residents who don't visit or pay attention to what happens there the rest of the year. I hope now that they know about it, neither of them will dig into the sale.

"That's quite a decision. That farm was in your family for four generations?"

Lennon sips some water. "Five," she answers quietly. "But things change. I needed to fund my journalism career."

I never told Lennon how my mom freaked out about the money I gave her. I'm sure my father was angry about it too, but we mostly communicate through my mother when we're in different places. They both know Lennon didn't need to sell her farm to afford college, and the fact she did is throwing them both off-kilter.

The doorbell rings, and my mother flies to her feet.

"That must be the St. Jameses!"

My father stands as well. Lennon and I follow suit, trailing after my mother toward the entryway.

Sophie is standing with her parents, surrounded by several bags of luggage. She smiles when she sees me, but it dies when she sees Lennon next to me.

I'm clearly not the only one who had details about this trip sprung upon them last minute, I guess. It explains why she didn't mention this when I ran into her on campus a week ago.

I introduce Lennon to Mr. and Mrs. St. James while my mother embraces Sophie like a long-lost relative. Once all the greetings and introductions are done, Sophie and her parents head upstairs to get settled in their rooms. My mom disappears into the kitchen to heat the food the chef already prepared. My father goes to get more firewood.

"Having fun?" I smirk at Lennon.

"Yup." She gives me a wide, fake grin.

"Jake texted me earlier. His family is here, and Colt came

with him. They're coming over at eight to go sledding. There's a hill close to here."

"The Barneses have a place here?"

"Yeah. They follow my parents' lead when it comes to most things. Including the real estate market."

Lennon shakes her head. "Of course they do."

Dinner is some sort of chicken dish. The table atmosphere is uncomfortable.

For the first few minutes, the only sound is silver utensils clinking against china as everyone serves themselves food. Then, my father and Sophie's start a hedge fund conversation filled with business terms that I could probably follow if I wanted to.

I don't.

"So, Lennon, you grew up in Landry?" Sophie's mother asks mid-way through the meal.

Lennon quickly swallows and nods. "Yes, I did."

"It's such a lovely town. We were just there for the Cup a few months ago. So much character and passion. It's hard to find that these days."

"Landry is one of a kind," Lennon states.

"And you just transferred to Clarkson this semester?"

"Yes. I was at Richardson Community College up until then, so I could live at home."

"What an exciting change. How many years do you have left?"

"Just one. I'm a senior," Lennon tells her.

Mrs. St. James's eyebrows raise. "I didn't realize Clarkson admitted new students as seniors."

"They do if they have a four-point-oh," I interject.

Lennon smiles modestly. "I've always liked school."

Sophie's mother glances between me and Lennon, smiling. Thankfully, she's never been as aggressive about shoving me and Sophie together as my mother has been. "You and Caleb are such a cute couple. Was it love at first sight between you two?"

The table falls silent. Sophie's looking down at her plate. But both of my parents' gazes are fixed directly on Lennon as they await the answer to the question neither of them has ever bothered to ask.

Lennon laughs. So do I. "Uh, no. Definitely not. I was actually really proud of being the only girl at Landry High who wasn't sucked in by the Caleb Winters charm." She glances at me, and I smile. "Turns out I'm not immune to it. We got assigned on a school project together senior year. Then, I had to write an article on him. Eventually, even I had to admit he's a pretty amazing guy."

"I read that article. It was good," my father comments. I glance at him, shocked.

Lennon appears equally surprised. "Thank you."

"It must be nice to be back at the same school again," Sophie's mother states, turning the attention back on Lennon and me.

The words are innocuous enough, but her eyes bounce back and forth between us. She's probing our past to try and foresee our future. Maybe I was wrong, and my mother isn't the only matchmaker sitting at this table.

"Yes, it is," Lennon responds.

"There were some Matthews horses winning the Cup for several years," Mr. St. James states. "Those yours?"

"My grandfather's, at the time. Now, yes, they're mine."

"That's quite a responsibility."

"At the moment, we're the ones horse-sitting." My father chuckles.

Any goodwill toward my father following his compliment quickly vanishes. "When was the last time you were out in the stable, Dad?"

"I was merely joking, Caleb. Of course we're happy to host the Matthews horses while Lennon enjoys herself at Clarkson."

I clench my left hand and release the fist. "Especially since they're staying in my *half* of the racing business."

My father's eyes flash with anger. That was another unpleasant surprise for him at my grandfather's will reading.

I didn't just get the farm itself, I also got half of the lucrative business known as Winters Stables that's headquartered there. It's a sore spot I rarely press, and something I'm certain he didn't want the St. Jameses to know. Knowledge is potential weakness, if you ask my father.

The doorbell breaks the charged silence.

"I'll get it." My mother starts to stand.

"No, I'll get it. It's Colt and Jake." I stand and toss my napkin on my chair before I stalk toward the entryway.

The door swings open to reveal two of my best friends. "Fuck, am I glad to see you two," I tell them.

"Really? How come?" Jake asks, grinning.

"Yeah. You normally love spending time with your parents," Colt adds.

I scoff. "Come on in. Everyone is in the dining room."

Colt and Jake follow me deeper into the house. Lennon stands from the table as we walk in.

"Matthews!" Jake ignores everyone else and heads straight for Lennon.

He gives her a big hug and then passes her off to Colt, who does the same before focusing on my parents.

"Hi, Mr. Winters. Mrs. Winters," Colt greets.

Jake repeats the greeting, then adds, "My parents say hi too."

"They should have come over with you boys," my father says.

"Nah. They hate sledding," Jake replies, grinning, then looks to me. "You guys ready?"

"Yep," I reply immediately. I've been ready to leave this house since we arrived, basically.

I catch Lennon's eye. She tilts her head toward Sophie.

"Do you want to come with us, Sophie?" I ask, silently praying she'll say no.

To my relief, she does. "I'm good, thanks. You guys have fun."

I grab Lennon's hand and tug her toward the entryway. Jake and Colt are right behind us.

"How much are you regretting coming?" Jake asks Lennon as we pull on our winter coats.

She laughs. "It hasn't been that bad."

"*Massive* regrets then," Jake surmises. "Mom and Pop Winters are arctic cold."

"They're just a little chilly," Lennon replies, magnanimously.

"You're too good for Winters, Lennon," Colt states.

I flip him off as I pull on my snow boots. "I'm trying to keep her from figuring that out, Adams."

"Better lock it down," Jake advises. "Just a matter of time. Surprised it hasn't happened already. They'll be married with two point five kids before you get your first girlfriend." He grins at Colt.

"How the hell do you end up with half a kid?" Colt asks, looking confused.

"I have no idea, actually. I've just heard people say that. It's a saying, right?" Jake says. "I didn't just make that up?"

I'm laughing too hard to answer him as we leave the warm

house. The loss of heat makes it feel especially freezing out. Darkness surrounds us. The only hint of light is the moonlight glittering on the frozen surface of the snow.

Jake parked his SUV right outside the front door, so it's not a long trip to the car. Colt climbs into the passenger side while Lennon and I pile into the back.

It's a short drive to the slope. The overlook has a drop that's steep enough to spark adrenaline but not suicidal.

Jake brought five different sled options in his trunk. I grab the largest and Lennon's hand.

Colt and Jake take off immediately, their shouts the only indication there's anyone else out here in the wilderness with us. For the first time since the uncomfortable stretch of time known as dinner, Lennon and I are alone.

Instead of comment on how unpleasant it was, I decide to adopt Lennon's attitude from earlier and just enjoy the moment. "Want to sled?" I ask her.

Her lips quirk, the movement barely noticeable in the dim light. "Yeah. Sure."

I settle into the back of the plastic sled. Lennon climbs in between my legs, the warmth of her body counteracting the chilly air. The sky is spread out like an inky blanket above us, peppered with pricks of light and the beam of the moon that illuminates the barest outline of craggy mountains around us.

This is one of those rare perfect moments.

It's tangible, the knowledge I'll look back and remember exactly how I felt during this precise point in time.

"I'm glad we came," Lennon tells me.

"Yeah, me too," I reply.

Then I shove off, sending us into motion to slide down the side of the snowy mountain.

CHAPTER THIRTY-EIGHT

LENNON

I have no idea how I got myself into this.

Actually, that's a lie.

I'm desperate for some small sign of approval from a woman who's alternated between acting as though I don't exist and demonstrating her mastery of the back-handed compliment. I know Caleb's relationship with his parents is strained for reasons unrelated to me. I also know if he had to choose between me and them, he would pick me. I don't want him to have to, though.

And that's why I'm stuck in a gondola, next to a woman I'm sure strongly dislikes me, climbing up the side of a mountain. The cliff I'm trying to talk myself off of in my head is only slightly steeper.

I assumed Abigail Winters owns a chalet in Aspen for an excuse to wear faux fur and host fondue parties. Her invitation to ski this morning was a totally unexpected one. Caleb tried to insist on coming with us, but his mother said it would be a nice opportunity to get to know me. I couldn't argue with that, and neither could Caleb.

So, here we are.

She hasn't said a word directly to me since we left the chalet. Everything has been an instruction to someone else, to drop us off here and put our gear there. I've followed along, trying not to think about how I'm just as uncertain about skiing as I am about spending time with Caleb's mother.

"We're nearly at the top." Abigail finally speaks, startling me. At this point, I figured she forgot I was even here.

Maybe I should have broken the icy silence first, but I'm not sure what to say to her. Part of me resents the disdain she's made obvious. Part of me doesn't want to say something stupid around her, because she's Caleb's mom and that will always mean her opinion matters to me.

"Great." I aim for enthusiasm but fall short around apprehension.

"I know I haven't been very welcoming toward you."

It takes a minute for her words to register. She's always hidden her contempt behind small snubs. If I ever confronted her about her behavior, I assumed she'd deny it and act like I was crazy.

"I grew up in Landry, Mrs. Winters," I reply. "I'm used to it."

"I'm not so heartless as to blame you for your parents' shortcomings, Lennon. To be perfectly honest, I think the town's perception of your family is quite ridiculous. Unfortunately, it hits a little closer to home for me."

"I don't know what you mean," I respond.

"I know you don't," Abigail says, glancing out the window at the snowy landscape, then back at me again. "I think I knew we'd be having this conversation ever since I saw Caleb go over to you after Richard's service. Austin was convinced you were a fling to Caleb from the first moment he told us you were dating. I knew better. Caleb could barely get the words out without grinning."

At that, I smile.

"Austin and I haven't had the easiest life together. There have been good parts. There have also been some bad parts. The worst was when Caleb was in fifth grade. Richard was gearing up for another run against advice and already having health issues. Austin traveled back to Landry a lot. On one of those visits, he… reconnected with an old high school classmate of his."

Realization hits me like lightening. I connect the dots. "My mom."

Abigail nods. Her lips are upturned, but they're defined by sadness, not humor. "I know you're not to blame for your parents'—for your mother's—actions, Lennon. Like I said, I think the fact that others do is silly and short-sighted. But some of those actions nearly destroyed my marriage. My family. You're a constant reminder of that."

"Does Caleb know?"

"No," Mrs. Winters replies swiftly. "He knows Austin and I have had our challenges. But not…" *Cheating*, I fill in. "I'm not asking you to lie to him," she continues. "But I want you to know I've made my peace with the past now. The actions of two consenting adults are nothing you can or should atone for. I didn't really believe your relationship with Caleb was temporary, but I hoped it would be, and I'm sorry for that. I was worried you would limit him. Keep him in Landry. But seeing you together yesterday and this morning… I've never seen Caleb happier. He won't hesitate to choose you if there's a choice to be made, but I never want it to come to that. Selfishly, I just needed you to know why I've acted the way I have."

I nod slowly, trying to absorb the bombshell she just dropped on me. Did Gramps know? I'll never be able to ask him. Maybe it's for the best. My mother was complex, and her relationship with Gramps was just as complicated.

"Should we ski?"

I glance outside and realize we've made it to the top of the mountain. My head is still spinning from Abigail's revelation.

"I'm a terrible skier," I admit. "I got invited to go with a friend in seventh grade, so my dad tried to teach me out in the field with boards strapped to my sneakers. It didn't help. Might have made me worse, actually."

"Did you spend much time with your father growing up?" Mrs. Winters surprises me by asking.

"No." I laugh. "Didn't spend much time with him at all."

"My father wasn't around much either. Always off chasing the next business venture."

"I wish that's what my father was chasing," I reply dryly.

She nods in understanding. Until a few minutes ago, I was certain there weren't any secrets about my family in Landry. All our dirty laundry has been hung out for years.

The gondola's doors slide open, revealing a black mat covered with snow that's been condensed and carved.

Abigail exits first. I follow her lead, hastily looping the straps of my ski poles around my wrists. I was hoping these could be used to slow or stop. Everyone zooming down the slope seems to be using them to go faster.

"Ready?" Abigail asks, snapping a pair of goggles into place.

I swallow. "Yep."

"We'll veer left first, then tilt to the right, then back again. Nice and easy."

She's off before I say anything. I take a deep gulp of cold air, then shove off from the snow. Despite barely brushing the frozen surface, I'm in motion immediately. Wind rushes past, chilling my ears and making my throat burn. I hastily close my mouth.

The motion is smooth. It's not the rocking feeling I typically associate with crossing the ground at this speed. It's a glide, even and direct.

Abigail turns to the right, sending a spray of snow off to the side. My attempt to mimic her is nowhere near as graceful, but it results in me heading to the right rather than straight into the pines that line the edge of the groomed snow.

It becomes a rhythm. Left. Right. Left. Right. Left. Right.

Down, down, down, until the trees lining the path disappear and we're at the bottom of the mountain, staring at the massive lodge.

"Wow," I say. I turn slightly, and a couple of handfuls of snow go flying off to the side. The spray makes me feel like a professional skier.

"You made it," Abigail tells me. It's hard to tell beneath her scarf, but I think she's smiling.

"Yeah," I pant. Residual adrenaline is warming my blood.

"Shall we go again, or get a drink inside the lodge?" Abigail asks.

Another run sounds like tempting fate. "I'm a little thirsty."

This time, she definitely smiles.

We unclip our skis and clomp inside the lodge in the uncomfortable boots. It's strange being inside such a formal, fancy atmosphere dressed in heavy snow gear.

"Table for two, miss?" A waiter wearing an actual tuxedo appears.

"Please," Abigail replies.

"Right this way."

He grabs two menus and heads for a corner table that overlooks the bottom of the mountain. Thankfully, it's a short walk from the entrance. I'm less graceful in the boots than I was in the skis. Abigail makes it look effortless.

"I'll be back shortly to take your order." The waiter fills our glasses with water, then disappears.

I shrug off my jacket before opening the menu and surveying

the contents. Lobster, caviar, venison, and steak are the first four menu options. I close it and take a sip of water.

Maybe I chose wrong. At least hurtling down the mountain, I didn't have to make small talk. I'm bad at it under the best of circumstances. This isn't those.

"What can I get you ladies?" The waiter has already returned. I guess the nicer the place, the faster the service.

Abigail glances at me. "Is noon too early for alcohol on vacation?"

Her tone is almost...teasing. I swallow and shake my head. "I don't judge."

Too late, I worry she'll take the response as a dig. But Abigail's expression doesn't change. "A Bloody Mary, please. And some french fries."

I blink at her. That's about the last order I would have expected.

"Lennon?"

"Uh, I'll have the same. Thanks."

Abigail looks out the window as our waiter disappears, seemingly lost in thought. I fiddle with the hem of the tablecloth.

"You're hoping to become a journalist?" she asks me suddenly.

"Yes," I reply. "We'll see. It can be a tough career to break into."

She nods. "You will. Austin wasn't the only one who read the article you wrote on Caleb in high school. You're a very talented writer."

"Thank you," I respond.

"You two weren't dating at the time?"

"No. I'd started to develop some feelings, but we weren't dating."

"Why not?" Abigail flushes as soon as she asks the question. Actually looks embarrassed. "Sorry, it's none of business."

"No, it's fine. I, uh—" I look outside, then back at the table. "I was worried. I didn't want to fall in love with him. Our lives were so different. He was *Caleb Winters*, this huge deal. I didn't want to get hurt. To admit I cared just for him to leave and never look back."

"That's understandable," Abigail says.

I nod. "It didn't make a difference, though. Even knowing I could get hurt didn't change how I felt. So I admitted it to him, still thinking we wouldn't last. But he…"

"Looked back," Abigail supplies.

"Yeah." I smile. "He did. Has."

"Here you ladies go." The waiter returns, setting down two glasses filled with red liquid and garnished with celery and olives on the table, followed by a steaming plate of fries. "Anything else?"

"We're all set, thanks," Abigail replies.

Once the waiter is gone, she raises her drink and tilts it toward me. "Happy Thanksgiving, Lennon."

Hastily, I pick up my glass. "Happy Thanksgiving, Mrs. Winters."

She laughs. "Call me Abigail, please."

I smile before sipping my drink. It's good. Fresh and zesty, with a hint of spice. I can't taste the alcohol at all.

"I took a journalism course my freshman year at Emory," Abigail tells me as we dig into the fries.

"Really?"

She nods. "I decided pretty early on it wasn't for me. I probably should have dropped it, but I was raised to believe that the worst thing you could be called is a quitter. So I stuck it out. Back then, I thought I'd have a few years on my own to try lots of things on for size. I met Austin, he proposed, and I knew I'd never have a career."

"Did you want to?"

"I never thought about it. Richard was a rising political star; Caleb had just been born. It was easy to get swept up in being a Winters."

"I'd imagine so," I reply.

"You'll find out soon."

"Caleb and I are a long ways off from that," I say quickly.

Abigail smiles. "Caleb and Austin don't have much in common. Caleb's grown up into twice the man Austin will ever be. But they're both charming and persuasive. It might come sooner than you think."

She laughs at my expression, then asks me another question about Clarkson. And shockingly, it feels...nice.

The bedroom door creaks open quietly. A few seconds later, the mattress dips. I roll over, blinking at Caleb.

Everyone was gone when Abigail and I returned to the chalet. Caleb was hanging out with Jake and Colt, the St. Jameses had headed into town, and Austin had a meeting.

I came upstairs and worked more on my essay for the Fulright Fellowship application. At some point, I fell asleep.

"Hey."

"Hey."

"You're smiling," he comments. "And your legs don't look broken." His hand runs up my leg, resting on the curve of my hip.

"We only went down the mountain once," I confess. "But I survived."

"Once? What time did you get back?"

I glance at my laptop. "About an hour ago."

"You were gone for a while, then."

"We went to a restaurant afterward."

"Really?"

"Uh-huh. Your mom ate *fries*."

Caleb chuckles. "Wow."

"Also…she told me some stuff. About her and your dad."

Up until this exact second, I hadn't decided whether to tell Caleb about what his mom mentioned to me.

"What stuff?"

I pull in a deep breath. "She told me he cheated on her. With my mom."

I'm expecting shock. Disgust. Anger. Not for him to calmly blink and say, "I know."

"What? How?"

"I broke into the safe in his office once, sophomore year of high school. I was bored and we'd just had an argument. There was an old receipt in there for some fancy jewelry. And the delivery address was your family's farm. Pretty easy to do the math. I knew what their relationship was—is—like. I'd be surprised if there haven't been other women, honestly."

"So you knew that was why your mom disliked me so much?"

"I figured that was part of it," he replies. "But don't let her use this as some get-out-of-jail-free card, Len. You're not responsible for what your mom got involved in. It should never have mattered in the first place."

"Your mom thinks you don't know."

"She's always wanted to pretend like we're this perfect family. I knew it would hurt her, knowing I knew. So I've never said anything about it."

"Were you ever going to tell me?" I ask.

"Probably not."

"Why not?"

"It has nothing to do with us, Lennon."

"We're talking about our parents! It's weird. Gross."

"We're totally on the same page there. But what does it change? Do you love me less?"

"Of course not."

"Do you know what I'd say to your mom if I ever got to meet her when she was still alive?"

"Stop gambling at the track so your daughter and your father don't end up broke?"

He chuckles. "No. I wouldn't ask her about my dad, either. I'd thank her for being the person who brought you into this world."

Heat floods my cheeks, and I look away from him. "For fuck's sake, Caleb. You can't just *say* stuff like that to me."

Caleb's always been far better at expressing his emotions than I am, but it's moments like these when I realize just how far out of my league I am with him in the romance department. I have no idea where he gets it from. His parents certainly aren't a model relationship.

Caleb laughs and rolls onto his back. I climb onto him, settling on the center of his chest and listening to the reassuring thud of his heart.

"Do you ever think about how far we've come?" I whisper.

"What do you mean?" Caleb murmurs back.

"I mean that the first time I saw you, I never thought we'd end up here. Never thought you'd be the person I'd be lying beside almost eight years later."

"Yeah, I think about it," he murmurs.

I close my eyes and snuggle closer.

CHAPTER THIRTY-NINE

LENNON

I 'm in the library, studying for finals with Amanda and Eric, when my laptop pings with an incoming email. I glance at the screen automatically, then freeze. Click.

We are delighted to inform you that you've been selected to receive the Fulbright Fellowship...

That's as far as I get, before a squeal leaves my lips.

"What?" Amanda asks.

Wordlessly, I spin the screen around so they can both look at the email.

"Holy..." Eric starts.

"Oh my *God*, Lennon! That's amazing!" Amanda says.

I'm still speechless. I thought applying was a long shot, at best. It never really occurred to me that I might actually *get* it.

"This calls for celebratory coffee!" Amanda decides, standing from the table.

We walk through the first floor of Clarkson's library, which has quickly become my favorite building on campus. It looks like something you'd find in a medieval castle in Europe. Dark wood, majestic arches, and the soothing scent of old paper. It's nothing like the metal shelves and generic tables in the Landry High library.

The walk to the nearest coffee shop isn't a long one. The school's architect must have figured studying and caffeine make sense in closer proximity. Amanda and Eric talk excitedly about the news. They both sound awed, their attention on me almost reverential.

I'm dazed, still in a state of shock, trying to remember the list of important papers the fellowship works closely with. It's overwhelming, and I can't decide if it's in a good way. Options are good; choices are challenging.

Fallen leaves crunch with each step along the paved paths. Only a few curled shapes are stubbornly clinging to the branches overhead. It's hard to believe the fall semester is almost over. That half my time at Clarkson is almost over.

We reach the coffee shop. I order first, then step to the side so Amanda can. It turns out Eric knows the barista, and Amanda and I exchange a conspiratorial glance when they keep chatting long after the amount of time it would take for him to choose a drink.

Finally, he joins us. Before any of our drinks arrive, the bell rings with another customer. It turns out to be Michelle Hodge, who usually sits behind me and Eric in our shared journalism class.

"Hey, guys," she greets, walking over.

"Hi, Michelle," Eric replies. "Guess what? Lennon got the Fulbright Fellowship! Can you believe it?"

Michelle glances at me. I'm expecting the disappointment on her face. Almost every journalism major at Clarkson applied. Including her, it seems.

But I'm not expecting the ire. "Must be nice to know people in high places." She scoffs.

"Excuse me?" I laugh, thinking she's joking.

I'm the last person with family connections. I don't have *any* family members, let alone connected ones. Maybe she's confusing me with someone else? We've only exchanged the barest of small talk and only a couple of times.

"You're dating Caleb Winters, right?"

"Uh, yeah."

"George Coleman is the chairman of the Fulright committee. He's also buddy-buddy with your boyfriend's family."

"I...didn't know."

Michelle scoffs. "Well, now you do."

She walks away, leaving me stunned for the second time today.

"She probably doesn't know what she's talking about," Amanda tells me. "She's just jealous."

I manage a smile, but I'm even more distracted on the walk back to the library once we've gotten our drinks. After ten minutes of getting nothing done, I give up.

"I'm going to head out. I'll see you guys later."

Amanda and Eric nod. They've both made efforts to cheer me up since we ran into Michelle, but I know only one thing will have any effect on my mood.

I need to talk to Caleb.

On the way out of the library, I pass Sophie walking in. I send her a small, tight smile and continue walking.

"Lennon!"

When I turn back around, she's jogging down the library steps toward me.

"I know I've been kind of a bitch to you," she blurts, as soon as she reaches me.

"Um..."

She continues like I never spoke. "If it makes any difference, it's never had anything to do with you. You just got caught in the crossfire, because I want him, and he wants you."

Now, I have even less of a clue what to say.

"I thought Caleb was using you to piss off his parents. I underestimated how much you mean to him. So…I just wanted to say sorry. Good luck with finals."

Thankfully she leaves before I have a chance to respond, because I have no idea what I would have said.

I continue down the rest of the stairs and across campus. It's a long walk to Caleb's off-campus house. I don't realize *how* long, until I've walked too far to turn back. It's always seemed like such a short drive.

I finally arrive just as it's getting dark out.

Drew is the one who answers the door, his face splitting into a wide smile when he sees me. "Lennon! Caleb didn't mention you were coming over!"

"Is he here?" I ask, my tone a sharp contrast to his. Night instead of sunshine.

Drew's eyebrows knit together as it registers. "Uh, yeah. Come on in."

I head for the living room, since I can hear the commotion coming from that room. They're watching football instead of baseball, for once.

Aside from Caleb and his housemates, there are a bunch of girls in the room too. I ignore everyone except Caleb, too upset to care about being rude.

"Can I talk to you?"

He stands from his seat slowly, confusion written all over his face. "How did you get here?"

"I walked."

"You *walked*?"

I don't answer, leaving the living room and heading for the stairs. Caleb reaches his bedroom a few seconds after me.

"What the hell is going on, Lennon? If you wanted to come over, I could have—"

"I got the Fulright Fellowship."

His expression immediately transforms, lighting up with pride and excitement. But nothing knowing. No sign he suspected it. "That's amazing. Congrat—"

I don't let him get the whole word out. "Do you know George Coleman?"

"I...sort of? He's good friends with my dad, used to come over a lot when we lived in New York. I think he did some journalism stuff, actually. Why? Do you want me to introduce you?"

"He's the chair of the Fulright committee, Caleb. He's the one who decides who gets the fellowship."

"Decides who gets the fellowship... You think I *set this up*? That I had them award it to you?" Caleb shakes his head. "Seriously, Lennon?"

"I don't know what to think, Caleb! One girl already told me to my face that's why I got it. That's what everyone else will think too."

"Who cares?"

"*I* care! Did you pull some strings to get me in here too? Is the dean your godfather or something?"

"Lennon, listen to yourself. Did you ever consider you're just an amazing candidate and that's why you got it? I doubt George even knows you're my girlfriend. My dad talks business, mostly, even with his friends."

"He knows."

"What? How?"

"Because I wrote about you in the damn essay, Caleb!"

Caleb pauses, obviously not expecting that answer. "I still

think you're overreacting," he finally says. "And I don't think it has anything to do with the fellowship."

"What do you mean? What do you think we're talking about?"

"I think you're freaking out because you don't want it, Lennon. Because you didn't think you'd get it, and since you did you feel like you have to take it."

"Well, you're *wrong*."

But I'm not sure he is, actually.

"Fine. What do you want me to do, Lennon? Call George and ask him why he picked you?"

"No. I just...I just need to think." All the outrage that fueled my walk over here has fizzled, leaving me feeling confused and empty.

Caleb takes a step closer. "Lennon..."

"I'm sorry. I shouldn't have come over."

"You can stay. We should talk."

I shake my head. "We will. I just... I want to be alone right now."

"Okay. I'll drive you home," he tells me.

Neither of us say a word, the whole trip back.

CHAPTER FORTY

CALEB

My knee bounces nervously as I sit on the bench, waiting for Lennon. We've barely spoken since I drove her home last week, the day she learned she got the fellowship.

I did some research, as soon as I got back to my house after dropping her off. She was right; George Coleman is the chair.

I was more concerned with how all of the papers associated with the program are located in Boston, New York, or Los Angeles.

All cities home to professional baseball teams. Out of thirty, that gives me about a three percent chance of ending up in the same place as her.

We've overcome worse odds. I'd bet the number of couples who make it long distance for three years is pretty low.

But it won't be easy.

Students start spilling out of the brick building. My knee bounces faster.

Tomorrow is the last day of finals. I'm going to New York, to attend a charity event my mom organized. Lennon is returning to Landry to stay with Cassie.

Neither of us have planned past that. Since an organized trip never came together, Colt wants to go to his folks' lake house again. Jake is angling for a return trip to Aspen. How today goes will probably determine what I decide.

My mom invited Lennon to New York unprompted, which made me hope she really is changing her mind about us, which she managed to convince Lennon of over Thanksgiving. Lennon declined, since it's Cassie's birthday this weekend and she's having a big party. And since she's going back to Landry on Saturday, I feel like I have to do this today.

Lennon appears, talking with her friend Eric, who's hanging on her every word. I don't know if she actually believes he's just extra friendly toward her instead of harboring a crush the size of Kentucky, but his interest is obvious even from this distance.

I didn't tell her I was coming. So I'm half-expecting Lennon to pass by in the swarm of students instead of stopping. But I watch her say something to Eric and then walk this way, only stopping when she's a foot away. He tracks her departure, only looking away when he catches me staring.

"Hi," she says, then yawns. There are circles under her eyes, and her brown hair is knotted in a messy bun on the top of her head. She looks beautiful.

"Hey." I stand. "Wanna go for a drive?"

Lennon eyes me carefully, obviously trying to figure out what's going on. Weighing my mood, the same way I'm feeling her out.

The past few days are the longest we've gone without talking since we started dating. It's felt weird, like I had a limb missing. But I get why she's needed space. We both have big decisions to make and more complicated choices than most people our age.

Finally, she nods.

We join the crowd of students, walking side by side until we reach the student center parking lot, where I left my truck. I open the door for Lennon, making sure her backpack is tucked in the footwell before closing the door.

When I climb into the driver's seat she's tugging the elastic out of her hair, letting the long strands loose and running her fingers through the knots.

She looks over at me. "I'm sorry, Caleb. I was stressed and upset. Even if you had interfered, I know it would have been from a place of love."

"If I had interfered, it would have meant I don't know you at all. You're the proudest person I know, Lennon. You think I don't know you want to earn everything you get?"

"You threw our English final senior year," she reminds me.

"That was different. I didn't blackmail Mr. Tanner into giving you an A. I just didn't write the essay. And that was partly because I was upset and distracted, not just because I wanted you to be valedictorian."

"I turned it down."

"What?" My hand freezes, right as I'm about to turn on the truck.

"The Fulright Fellowship. I turned it down. And not because I think it was handed to me. Because I didn't want it. I want to apply to a bunch of papers and try writing in different departments, not have to follow a pre-determined program. And... I want to see where you get drafted before I commit to living somewhere." She pauses, searching my face. "Are you mad I didn't talk to you before I decided?"

"Of course not. It was your decision, Len."

"I want things to be *our* decision," she says. "With this, I was just worried you'd tell me I was walking away thinking I only got it because of you."

I start the ignition. "I think you made the right decision."

"Really?"

"Yeah." I pull out of the parking lot and start driving on the main road, wondering how long it will take her to figure out I'm not heading back to her dorm or my house. "How was your exam?"

"Fine." She pauses. "After tomorrow, there's just one semester of college left. It's crazy."

I nod, flicking on the stereo for some background sound. Lennon yawns again, then leans back against the seat.

As soon as I turn onto the highway, she sits up straight. "Where are we going?"

"Home."

"Caleb. I have a final tomorrow."

I nod. "Me too. We'll be back by then. I promise."

She still looks confused and uncertain, but doesn't question me again until we're in Landry and I continue past the turn-off for my family's—*my*, technically—property.

"What the hell is going on?"

"You'll see."

Lennon inhales sharply, when I flip my blinker on and then turn into the driveway that leads to Matthews Farm. "We're trespassing."

I say nothing.

"Seriously, Caleb. This is sweet. But we can't..." Her voice trails as we pass the barn and the farmhouse comes into view. I park in the center of the yard, overgrown with dying weeds, and climb out of the truck.

Lennon scrambles out after me a few seconds later, spinning around in a slow circle as she looks around.

"They haven't changed anything," she says. "I was sure..." She glances at me. "Well, I figured it would be a pile of rubble by now. The house is too small and the barn could blow down. It'd be easier to rebuild everything. I didn't think—" Her voice catches. "I didn't think I'd ever see it all in person again." Lennon visibly composes herself, then turns toward me. "We should really go. This is illegal."

I lean against the side of the truck. "You sure? Last I checked, you could do whatever you want on your own land."

All of a sudden, I'm staring at a statue. Lennon looks at me, her face frozen in total shock. Finally, she breaks through it, glancing at the farmhouse, then me. The barn, then back to me. "You didn't."

I open the truck door, grabbing the piece of paper from the glove compartment and then walking over and handing it to her. "Technically, it's your land. Still. I kept the deed in your name. And if you decide to sell it a second time, I won't interfere."

Lennon takes the paper, glances at it, bites her bottom lip, and then looks out toward the east pasture.

"But if we're making decisions together, for whatever it's worth, I think you should keep this farm."

"For what?"

"To live on. To get married on. To raise a family on."

She turns toward me then, raising a hand to tick fingers off. "You don't want to live in Landry. You could get drafted anywhere in the country. This farm needs a ton of work. There's—"

I grab her hand before she can lift another finger. "I think you rushed on selling this place, Lennon. If it's not what you want, that's fine. But don't put it on me. Don't say it's not where I want to be. Don't assume you have to live wherever I get drafted. And last I checked, you have plenty of money."

"From *you*." She huffs. "I never would have taken it had I known—"

"I know you wouldn't have. That's why I had a real estate

attorney bury the sale through one of the corporations my grand-father left me, in case you looked. But it's done. And you can undo it, if you want. But I hope you won't. People don't retire from professional sports at age sixty-five, Lennon. Me playing won't be forever.

"You've got roots here. But so do I. Just as many. Perception is all about perspective. I didn't have any when we were younger. Not when it came to Landry. To me, it was a town full of nosy snobs who revered the man who barely gave me the time of day if we weren't in public. I see it differently now. I can picture our lives here. Holidays and weekends and regular days. Kids."

I look over at Lennon, and that's when I realize she's crying. Ribbons of salty water streak down her face, the fading light still enough to illuminate them.

"Okay," she says.

"Okay to what?"

"To all of it. You just described my perfect life."

I stare at her, emotion clogging my throat.

I was worried about how this conversation might go. No matter my intentions, I went behind her back and undermined a decision she made. Best case, I thought it would take her a few days to get used to the idea. To think everything over and consider keeping the property.

"I've gotten estimates from a few construction companies. The farmhouse really needs to be gutted. New electric, new plumbing, new well. And all but one has suggested leveling both barns and building new. And then on the fencing it seems like—"

"Caleb." She interrupts me.

I look over. "Yeah?"

"You know I'm in love with you, right?"

I exhale, long and low and relieved. "I know."

"Good."

She walks over to me, not stopping until our bodies collide. Her face gets buried in my neck, her arms wrapping around my waist.

"Thank you," she whispers. "For telling me that and for every single thing you've done to show me how you meant it. Especially this."

CHAPTER FORTY-ONE

LENNON

Six Years Later

"He's home! He's home! He's home!" Tiny feet pound the hardwood floor.

Hazel breezes past me, almost taking off the screen door clear off the hinges before she reaches the front porch.

"No running in the house!" I call after her, rising from my seat at the kitchen table.

Hazel doesn't reply, not that I expected her to. Not that I actually thought she would listen to me. And if she *had* answered, it probably would have been to tell me she's no longer inside, so she can run.

Unfortunately, she inherited my love of logic. And arguing.

I follow her outside, reaching the top of the porch steps just in time to see Hazel leap into Caleb's arms. He spins her around, the sound of her laughter carrying across the air in the October breeze.

Hazel starts chattering away immediately, filling him in on the drawings she did this morning. The peach pie she helped me make that's currently in the oven. About how she galloped on Stormy yesterday. By galloped, she means trotted, but Caleb is ignorant enough about horseback riding I'm not surprised when his expression isn't concerned.

Instead, he looks completely at ease as he watches our daughter fill him in on everything he's missed in the past two days since they spoke.

Caleb only looks away from Hazel when I step on a squeaky stair. I'm surprised one even exists. Matthews Farm is almost unrecognizable from my adolescent memories. There's no longer an inch of this property that hasn't been repaired, painted, or trimmed.

Caleb's gaze meets mine, and he gives me the secret, special smile that still gives me butterflies.

I descend the rest of the stairs slowly, trying to compensate for how my center of gravity seems to shift daily.

Hazel scrambles out of Caleb's arms and starts racing toward the house. "I'll be right back," she calls over one shoulder. "I'll be right back, Mom," she tells me as she passes by.

"Okay." I laugh. I'm guessing she's just remembered she left the art project she worked on all morning upstairs in her room. The excitement of Caleb's arrival was clearly enough to make her forget about it until now.

"Hi," Caleb greets as I approach, grinning lazily as he looks me up and down.

"Hi," I reply, taking him in too. The dark hair, the strong arms, the crinkles in the corners of his blue eyes that are the only indication he's fourteen years older than the first time I saw him.

His smile turns wicked. "You look *good*, Matthews."

Matthews hasn't been my last name for years, but hearing Caleb say it makes me feel seventeen again.

"I look like a whale, Caleb."

"Just your belly."

I scoff.

"I'm kidding." Caleb takes a couple of strides forward, so my bloated stomach is touching his. "Seeing you pregnant with my kid is actually sexy as fuck," he whispers to me, right before he kisses me.

I melt against him, as much as my belly will allow. He hasn't been home in three weeks. Not the longest stretch we've been apart—not by a lot—but distance never gets any easier. Especially when you're separated from someone you love as much as I love Caleb Winters.

This reunion is especially sweet. Not only because we're close to becoming a family of four, but because we're through the last separation in what has felt like an endless stretch of them.

Caleb was drafted to play in Chicago after we graduated from Clarkson. Not as far as he could have gone, but not an easy commute from Landry.

We split our time between Illinois and Kentucky as best we could. I spent a year working freelance for larger papers in the city, before starting a full-time position at the *Landry Gazette*. That limited my time in Chicago, especially once I found out I was pregnant with Hazel.

Caleb had already told me he intended for this season to be his last before I found out I was pregnant again. We weren't trying, but we weren't being careful either. Neither one of us was surprised.

And I'm glad he didn't feel pressured to make the decision about retiring. Equally relieved I won't have to take care of a three-year-old and a newborn on my own. I'm able to do most of my work for the paper from home, and we have a couple of barn staff who help out with the barn work, but it's still a lot to manage.

But more than simply having someone to share the workload with, I miss *Caleb* when he's gone.

"Is the pie done?" he asks as we head for the front porch.

"Yes, but it's for the party tonight." I glance at him in time to catch his grimace. "You forgot."

"More like I temporarily removed the knowledge from my brain."

"I got him a tie. I didn't know what else to get. Plus, every time I see him he's wearing one, so I figured it would get some use."

"Thanks, Len."

"You going to make it tonight? You look exhausted."

"The guys set up a whole goodbye thing. It went late and was a little crazy."

"A little crazy? So drugs, clubs, strippers?"

Caleb rolls his eyes. "It was not that wild. It was mostly getting wasted at sports bars and rehashing old games."

"Landry's going to be a real change of pace, huh?"

I've lived here full-time since I had Hazel. This is Caleb's first time returning with no plans to leave.

"A *welcome* change of pace."

"Good."

Caleb holds the screen door open for me. "How many people did my parents invite?"

"Hazel said five hundred, but I'm hoping she's wrong."

"How would Hazel know?"

"Your mom took her for the day on Tuesday. They were party planning the whole time."

Abigail Winters may be aloof and reserved around many

people, but she dotes on Hazel in a way that reminds me of Gramps. Ever since she was born, Abigail and Austin have spent at least half the year in Landry, most of it with Hazel. They'll never be the sort of in-laws that feel like a second set of parents, but my relationship with them is far closer than I ever imagined it being. They're thrilled we're expecting again.

Caleb follows me inside the front hall just as Hazel comes flying back down the stairs, clutching a piece of paper in her tiny fist.

"Here! Here!" she shouts, shoving it at Caleb.

He drops his bag by the door and takes it from her, crouching down to inspect it more closely.

"Is this me?" Caleb points to a stick figure standing next to a white and red ball that's about the same height.

Hazel nods emphatically. "With a bawseball."

"Baseball," I correct.

"And this is Mommy?" Caleb asks.

"Yeah and me and Stormy too."

I peer over Caleb's shoulder at a stick figure that is apparently me next to a shorter one with brown hair and blue eyes that must be Hazel. Stormy takes up the most real estate on the page, as a brown blob in the background.

"It's beautiful, Haze," Caleb tells her.

She nods. "You're welcome." I hide a smile. "I'm going to get ready for Grandpa's party," she announces, bounding back up the stairs. I'm exhausted just watching her.

"How many people did Grandma invite?" Caleb calls after her.

"Five hundred," Hazel calls back as she heads up the stairs.

"Unbelievable," Caleb mutters. "Does she even know that many people?"

"You know she does. People are probably flying in from your dad's office in New York."

Caleb rubs his forehead. "Okay. I'm going to unpack. Maybe nap."

"Okay." I head for the kitchen. "I'm almost finished with my article for this week. We have to leave for your parents' by six."

Caleb sighs, then nods.

Caleb

The drive to my parents' takes ten minutes, instead of the usual five. Both sides of the driveway are lined with cars, beginning right after I turn through the gate.

"Maybe she said five *thousand*, and Hazel heard five hundred," Lennon comments, from her spot in the passenger seat.

"Haha." I can feel a headache forming at the thought. I didn't drink much last night, but I didn't get much sleep. In addition to celebrating the end of my career, the guys were drowning their sorrows about not making playoffs. I was relieved we didn't, which is one reason I know I made the right choice retiring when I did.

Now that I'm back in Landry, all I want is to be alone with Lennon. Preferably in a bed, naked.

Instead, we're heading to a fancy party that will undoubtedly include a lot of people I have no interest in talking to but will have to make nice with anyway.

Hazel starts kicking the back of my seat half-way up the driveway.

"Hazel. No kicking."

She keeps kicking.

"Listen to your dad, Hazel," Lennon says.

She keeps kicking. "Party!"

"If you don't listen, you won't get dessert tonight. There's peach pie *and* Grandpa's birthday cake, so you'll really be missing out."

She keeps kicking.

Lennon sighs, quietly. "She's stubborn," she mutters to me, under her breath.

"Wonder where she gets that from."

"I don't know what you're talking about."

I raise my voice. "Hazel. Stop kicking, or no riding for a week."

Finally, the pounding against the back of my seat stops. I glance over at Lennon. "She got that from you too."

"When our son is breaking every window on the property with a baseball, I'll remember that."

My head snaps toward her. "Are you talking hypothetically?"

Slowly, Lennon shakes her head. "I saw it on one of the tests they ran at my appointment last week, by accident. The tech felt so badly, and I hadn't decided if I was going to tell you. I know we agreed we weren't going to find out again."

"It's a boy?"

"Yes."

"Wow," I whisper. I've had to travel regularly for most of Lennon's pregnancy. Aside from seeing the bump, this is the first moment where it's really hit me we'll have another child in a few months.

Now, more than ever, I wish we were at home and alone. But I can't miss my father's fiftieth birthday. We're nowhere close to the relationship I plan to have with my son, but we're on much better terms than we were for most of my life.

I drive all the way up to the house, managing to squeeze in between two cars right in front of the center walkway. All the trees and bushes have been wrapped with twinkling white lights, illuminating the whole yard.

Lennon climbs out of the passenger seat with her pie, while I unbuckle Hazel from the back. We head around the side of the house, toward the back patio where the party is being held. It's a balmy fall evening, ideal for an outdoor gathering. Knowing my mother, she had a tent on standby in case it rained and heaters lined up in case it was cold.

"Grandma!" Hazel begins struggling in my arms as soon as she spots my mom. I set her down, a smile automatically forming as I watch Hazel run over to her.

My mother stops talking mid-conversation, leaning down to listen to my daughter. The hem of her dress drags on the dirty patio, and for once she doesn't seem to care.

Hazel is still talking exuberantly when Lennon and I reach them. The women my mother was talking to excuse themselves, leaving us to a family moment.

"Caleb!"

"Hey, Mom." I lean in to give her a hug.

"It's so nice to have you home."

"Thanks. It's nice to be home."

My mom smiles, then looks to Lennon. "You didn't have to bring anything, Lennon."

"I know," she says, before handing the pie over. "I just had the ripe peaches and wanted to contribute something. You don't have to use it tonight, I'm sure you planned for plenty of food. It'll freeze well."

"Thank you. That was very thoughtful of you. I'm going to put this in the kitchen. Caleb, you should say hello to your father. He's standing over by the grill."

I tug at my tie and nod. Thankfully, Hazel erases some of the awkwardness that sometimes lingers between us.

"I see Grandpa!" she announces, then makes a beeline for my father. Just like my mother said, he's standing next to the grill, talking with a group of business colleagues. By the time I get to the grill she's in my father's arms, telling him all about the pie Lennon made and the tie that's his birthday gift.

"How old are you?" she's asking my dad.

"Fifty," he tells her.

"Wow. That sounds old."

All the men around my father laugh uproariously.

I step forward. "Happy birthday, Dad."

"Caleb!"

He holds a hand out to shake, since he has his arms full of Hazel. She leans into me once I'm in reach, wrapping her small arms around my neck and clinging to my chest. "I'm hungry," she says.

"I'll take you to get some food. Give dad a minute to talk," Lennon says. "Happy birthday, Austin."

"Thank you, Lennon," my dad says, before she and Hazel disappear into the crowd.

"How's the arm?" he asks me.

I rotate my shoulder. "Still solid."

"Smart, leaving while you're still on top."

"Thanks."

"I know you have plenty of money. And you should enjoy your family, especially with the new baby on the way. But we'd love to have you at the company, now that you're out of the majors."

I nod, already expecting the offer. "I'll think about it, Dad."

He nods back. "Good." Then turns back toward the group of men. "You all know my son, Caleb?"

After visiting with my father's friends, I end up in a long conversation with the St. Jameses. I haven't kept in contact with

Sophie since graduation, but they tell me she's doing well, living in Los Angeles and working for an advertising firm. Colt, Jake, and Luke are all here, but we talk regularly enough there's not that much to catch up on. We make a plan to get together for beers tomorrow night, at Matthews Farm.

Finally, I find Lennon talking to her boss's wife, Mrs. Stradwell. Although Tom might technically still own the *Gazette*, Lennon is the one running day-to-day operations now.

"Hi, Mrs. Stradwell. How are you?"

"I'm good, Caleb, thanks. Congratulations on your retirement."

"Thank you," I answer, hiding a smile. It feels weird to hear that from people, when I'm not even thirty. "Do you mind if I steal my wife away for a minute?"

"Of course not. I'm going to grab some food."

I reach down and grab Lennon's hand, then tow her along the edge of the patio, toward the stairs. She glances around. "Hazel…"

"I just checked on her. She's with my mom, eating cake."

Lennon grimaces. "She already had one piece. She'll be bouncing off the walls when we get home."

"I'll hook her up to the hot walker."

Lennon rolls her eyes, but she also lets me pull her off the side of the patio and in the direction of the stables.

"Where are we going?" She has to half-jog to catch up with me, so I immediately slow my steps. "I was just about to get some water."

"Shit. Sorry. Let's go back and get you some." I was so focused on getting her away from the crowd, I didn't stop to think.

Lennon grabs my tie before I can take a step. "I didn't say I wanted to go back." Her lips curve upward as she takes a step closer and wraps my tie around her hand, pulling me closer.

Fuck it.

I kiss her, hard. She's expecting it. Immediately, my tie loosens and her hands are in my hair, pulling my head down closer to her level as she rises up on her tiptoes. Her teeth sink into my bottom lip for a second before her tongue slips inside my mouth, deepening the contact.

I haul her against me, letting her feel the effect she has on my body. Her baby bump is a noticeable curve between us, and it drives my desire higher. Some primal, animalistic part of me loves knowing that's my kid in there, that she and I are so inextricably linked.

We don't break apart until I distantly register the sound of voices. Someone else seems to be heading this way. I let go of all of Lennon except her hand and tug her toward the left, only stopping when we reach the side door that leads into the kitchen.

I key in the code and then pull her inside. Despite the shiny appliances, it's obvious we're in a barn. The stamping and snorting is an obvious giveaway.

So is the scent of hay and leather in the air. Knowing Lennon, I'm half-expecting her to keep walking into the aisle to see the new foals born this summer.

She climbs up onto the counter instead. "If you can't wait until we can do this in a bed, I'm at least sitting," she tells me.

I swallow a laugh. "I don't know what you're talking about. I thought you'd want to check on the horses."

As soon as I step between Lennon's legs her hands are on my belt, deftly unbuckling before unzipping my slacks. I hiss as she fists my erection, a sudden rush of desire jolting my system like an electric shock.

"Kiss me," she whispers.

I step closer and tilt my face down, capturing her lips with a long, heady kiss. My hands slide up her bare thighs and under her dress.

Her lacy underwear is soaked. I'm so hard it's painful and if our absence wasn't already noticed, it will be soon.

So I simply tug the lace to the side, not bothering to pull her underwear off or to take my own pants off. I thrust into her, muttering curses as wet heat clenches around me.

Finding someone you share an intense emotional connection and a consuming physical attraction with isn't a common occurrence.

I know what Lennon and I share is rare. I knew it in high school and college, and I'm even more certain of it now.

She'll always be it for me.

Clothing constricts my movements some, but my shallow strokes don't really matter. I'm already close to coming and I can feel Lennon's inner muscles fluttering around me, suggesting she's close too.

This wasn't about wild, crazy sex. I just needed a hit of her, because no matter how much I touch Lennon, it's never enough. And if she wants a bed, I'll fuck her all night when we get home.

"Harder," she begs, digging her nails into the back of my neck and rocking her hips against mine.

I quicken my thrusts, then slip my hand between our bodies and rub right above where I'm filling her.

Lennon comes with a cry that sets off my release, spilling into her as bliss spreads through my body. The sweetest sound in the world is her calling out my name.

We're both breathing heavily, when we separate, laughing like teenagers as we fix our clothing.

But we're not. We're adults. Parents.

And all the things that seemed like big challenges when we were younger are obstacles we've overcome.

I help Lennon off the counter. She clings to me, as we walk through the dark kitchen back toward the door. The only source of light is from the moon, spilling in through the windows.

She keeps holding my hand once we're outside. We walk back toward the house with our fingers linked, swinging them between us.

I glance over, studying her profile in the moonlight. Wondering how I got so lucky as to end up here, with her. Exactly where I want to be.

"Hey, Lennon?"

"Yeah?" She glances over, blushing a little when she realizes I'm already looking at her.

"We made it."

Lennon inhales, like she's pulling my words in with the oxygen. "We made it," she repeats.

We share a smile as we keep walking.

This isn't the way I thought my life would turn out.

I didn't think I'd be living in this town or walking next to this girl.

Sometimes the best things in life—the best *thing*, love—can come out of left field.

THE END

ACKNOWLEDGMENTS

First off, thank YOU for reading Caleb and Lennon's story. Of all the characters I've written, they are the two who have stuck with me the most. I hope you loved them as much as I do.

Mary Scarlett, I could not possibly love this cover any more. You captured each detail perfectly and I smile every single time I look at it. I'm in awe of your talent and can't wait to work with you again!

Britt, your comments on this book kept me laughing nonstop while editing. I'm so glad you connected with this story and appreciate you going above and beyond throughout what turned into a very long process. Thank you, thank you, thank you!

ABOUT THE AUTHOR

C.W. Farnsworth is the author of numerous adult and young adult romance novels featuring sports, strong female leads, and happy endings.

Charlotte lives in Rhode Island and when she isn't writing spends her free time reading, at the beach, or snuggling with her Australian Shepherd.

Find her on Facebook (@cwfarnsworth), Twitter (@cw_farnsworth), Instagram (@authorcwfarnsworth) and check out her website www.authorcwfarnsworth.com for news about upcoming releases!

ALSO BY C.W. FARNSWORTH

Made in the USA
Coppell, TX
10 November 2024

39925885R00308